T0354490

A
Haunting
Obsession

Anthony Morel

iUniverse

A HAUNTING OBSESSION

Copyright © 2019 Anthony Morel.
Author Credits: Jim Betts

All rights reserved. No part of this book may be used or reproduced by any means, graphic, electronic, or mechanical, including photocopying, recording, taping or by any information storage retrieval system without the written permission of the author except in the case of brief quotations embodied in critical articles and reviews.

This is a work of fiction. All of the characters, names, incidents, organizations, and dialogue in this novel are either the products of the author's imagination or are used fictitiously.

iUniverse books may be ordered through booksellers or by contacting:

iUniverse
1663 Liberty Drive
Bloomington, IN 47403
www.iuniverse.com
1-800-Authors (1-800-288-4677)

Because of the dynamic nature of the Internet, any web addresses or links contained in this book may have changed since publication and may no longer be valid. The views expressed in this work are solely those of the author and do not necessarily reflect the views of the publisher, and the publisher hereby disclaims any responsibility for them.

Any people depicted in stock imagery provided by Getty Images are models, and such images are being used for illustrative purposes only.
Certain stock imagery © Getty Images.

ISBN: 978-1-5320-6330-5 (sc)
ISBN: 978-1-5320-6331-2 (e)

Library of Congress Control Number: 2018914249

Print information available on the last page.

iUniverse rev. date: 11/29/2018

Preface

Note from Author: Anthony Morel

I am truly gifted with a keen, visionary mind drawn to perfection. The harmony of beauty cleanses my inner soul, giving me a sense of tranquility and serenity. Maybe that is why I am an architect who attempts to create beauty by the ocean side. This novel was possible because of my intense connection with my passion. A soulful union with my imaginative perspicacity allows me to relate to my inner wealth of perception and desire. This novel reflects that intensity, for without such fervor, I could never have written this story.

Note from Tony Christian

I didn't realize the symbolism of the continual dreams. Each dream lured me in closer to her realm of grandeur, where I experienced intense emotions filled with serene bliss. She enclosed me within her aura of mystique. But there was something else—a haunting sensation. Fear was riding on the surface, barely detectable. A hint of its presence aroused my passionate fervor, yet it was tempered by doubt and curiosity.

I never imagined my enamored curiosity would turn into an obsession, not until I realized the recurring dreams carried a continual theme, conveying a journey to lost times and breathing life into past memories of the same woman. The woman symbolized the very essence of poetic purity and beauty. As my dreams took me to more distant memories, my curiosity turned into an intense obsession—an obsession of discovery. Were the remote memories of this alluring woman just remembrances from a milieu of fantasies or foregone realities? My story begins here, and you can make your own judgment as to whether or not I indeed have a proclivity+ for obsession.

Prelude

Fate: The Gatekeeper

Fate has no boundaries and no limitations. Its presence has been endless since the dawn of time. It is present before our souls become born. It stays with us when our souls leave our physical embodiments, searching for other entryways to continue our journeys on a different path. Each pathway is mapped in such a way that our journey remains unique, filled with the expected and unexpected, so that we will never forget that odyssey whenever the pathway ends. Then the journey will begin again. We might sense both anticipation and wariness regarding what our next journey will have in store. My journey here and now has many concurrent paths, for reasons yet to be known—passageways that seem to have no end. Some are real, and some are only dreams. Which ones are fantasies? I do not know. But each stopover is a hiatus, a destination where I will reside, and when I disembark, I engage with limited time, for my journey restlessly awaits my return, and I must get on board for my next stop on this endless run. Each departure is filled with renewed memories of once-forgotten times in foregone eras filled with the joys of love and sorrows of despair. Fate can be merciful yet cruel. It makes the rules; it's the final judge and jury and passes judgment purely on its own. It makes us wonder, unwilling to share what is to come, for it controls the deck when it's ready to deal. Who gets what? Maybe we were never meant to know.

But I wonder. What if we break the rules? What if we decide that this chosen path is not to be? What if we end it to appeal to fate for another try in a place, a destination, we have been before? Would fate hear us? Yes, the gatekeeper will decide on our appeal. If the end is indeed self-imposed, then one verdict is in mind: guilty. Guilty as hell! Doomed to eternal damnation. But if the journey proceeds to its destined end, then the verdict is an acquittal, and our plea to another place is now at the mercy of the gatekeeper. But beware of what you ask for. Without a doubt, you will be there. You will be on a special one-way journey to a foregone memory, that one event that brought you here. This chosen passage will be your last to give what you seek: immortality. Your chosen path is locked in time. Behold, the path you chose from that eventual day is to last forevermore. It's the gatekeeper's judgment to decide if our chosen paths will be hosted by heaven or hell.

Before the Event

I sit here thinking, waiting to begin this hour interlude. I have been told I experience hallucinations caused by deficits in the brain, resulting from cerebral damage or chemical imbalance. The synapses in both cerebral hemispheres are not communicating the way they were meant to. The signals misfire, which can modify my perception. These pretentious doctors and their anemic prognosis assume these aberrations were brought on by sudden emotional or physical trauma. They're so sure of themselves with their diagnosis. Their posture is smug and self-congratulatory as they relay their verdict, despite my wariness.

Further tests result in a more precise diagnosis, pointing to a rare genetic disorder as the underlying cause: paramnesia, a memory disorder that surfaces when the synapses short-circuit. Then my perception cannot distinguish between fantasy and reality. I'm unable to perceive fantasy and reality as different states of mind, and this continues until the short subsides. Even then, I cannot specifically detect what part of the episode was real and what was fantasy. It's a recurring, rare, complex disorder that, from my perspective, commits me to a continual state of angst, as if I'm walking along a tightrope over a bottomless chasm, not knowing which side is real and which is fantasy. Unless this issue is resolved, it will, over time, drive me to contemplate the unthinkable.

The disorder surfaces without any foretelling symptoms. It will then gradually retreat into a dormant state for an undetermined period of time, and my perception resorts back to normal until the short-circuit decides to run its course again. These periods of perspicuity can last for hours, days, weeks, or months, but the windows of quiescence are getting smaller. It has become apparent, to my growing concern, that these brief periods of normalcy are becoming shorter in duration and less frequent. The perceptive disorder, once infrequent, is now boldly gaining a foothold in my realm of reality. It's a definite yellow flag, but I have been unwilling to disclose it to the doctors. My reluctance to reveal it comes from my desire to avoid their excessive, futile attempts to further examine me as if I am a rare aberration that requires constant observation.

I try to recall when I first detected this anomaly. I can't pinpoint the exact first instance but am aware of when I first noticed the aberrant disorder during moments in several of my dreams. The dreams exasperated my condition. I knew when the dreams started, but from there, it became a guessing game. My disorder intensified to a heightened state when the dream was nearing the end. Instead of the dream relinquishing control, it merged into my conscious state. One dimension flowed seamlessly into the other dimension to the point where the dream's fantasy fused into my reality, resulting in a surrealistic view, a pseudoreality. It persisted until the brain signals detected the abnormality and attempted to self-correct. Then the fused perception would unexpectedly end, releasing me with a suddenness.

My condition still remains a mystery to the experts. They've never mentioned dementia or a brain tumor. It's likely induced by the trauma from an event, they say. But truth be told, I know it is a genetic condition that was prevalent when I was brought into this world. During my younger years, a hint of it would surface but quickly dissipate before it could be detected as a potential malady. Then the event happened. It got worse after the event. Despite all the questions and discussions by the experts and despite the complexity of my condition, when I'm asked to describe my condition, I cannot seem to get beyond the basics, and I continue to resort to simply stating that there are times when I cannot distinguish reality from fantasy.

Yet now my wariness has become more in tune with my disorder's complexities when I start to hallucinate. Remembering the doctors' discussions, I realize that my condition can precipitate more cerebral maladies, which explains my hallucinations. I've become more fully aware of the emotional implications of my disorder. The implications are significant, potentially triggering a myriad of emotional, psychological, and physical problems ranging from complete emotional withdrawal to psychopathic tendencies.

Despite the implications, my dignity and pride are still intact as I resort back to the simpler, safer view of my condition. My defensive posture immediately surfaces, and my irritability is apparent as I feel victimized by the endless clinical intrusions. I feel I'm being analyzed constantly, as if I'm an aberration of the human race. With more conviction, they relay that my condition might be a continual, persistent malady, might trigger more cerebral chronic illnesses, or might resolve itself eventually. It most likely will continually persist with occasional periods when my perception temporarily returns to normal. But these brief intervals of normalcy occur purely at random with indefinite duration. There are too many unknowns, too many variables that never remain static. Maybe the reason for all their questions is to dig further to come up with a more formal medical term so they sound authentic with their pretentious dialogue.

So here I am, absorbing one of these brief interludes of normalcy. I sit patiently as I start this hourly session with my doc, waiting for the right moment. His probing questions try to get inside my mind. Even I cannot accomplish that feat. But I'll give it a try. What do I have to lose? I have a lot to gain. *Well*, I think, *we will see, won't we?* I sit there waiting for the same two initial questions that have been shoved at me during every session.

The chair I'm sitting in is large—too large. The height of the chair is lower than where the doc is sitting—a psychological ploy to maximize my insecurities, I surmise. I lift my gaze to meet his solemn look. As before, my observation does not alter. He looks like a psychiatrist. He's not handsome in the typical sense, more of a sturdy, stoic, steady, dominating appearance. He would definitely stand out in a crowd. His suit is immaculate and expensive looking. His shoes appear to be made of Italian leather. His attire gives the immediate impression of vanity— how others perceive him is important to him.

He seems self-contained and dignified. He has a full head of hair— medium-length brown with a hint of gray and sideburns slightly longer than usual. I would say his age is in the midforties. He's a little taller than average; I would guess just over six feet. He is not too thin and not overweight—I would guess between 180 and 200 pounds. His square chin juts outward, giving me the impression of stubbornness, arrogance, pride, and egotism. He has a thin mustache that adds a pensive look. I can see how one could easily gain an impression of smugness, self-righteousness, and self-importance.

His brown eyes are partially closed yet intense. His glasses seem too small—probably reading glasses or glasses worn just for impression's sake. Even with his full, angular face, the glasses have the appearance of being disproportionate to his face, maybe due to his square, jutting chin but more likely due to the contrast between his undersized glasses and his protruding, thin nose. His acute gaze strikes me—never a blink. His eyes are always focused on me, never wavering. But there is an oddity to his gaze. His right eye has an intense glare continually focused on me, as if conveying continual suspicion, watching every move, each subtle hint provided by my body language. His left eye has a flat gaze, more of a subliminal stare that is absorbing and processing information that will prove instrumental when forming opinions. His gaze holds steady. It's as if he is just sitting there noncommittally, deep in thought. *A mind game*, I think to myself.

Impatiently, I sit here waiting for him to make the first move. His opening move is a question that has a low and patient yet accusatory tone. I sit there listening to his initial question, trying to remain calm. "Why are you so compelled? Your obsession is so full of yearning, yet you say it is without purpose," he says. "Your dreams. You live for your dreams. Yet when awake, you feel nothing. So tell me—what do you feel when you dream?"

Surprise, surprise. New questions. Could it be that he is sincere in wanting to find the root cause? Is this a change in his approach? The onus is on me now, as if I have the answers. Well, maybe now is the right time for a response. But to do this properly, with insight, I first have to relive this experience since it was so long ago when it first started.

"There was a time," I respond, "far enough back that I have to struggle to remember. I am not sure of the year. I am not even sure if it was in this lifetime." I say this with definite sarcasm. "Kind of sounds like a magic fairy tale. Oh, so beautiful and marvelous. Perfecto." I snicker. "But no!" I shout. "Just the opposite. A damn demon from hell! I warned you, Doc, so don't look so startled. Not a good pose for a doc in your profession. You are dealing with someone who has no soul, cannot feel, and has no empathy.

"Sorry, Doc. Kind of stumbled there. Strayed slightly off course. But considering, it is to be expected. Hm, now, how do I feel? Well ..." I pause, acting as if I have to dig deep for an appropriate response. But that is just a ruse; my response is always immediate, cocked and ready at a moment's notice, with no hesitation necessary, as it lives within me, always in relentless pursuit. It is a cross to bear every second of every hour, day in and day out—a constant reminder waiting patiently for the moment when I will shout without restraint, "Lost! Aimless! Hopeless! Without a soul! Without emotion! Inability to feel anything!" I speak the words as if they are well rehearsed but vented with rage, the anger carried with every word as a flaming torch of hatred.

I realize I am off the couch, leaning in with my eyes glued to his—never a blink. I sit back down in an attempt to reconcile with my emotions. "I like to use the word *soulless*," I say with still a venting edge to my spoken words. "Kind of says it all—a complete loss of worth. Why, you may ask? Well, I have always felt that way. Maybe because I felt I was born without a soul, without the ability to feel. If God bestowed a soul in every being, I was the one he must have overlooked. And to be blunt, I do not think it was an oversight but was intentionally overlooked. I felt it when I was born. Maybe not in that first year but later. After a few years, I sensed something amiss. A promise that, once revealed, held no promise, just a layer of shattered would-be dreams, a layer of dust from decay, never materializing. Oh, I saw how that look of hope from those close by turned rapidly to pity and sorrow. Trying so desperately with their own spin, relying on their home-grown excuses for my lack of response. But there was no hiding the fact. When they looked into my eyes, it was apparent that what they saw was a complete void, an abyss into a black endless pit, filled with nothing but emptiness. The pain and disappointment were just too much for them to bear. They gave up and just accommodated me to appease their pain of guilt. But you see, if I cannot feel, then for me, there is no pain. But that is the epicenter of my anguish—that I cannot feel. Anything.

"Was there anything before, you ask? Anything that provoked some lift to me?" *Before* is a word that triggers some significance, some vague remembrance, and my expression clouds with a smidge of doubt, fear, and anger. A memory just barely surfaces before submerging underwater, sinking back toward the bottom, masked by layers of denial, too deep to surface. *Before!* My head spins with a hint of long-past felt emotion. My current setting reemerges as I listen to him repeat the question; then he just sits there waiting. Waiting for what? A response—yes, that's it. "Not that I remember," I quickly answer without further hesitation. But, I think, there was a hesitation. A breakthrough? Did he notice that?

His stare is unusually intense. It's an odd look. I've never beheld this look since my first session. Why is he looking that way at me? And why the smile? As if he knows something I don't. But he knows what? What the hell did I do? Was I too tense? Too hateful? Too passive-aggressive? Passive-aggressive—yes sirree, he mentioned that in our first session, when I just started. I thought, *What in the hell does that mean?* But you know, it was my first session, so I never asked. I just sat there and took it all in. But now this new look, this certain glare, reveals a red flag. Not a yellow one. I've detected something that immediately surges past the yellow and hits the red zone dead-on—bulls-eye. Should I be aware of his thoughts? How do I ask without giving myself away? He looks at me as if it is a secret, and I have to guess what it is. His stare forces me to divert my attention and look for something to focus on just to avoid his damn stare. He is searching me for something amiss. But what? Should I ask? Oh no, never—not a good idea. My paranoia is getting the better of me. I've got to watch it. But oh, the hell with it! So what? It is my damn hour! I control the deck, and I am the one holding the damn ace of spades!

Quickly, I return to form. Impatiently, I respond, "My memories before are absent." Now, there is an irony. "You keep asking if I have memories of anything from before. Before what? *Before* implies a pivotal moment, a milestone, a marker, a turning point we can use as a reference point when referring to a before and after. As in the parting of the Red Sea or, on a more personal level, when your spouse wakes you up at three o'clock in the morning to say it's fucking over. So that being the case, I have to remember the event that divides the before from the after. If I have no memories of the event, then I have no memories of the before. The before becomes a lost entity. Before what? How can I remember anything before if I do not remember the before event? If there is no point of reference, then the question becomes moot!" I shout. "The after? For lack of a better word, yes, I have total recall. Not much to remember there," I say with a sarcastic smirk. "Very simple: my whole life is one constant after.

"Excuse me again. I keep getting derailed—part of the territory. Can't maintain focus." I laugh, even though I am not amused. I am thoroughly pissed off. My warped brain cells keep wandering off out of boredom. *Now, where was I? Oh yes, wandering.* "I wander through my dull, repetitive days with no purpose, just existing, waiting for the day when I will decide to cash it in. Yes, I think about it every day, exactly at the same time: upon awakening and at night, when the despair becomes too heavy a burden and I'm waiting for my dreams to begin so I can escape. They're my salvation—where and when I can feel. I feel intensely in my dreams. But these emotions do not cross over with me to my waking state. They leave me and let me burrow deep into my shell of emptiness, so no help there.

"You ask why. Do you mean why I tried? To attempt the unthinkable? Well, unthinkable from your perspective. But obviously, it appears I gave it some thought. I guess we have proof of that, or else I would not be here. Right, Doc?" I ask with a sarcastic tone.

There's no response. He just sits there with his eyes glued to mine without a twitch—no compassion. He's just there, solemn and stoic, a poker face if there ever was one.

"You are the judge, Doc, so make a judgment. We do not have much time left. What? Fifteen minutes before my hour is up?" I look back impatiently. I sit there twitching; my patience is running thin. I feel like running but have no idea where to go. My memories return to the point in time that brought me here. The reality of that time returns as vividly as ever. Its impact hits me again with as much force as it did then. I do not want to remember. The pain is too intense. But I sit here with that day still so very real. I do not know how it turned out at the end. That's blocked. I can't remember the rest, and maybe that is best, for once realized, it would truly take my sanity away. Then I would know that judgment has been passed, with the sentence being insanity forevermore. Painfully, that day returns with relentless pursuit, unforgiving. It is not fair, but what is fair?

2

Downward Spiral to Hopelessness

It is nighttime, not a good time. My mind races; I think out loud. At times, I have an internal dialogue with myself. My memories perform another encore, my thoughts laced with finality. Midnight is drawing closer; I have two hours to spare before the stroke of midnight signals the end of another day, before the next begins, which I am not committed to. Today marks my end. I have thought about it repeatedly, and it's finally coming to a head. I've gone so far as to invest in several means to end it. I purchased a gun, a hunting knife, and bottles of sedatives and volumes of liquor, each capable of ending it in large enough dosages. But I'm undecided on how to do it. I just can't make a decision. You see, that comes with the territory: indecision. I never have the forethought, fortitude, or courage to actually do it, which makes me even more remorseful.

That night, my swing hits bottom. It just does not matter anymore. I close my eyes and point a finger to blindly pick which instrument will be my guillotine. Upon opening, my eyes connect with my instrument of death, the gun—a Magnum .44, a Dirty Harry special. Well, what do you know? A catharsis hits me. I view it, mesmerized, my gaze beholden to the instrument, worshipping it as my personal savior and release, an end to end all. *Impressive. The perfect instrument.* A part of me finally gets it, for if I am going to do it, then I should make sure there is no chance I will screw it up. To make it interesting, I decide to play Russian roulette. Now, there is a twist. With death staring me in the face, I suddenly have come up with the only creative idea I have ever had! I laugh at the absurdity, the irony, crazy like an aged drunkard. But that does not matter anymore, for my mind is settled. There is no turning back.

I grab the gun, place one bullet in the chamber, spin the chamber, and bring the barrel to my head at the temple, with my finger wrapped tightly on the trigger, with conviction to follow through. I do not close my eyes; instead, I look at myself in the mirror to see the look in my eyes as I am about to die. It is funny how the eyes dilate and change in the intensity of the color as the mind absorbs the impact of what it is about to do.

I take a moment to look at my reflection in the mirror—one last insightful observation before I enter a new world of dark, hidden unknowns. "A checking out, using today's jargon," I say with sarcasm. "The years I have endured, and it comes to this very moment. Been through a lot," I note with a tone of anger. It's too late now. Everything about my existence has gradually worn me down. The angst, anger, depression, irrepressible sense of paralyzing vulnerability, and endless hours of failed therapy have all contributed to an empty, joyless, emotionless life. I have endured too much pain since the event to the point of exhausting my patience.

I close my eyes, attempting to remember when I was younger a long time ago. A few cloudy recollections surface. But without more memories, the faint recollections are for naught, just a tease to trigger my curiosity only to lead to a dead end. I am surprised I remember anything that far back, since everything else is a complete blank. I open my eyes again and see the image of myself as a much younger man, before the struggles intensified. Definitely not someone unappealing—a young man in love. Confidence was never a problem. I'm a handsome man with solid features. I have a full face with blue eyes; a broad, square chin with a slight dimple; a full head of medium-length brown hair; and sideburns that extend down to the earlobes. Everything is in proportion with a sturdy nose and a fully formed mouth. My eyes are my best feature. They're deep blue but sometimes change to a mix of blue and green, depending on my mood. When I smile, everything lights up. I seem to always draw respect, and I assume my overall appearance is a factor. I feel I present an impression of someone sturdy, masculine, dignified, intense, deep, pensive, and inherently intelligent. I feel fortunate that I have these attributes.

The youthful image facing me gradually gives way to another face. The transformation is startling. Every detail is portrayed with startling reality as the torment and physical aging take their toll. It's a face that shows the years of affliction. The face looks like me but somewhat older. I see my inner struggles, with relentless torment etched onto my face. It still looks dignified, but something else is there, something hidden in the wrinkled, etched lines around my eyes, something that epitomized the culmination of this relentless journey: a loss of hope, lack of faith, and posture of giving up. I raise my hand and feel each wrinkle, each line I perceive in my reflection. Each touch by my fingers brings forth the pain and anguish unique to each wrinkle or etched line. I'm still a handsome man but a man who shows too many years of living with too much suffering.

I grow weary of remembrance. I look down toward the gun. I'm more determined than ever to make this be the end. The purpose of life is absent, just a shell of nothingness. I look at my finger resting on the trigger, waiting for the commitment from me to proceed.

I press on the trigger with my eyes wide open, staring directly into the mirror, acutely focused on my reaction. I actually see a smirk: the outer edge of my lip notches upward with a "To hell with it" attitude when I pull the trigger. There is just a click, and I see slight relief in my mirrored expression. *Coward*, I say to myself. *At least have the guts to be determined to pull this off. At least die with some form of honor.* In case you are wondering, there is honor in ending it all in some parts of the world, such as the Far East. There, it is highly accepted. In fact, it's an honorable means to an end. Here in the grand USA, well, it is considered a felony. Imagine that. We have personal rights, but deciding to end it at our discretion isn't included. We have gotten to the point where our birth-given rights don't matter anymore. If we even think about it or attempt it, we are thrown in jail or, worse yet, a psych ward, along with inmates intent on making our lives a living hell. Isn't that the reason we decided to end it? Does that make sense at all? Okay, I've got to stop; I'm getting too pissed and too wired. I need to have some composure to focus on this fateful task. After all, it is what it is. Now, there is a screwed-up phrase. Talk about one simple phrase that paints a complete picture of dormant impotence. One's using it signals complete, inert, ultimate passivity. God, that's such a Freudian interpretation. But look who's talking. It is I who is going to end it ASAP, and you can't beat that for passivity.

I take the gun back, spin the chamber again, and place the barrel to my temple. I pull the trigger again. *Click.* Then I do so a second time with the same result. *Oh, the hell with spinning the chamber. Just keep pulling the trigger until that one special final pull will result in one fatalistic wallop, exploding through my temple, obliterating every piece of brain tissue I have in this flawed, tiny thinking mechanism that isn't capability of anything.* It is a wonder I even think of this, but maybe since this is my last testament, my empty, uninspiring mind relishes my demise by helping me with my first insight to assist in my destruction. I turn to face the mirror and repeatedly pull the trigger, waiting for then magical moment when, with a sudden flash, all the lights will perish, and then an infinite set of unknowns will fill the gap.

I must pull the trigger fifteen times with a gun that only has the capacity to hold six bullets. Nothing happens. I pull the gun away, determined to find the bullet I placed in the chamber. It is still there. *Maybe the firing pin,* I think. I go toward the window, open it, and fire away into the midnight air, aiming at the partially obscured full moon, and then I hear the blast. Perplexed, I load another bullet into the chamber, more determined than ever to pull this off. Once started, I have to end it. What is that saying? *I need closure,* I note with a satirical laugh. *God, that is funny. Okay, let's be sure I have not made a mistake through my clumsy efforts on such a simple task. Just check the chamber, find the bullet, and pull the trigger until the lights go out. How simple. Impossible to screw this up the second time around.* Well, I try again with the same result. Is this a joke instilled upon me by fate? If so, why? I look at my reflection in the mirror and see a look of utter failure. "Could not even self-destruct!" I shout vehemently at my image.

From behind, a voice speaks. "Tony, what are you trying to do? God, please stop. It's me—Cassandra."

I look in the mirror, and behind me is her image. I experience a piercing shock of recognition, an instant recollection provoking hidden memories to trickle down into my consciousness. I'm paralyzed with stirred emotions—emotions I have not felt since our last engagement so long ago. It is Cassandra. I turn to face her. I look to believe the unbelievable. I cry out in shocked disbelief with tearful anguish, filled with confusion, my mind reeling with hypnotic uncertainty, disbelief of what appears before me. My attention diverts to her presence, incognizant of my fingers, which are still tense, with one finger pressed to the trigger and the pressure mounting unknowingly from the reaction to the suddenness of her appearance. I hear a shot bearing down on me. Cassandra has a look of surprise tinged with horror as she looks at me with her hands reaching out toward me. "Tony," she gasps. "No! My God. Oh no. Not now, after all this time. So much time and effort. I heard the shout earlier and knew it was you, and I rushed here. Tony, I know. It is okay." I turn as if in slow motion toward the gun in hand. I smell the residual odor from the spent shell as it ejects and floats effortlessly to the floor. My eyes reconnect with Cassandra. Reality floods in. Our last engagement—the before. God, the event. Before and after—it all comes flooding back. Cassandra, my before, reaches her hand toward my face. "Tony, I loved you before, and I'm in love with you now."

Then there is nothing, a complete blank; I'm finally crossing over to another world, that of unknowns. I'm floating endlessly, alone in the middle of nowhere, riding the tides as the ocean waves carry me back and forth between distant memories that hold no reference. I'm rising with the tide on top of a small raft with room just for two, in the middle of a vast ocean, floating with ease. But to where? I see her; her head is bobbing just above the surface. I start paddling toward her, trying desperately to reach her. There she is: Cassandra, my before.

She's the same as last time. When my recollections confront me with a brief glimpse into that pivotal moment, it all disappears. It is a vacant memory escaping to a place unbeknownst to me, behind a wall; a wall of denial, buried by a subconscious effort for self-preservation. Memories race to that one destination that lies beyond the wall of sworn secrecy, where I no longer remember that day or the rest and am unaware of the event, the before, and the after. My memories are just able to hold on to the now. Maybe there is compassion after all. It is just a guessing game now. I sit here with no remembrance of it, just a dead-end street. A sign at its end says, "No admittance. No trespassing from here on. The entryway will reopen at an undetermined date. Once secure admittance is possible, a safe passage will be made to the place behind the wall."

Summer Retreat

I do not know exactly how young I was when we first met. I am not even sure of the year. I just know that it started during a hot, dry summer. It was an old country town, Neverland, where we had our summer home. It was a getaway from the big-city life, an escape to a more civilized life where people were more than just productive measurements and statistics to serve the affluent. There, prosperity had a different meaning and was measured by the human spirit. Those small towns in the South were becoming fewer in number, still surviving the pressures of progress. That town was one of only a few still remaining in the southern tip of Appalachia, with a population of maybe twenty to twenty-five thousand, nestled in a valley surrounded by the Blue Ridge Mountains. There was not a lot going on there as far as events; it was just a small to medium community with a downtown of only a few stop signs. It was not poor but more of a summer retreat for those who still believed in the art of socializing. If you looked in any direction, you saw miles of open fields and small country roads that ran out to the base of the mountains and then wound their way up, forming a network to connect the small communities scattered throughout Appalachia. That was before the expressways and turnpikes, which turned many into ghost towns. The main exit out was the Blue Ridge Parkway, which wove you through the mountainous chain of those laid-back communities.

In our town, each house was located on an average lot of several acres. The houses were large, with huge swing porches supported by massive columns, two on each side at the front of the house. Most of them were white with wooden wraparound porches, with one or two swings in front at each end of the porches. In between the swings were at least half a dozen white wicker rocking chairs for the evening chat ritual, wherein endless stories were told, dating back to the younger days when that southern town was in its prime. The ceilings all were at least fifteen feet high. Most houses were one or two levels, with a few reaching up to three. The homes were from ten to more than fifty years old and well constructed, with several bedrooms, each large enough to accommodate two or three guests; a huge living room; a sizable dining room; and a multiple-purpose kitchen. Each room, except the kitchen, had ceiling fans that helped keep the place cool since, at the time, there was no air-conditioning. Each room had numerous windows that kept the inside bright and fresh, adding to the jovial atmosphere.

Massive trees, mostly oak and maple, were plentiful, which provided enough shade, keeping the home's interior cool. The maples were mostly at least a century old, with many of the oaks well past the century point. The oaks and maples were massive structures. The maples in front of our house were at full blossom during the months between June and August, forming a perfect symmetrical shape thirty feet across and stretching upward to forty feet. The blossoming reached its peak for just three months, but those three months were filled with enough memories to last several lifetimes. The oaks, which were massive structures, were endowed with sturdy limbs protruding out twenty feet and rising to fifty feet in height.

The town was filled with joy and laughter. Every home and each landmark had its own story, which filled the rumor mill, providing more than enough storylines to capture an eager audience nightly. Everyone would sit on the porches, listening attentively, each craving more. The elderly listened with nostalgic memories, and the young listened with vivid imagination. Fear was nonexistent, and locks were unheard of. Many nights during the summer, the doors were left unlocked, and during sweltering summer evenings, they were even left partially open. The windows opened wide, letting the screens flutter in the evening breeze. Of course, the old railroad tracks ran through the middle of town, sort of a dividing line that, unfortunately, grouped the population based on what one could afford, which was typical of most small to medium southern villages. Despite the social grouping, there was money held in the town, as evidenced by the large southern-style homes.

Even though the town was nestled within a mountainous valley, you would never have known that it was a well-to-do community, as it was enclosed by the Appalachian Mountains and had mostly old blacktop roads. Maybe that was its appeal: it was a stopping point off the well-traveled road called progress. It was a detour to a place where things held fast, remaining as they'd been decades before, to bring back the comfort of familiarity. It was a place where traditions and values never changed but remained as constant reminders of times when they were more valued. We had our southern drawl, but it was more of the Georgia-style accent, with lengthened, drawn-out vowels rather than the twangy drawl found in the hidden communities scattered throughout the mountain chain.

4

The Beginning: Cassandra

We would visit our old southern home during the summer months. It was more than a temporary stay, as we extended our visit to last the entire summer. My parents were professors, and that was their summer sabbatical, an escape from the big city located two hundred miles away.

On one of those hot, sunny summer days, I was perched high on an old oak limb, sketching out images on my sketch pad as I conjured up shapes of storybook villains and heroes from the various formations of cumulus clouds that floated by. I must have been around fourteen years old and had a fertile imagination fueled not only by numerous comic book heroes but also by the heroic deeds of a prince helping a damsel in distress, rescuing a princess of some enchanted land from the evil sorcerer. My mind rehearsed heroic feats, saving the princess so she could become queen of a magical kingdom.

Then I heard a voice calling to me: "What are you doing up there?" I looked down and saw a young girl about the same age looking up at me with a mixed expression of amusement and bewilderment.

"Hi," I responded. "Up here, I am closer to the clouds, where the knights and princesses live."

With a genuine laugh, she replied, "That's silly. There are no knights or princesses who live in clouds."

"Well," I responded, "each cloud up here resembles a knight, prince, or princess. Each cloud resembles something. You see that one over there? A princess with her gown flowing behind her. You see that other cloud? That is the prince's horse. And over there is the prince who will ride his horse to save the princess."

She looked at me with a quick, cute, amused smile, her eyes eager to see. "Why would the prince try to save the princess?"

"Well, because all princesses should be helped by their princes," I replied.

She smiled and laughed out loud. "How do you know this?"

"That's easy, for every story has a prince and princess. Have you ever seen *Snow White* or *Sleeping Beauty*?" I asked. "The fair maiden was rescued by the handsome prince, and she turned into a beautiful princess. Have you seen *The Wizard of Oz*?"

"There was no prince in that movie!" she exclaimed with a stifled laugh.

"Well, there was a knight," I responded.

"But he did not act like a knight," she said.

"Oh yes. He did. He threw the bucket of water at the witch and killed the witch and saved Dorothy. So he was her knight."

She laughed again. "You're funny."

I returned the laugh and asked, "What is your name?"

She looked up, kind of shy at first, and then proudly said her name was Cassandra. "And what is yours?"

I looked down at her, and with a smile, I replied, "Tony."

"Tony, can I come up there to see?"

"Sure," I said, and I climbed down to give her a helping hand.

"I can climb up there, for I am not weak," she said proudly. But she took my hand, allowing me to pull her up to the giant oak limb. We were near enough to other limbs to steady ourselves. The trunk of the oak was thick enough to support both of us as we leaned back to watch the massive cloud structures roll by. I showed her my sketches from each cloud formation and explained which ones were knights, princes, princesses, and evil sorcerers. She looked up at the billowing masses floating by, each a different shape, and accurately matched each to its sketch, remarking on having such magical qualities and adding more detail to each as I eagerly captured her surprising input into each drawing. I was amazed at how rapidly we harmonized. It was obvious she too had the gift that most artists had: a fertile imagination.

Hers was unique in that her mind partnered with mine seamlessly, as if predestined.

She then pointed to a large, floating structure far away. "You see that over there? That is the ugly warrior coming to capture me and take me to his dungeon."

I looked over to where she was pointing and said, "The prince will save you and carry you to his castle, where you will command everyone who lives there."

We both laughed and continued our fantasies as the day wore on. Hours went by, and we were never at a loss for words, using our imaginations to create what seemed like endless scenarios and capturing each in the sketch pad, signed with both our names. Dinnertime was approaching, and I looked at her and wondered where her home was.

She responded with a sheepish grin, "I was brought here to keep you company, Tony."

I looked at her, bewildered, but caught her meaning. I looked across our lot and saw a large home with a wraparound porch and a white picket fence in front. "Is that your home?"

"Yes, we just moved here last week."

I pointed to the house in back of me. "We came here two weeks ago."

From far away, I heard a woman call out, "Cassandra, dinnertime!"

"Tony, I have to go now."

I tried to help her down, but she insisted she could climb down herself. I let her, and I watched with amazement, for she climbed down the tree as if she had done it a hundred times before. She started walking across our yard to her house. Midway, she turned around. "Tony, glad to meet you," she proclaimed with pure, genuine honesty.

It took me just a few seconds to reply, "Glad to meet you, Cassandra." She looked at me with joy and giggled an affirmative response. "Cassandra, can you come back after dinner?"

She looked at me and then back at her house, and as she walked gingerly toward her house, she turned and smiled. "I will try," she responded. "When you see me up there on the limb, waiting for you." Then she ran to her house and up the porch stairs, opened the door, looked my way, and disappeared inside.

I sat there on the limb, just staring in her direction. I was young, but my heart did a flutter, and I was glad we'd met.

My mother called out that dinner was ready, and my stomach started rolling with hunger. I climbed down and walked halfway to the porch steps. I turned toward Cassandra's house and thought, *I too will be waiting.* I must have been famished, for I ate wholeheartedly, absorbed by the thought of meeting Cassandra and unaware of the after-dinner talk about the day's events. I was in no mood for dessert, which was unusual since that was my favorite part of dinner. Anxious to get outside to see if Cassandra was waiting, I asked if I could leave the table. Everyone must have wondered why I was turning down dessert, and they asked if I was feeling okay.

"Of course. Just want to go out before it gets too dark," I said with a tinge of impatience.

My dad spoke up. "Boys will be boys. Just put your dishes in the sink."

I immediately slid back my chair, raced to the sink, hastily dropped my dishes into the sink, and hustled toward the front door. I ran out onto the porch, looked out toward the giant oak, and saw Cassandra up on the oak limb with a pencil and scratch pad, staring at the cloud formations, which by then had a pinkish hue.

She looked down at me and said, "Join me in my kingdom, and let's dream together."

Without a response, I eagerly climbed the tree and sat next to her, and we both shared more fantasies. Time passed by effortlessly, and dusk approached as the pink clouds turned to shadowy forms. We both knew we had to get home before it became too dark. I asked her if she would be there tomorrow.

She responded, "If that is your wish, I will be here."

I listened to her as she replied with an inner smile. Her answers held a quality of uniqueness with a hint of mystery, and I had to take a minute to interpret them before replying. It was not only what was said but also the manner in which she replied, which made me feel as if I were being greeted with the warmth of a summer sunrise. I responded, "Yes, I would like that."

We sat there staring at each other, and then we both grinned with gleeful laughter filled with joy. She climbed down and ran across my yard to her house.

I called out, "Cassandra!"

She turned around and said nothing; we just looked at each other. Her face lit up with a thousand smiles, and she disappeared into the house.

I sat there absorbing the moment and whispered, "Cassandra, I am glad we met." As I turned back to my house, I caught her looking out through her downstairs window, and she waved to me and threw me a joyful kiss.

I spent the early part of the night in my third-floor bedroom, looking out the window across our yard toward her house, wondering what she was thinking and hoping she would look out through her downstairs window one more time before I went to sleep. I turned my gaze up toward the night sky and caught several shooting stars chasing each other's tail. My gaze locked onto the two bright stars that shined with a brilliant glow during the summer months, and I gave them names: Cassandra and Tony. I could hardly wait until tomorrow to let Cassandra know. We would talk, daydream, and sketch our fantasies all day until it was dark, and then I would point them out to her: Cassandra and Tony, the two brightest stars in the sky. *If only today were tomorrow so I could eagerly point them out in the star-filled night.* As I turned toward my bed, I looked one last time out my window to see if by chance she was there at her window. I glanced at the window on the top level and saw her standing at the window, looking in my direction. She waved again and threw me another kiss before she turned off her light. My excitement kept my sleep at bay, but eventually, my tiredness took hold, and I turned toward my bed, too tired to think. My dreams carried me to a faraway magical kingdom.

Emergence of Rapture

It was morning, and I was awake at sunrise. I heard the typical routine of my mother getting breakfast ready and hurriedly put my clothes on, anxious to look outside to catch any glimpse of Cassandra. Before I got to the hallway, my mother called out, "Breakfast first!" Her voice was stern enough that I complied by turning around, heading to the kitchen, and taking my seat as the adults shared their plans for the day.

I nervously swung my legs back and forth, my energy ready to burst through the seams, as I waited for the eggs and sausage to be passed around the breakfast table. When the serving was passed to me, my anxious hands almost dropped the plate with nervous fingers. I scooped up a generous helping of scrambled eggs and gobbled them down, finishing with a glass of milk. I tried to peer down the hallway toward the front door, hoping Cassandra was there waiting. It felt like hours at the table, but the truth was, it was just short of an hour. Giving in to my impatience, I asked to be excused.

"What is wrong with you, boy?" my mother asked jokingly. "Okay, place your dishes in the sink before you leave."

I jumped out of my seat, brought my dishes to the kitchen, and rinsed them before placing them in the sink. I then raced through the hallway toward the front door, my heart racing with anticipation. The grandfather clock that stood next to the door had just finished its last chime signaling nine o'clock. I swung open the door, raced to the giant oak, and looked up. Cassandra was there, but she'd climbed higher to a larger branch.

"What kept you so long?" she teased as I started climbing. When I got to her, I turned to sit by her and noticed the fragrance around her hair. She'd placed a red rose with a rubber band to the side, and it gave off a soft fragrance. Noticing that I was looking at the rose, she moved her head toward me so I could catch its scent. I bent my nose closer to the rose and felt the softness of her hair. I reached out with my hand to touch her hair. Upon my doing so, she pulled back and raised her eyes to mine, and our eyes connected. We just sat there with our gazes fixed, uncertain what to do next, both with a hint of a special feeling but not yet understanding its meaning. The silence was lost when Cassandra opened up with a smile, asking if I liked the rose.

"Yes," I replied, "and I will order a dozen so that you have a rose for every day."

"Oh, Tony, your wishes are your dreams." She laughed.

"My wishes become my dreams, which become true," I responded with a note of sincerity.

She looked at me and said nothing for a moment. Then a sudden smile appeared when she raised her hand in a princess-like gesture and graciously thanked me. "A red rose a day from my Tony," she proclaimed with her unique tone of genuine mystery. "Look that way, Tony, and you will see the prince and princess in the clouds. See over there? The princess is sitting on her throne, and her prince is by her side to protect her."

I saw where she was pointing, where huge cumulus structures moved swiftly our way, and viewed with amazement her sketch and what she'd captured with her artistic flair. It was obvious she had a gift, and I responded with an awed confirmation. We sat there until noon, drawing sketches as we fantasized our way through the cloud formations as they floated overhead. Noon arrived, and both our mothers called out for us to have lunch. Before we climbed down the oak tree, we promised each other we would meet at the old country road at the corner of our lot, which led to an old fishing pond about a mile toward the backwoods. She had never been there, and with anticipation, we both agreed to meet at one o'clock.

Thankfully, lunch was a quick grilled cheese, which I gobbled in one bite. I was out the door in a flash and saw that Cassandra was waiting. "Did you have lunch already?"

She bent down to hand me two bamboo fishing poles while she picked up a basket with sandwiches for both of us. "In case we do not catch our lunch," she said jokingly. It did not matter that I'd already had a sandwich; I looked forward to sharing lunch with her. I carried the fishing poles as we strolled down the country road barefoot toward the fishing pond. That sunny afternoon was near record temperature, and the old two-lane country road was freshly blacktopped. We kept hopping off onto the grass to cool our feet until we hit a spot that was completely shaded. There was not a worry in the world during that special afternoon. I can say with certainty that one day was the day I felt most at peace. God only knew then what was in store for us.

We arrived at the pond, and by that time, it was late afternoon, so the fish were nibbling. We laid the blankets down, swung our poles out, and rested them on the grass, waiting for a bite. The pond was circled by trees, but if you looked straight upward, you could see the opening where the clouds would float by. We grabbed the sandwiches from the basket, along with two bottles of Coke. We gazed at the formations that lazily floated by, continuing our sketches from our fantasies about warriors, knights, princes, and princesses. We must have fallen asleep, and when we woke up, it was near twilight. Realizing our parents were probably worried, we packed up and started heading back, forgetting about our poles. Our walk was slow, for neither of us wanted our day to end. She broke the silence. "Tony, I am glad I met you." I looked at her and held her hand as we walked back.

"Me too, Cassandra. Me too," I responded softly.

6

Summer of Love

Those days of meeting up high in the old oak tree and at the old fishing hole and talking about our hopes, dreams, and fantasies continued throughout those summer months. Every day became a treasure chest of discovery and wonder. There were early evenings when, just as it was getting dark, up high, nestled cozily in the oak tree, we would hear the far-off train whistle. Its lonesome call carried through the nightly silence, catching nature's creatures' imaginations and beckoning all to listen to the soulful, wishful sound while fading off in the distance. Cassandra and I keenly listened, fantasizing that the mysterious nightly train was taking us on a journey toward a magical kingdom where every wish we made would come true. As each day passed, our connection grew, and our bond gained a permanence. We became inseparable and shared each summer event. Each new day arrived with its own agenda, planned with a sense of adventure by both of us. I knew that no event would go by alone; all would always be shared together. We walked for miles to the downtown area to experience the marching bands during Memorial Day. We spent the Fourth of July at the pond to watch the fireworks. We would sneak into the town's one outdoor theater to watch from the refreshment arcade, listening to the speaker from the nearby vacant lot. The theater in the center of town became our private retreat. When heroic movies played, we'd use our imaginations to escape to a magical faraway land. Our summer became our special interlude, and we formed a bond that would last a lifetime, unaware at the time of the consequences of our connection. The soda fountain owners always had reserved spots at the counter for us, and when we walked in on a summer afternoon, the fountain clerks greeted us by name with genuine smiles, as if our visit made their day a little bit brighter, and they'd place our chocolate shakes at the usual spot where we sat.

As the summer flew by, our bond grew stronger, and our ties intertwined to further strengthen our connection. July turned into August, and our elated spirits continued. At times, we were somewhat dispirited, reluctant to acknowledge our most memorable summer drawing to a close. Our shared unease about the summer's end brought us closer, as we realized our companionship was evolving, strengthened with ties of endurance. Our memories were infused with dearly felt emotions that turned that summer into more than just a summer retreat.

During the second half of August, our buoyant jubilation had moments of pending loneliness when we shared our concerns and formulated plans for the following summer. The last week in August soon arrived, and we both were dreading the day when we would say our farewells. Our desperate loneliness was cushioned somewhat by our commitment to meet again the following summer with a renewed agenda. The pained uncertainty made us wish that summer would last forever and our connection would have no end, but reality told us otherwise, and we discussed the unknown variables, hoping each turned out in our favor.

The last weekend of August arrived. It was Friday, and we were going our separate ways on that Sunday, with our families' departures destined to proceed in opposite directions. Friday morning, I woke up and lay in bed for a while longer, thinking about Cassandra. My thoughts were filled with pending despair; I was unable to face the inevitable separation in three days. Fear and uncertainty consumed me, leaving me with paralyzing loneliness. I fought back tears, intent on making that day unforgettable, as I launched up onto the floor to take a shower and get ready for the day and Cassandra. Half an hour later, after taking a few extra minutes to groom myself, I hastily retreated downstairs, listening for the usual morning routine. As I drew nearer to the bottom steps, I heard the breakfast preparations, a comforting routine I associated with that memorable summer. But the comfort was short-lived, for upon reaching the hallway leading to the kitchen, I saw suitcases piled high in my parents' bedroom, bringing to the forefront summer's end. My solemn despair struck fast, bringing with it a feeling of solitude. I walked into the kitchen and took my usual spot at the table. Breakfast was not ready yet, and my mother took notice of my dejected posture and asked if I was feeling okay. I looked up with a despondent expression and replied weakly, "No, I am feeling ill. I am going back to bed." My mother came over and felt my forehead. Then, with a look of concern, she agreed I should go back to bed, and she would come up later that morning to see how I was feeling.

With a tinge of guilt, I rose from the table and then departed for the living room hallway stairs leading to my bedroom. I kept my head down so I could not see the suitcases, which would remind me of summer's end. Upon reaching the stairs, I looked back to see if anyone was looking and darted toward the front door. I ran out onto the porch and looked up, but I did not see Cassandra. My heart took a sudden drop as the first wave of loneliness slammed into me, leaving me with a panicked desperation. *Has she left already?* That was my immediate concern. *Without even saying goodbye?* Now I really did feel ill, and a wave of dizziness overwhelmed me as I walked unevenly toward the giant oak. She was not there. My vision pictured us together up high, and I saw images from memories of the cherished, timeless, precious moments from our summer engagement. My loneliness turned into a worried frenzy, which soon became deluged with nausea when I retreaded back to the house, dejected. I was lost in a complex web of emotions as I went back upstairs to sleep to replace my fears and uncertainties with dreams of Cassandra and our first meeting, of priceless memories during these precious months, of faraway places where life consisted of just our hopes and fantasies. Soon I fell asleep, and my dreams escorted me back to that place and time where fantasies always became true.

7

Commitment to Love

It must have been only an hour later when I felt a palm against my forehead. I opened my eyes and saw my mother. She said I did not feel warm, and maybe the fact that we were leaving Sunday had caused me to feel ill. I said with a hint of uncertainty that I felt better. I then decided to ask about next summer. She replied, "Tony, please don't worry; we have all intentions of returning next year." My spirits lifted immediately, and I needed to tell Cassandra. Then I remembered that earlier that morning, Cassandra had not been there. My mother, sensing my turmoil, said, "Tony, the young girl next door, Cassandra, stopped by ten minutes ago and asked for you. I told her I was going upstairs to check on you and would let you know. She told me she would be waiting for you at your usual spot." I looked at my mother and then shot out of bed, ran downstairs, raced onto the porch and to the oak, and looked upward.

There she was. "Cassandra!" I called out, and I immediately started climbing to be by her side.

"Tony, I am sorry I was late, but I had to pack this morning." She turned toward me, her eyelids red and swollen.

"Cassandra," I said, "what is wrong?"

She faced me, and I brought her head to rest against my shoulder. Her tears poured out as she whispered, "Tony, I do not want to leave. You are my prince, Tony." I held her there, keeping my tears in check. We both remained quiet, but our feelings spoke volumes. We held each other, no longer speaking a word, for our comfort fed our souls with unspoken promises.

After a period of time, her sobbing slowed to an even, breathless sigh, and the warmth as she exhaled her worries felt like a warm summer breeze against my neck. I moved her head up toward mine so I could see the vibrant sapphire in her eyes. "Cassandra, you are my princess forever. Wherever you are, I will be there for you if ever you need me." She laid her head on my shoulder, and tears of joy slowly spilled onto my cheek. As each drop fell, our hearts became more as one. When the tears slowed, I told her my parents were coming back next summer.

Her eyes lit up, and the glow of hope returned with prominence. She replied, "I asked my mother the same question. They too are returning next summer." Relief flooded our eyes, and as we held each other close, not wanting to let go, already in the back of our minds, we were both formulating plans for next summer.

We felt a temporary respite from the yearning and loneliness. Dismissing everything but that day and our plans, we descended the tree, ready to walk to the fishing hole. When she climbed down, she reached behind the tree to grab a basket full of chips, peanut butter sandwiches, and two bottles of Coke. It was midmorning, and without a minute to spare, we took each other's hand and briskly walked toward the old country road, richly filled with memories from all our walks during that momentous summer. We took our time once on the country road, for now our hopes were soaring, and our yearning for each other's companionship was reflected in our walk as we strolled hand in hand toward the old fishing pond. It was nearly our last time at that old pond for the summer. We spent hours holding each other close side by side, not wanting to let go. We sketched each hero, warrior, knight, prince, and princess we perceived from the endless cumulus formations that floated by that afternoon. We laughed, cried, and bravely kept our hopes up as we started to make plans for next summer. I could tell we both were working hard to keep the Sunday deadline at bay. Yet Sunday's deadline was not my only prominent thought. A nagging suspicion of being observed, watched, ran up my spine. That was not the only instance; a number of times during the summer, I'd detected something or someone observing with malicious intent. That instance, though, was more pronounced and prompted a gut feeling that caused me to glance away toward the surrounding willows to intensely scrutinize the surrounding foliage to detect anything unusual that would justify my wariness. I saw nothing out of the ordinary, just a normal setting, and with residual hesitancy, I attributed my creepy feeling to overwhelming stress, as my emotions regarding Sunday's planned departure consumed me with sorrow and worry.

For the time being, I did not relay my concern to Cassandra, to protect her from any more stress than she already had with the pending departure. "Hey, Tony, where are you?" Cassandra asked as she reached out to stroke my face.

"Daydreaming about us," I responded with sincerity.

"I am right here. By your side." She took my hand and turned me toward the pond. "Let's make a wish, my prince."

As the sun started fading away, the cloud formations cast a pinkish glow overhead, and we picked up several stones, each carrying a wish. We took turns tossing each stone farther out into the pond, hoping we could make a bull's-eye exactly in the center, where a promise would then most surely be fulfilled. We held hands as we both used our other hand to throw each of the last two stones out toward the center. Bulls-eyes—both landed together right in the center, and we jumped with joy and held each other with one promise shared between us, which now we knew would come true for sure.

Our promise secured, we walked back to the country road, realizing the sun was setting, and the full moon was already announcing its presence. We looked up at both and remarked on the autumn full moon's prominence. We stopped right there as dusk was settling in. Nature's creatures must have sensed our mood, for they started their symphony of music as we glanced upward. I looked upon Cassandra and saw the moon's glow reflected on her face, and she turned toward me, her eyes glistening with fresh tears. I stood in front of her and held her face in my hands as I moved forward to kiss her gently. A moment of pure magic traversed through our senses, and I left her lips, looked up into her eyes, and saw an angel. She then brought her lips to mine and kissed me softly, her fingers gently pressed on the back of my neck, holding her kiss a little longer to make sure we remembered our kiss until we met again next summer. Our emotions spiked, causing a sense of uncertainty because of their newness, yet we were filled with want and desire. That was the moment our connection was sealed. Bonded with fate, we pulled away reluctantly and beheld the darkened sky solely occupied by the full moon as we both envisioned its wink with a romantic smile.

We turned back in the direction of our homes, sharing a newly discovered set of emotions between us. The impact rippled through us, revealing a new awareness, yet we were not sure how to react. Despite the yearning, with all its dubieties, we both knew without doubt that we never would separate without a promise to return. We planned for the next day, the summer-end holiday, with all its parades and festivals. We would meet the next morning in our favorite spot: high up in the old oak tree. For the time being, the next day was all that mattered.

As we came into view of our homes, we heard the joyous laughter of the crowd assembled on my porch. It was a pleasant surprise that Cassandra's parents had joined in the festive occasion. Everyone noticed our return but asked not a question. I was sure they were aware of our connection and did not want to intrude. They asked us to join, but we declined, deciding to use the old swing hanging down by the old picket fence, under a large maple tree. We reached the tree, and she sat on the swing and started to swing back and forth. I stood beside her and helped her momentum as she swung higher up toward the stars. The summer wind was warm and flowed gently against our faces. I could see her short blue-black hair flowing lightly across her perfect face as she looked up at the multitude of stars, a beholden view of the vastness of our galaxy, when it suddenly dawned on me. I beheld the two brightest stars that were most pronounced during the summer months, remembering when I'd first spotted them back in June, the night after we first met. With an excited gesture, I said, "Cassandra, look here to our right. The two that shine the brightest—I named them after us when we first met." I pointed the two out.

She gazed up. "Tony, they are beautiful."

"The one there that shines with brilliant color I named after you, Cassandra, the princess. The other I anointed Tony, the prince."

She gazed at the stars, holding my hand, her feet planted on the ground, and said, "They are so stunning. Their brilliance is a symbol of our connection." Then two comets streaked past us, each flowing directly in front of each star. She turned and looked at my eyes. "Tony, my prince, never leave me without promising to return."

"Forever," I replied, and we hugged again.

Our day together was soon to end, as we both had to rise early to celebrate the next day's holiday events. We wanted to capture everything since it was our last day together for the summer. We had a lot to cover tomorrow, as we had to also plan for the following summer to come.

"Tony," she said, "tomorrow is to be a busy day, and we must get some sleep."

Exhausted, I replied, "Yes, I see your parents getting ready to leave. I will walk you back to the porch."

We walked hand in hand back to my porch, where Cassandra came near and whispered in my ear, "Until tomorrow, my dear prince." She then walked up to where her parents were saying their goodbyes and called it a night.

8

Eventful Day Before Summer's End

The following day arrived. I woke up at sunrise with anticipation, pushing everything else to the wayside. I thought to myself, *Today is going to be a very special day, and tomorrow will remain tomorrow.* I dressed and hurriedly ran down to the first floor, almost tripping over my untied shoelaces as I breezed through the hallways toward the kitchen. I kept my eyes glued straight ahead, not allowing myself to be distracted by anyone who might be packing up for the trip back to the city tomorrow. I stopped in front of the kitchen counter, grabbed a handful of biscuits, and tossed them into a plastic bowl before racing back toward the front door.

I heard my mother call after me, "Tony, you are going to miss breakfast!"

"This is my last day here. I am not hungry and will be back for lunch," I quickly replied. I was out the door before my mother could respond. I was on the porch and jumped down to the path that led to the oak tree. I held the bowl of biscuits in both hands as I arrived. I looked up, and there she was, dressed specially for our last day together, with two red roses, one pinned to each side of her hair. "Cassandra, I have some biscuits for breakfast."

"I brought the basket full of sandwiches for the pond. You can put them in the basket," she replied. I walked around to the back of the oak tree and placed the biscuits in the basket, leaving the empty bowl beside the tree. I grabbed the lower branch and pushed myself up, hanging on to the upper branch for support. I climbed upward branch by branch, realizing Cassandra was up even higher, near the top. I wondered if the limbs that high were sturdy enough to support us both, but my concern was relieved upon my seeing Cassandra as I drew nearer. She'd found a resting place against the trunk where two main branches reached out and then turned upward. The spot was even better suited for us than the previous ones we had used. I continued climbing until the clouds seemed to be right overhead. Finally, I grabbed the limb that supported Cassandra and pulled myself up, finding a spot to sit beside her.

"Cassandra, I like the roses, and you look so special dressed up for this occasion."

"For you, my prince," she responded with a twinkle in her eye, her head lifting to catch a glimpse of an unusually large cumulus mass floating by right above us. We could see both the prince and the princess within, looking down at us. "Tony, there. You see? There we are."

"Yes, I do," I replied. Clear as day, I could see Cassandra and myself, a princess and prince in the formation, and I swore I saw a pair of red roses in the princess's hair. She gave me her sketch of us, as viewed by her perceptive eye. That sketch was special, for she held her heart in her hand as a gift to me to be treasured as a token of her undeniable connection. It was a special gift we shared that has been with me ever since.

We just sat there for what seemed like hours, holding hands tighter than usual to hold on to that summer, wishing for an extra day to lift the weight of the inevitable departure the next day. The next day, a sentence would be bestowed upon us to separate us for reasons we knew were valid but took personally. The bond we had formed would be put on hold with an unknown future. Reality—that was what the adults reasoned. But truth be told, the reality of the next day hurt with unbearable sorrow. It seemed unfair to be presented a gift that touched us deeply only for fate to take it back, uncaring of the consequences. We were too young to totally understand, but life's reality in our minds was full of pain and sorrow. For a brief moment, we sat there just feeling the comfort and security of our companionship. We shared those feelings without saying a word, for there were no words to describe.

We became aware of the passing time and realized we should have left for the pond an hour ago. We hurriedly climbed down the oak, hastily retrieved the basket, and headed to the country road. We walked more briskly because of the lateness of the afternoon. We had so much to do and not enough time in the day to fit everything in. We were determined, though, as we hastily ran down the country road hand in hand. I was surprised at her energy and speed. She pulled me forward as we hastened down the open road. We slowed down, realizing once again that our last full day was moving too fast, and we attempted to stretch the passing day further out to absorb every moment. Way off in the distance, we caught sight of a dark sky filled with thunderheads, and we heard its wrath from afar as it lit up mounting dark cumulus structures, announcing its forewarning with a thunderous rumble and sending shock waves of echoes throughout the mountainous surrounding terrain.

We were not sure which way the storm was heading, as its pace was slow. It seemed to just stay there unmoving while surveying which direction to proceed with its advance. We only had an hour left before the parade would start, so we slightly picked up our pace, heading to the pond, determined to make the most of that hour. We reached the pond, laid our blanket down, and grabbed the basket. We had not had a bite to eat since breakfast. We eagerly brought out the sandwiches, opened the bottles of Coke, and dug in with joyous laughter. We had not bothered to bring our sketch pads and instead filled the hour with unrestrained exuberance while planning the events for the following summer. Our worries about the next day were on temporary hold, as our excited plans kept them at bay. By the time we'd finished our first round of planning, when we looked up at the fading sun, we knew we were missing the parade. Determined to catch the start of the carnival, we started to gather everything for our return.

Off in the distance, we heard a roar, a clap of thunder, and we turned to fix our gaze on the dark cumulus clouds marching in fast from the nearest surrounding mountain—the approaching storm front. The ominous view spurred my imaginative fantasy, and my mind vividly transformed the dark, massive approaching structure into an evil sorcerer. The sorcerer was racing across the skies to invade our magical kingdom with malicious intent, with one purpose: to challenge our bond, separate us, steal the princess away, and carry her to his castle filled with malign pretense. I wished with all my might that I could ride to her rescue and save Cassandra, my princess. A gust of wind blew across our faces, and we both could feel the electrical charge in the air as we were brought out of our trance back to the present. We rose, grabbed the basket, and ran toward the surrounding forest of trees to find a safe haven under a canopy of weeping willows by the pond.

We reached the willows just as the first few raindrops landed, and the sky turned an inky gray as we huddled by the huge trunk, under the willow foliage, which shielded us from being drenched. The storm was bent on destruction. We saw the line of rain invade the entire area. Bolts of lightning lit the forward advance, followed by a tremendous series of claps of thunder announcing the storm's arrival. The winds shifted, driving the rain in our direction and forcing us to run to the back side of the willows to shield ourselves from most of the deluge. I lifted the red roses from Cassandra's hair, placed them in the basket, covered it with the enclosed napkins, and wrapped my arm around Cassandra with my jacket covering our heads, with the basket nestled between us so it would stay dry. We sat there with our cheeks touching and our hands held tightly, waiting for the thunder burst to be whisked away. It lasted for just a half hour, and then the rain moved on, marching across the open fields toward the surrounding mountains, another kingdom to conquer. The sun came out as it pushed open the remaining storm clouds to reveal a perfect blue sky. *If only tomorrow could be so easily resolved*, I thought. I lifted my jacket off our heads. We were not drenched by the deluge but were wet to the point where our clothes clung to our skin. *In an hour, our clothes should dry*, I thought, *since the temperature was well into the nineties*. Cassandra stood up, her clothes clinging to her body. She saw my gaze, and then we both became red-faced, aware of what we felt but awkward with our emotions. Our eyes met with an acknowledgment that as the summers became several, eventually, we would engage. We exchanged the message wordlessly, a commitment that we beheld with promised certainty.

A sudden movement caught in my peripheral vision. I turned immediately toward the surrounding willows. Across the pond, I detected the movement again. But this time, I saw a reflection from the sun's glare. I moved closer to the pond, my protective instincts heightened, ready to thwart a potential threat. The sensation I'd had earlier that week at that exact location reared up, crawling up my spine as my anticipation of possible danger grew to an alarmed state. This time, Cassandra took notice, reactively covering her breast with crossed arms as she too felt the same prickly sensation. She grabbed my arm, peering over my shoulder, staring intently across the pond. We just stood there waiting. Every passing second seemed like minutes. Our bodies were both in a flight-or-fight stance, not sure which response would be triggered. A movement occurred again, this time more noticeable, as the foliage separated to give us a glimpse. With relieved sighs, we welcomed the sight of a deer with gorgeous antlers. We broke into cries of relief as we hugged each other with a reassured release from the stress. The deer took notice as it raised its head and stared directly at us with no noticeable fear. It stood there for what seemed like minutes before bowing its head, an obvious welcome gesture. It then raised its head again before turning away from the pond and disappearing back into the dense foliage.

The relaxed state from the tension-filled moments brought with it a temporary reprieve from our desperate heartache at Sunday's departure. We sat for another hour, lying under the sun as our clothes dried. I pulled out the roses and pinned one to each side of her hair. Both roses blossomed further, opening wide to reveal their radiant color. We'd missed the main holiday event held downtown but were determined to catch the carnival later that evening to celebrate one more time before the day closed. It was our last evening together before the next morning came.

We went back to some worry from our parents. The remarks were plenty from concern, and I had to plead for their permission to go to the carnival as long as we were home by eleven thirty. I skipped dinner, and knowing it was our last night, they finally conceded and pressed the importance that we come home at the anointed curfew. I went back out with twilight approaching fast and sat under the oak, waiting for Cassandra. Thirty minutes went by, and I was still waiting for her, wondering if she was grounded. I heard her call my name as she dejectedly walked toward me. I asked if she was in trouble. She just sat next to me, saying nothing. Finally, she told me it was okay if we went to the carnival, but she only had an hour because of the early start to the big-city morning. We left for the carnival, trying to keep our spirits high.

As we neared the downtown area, we could hear the intoxicating laughter and cheers from the excitement of the thrill rides. Upon our seeing the carnival lights, our moods lightened, and we broke into a run to the entrance to make the most of the hour. After we entered the carnival grounds, we went to the arcades, where the carnival barkers called out to the visitors to try their skill at the various booths, which featured shooting ranges and basket shoots. I picked the nearest booth, which featured a shooting gallery of moving targets. You got ten shots for a dollar, and hitting the bulls-eye on five would get you a giraffe. Hitting all ten would win the grand prize of a large panda bear. It took me five attempts, but on the last try, I hit all ten dead in the center. Cassandra picked the giant panda, which I carried while we ventured to the fortune-teller.

As we neared the wizard, my anticipation became tempered with an eerie sensation upon my noticing the wizard's eyes, which seemed to come to life, following our every move. The wizard's eyes appeared to be glued to my presence, following my every movement, making eye contact. I could not seem to break the connection as its hold on me drew me into a hypnotic fugue. My concentration fragmented, and every notion was tossed aside, as if the wizard were searching my mind and examining every thought. My mind seized on a memory of some distant, mystical acquaintance who was somehow associated with the wizard. What chilled my soul was that the odd remembrance felt eerie and real yet too vague to discern more, sort of like déjà vu. I'd had the same eerie sensation when at the pond, a feeling of being watched. My back tingled with chills running up my spine, spurring up paranoid suspicions. I felt someone yanking my arm, jolting me out of my fugue. I realized it was Cassandra, pulling on me with genuine concern. "Tony, where are you?"

I replied that I was just tired, and my mind was drifting from fatigue. "Tonight is our last night for the summer. So let's enjoy what we can and not worry."

With a worried look, Cassandra agreed, and we returned our attention to the summer evening and the festive carnival atmosphere. I turned back to the wizard, hiding my alarm, when I noticed the wizard had his eyes closed but with a hint of an amused smirk. Tossing all my suspicions aside, assuming they were related to the stress of our departure, I focused my complete attention on Cassandra as I inserted a dollar for the wizard to tell us our fortune: "Tomorrow is not the end but the beginning of something special." I read it to Cassandra, and she gleefully accepted it. Our moods lifted higher.

The evening turned into night. The jubilance of the crowds filled the atmosphere, with the rides in full swing, and everything—the crowds, the events—seemed to be moving effortlessly. We lost track of time, and then, unexpectedly, we caught sight of the time on the lit clock mounted high on the village hall nearby. We realized we had just thirty minutes before curfew. We searched for the entrance, and dodging the crowd, we left and briskly walked back. It took us an hour to get home, and once our homes were in sight, we agreed to meet at the old oak tree in the morning. Hurriedly, we both ran to our houses—surely to be greeted by stern lectures. Once inside, I walked down the hall and saw everyone gathered in the dining room. I met no harsh words, just a "Glad you made it back. Did you have fun at the carnival?"

"Sure. It was great," I replied, and then I asked about the next day. I found out that our departure was scheduled for noon. Upon hearing that, I decided to go upstairs to get an early sleep for an early rising.

9

Summer's Tearful End

The eventful morning arrived, and I was more tired than usual because of a late, restless sleep. I looked at the clock: 9:00 a.m. Only three hours were left. I jumped into my clothes and ran downstairs, ignoring breakfast. I ran out the front door to the old oak tree and searched for Cassandra. I saw her dashing across the yard, calling out my name. We hugged each other, both weary of what lay ahead. Without saying a word, we started off toward the pond—our last visit to the old fishing hole during our summer retreat. We walked the old country road and thought about the first time we'd met. We walked hand in hand, our pace slow, as if we could delay our deadline. I was the first one to speak, and my voice carried a lonely tone. "Cassandra, I will write. Every day until next summer." I waited for her response, but instead, there was just silence. "Cassandra, will you write me?"

She stopped and turned toward me. "Yes, Tony. I will write you twice a day until next summer." Our hearts ached with every breath. It was almost impossible to keep our emotions in check, so we continued the silence, just walking hand in hand toward the old fishing pond, our thoughts in tune with each other's, both breathing in every moment before it was time.

We reached the old pond and sat there, just listening to every sound, viewing the billowy masses floating by, and watching the fish search aimlessly for their morning brunch. Everything seemed relaxed, with no worry in sight, just repeating a routine that never changed. It must be nice, we thought, to be able to carry on with life, not concerned about life's interruptions, where everything was safe and carefree. It must have been an hour, and upon realizing it was almost eleven o'clock, we knew we needed to head back. We each took a stone, and we held hands while we threw the stones out toward the middle and again hit the center. We knew our wish, and we both smiled, knowing that for sure next summer, we would meet again. We turned and walked the country road back to our homes. As we came near, we could see our parents loading up the vans. We made one last trip to the swing, and we agreed to meet at the old oak tree with our phone numbers and addresses.

Thirty minutes later, at eleven thirty, we met. We stood there and just looked at each other. Several tears rested on Cassandra's cheeks as well as mine. "Cassandra, I will never leave without a promise to return," I told her as I held her near.

"Tony, I will always be there waiting for your return." We carved our initials on the trunk of the oak tree, with a heart that connected us. We exchanged our addresses and phone numbers and then started back in different directions toward the family vans. We both stopped midway, turned around, and ran toward each other to hug one last time.

Cassandra came close to my ear and said, "Tony, I love you." She pulled out a rose from her hair and gave it to me. With the rose, there was a note: "I love you, Tony."

I pulled her close to me and told her, "I love you, Cassandra. I will always love you." We held each other close, desperately hanging on, our tears gently flowing, and then we kissed each other softly.

The next moment, I said, "Until next summer. I will write often. Every day."

Cassandra, her eyes conveying what words cannot describe. Her emotions no longer contained, responded with a suddenness, "Tony, I love you. I will write every day, planning our next summer with each day filled with love, and new memories to be cherished forever". She rushed towards me and hugged me, holding me close with a reluctance to let go.

I shared her desperation and whispered in her ear, "I will always be with you, heart and soul." I then gave her my sketches. "Cassandra, a token to be viewed when you are lonely, and when we return next summer, we will start a new chapter of sketches—and then another for the following summer."

"Tony, I can't take this from you. It means too much to you."

I listened to her reply, sensing that deep inside, she would treasure the sketch book to remember our special summer and look forward to next summer. It was important to me that she have it. "Cassandra, it has no meaning to me if only viewed by me. It is best left with you as a token from me. A token to be used on your return journey back here to join me for our next chapter of sketches. When you are home and you see the two stars that shine the brightest, think of me, of us, and include your dreams and memories as new sketches in our sketch pad. New sketches to be shared by us when we meet again."

She looked at me, took the pad from me, and held it tightly against her chest. With teardrops forming, she held me close, as if I'd given her a priceless gift, one she would cherish forever. "Tony, I will treasure this with my most secret dreams to be shared when we meet again." She kissed me on the cheek, near my ear, and whispered softly, "Forever, Tony. Never leave without saying you will return." As we parted, we connected on a richer, deeper level, both too young to capture the significance, but our eyes spoke volumes as we both sensed something we knew would grow to a higher level of grandeur. Then we went our separate ways to our vans, where our parents quietly waited without a word, aware of our tearful goodbye and exchange of promises for next summer's return.

We did not look back as we headed to the vans; the pain was pure torture. But once seated in the rear of the van, as my family started to drive down the driveway, I dared to look back out the rear window to catch a glimpse of Cassandra. She was there in the van, in the backseat to catch a glimpse of me. Our eyes connected, and we blew each other a kiss as our vans made their turns in opposite directions, each headed to its destination. I turned around one last time, and there she was; her eyes never left me until we were out of sight.

I felt lonely as our van started to climb the mountain. *Why?* I asked myself. *Why is life so full of pain?* I felt my heart breaking with unbearable sorrow. My thoughts were too weighted to carry. I felt I would never get over this. The pain was too much for me. I thought about reaching for the door handle to jump out and run back to our summer home to find Cassandra there waiting for me. I heard a faint weeping, felt the first crack in my heart, and then realized the distant weeping was my own heart crying out with remorse. With quiet sobs, I buried my head in my hands. The van was quiet, as if everyone could feel my despondency. I heard only the hum of the tires and the soft cries from Cassandra. I then heard her words floating in from the partially open window: "I love you, Tony." It was music to my ears and magic to my heart.

I looked up with red-rimmed eyes and softly replied, "I love you too, Cassandra," and I saw my words float out the window to catch up with Cassandra so she could hear my reply.

10

Consummation of Love

That was our first summer. We shared the following summers in that small southern town. Our days were always full. We were constant companions, and eventually, our companionship turned into a relationship in which we were considered a couple. Each summer was like magic, yet toward the end of each summer retreat, the pain and sorrow were always there. We made sure we wrote constantly—not every day but at least once a week. A week never went by without us writing. We read about each other's experiences in the big city—school, the gossip, the changing times, and everything else to share. She joined the cheerleading team, joined the music class, and took up piano and dance. I wrote that I tried out for the baseball and football teams and made second string as wide receiver. Honesty was never a problem for us, as our trust in each other was unchallenged. Someone asked her out to one of the school dances, and she wrote to me for my thoughts. I wrote back that it would be only fair to her to go. She did go out, but fortunately for me, she wrote that the boy was just a friend. I had a lot of opportunities to date and kept many friends, but truthfully, my heart had belonged to her since our first encounter at the old oak tree.

Our lives became enriched further with each passing summer. We were like an anchor to each other, constantly in each other's mind and always there for support. The stretch of time between our engagements brought unbearable loneliness as a constant companion. When each summer retreated to begin its voyage to a distant yet unforgettable memory, our separation became too much to bear. The departures were a gray shadow. With each passing summer, as the summer drew to a close, the departure became more intolerable. With each departure, the shadows of sorrow grew darker, spreading outward and turning a sun-filled, cloudless sky into one with heavy overcast, and the threat of downpour was a constant visitor. As the summers progressed, the dreaded departures dominated our minds earlier each summer. Eventually, the dread painfully seeped into our minds during midsummer, despite the eventuality of our separation being still more than a month away.

When spring arrived, the loneliness started to lift, yet our patience wore thin with increased anticipation of our summer engagement. The springs, in a way, were the longest; each day felt drawn out as we counted the days one by one till the day we desperately wanted and hoped for. That was when we started to plan for a different route, one in which, at summer's end, our companionship would not end but would continue on a different path. We were nearing graduation, and our plans as a couple were just beginning on a more permanent level. We agreed that next summer, after graduation, we would never separate again. We discussed our college plans, and we both decided to transfer to a college where we could live together. Our plans became even more far reaching as we discussed marriage and eventually a family after graduating from college. We still visited the old oak tree and swung on the swing under the maple. Our visits to the pond remained frequent. But our experiences were now more cherished with the expectation of never separating again. We'd always dreamed the same dreams and wished the same wishes, but now everything about us had more permanence. We made each plan for the long term, no longer for the interim. Now the focus was on our relationship and marriage.

We had loved for many summers, and we fell in love that summer before graduation. It was then when that special moment arrived, the moment that embraced the relationship, a confirmation of each other's commitment. That moment was always there, subliminal at first, born on that first encounter, an undercurrent just below the surface, and gained substance as it developed with the passing of each summer, until that first recognition that ran through our veins triggered an onset of emotional awareness and uncertainty—that defining moment when everything was aligned so that it became undeniable, when both of us realized it was time to express our precious gift of love intimately and share it between us. Youthful dreams of princes and princesses became a soulful bond with young adult aspirations. From the first day we met to that moment of intimacy was a gradual process, which we accepted and treasured, both assured that the most enduring, meaningful, and lasting relationships were the ones that evolved naturally.

We were not shy, as we once had been with our stirred emotions. Our first intimate encounter was by the pond on the Fourth of July. We watched for the start of the fireworks, and we both knew our magical road we had traveled would turn into something more special, a turning event wherein our commitment to each other would be confirmed. The darkened sky turned into a rainbow of colors when the fireworks started. We hugged each other, our faces turned upward to catch the theatrical performance. At that moment, an umbrella of colors exploded with brilliancy directly overhead in anticipation of our commitment. We turned toward each other, our eyes mirroring the celebrated colors, and delicately undressed each other as we made our seductive foreplay an erotic prelude to our precious commitment. We made love as the fireworks spread their vibrant colors over us with jubilation of that transcendental moment. It was magical, more than we'd expected. It was fast and furious at first, with our bodies meshing together with an intensity that signaled the long wait was over. We repeated our lovemaking once again but more slowly; we both took our time with an encore of foreplay arousing our senses with heightened tension, quivering in wait until the moment would arrive. Our erotic passion was in complete harmony; our bodies moved in unison, capturing every movement until we both reached orgasm together. We shuddered in each other's arms as the waves of climax swept through our system time after time. We made love repeatedly, our need to consummate compelling, and we climaxed repeatedly, holding on to each other as if never to separate again. Our energy finally spent, we descended from our euphoric high gradually, holding each other close, our bodies soaked with our pheromone-scented sweat, feeling the beating of our hearts in perfect harmony. Our nervous systems still quivered from the emotional depth of our sexual encounter. We were like two thoroughbreds pacing continuously, waiting for the adrenaline to subside from a record-breaking, climatic run.

We stayed that way past the fireworks, and the lit celebration now appeared from the surrounding lightning bugs. Nature's animals must have sensed our romance, for the frogs announced their mating calls. That Fourth signaled a turning point, one in which our souls connected on another level. The connection was undeniable. It defined immortality as our bond continued intensely during that summer.

Admirer's Fallacious Romance: Jealous Revenge

I could not bear it any longer. There was too much to absorb. I had to look away, yielding to my imagination, conjuring up disturbing visions far worse than what I'd just viewed. One word stood out like a flashing neon sign. Endless repetition hammered away at me, with each letter becoming more intense until my pupils felt singed. The light was blinding, a laser piercing my soul. Betrayal! So this is your way of being faithful to me. All those mornings back in the city, where we used to meet. Those coincidental encounters. At least that is what you jokingly called them. But, my dear, I saw behind the charade. They were never at random—maybe once or twice but not when our casual encounters were several times a week. I know you planned this. You must have given our rendezvous a lot of thought due to our perfect timing. Despite the obvious, I welcomed these charades.

I picked up your intentions immediately. Your eyes held the truth of your desire—a desire for intimacy with me. What is that saying? "The eyes are the mirror to the soul." Yes, that's it. It was just a matter of time before we committed. I was waiting for the right moment when you would make the first move. I find it erotic when the woman becomes the pursuer. Yet you could not overcome your shyness. That was when I decided to lead.

From the beginning, it was apparent you savored those moments.

I loved you the first time we met. It must have been obvious, for I lived for those moments. Those precious times became my sole focal point. We both knew the time was near for us to take the random encounters a step further. I planned a surprise for you on our next encounter: a key to the resort located several miles from the city, with a ring attached. I wanted to present the ring after we made love, but I could not hold back any longer. I needed to see the look of amazement when you opened your gift. It would have made our intimacy seem like heaven. But you missed our meeting. I stood there outside the café, waiting for you, but you never showed. That was the moment I'd dreamed about, the one defining turning point, the pivotal moment we both anticipated: a consummation of us as a couple. Because of your frivolous thoughtlessness, my plans were for naught. You weren't there. Why weren't you there? That was the nagging question that consumed me. The question persisted. Night and day, the question became more pronounced, causing painful headaches, as if driving a spike into my head. The tortuous, throbbing, sharp pain got worse, insistently plaguing me with the same question, until I had an answer. The incessant question became maddening. The same question sounded over and over, each time driving another spike into my frontal lobe. The pills were the only relief that distanced the agony for a while. But the nagging question kept ramming into my head. There was only one solution.

It then dawned on me that it was summer break. You'd mentioned that you would be going to a summer retreat, Neverland. What a strange name for a summer retreat. It was difficult to find, yet my persistence was rewarded. I can't fathom how a small town hidden in the mountainous terrain could have such appeal to you. I rented a car and drove there. Then, as I was searching the area, I saw you with him. I saw the expression on your face when you looked at him and the way your eyes conveyed your thoughts. I decided to follow you for the next several weeks, until now. I have one word for you: *whore.* You are a two-faced, unscrupulous bitch! You are a deceitful harlot! You will pay for this. I loved you, yet you have betrayed me. I am torn between pleasure and hatred. The artistry of our sexual intimacy would have been intoxicating, providing a tone of symmetrical fluidity in motion. It would have soothed our souls. But now my soul has been injected with hatred. What was once perceived as sensual poetic beauty now is fused with complete chaos. The thought of sexual intimacy triggers a different response in me now: anger, unendurable pain, and revenge. The thought of you making love to him repulses me and fills me with rage. Our moment together was to be magical, and we were to remain inseparable. Now this hatred I feel turns my vision into a nightmare of turmoil filled with poison. I perceive everything with a backdrop of crimson. Everything I feel is torment now. This torment consumes me with intolerable pain. It started with your deceit, Cassandra. Your unfaithfulness is unforgiving. My observation of you over the past month has eliminated any doubt of your guilt, and now this final act of deceit has spread the guilt to both of you. You are the very essence of betrayal. Why is it that the female gender has no guilt and no remorse when cheating on someone who is in love with them?

Now fate has brought me here to this summer village. Fate wanted to show me what you have been doing behind my back. I am not sure how this Tony guy will react if I show up, and frankly, I don't give a damn. For now, I just want to observe. This is my test of your faithfulness. So far, you have failed miserably. How could you make love to this guy and say you love me? Maybe you need a refresher course on being faithful when you return to the city. I will be back another time. Maybe tomorrow. I definitely will be back when you return to the city on Sunday, and then I will decide. I have too many plans to make tonight—plans I need to make concerning us, Cassandra. Those plans do not include Tony. Is that his name, Cassandra? Soon, Cassandra. Soon we will make love. Then you will realize that this act of making love with him was child's play. After we make love, you will enter through the gates to ultimate pleasure. Fate arranged o$ur encounters. It is fate's promise to me, and, Cassandra, I always follow up on promises.

12

Engagement to Cassandra

The last weekend for Cassandra and me moved in quicker than before. All the plans we made about next summer, college, living together, marriage, and our vow never to separate again kept our hopes held high. But our separation that summer would be especially difficult, in large part because of our intimacy and long-range plans. Our heightened awareness with hopes and dreams also brought a heightened sense of anxiety. There was more at stake, more things could go awry, and the potential consequences were more painful. It all came to a culmination during our last weekend before the summer's end. It was our last Friday toward the end of August, and we relished every single moment together. Our long-term plans were final. If all proceeded as planned, all of the dreams and plans we'd made over the past summers with our youthful fantasies would come true. That weekend was to be our last for the summer. Another chapter of a storybook romance would end, and the mood was filled with mixed emotions. We'd had an unforgettable summer of intimate moments and falling in love, which had brought with it a desperation; we needed to share our last Friday in private.

We decided upon the outdoor theater, a place where we could share precious moments in solitude as a couple to talk about our deepest secrets and desires without any interruptions. The long-running romantic movie playing that night made it even more special. We borrowed my family's van for the special evening and arrived early to firm up our plans for next summer. Our hopes were especially high that night as we talked, but soon the pain of separation inevitably came roaring back. Our helpless feeling at separating again had been held in check for too long, and it resulted in a longing we had not felt since that first summer when we departed.

We climbed into the back, where we could hold each other close to reassure ourselves that soon what we hoped and planned for would become a reality. We watched the movie with impassioned interest, not speaking a word as we felt the intense emotions of the movie, in part due to the reality of our separation occurring in just two days. As we became more tuned in to the movie, it was apparent that the theme resembled our lives. The story was of a couple who met as young teenagers and over time fell in love. It was their last night together before they would separate. As with us, their story had an element of uncertainty of what tomorrow would bring. The resemblance was uncanny, sending eerie chills up our spines; both of us were mesmerized by the unnerving parallels. He was a marine captain during the height of the Iraq War. News arrived that he'd been assigned to the front preparing for the final invasion into Bagdad. He was scheduled to leave the following morning. They were faced with an uncertain future, but despite their hopes and dreams being on temporary hold, their commitment to each other was undeniable, and they made passionate love that night to treasure that moment forever. But fate would intervene with malicious intent. Fate can be cruel, merciless, and uncaring, dealing cards to whomever it chooses, and hopes become unbearable sorrow.

We were glued to the screen, hoping that what we feared would not happen. The following morning arrived for the couple. At four o'clock sharp, there was a knock on the door. His unit's bus was in front, waiting to deliver him to the airbase for transport overseas. In the last minute when he turned to his fiancée to reassure her with a farewell kiss, the look from his wife revealed her mate's demise. That was their last encounter. He never returned. Word arrived that he'd been killed in action. When his fiancée received the news, she half expected it. But no one can be fully prepared when fate knocks at his or her front door. The letter was delivered, a whole lifetime of experiences reduced to one page: "Sorry to inform you, but …" How many ways can "missing in action" be conveyed? It still has the identical meaning. From that point on, she would be beholden to just memories, which would fade with time, but the pain always would be there, never to be forgotten. The harbinger of death became too much for her to bear. Cassandra and I could not continue watching the tearjerker. There were just too many parallels.

The tearjerker jolted our souls with uncertainty, causing us to think that if something happened to us, then that would be our last time together. Our fears overwhelmed us, and Cassandra wept on my shoulder. I held her close as she whispered in my ear, "Tony, make love to me tonight. Make love as never before."

A silence followed. I sensed her pensive mood. "Let us forget about precaution tonight. I want to feel you tonight, and I want you inside me, to become part of me," she said. I held her tighter in agreement. I slowly pulled down her panties as she undid my belt and slid down my pants. I was ready, as she was. She climbed into my lap and raised herself until I was just inside her, and then she slowly slid down as I pushed farther into her. We both knew we were taking a chance, which propelled us to a higher level of ecstasy. Secretly, we both wished that one moment of lovemaking would be the one when we could no longer separate ever again, because we would marry to care for a baby. That carried us to an even more potent level of eroticism, and we made love feverishly with such intensity that we couldn't stop.

With each intimate thrust deeper inside her, our sexual prowess reached its peak, and our sexual urge surpassed our primal hunger, creating a need to become one celestial star to capture all of the universe's energy and fuse it into our souls to ensure that our soulful bonding would remain joined for infinity. We both felt vibrant shudders traverse through our nervous systems, following the neural passageways to trigger our synapses to provide one seamless connection between our physical and emotional stimuli. We became one being. We were able to feel each other's heartbeat, taste each other's pheromones infused with our powerful sexual scent, and feel each other's tremors as wave after wave of climax brought us to a cathartic eruption of pheromones. Our sensation was so all-encompassing that we felt our souls fuse as one; I was nestled in her womb, connected to her soul, ready to give birth to our new soul as one for infinity. Our souls joined on an immortal plane, as evidenced by her scream of ecstasy when she passed her threshold, and our euphoric release was magnified a thousand times, bringing us to a frenzied state. Her vaginal muscles closed and held me in as we both climaxed repeatedly with a torrid flow of our sexual release. Our climatic response was so acute that we both absorbed the pain and exuberance of our past memories up until that moment, when our souls bonded on a level reserved only for celestial beings. We loved as if it were our last time, kissed as if it were our last kiss, and climaxed as if there were no tomorrow. Our lovemaking persisted relentlessly, reaching new euphoric heights that only we could achieve and satisfying a hunger that only we could fulfill, until our urge was satisfied and every ounce of our energy was spent.

We lay back, nestled close to each other to feel each other's warmth and comfort, holding on tightly for fear of letting go. I felt her warm breath on my neck. Her warmth was like a ray of sunshine upon first awakening on a summer morning. I moved my lips toward her ear. "I love you, Cassandra, with my entire being."

She responded as she came closer to my ear, "Never leave me without a promise to return. I love you, Tony. I would die without you." I felt her tears mix with her warm exhalation upon my cheek. I placed my hand on her face and lifted her face toward mine as our eyes connected. With a final wave of release from our euphoric high, our nervous systems sent quivers to the forefront. Our reactions were vivid as we watched each other's response as the last tremor from our torrid lovemaking was spent. We looked at the clock on the dash and became aware that only fifteen minutes were left before the movie would end. Quickly, we dressed and exited the rear door to move to the front just as the movie ended. We sat there for a while to fully absorb the evening. We did not say a word on the way home, for there were no words to describe what we felt. We conveyed our emotions on a soulful level, where conversation was emanated by transference, sustaining our intimate bond as we drove back contentedly from a euphoric night of our intimate encounter. It was nearly one o'clock in the morning. It was late, and we both knew that the next day would be an early riser. After I parked the van, we left the van to go to our homes. We turned toward each other. I held her and told her that next summer, after graduation, we would marry and attend college together as a married college couple.

She looked at me with tears in her eyes and held me close. "Yes,

Tony. I will be your wife." We'd finally decided on the final step to our lasting plan. We kissed feverishly, confirming the essence of what we'd just said, and set a time to meet the next morning: nine o'clock. I walked her to her door, where we kissed again, not wanting the night to end. She opened the door, and upon entering her house, she turned toward me once more as she whispered in my ear that she loved me with all her heart and wanted us to have a baby.

I listened with an earnest heart, wishing the same. "Soon we will bring a newborn into this world," I replied. She closed her door, and I walked back to my home to dream the rest of the night away.

The following morning felt as if it would be our last day on earth. We both ignored breakfast and rushed out toward the oak tree exactly at nine o'clock. Our eyes spoke volumes. We held on to each other intensely, not wanting to let go. That departure was different. It was different in that it would be the last time we would be separated. We were in love. We'd made love and taken a chance last night. We were not sorry about it, and we would do it again. But this time, we felt that everything was on the line. Our future was almost there as a couple, and that made us fearful, for if anything went wrong and got in our way, the result would be more climatic. But maybe because of the aftermath from last night's movie, we were too cautious, too fearful of what could go wrong. One scene, still clearly vivid in my mind, of the wife in shock had triggered our caution and ignited our fears. With just ten minutes left, we hugged and kissed again and went to the old oak tree, where we carved our names as Mr. and Mrs. We looked at each other, and I asked her to be my wife before we would enter college. "Tony, my love, yes, I will marry you."

I reached into my coat pocket, pulled out a gift with a red rose attached, and gave it to her. "Please open it, Cassandra." She looked at me with surprise, filled with hope. With nervous fingers, she lifted the rose from the box and placed it firmly in her hair. She removed the wrapping and opened the box. The gleam of the diamond engagement ring was brilliant. She stood there speechless and looked at me with awe.

The tears came, and she grabbed me and kissed me as she shed tears of joy until there were no tears left. "Oh, Tony. Yes, yes, I will be your wife. I am so in love with you. I will wait for you until that special moment when I say, 'I do.'" My heart filled with love and passion. I took her in my arms and pressed my lips to hers in a kiss to last until we would meet again. There were no words to describe our emotions. Our tears were many. We promised with our hearts that this separation would be our last. We would never separate again. We kissed again, our lips reluctant to part. That kiss sealed our engagement, and then we lifted our eyes to convey our deepest love.

We walked to our vans and showed both our families her ring. Everyone was surprised, but I knew they had been expecting this, and their joy for us was sincere. We kissed again, I watched her walk to her van, and then I turned and slowly walked to our van. This time, the pain was too much too bear. Everything seemed to move forward in slow motion as we both left for our vans. I watched her van drive out to the country road where we'd met so many times, filled with memories, but this time, when we reached the country road, we would go our separate ways and turn in opposite directions toward our city homes. We could not look back as we made our turns, but just before our vans finished their turns, before we were no longer in view, we felt compelled to look back, and she pointed to her engagement ring on her finger and blew me a kiss. I waved and blew back a kiss as our vans climbed their way back up through the mountains. My heartache was torture. I wished I would have given her the ring during the movie at the outdoor theater while we were making love. Maybe if I had, our journey would have taken a different path, one that would have had more permanence, and our separation would have been a thing of the past. I could not bear to think anymore, for the pain was too great to bear.

The old southern town remained the same, unchanging in an increasingly complex and changing world. From one viewpoint, meeting on summer retreats at that old southern town held our promise intact. It symbolized our unchanging love. No matter what happened during those months apart, when changes were forced on us to survive, in our hearts, we held that southern town as our special place where our love would be cherished and protected. It would never change but only intensify, shielded from any change that could harm both of us. Just the anticipation of returning to the summer town held our belief that our love, which had started in that town, would, like the town itself, be protected and never change but only strengthen with time.

13

Falling from Grace

That was the summer before high school graduation. It was to be our last during those vulnerable years when youth's naïveté shielded our hopes and dreams from life's harsh truths. The following summer— after graduation and before leaving for college—was to be the defining summer for us, wherein we would begin our journey of marrying and becoming a couple living together during our college years.

My hopes were slammed into oblivion by fate's cruelty. Cassandra was not there. She never arrived for that special summer to begin our plans. We'd both earned scholarships to colleges. But that first day, when I returned to the old oak tree, she never showed up. I wrote to her several times with no response. Her letters had stopped a month ago. I called her repeatedly without any response. My soul felt unhinged. I could not accept what was becoming obvious. My sleep escaped me; my days and nights were consumed with thoughts of her. The moments when I would nod off from pure exhaustion were haunted with memories and visions of her. Dreams I'd never encountered before presented haunting images of her. Each image portrayed an atmosphere of elusiveness and longing, leaving me even more exhausted. Her images were pure and clear, but there was a hint of despair. A tone that was barely audible would, on unexpected occasions, be revealed as a high-pitched shrill, one that I discerned as pure terror. The shrill eventually would evaporate into just a faint, stealth-like echo. I was on the verge of becoming ill, realizing that my own deep-rooted insecurities of her disappearance were overwhelming me with worry. I had to come to terms with one fact: she was not there, and she might never be there again. The pain at summer's end with our departures did not compare to the pain I held then. I felt my heart break into tiny fissures, each spreading outward and shredding my soul into fragments. I was unable to sustain any hope and, under the weight of despondency, spiraled into an endless tunnel of pending doom. I felt dead in soul and mind. I had to pull myself together with college approaching. Eventually, I conceded to what was becoming obvious: maybe she'd found someone. I eventually stopped waiting and hoping. However, in the back of my mind, there was a secret place where I had a vague odd feeling that one day we would meet again.

The summer was just half over when, in mid-July, I elected to return to the city on my own. I made one last visit to the old fishing pond, which was still there as if nothing had changed. I went to the old oak tree for a last look at the carvings we'd made that first and last summer. A wave of memories passed through me, causing me a tearful sorrow, one that caused a persistent ache that traversed throughout my soul. But despite the tormented cross of loneliness, I came to terms with her absence. I wished her luck and hoped she'd found her love in life.

14

Cassandra's Letter

I returned to the city and started packing for college. In the process of packing, I searched the mail the postman had saved for us during our absence. I sorted through the mail piece by piece, and one envelope caught my eye because of its familiar handwriting. It was addressed to me. I took it from the bundle and noticed no return address. One immediate thought crossed my mind: *Could this be from Cassandra?* It had to be. But if so, why no return address? I brought the envelope closer to detect any scent. Yes, it was there—the scent of a fresh rose. My intense longing for Cassandra focused on that very moment. I felt my total existence hinged on what was about to be revealed. The message had to be from Cassandra. I was both excited and cautious about opening it. Yet the more I thought about the letter, the more my sense of caution escalated to the next level. The absence of a return address triggered my hesitation and spurred more uncertainty. What if it was news I did not want to hear? Why had it taken her so much time to write? What if the letter was a plea for help? Even if it was bad news, I had to know, regardless of the intent. I delayed opening it for a while longer, for at least five minutes, but finally realized that my reluctance to open it was due to an unfounded anxiety.

I almost succeeded in convincing myself there was no need to be concerned. My curiosity finally overruled my hesitation, and I opened the letter. Out came a red rose enclosed in a small plastic bag along with a letter. My surprise was obvious. My smile was convincing, and my eyes were filled with renewed hope as I excitedly picked up and opened the enclosed rose to catch its fragrance. Memories flashed before me, bringing tears of longing. For sure, the letter would convey what I have been anticipating since the last time we'd met. I picked up the folded letter lying there waiting for me to open it, yet I reluctantly decided to pause once more before reading. My patience was locked in a struggle, wanting to give in. I wanted just a little more time before opening it to let the exuberant feeling sink in and fully absorb the long-overdue sense of relief, a calm I hadn't felt since our last summer. But unbeknownst to me, that calm was the prelude before the tempest, like the dead calm a seaman experienced out in the middle of the ocean with no land in sight, when nothing moved, the winds were nonexistent, and not a sound could be heard for hours, only for him to be surprised by a monsoon of beastly proportions. I should have instinctively picked up the foretelling signs, sensing the lurking portent. All the yellow flags were there, a prophetic omen of things to come, but my desperate hope blinded me. So much time had passed to that point. For that interim, quietude was just what it was—a temporary respite to prepare myself for the shock of my life.

I cautiously opened the letter, and my eyes immediately took in the first sentence. My mind was on hold until I read further and could assess its meaning.

> Tony, I have a lot to say, but this one letter will be brief for reasons I will write later. I am not sure if you were at our summer retreat, but if so, you know that I did not go to the summer town this year. I want to apologize for not being there but also, more importantly, for not telling you before the summer started. There is a reason why I was not there. I have to tell you something, and I hope you can forgive me.

I paused for a few seconds while I prepared for whatever was next. I knew it was not going to be pleasant, and I had to glance away to catch my breath. I'd had no idea my breathing was so shallow all that time, but there was no doubt now, with my pulse etching upward as my heart raced. I expected the worst. I took a few minutes more, bringing back memories of past summers when we'd sat up high in the old oak tree. I thought of the old country road, with just the two of us walking gingerly because of the hot tar to the old pond. I remembered it vividly, especially that one afternoon when everything was perfect. It was the only time I'd felt that way, and I doubted that special feeling ever would encompass me again. I soon realized that maturing into adulthood brought with it baggage with your signature firmly stamped into the leather—baggage filled with what we perceived as life necessities, which would eventually all end the same way: suffocating, agonizing problems that wore us down to just a shadow of who we once were. Tearing myself away from the tunnel I was in, with gritted resolve, I turned back to the letter and read on.

> For love and honesty, Tony, our most precious gifts to each other, I need to be truthful with you, as you are my heart and soul. Lack of truth between us would result in the ultimate portrayal of deceit. The absence of truth, with no disclosure, would only end in our dissolution. As painful as this will be, I must reveal to you why I wasn't there for you this summer.

> Last year, after the summer's end, the friend I wrote to you about—Matt is his name—well, our friendship eventually became more than just a friendship. I wasn't sure how I felt about him. But in between those magical summer months, the loneliness became unbearable. Love and loneliness become an inseparable couple. And the more intense one side becomes, the more unbalanced it becomes. Something eventually gives, no matter how important. But that is what loneliness can do. It can make us desperate. Matt sensed my loneliness. He was always there when my loneliness became almost intolerable. We began to have lunch together, and eventually, it led to several dinners. Tony, I am having a difficult time writing this, but I must. Forgive me for what I am about to disclose. It pains me to tell you this. I got pregnant. To this day, I cannot

explain my actions. If you only knew how much I missed you. If you only knew the depth of my love for you. But to bring a new life into this world was equally important. To have a normal life for the baby, we decided to marry. I felt that a marriage could last without the couple being in love. But, Tony, I was wrong. He said he was in love with me, but I was not with him. That, Tony, belongs to you.

It does not end here. Tony, the worst is yet to be revealed. I don't know how we have come to this moment. It is not your fault. The fault is mine and mine entirely. We had our entire future ahead of us, and my personal weakness has caused a serious fracture in our relationship. You must feel cheated by me, and I have no excuses that would justify my actions. It all seems surreal to me. Even I do not comprehend my actions. I need to understand, as you surely must. I need to replay the details to make sense of all this. But more importantly, I need to reveal to you the details. To reveal my story for both of us. For me to forgive myself and for you to feel the intensity of my ordeal, and I hope to forgive. I have been unfaithful to you, and you and I both know that you need to make judgment on our connection. Your decision about me must be based on all the facts. After you hear my story, you will have all the facts before you and will be aware of my emotional turmoil before you pass judgment. I have always felt our connection existed at the spiritual level—that our souls were intertwined. We both knew it when we first met under that oak tree. Because of this connection, I feel it is my obligation to reveal the truth, to be honest with you. If our connection is to continue, it must be based on the truth. Otherwise, our connection will be based on lies and will fail. Once everything is revealed, I will accept your decision.

Here is my story. As unreal as it may sound, this is what
I have lived through since our last summer.

I stopped reading for a few minutes. I felt tired—more of a mental
fatigue. I was feeling every intense moment relayed to me in Cassandra's
heartfelt letter. She was right. There was a soulful connection between
us. It had been there when we first met. That connection carried an
obligation between us. I needed to know what had happened in order
for us to heal. I already knew I wanted our connection to continue.
Our love was strong, resistant to any obstacle. We both realized that
without emotion, without love, one had nothing. Yet I had to understand
Cassandra's turmoil; it was necessary to heal the divide. My mental
weariness persisted, but I had to read on. I had to understand and feel
what Cassandra felt. I returned to her letter and continued to read.

I wrote you previously a letter that incited this
gruesome scene I am to reveal now. He found the
letter I wrote—that I had intentions to divorce him and
to return to you. That is, if you were to have me and
the baby. But that night, when he found the letter, he
came at me with his ferocious temper. He'd already
had a few drinks. A few too many. He found me in
the bedroom while I was getting ready for bed. He
pulled me up to face him. His eyes were filled with
hatred. A crazed look of insanity. That look could
only mean one thing: he must have found out about
my intentions.

But I did not know that he'd also found out about you.
In a jealous rage, he grabbed me by both arms and
wanted to know who Tony was. He told me something
you should know. He asked me if this was the same
man who made love to me by the pond. Remember
that evening by the pond when we made love? You
heard something. You sensed something. We saw the
deer. But now I realize that what you heard must have
been Matt. He must have been there on those other

occasions when you sensed something by the pond. His eyes, Tony. His eyes had a glazed look, one of crazed lunacy. I told him nothing about you.

He threatened me and held me down with his hands around my neck, squeezing the life out of me, until I would tell him who you were. I remained silent. My vision blurred, and I knew I was dying. But then that first day at the old oak tree came back. I remembered how I fell in love with you that summer, and that memory gave me the strength to fight back. With everything I could muster, I fought back. It must have taken him by surprise because there were a few seconds of hesitation; he was taken aback by such a sudden outburst. That is when I bit him, taking a chunk out of his hand as he loosened his grip. The pain must have caused him to lose focus as he brought his hands up in response to the pain. His weight shifted to one foot as he raised his other foot to send a crushing blow to my face. But just as he was ready to stomp on me, I brought my knee up and kicked him in the groin. I pushed him off me and somehow managed to free myself, and I ran down the hall toward the stairway. But he came after me, his anger bordering on delirium. He caught me and threw me against the wall repeatedly until I almost blacked out, and then he thrust me down the stairs. At first, I did not know what had happened. But I saw the blood around me. The pain was intolerable. I was not aware from where I was bleeding. I feared I'd lost the baby. I looked at the crimson pool encircling me. God help me. If I did loose the baby, the tragedy would be unfathomable. The living essence of a soon-to-be newborn, only to forever lose that chance. As the blood continued to spread out around me, the very thought of the potential tragedy was filled with a mind-numbing paralyses. My sorrow and pain were enormous and channeled into a fierce hatred. I lost myself. Without realizing what was happening, I became hysterical as I brought my hands, covered with blood, to my face, smearing the sanguine fluid over my face and neck.

I raised my head and then looked up at him, my eyes glued to his every movement. There was a moment of alarm from him as he momentarily stopped at the top of the stairway. I must have looked like the devil himself, for I swear I noticed a flicker of fear run through his eyes. I was ready to face him. To fight until one of us was dead. I shouted at him. I called him a fucking bastard and a coward. I broke out into insane laughter, which escalated into a high-pitched scream as I rose to my feet, trying to keep my balance with all of the blood on the floor. But even if I had fallen, I would have crawled my way toward the stairs to get at him. There was to be only one way for this to end: either he or I would be dead.

A deadly silence followed. I moved toward the stairway, slipped on my blood, and fell to my knees. But my intense hatred for this man pulled me forward. All that could be heard was the wet swishing sound as I crawled through my blood toward the stairs with my eyes locked onto his. Then I heard a voice I did not recognize. A voice full of rage. I soon realized the voice was coming from me. I stopped and grabbed the side rail to pull myself up near the first step and shouted that I'd never loved him and was in love with you, Tony. I yelled that he would never be the man you are. He was just a fucking coward and loser. I yelled at him like a crazed woman that I would seek a divorce and leave him. I'd let his companions be just his fucking whiskey and rotting brain and liver until there was nothing left. Then he would finally see what hell was, for surely that was his destination.

He charged down the stairs toward me with a hunting knife. God must have been watching, for he tripped and fell on his way down, and upon his landing, the knife sliced through his sternum. I stood there staring down at the wasted body lying in front of me. The knife protruded from his chest. Blood was oozing from the mouth. I noticed a few air bubbles forming at his mouth as the blood bled out. I caught a slight movement as his chest rose slightly. I wanted to watch his last breath as death made its entrance. But I felt something else. I felt angry at God. How dare he take the lead by sending this man to death? That was my role. And I did not have the pleasure, the satisfaction of doing the task myself. Instead, I felt nothing. No triumphant thrust of my hand outward to rejoice in victory. No sense of personal closure. But upon further scrutiny, I realized there never would be closure. A constant pain would be my companion from here on. The pain is intense now, but over time, it will recede like a constant addiction that never leaves but stays with you—the craving is always there, varying in intensity but nonetheless a companion for life, never leaving, just becoming part of you. I saw his eyes start to open. I stood there, my hatred returning, and as I raised my foot to drive the knife farther in, I heard the front door bust open.

The medics had come after a call from a neighbor. They looked on and saw what must have appeared as a war zone, with two combatants battling until one was dead. They rushed to my aid, and after taking my vital signs, they put me on a stretcher and rushed me to the hospital. I don't know what they did for him. Hopefully they have shipped him to the morgue. That was the last I saw him. I was in the hospital for three nights. I had a severe cut, a concussion, and bruised ribs. The blood gushing out of me was from a wound to my midsection. I had to stay an extra day for the x-rays. Miraculously, my pregnancy was not harmed. Of all the pain I went through, it was nothing compared to the sick feeling I endured while I went through the ordeal to check on my baby.

Then panic surfaced when I found out Matt was in the same hospital and somehow had survived. I was discharged in three days. The police came and asked me if I wanted to press charges. I couldn't, Tony. All I could think about was getting away. I had to get away as far as possible to rid myself of him. I was scared to death of him. When he fully recuperates, he will look for me. He will try to kill me. That I am sure of. The only escape I had was to leave as soon as possible while he was still in the hospital. I hurried to my place and packed, and now I will drive to a place that is remote and far away. I will be on the road and be at my destination in a few days. I cannot disclose where I will be going. Not right now. When I get there and am somewhat settled, I will write to you with my new address. I am writing you this letter from my old address. Right after I mail this, I am leaving. I am telling you this because I want you to know why I was not there. I will write again once settled.

Tony, before I leave, I must forewarn you about this maniac. He may know your address. I wrote your address down as I was writing you the letter he found. I did not tear the address up and throw it away. I left it on the dining room table. I found it upon returning from the hospital. So he most likely knows where you live, Tony. If you are hurt, I will understand. I have not been fair to you, and I will not blame you for finding someone else. For now, I have to keep you out of harm's way. I can't see you now. Too much has happened, and I could not bring myself to look into your eyes. I could not bear seeing the pain I have caused you. So, Tony, maybe one day we can look back at this and dare take that chance again when I ask you to be my prince. For now, Tony, my prince, I am not that princess to be saved by her handsome prince. Maybe later, when I forgive myself and if you can forgive me. By the time you read this letter, I will be at my new destination. I should not ask you my next question. But I must. Could you please try to understand and focus on our special moments during our magical summers and wait for me to talk this through? If, at that time, you still want to leave, then I will accept your decision. Just remember: I do love you. I always have, Tony. I am sorry.

15

Tony's Quandary

I could not read anymore. The nausea hit me like a solid brick. I didn't have time to make it to the bathroom; I lurched forward, heaving my guts out until nothing was left. The dry heaves continued relentlessly. My gut was tied in knots. Spasms of searing, knifelike pain took my breath away, and my breathing came in short gasps. My body shook with agony while the impact of what I'd just read fully registered. I felt as if I were breaking into tiny fragments. I ran to the dining room, grabbed a bottle of brandy, and finished off several shots. The brandy tore into me like a flaming torch, and my stomach muscles tightened in a death grip before the alcohol started taking effect. My nausea was worse because of the alcohol, but I put up with it, and the spasms started to subside from the alcohol's sedative effects. My emotional upheaval was overwhelming but was no comparison to the ache in my heart. I had to sit as vertigo got the best of me. Too many mixed emotions were running through me. Emotions that were foreign to me. Emotions from all spectrums. I felt anger, deceit, betrayal, remorse, and sympathy. The intensity was such that I could not make any decision on how to respond. I just sat there numbly as all the memories paraded before me, bringing forth images of us through the summer months.

I tried calling her old number. "Unlisted" was the only response after repeated dialings. I restlessly paced the hallway leading to my room, trying to think of what I could do. I tried to think of something to no avail. I looked at the date on the envelope. She'd mailed the letter to me about five days ago. With no return address, there was no way I could find her. She was gone. The impact of that one word left me empty. I felt an emptiness filled with total despair. *Gone!* relentlessly repeated over and over in my mind until I could hear nothing else. It screamed in my head with such intensity that I thought my head would explode. My vision became an enclosed tunnel. The light became narrower, turning into a pinhole, until the lights finally went dark, leaving me in a void with a strange calmness, as if I'd given in, surrendering to fate's whim.

I fought to maintain consciousness while I took two double-strength aspirin. I sat down at the kitchen table to wait for the aspirin to kick in. My patience was nonexistent. I realized that it wasn't just the pain that distracted me. I was distracted by my tension; my anxiety was causing an anguish I hadn't felt since that first summer with Cassandra, on that unforgettable Sunday when we departed. I'd never thought I would experience such a devastating sorrow again. I walked over to the family room, opened the door to the hutch, and grabbed the bottle of brandy. I returned to the kitchen and poured myself another double shot. I virtually inhaled the brandy, and its mellowing effects started immediately. I felt somewhat subdued due to the effects of the drink but alert enough to attempt to think of some kind of plan. I needed anything that would help formulate a strategy to handle this nightmare. *The police report? But where?* It would be an exhaustive task to search for an assault-and-battery report unless I knew where to look, and that would be only if Cassandra had filed an assault charge. But how many assault-and-battery charges occurred over a month's span throughout the states? I walked over to the computer to search on the internet. After a few attempts, I realized this would not be a simple search. I would need to access a database that housed such information, and it would have to contain up-to-date charges. Was that even legal, especially searching for charges before a case went to trial? It also dawned on me that the same held true for emergency room visits because of HIPAA privacy regulations.

A stark reality hit me: there was nothing I could do. I could just carry on with my life, hoping and waiting for her call. I was devastated. I had never felt so hopeless. Cassandra was in trouble. Her life was in danger if her ex came after her, bent upon killing her, and all I could do was wait. It would be a torturous wait. My princess was in trouble, and her prince was helpless.

Days turned into weeks, and then a month went by without my hearing a word from Cassandra. I was at a heartbreaking loss. I was fearful that her ex had found her, and from there, all I could do was imagine the worst and hope for the best. Daily I listened to the news and scoured the paper. I searched for anything that related to violence or murder with a description of the victim. I found nothing that matched Cassandra.

One month turned into two. The pain was still there, just camouflaged by life's daily routines. That was all I was—just someone living a life infused with repetitive, mindless daily tasks with no purpose and no end. I felt myself sliding into a state of depression. It was slight at first, but the downward trajectory became more pronounced over time. Eventually, it got to the point where I was convinced I was suffering from acute depression, and worse, it was not letting go. It pervaded my soul, clinging to me like a leech sucking my lifeblood away until nothing was left.

16

Matt's Letter

Fall became winter, and then the beginning of spring arrived. It happened on one of those spring days that teased with a taste of summer. The temperature was in the midsixties. I'd just gotten home from my job as an assistant professor in the architectural field. I taught an innovative course: creative design. I searched through the mail, tossing immediately into the miscellaneous basket anything that seemed unimportant. Then I saw a letter with no return address, addressed to me and written by hand. I immediately grabbed it. For reasons I cannot explain, the touch of the envelope did not feel right to me. It felt course and rigid, unlike Cassandra. I did not spend any more time pondering whether I should open it, as I had last time. I felt that whatever the letter contained could not be worse than the last one.

I opened it with nervous anticipation, my fingers stiff from the tension. Before I had a chance to look inside, I dropped the letter from clumsiness, and as it landed on the floor, petals of a dead rose fell out of the envelope. A feeling of dread crawled its way up my spine as I picked up the rose, and the petals crumbled into pieces. Instead of being filled with the scent of birth and rich with color, the petals were fragments of what once had been, and the odor was akin to the scent of decay. The smell was more repulsive as I brought the decayed pieces closer. My vertigo returned, and my anxiety rushed back with a vengeance. I brought the rose up even closer to my face. The stench from the decay was similar to the reek of death. Pure panic ensued. I picked up the envelope and pulled out the folded letter. *Please, no,* I thought. *Please do not let this be what I think it will be. Not her death. There is no way I could handle that if it was Cassandra.* My hands shook with such tremors that I had to try several times just to open the envelope widely enough to pull out the letter.

I unfolded the several-page letter with eyes partially open. The words stood out, coming off the page. The heat from each word felt like a searing torch to my pupils. My mind initially could not interpret the message, held back from fear of overload. The words soon became more focused, with my mind taking in each word and struggling with the impact. The first paragraph stunned me immediately as I read.

> Tony. I assume that is your name. At least that is what she finally blurted out before she broke. There is no hope, Tony. It is a psychotic break. That means a break from reality. And the probability of recovery is almost nil. Nada. Absolutely zero chance, mister. Her state is catatonic. I was going to end it for her, but the state she is in is more of a suitable punishment. I mean, with death, the breaking point is instantaneous and ends when the last breath is exhaled. But this state she is in is one continual state of hell. Definitely a justified punishment for her affair with you. Eventually, her state of mind will have a degrading effect on her physically. A suitable punishment for infidelity. Quite a price to pay for a night of intimacy. Your fate is next, Mr. Prince. Just not sure what your punishment should be, but I do have a creative style, and I guarantee your descent into the pits of damnation will be one hell of a trip.

I stopped reading, unable to comprehend. I stood there and started over, pausing again when I reached the words *psychotic beak.* Tears started forming. Each drop pooled on top of those two words, as if my tears were attempting to drown out the impact, hoping that once submerged, it would dissipate, its meaning washed away by tears of despair. But it wasn't so. The words bled with each drop, becoming just a blackened smear, but the impact was still there, sitting there to torment me. My mind was desperate to maintain composure but losing the battle as pure panic seized me, nearly uncontrollable. I was bordering on a complete breakdown, trapped in a chamber of horror. Despite the building panic, another emotion was charging out with full force. An inferno of rage took control, driving me to read on.

Yes, Tony. She had to pay the price for violating my trust. You will never find her. She is mine. A ghost of her previous self, but she belongs to me. She is in a place you will never know. She did not love me. And if she could not love me, then I would not allow her to love anyone else. I took my time, Tony. I wrapped my hands around her neck and squeezed until she blacked out. Then I stopped to shock her awake. After a while, her eyes turned to a vacant stare. She must have known the end was near. Have you ever seen the eyes change just before the breaking point? A beautiful sight. You would be moved by it. You can see the soul retreating; the eyes are vacant as the psychotic break occurs. Well, finally, she told me she never loved me. She loved you. One last thing, Tony. You want to know what finally detached her from reality? When I told her I was sterile. The baby could not have been mine. That last look when she realized the baby was yours, I have to admit, was tragic. I almost felt pity for her, a rare emotion for me. She finally withdrew into a catatonic state. And you know, Tony, that was when I realized I did not have to end it for Cassandra. She already knew the end was here. The eyes, Tony. Do you know that when the break occurs, the life force leaves, and the eyes become soulless, lifeless, and empty? Oh, I wish I had a picture, which I surely would have included with this letter.

Your baby, Tony. Well, I assume it is yours. Tears you up inside? Remember the Fourth last summer? You made love to Cassandra. I have to admit it was intense. I was there across the pond. Just like the other time, when you noticed something and were surprised when you saw it was just the deer. The deer was not expected. But it was a perfect decoy. I remained hidden, using the deer as a shield. You were looking right at me, but all you saw was the deer. Did you know, Tony, that your lover and I made love? Back in her home, away from your summer home. Every morning, we met before work, and it was obvious she wanted me. Again, the eyes, Tony. The eyes reveal the soul, and it was obvious. So obvious that it was our turn. I am Matt. Recognize the name? I was the one always there for her. Can't say the same for you. Where were you, Tony? How can you make love to Cassandra and then just leave? Well, Mr. Prince Tony, I was there every day, and you weren't. What type of impression does that leave?

But after we married, I found her letter to you. After all that I did for her. What the hell did you do for her? At the end of the summer, you left her. And that is where I came into the picture, exactly at the center. Yet she loves you. I do not comprehend this. It does not conform to my logic. When love is given to another, it should be reciprocated. If not, then that contradicts nature's greatest gift. And that violates my rules. We are not talking about jaywalking or some idiotic traffic violation. This is about faithfulness, obedience, and loyalty. Whatever you want to call it, it is the very essence of the rules we must abide by. And those rules were broken by you and Cassandra. Both of you have deceived me. Deceived me on a primal level that is sacred to my soul. Since this is so personal, I have decided on your fate. As judge and jury, I will pass a verdict and punishment. It took me exactly fifteen minutes. Guilty! Cassandra is finished, with no mercy from me. So, Tony, you failed miserably. You were not able to save her.

How does this feel, Tony? Do you or Cassandra have an inkling of how I felt while watching you lovebirds? I can tell you that your reaction to what I write does not even come close to how I felt when watching you and Cassandra by the country pond. I guarantee that your heartfelt despondency at what I have relayed is just a minute sample of what I felt by the pond. The oddity, though, is I feel that I know you well. From Cassandra's last words, I feel I have connected with you. You will learn more about me as time goes on. What did old Bogart say in *Casablanca*? "This is the beginning of a beautiful friendship." Yes, perfect. Oh, we will get to know each other very well. There is a sadistic side to me, but what is life without some drama?

Now, Tony, you are part of this ménage a trios. There is no appeal here. Consider my verdict as final. Your finality is coming. And it will arrive. I am sure Cassandra must have informed you that I know your address. And guess who is coming to dinner? Me, Tony. I will bring my steak knives. They're brand new for carving. A feast for a prince. Is that what Cassandra called you near the end? Well, Tony, where was her prince when she needed you? Nowhere. You failed. You broke your promise. And here I thought a prince always kept his promise. So that means you are one damn liar. And one more thing for now. Our dinner engagement has an unannounced date. When you least expect it, I will show up. So keep the table set just in case an unexpected dinner guest arrives. Maybe tomorrow or maybe next week, next month, or next year. I do love suspenseful plots, Tony. They are such a turn-on. So I will see you later. Just you and me, sitting across from each other at the dinner table, and I will bring a bottle of wine. More of a farewell gift. We both will have a toast to your fateful end, Tony. Sweet dreams, fucker.

The impact of what I'd read was not registering. My mind was reeling, unraveling. There was no stopping the collapse. Every type of emotion hit me at once, each with a wallop. Blow after blow hit me with full impact, tearing my mind in every direction, ripping apart the fabric that formed the essence of me. I felt there was nothing left. Everything led to me. The unescapable truth pulled me down with unbearable weight, a truth I could not deny. I had not been there for her, and she'd paid the price, along with our unborn, who did not have a chance. Both were devastated due to my failure. I had lost everything. My hopes and dreams had vanished. Each dream, each memory, and each vision of those summer retreats, the country road, the old pond, and the old oak tree was buried in a graveyard meant for lost souls who had succumbed to death from repeated, relentless volleys from fate's cruel punches. Now it was my turn to take that leap into the graveyard to find my plot with the hole already dug out with such precision by fate. A wave of fear, anger, despair, and emotions that had no name swallowed me, infusing my soul with one thought in mind. Fate had dug the hole, but it would let me pull the trigger.

All the rooms spun around me. My mind seized up. The lights dimmed as I swayed back and forth and finally sensed my fall as I blacked out.

17

Abduction: Held Captive

Where am I? Those were the first words that surfaced as I came to my senses, struggling to breathe and become fully conscious. A current of sensory awareness was just barely out of reach, submerged under a rising tide of distant memories held back by a wall of denial. My eyelids felt like weights. I couldn't tell if my eyes were open. There was no discernible light, just a pitch-black darkness filled with a damp, musty odor. My back ached with nail-biting vengeance. I was lying on something cold—a metal table, it felt like. I reached down, trying to feel what was underneath me. My arms were tied to the table—not tightly but with enough play to allow my arms some movement. I had just enough room to be able to reach down and feel the surface I was lying on. The feel was smooth, as if the table were made of glass. It felt hard and ice cold. The cold sent aching spasms up my back, leaving my back muscles rigid and tense. I tried to move my body slightly, but the pain from the effort traversed throughout every inch of my body. My head throbbed with pain. I couldn't focus. Every thought seemed vague, as if it were caught in a web of confusion.

Behind me, a light came on. My eyes screamed with blinding pain, trying to adjust to the newfound wall of light. As my eyes adjusted, the circle of light diminished to a narrow beam, illuminating the area immediately around the table I was lying on. I tried to get up, but I was too weak to lift my legs. I attempted to lift my arms with minimum success, remembering the ties restricting my arm movement. I tried to lift my legs again, but the effort was in vain; I realized they too were loosely restrained to the table, allowing minimal movement.

Outside the perimeter of brightness was complete darkness. I scanned the dark perimeter, hoping for a glimpse of any other form of light. Even a pinhole of light would have provided some hope that the enclosed darkness was not endless. The surrounding darkness varied in intensity. I noticed there were several peculiarities—patches in the darkness that did not have the same consistency. Those areas were darker, a dense blackness of varying shapes that gradually blended with the rest of the dark background.

A sudden movement caught my attention. My gaze shifted immediately to the dense patches. A sudden shift occurred, too quick to discern further. But I detected it in my peripheral vision. It was subtle but did not go unnoticed. I held my focus on the dense areas. My gaze held steady, keenly alerted to any movement. A few minutes passed without further irregularities. I was tense. My imagination, I was sure, could have conjured up any oddity. I couldn't help but feel something ominous perched in the dark, just waiting to cause havoc. I listened intently to detect any sound, but the silence was deafening. It was too quiet and too dark, as if I were being observed or studied. I could not let my guard down. Something kept my senses on acute alert, highly tuned to detect even a needle dropping. I was convinced a presence was there within the room or chamber I was in. I could feel it—not physically but instinctively, with that sixth sense and its uncanny, radar-like ability to detect what we were consciously impervious to. I had an ominous feeling of foreboding, a sensation that crawled up my spine, wary of harmful intent. It was a waiting game to see who would make the first advance. *How stupid*, I thought, *for I am the one confined to this table. It is the other presence who has the advantage, and that being the case, why the waiting game? My only conclusion is that whatever or whoever is in this chamber is playing out this game either because it is fearful of me or enjoying the torment. Just watching me squirm with dreadful anticipation.* God, my paranoia was getting the best of me. I needed to back off before I totally lost it.

I diverted my attention toward the end of the table for any sign of movement. I detected more patches consuming areas with an intense shade of darkness, areas that appeared to have a greater density, giving way to my assumption that the patches were more than just a normal gradation of my perception but represented some forms or objects placed there to parley the waiting game with me as the potential victim. *Damn my paranoia returning with a vengeance. Just get me out of here.* Upon further scrutiny, the patches appeared to be just shadows. I felt a flicker of hope, realizing that my rationale was breaking out of my paranoid mind-set. But my rationale was short-lived, as I realized the shadows were irregular forms, each with a slightly iridescent quality that caused each shadowy form to appear as a ghostly image. The forms' ghostly, opalescent appearances occurred at varying intervals, alternating between dark, oppressive shadows and forms with prismatic appearances. Even though the forms changed their visual state with timed precision, there was no discernible change in position.

As I looked away momentarily, I suddenly returned my gaze to the shadows. There it was again: movement. There was no question this time. The movement had been still subtle but a split second longer in duration—a slight movement in which the shadows had shifted slightly, as if to avoid detection. A continual vibration emerged, causing a stealth-like noise that seemed to permeate the air from somewhere behind the shadows. I could not locate the source of the noise, but it filled the air with an ear-splitting intensity. It had not been there just a few minutes ago, when complete silence had filled the place.

Again, another sudden movement occurred. An unconcealed view just for a fraction of a second revealed a shift in the shadows. Were the shadows closer to me? It seemed the shadows had inched forward, forming a circle that was becoming tighter. The noise and vibration abruptly stopped, replaced with a numbing silence. The sudden contrast between the ear-shattering noise and the deafening silence was more alarming than the ensuing noise or complete silence. Within minutes, the light grew dimmer; the beam retreated to just a pinhole and was finally extinguished in the vast void of darkness.

There was absolute blackness, a complete vacuity of nothingness—no sight and no sound, just emptiness. It was too quiet. I had just my thoughts and runaway panic keeping me company. The only sound came from my shallow breathing. I took each breath slowly to avoid possible detection. I could hear my own pulse beating profusely from a rising tide of anxiety. My thoughts were racing, wandering aimlessly.

I was nervous with dreadful anticipation, surrounded by a vast sea of unknowns. *Is this what it feels like to die? An afterlife of lasting emptiness. Leaving one just with his or her thoughts. Remembrances of deeds good and bad. To absorb for an eternity of time. If so, it could only end one way: complete madness. Sinking into the pits of despair, where the silence is broken by those fellow souls who have succumbed to the inevitable form of lunacy. So this is hell. To be judged, and when the sentence is passed, to fall from grace to the very bottomless pits of soulful damnation.*

My thoughts rambled on. The uncertainty of what lay ahead paved the way to an avenue of fear, of torrid thoughts with aimless direction to an unending highway by happenstance, with no destination. The only sounds I detected were my breathing and heartbeat. Each beat and each breath melded into a rhythmic, muffled noise, as if I were underwater, where the noise was self-contained. I yelled out loud, expecting no response. Repeatedly, I yelled until I answered my own pleas. I figured if I were going mad, then at least I would create my own dialogue to keep myself company during my descent into the abyss of darkness.

Someone must have heard me, for the beam of light returned, intensely cutting into the darkness and illuminating the area immediately surrounding the table. The shadows disappeared, revealing empty air. Oh, the shadowy forms were there—I was convinced of that. I saw a flicker of the forms just as the lights turned on before they vanished. No doubt they were in hiding, but from what?

I glanced toward the foot of the table I was on. *Strange,* I thought. There above my feet was a red light that appeared to be suspended in midair. The light briefly switched to green before returning to a red status. A few seconds elapsed before a sharp pain traversed up the length of my body. Every cell seemed to be on fire. The pain grew intense, causing my body to constrict, with violent eruptions exploding from my vocal cords in a mournful cry. The pain was insistent, elevating my anguish to another level. My muscles started to spasm, making the pain intensely worse. I tried to lift my head, but my neck was so tight that any sudden movement was too overwhelming. I rolled my head sideways in both directions to stretch my muscles. The pain started to ebb, allowing my muscles to finally relax. I lifted my head as high as possible to detect any possible damage. I could only see my midsection, which was black and blue. I lifted my feet, and both had the same discoloration. *What the hell happened?* Panic ensued, which stirred a myriad of anxiety-filled questions. *How did I wind up here? Why am I here? Whoever is responsible for this must be truly mad. I fear that whatever is happening here is personal.* The lights flickered again and then suddenly extinguished into total darkness.

I heard something move near me. I reached out as far as I could with my hands but felt nothing. I heard it again. Something was sliding along the floor, making a slithery sound, as if dragging something. The presence felt closer. Something hit the table I was lying on. Then the movement stopped. I listened intently, waiting for whatever was moving to make any noise; my senses were acute, anticipating something hideous climbing one of the table legs and then scrambling along the table toward where I lay. I waited for any touch or sensation on my arms or legs. My body froze with tension, ready to pull back once the slightest touch was felt. *What was that?* I felt something hairy by my feet. *There it is again. Climbing around my big toe.* It felt as if several objects were squirming between my toes. I felt another sensation of something larger climbing up my ankle. *Maybe my imagination. Just pretend nothing happened, and it will go away. Maybe.* My body quivered with anticipation of the unexpected. It was not my imagination, I finally conceded. Whatever it was, it felt as if several were climbing up my leg. I lifted my head but not far enough to see anything. The slithery sound I'd heard before returned. It was closer to me. Then there was silence.

I could no longer contain my panic. I screamed until my vocal cords could no longer tolerate the tension. My scream broke into tearful sobs. I blurted out my questions with a strained voice. "Who is here? Why am I here? Who are you? What have I done to deserve this? At least show your face. Do not be a coward." I tried to move to a more relaxed position to relieve the cramping in my back. *Too much time has passed. Something is going to occur.* I could feel it. This vendetta was personal, but who? Someone sinister with an ulterior motive. Sometimes you just know that something isn't right—that the motives are all wrong. No words need to be said. Nothing needs to be communicated. It's just a gut feeling. Call it a sixth sense, but once triggered, it becomes a fight-or-flight syndrome. The only problem was, I could not fight or flee. The escalating tension trapped me, imploding inside me, wreaking havoc.

I just lay there for what seemed an hour. *What the hell happened?*

What is the last thing I remember? The fact was, I could not remember a thing. I was drawing a complete blank. The only recall I had was waking up there.

I heard footsteps outside the room I was in. Then a set of keys turned a lock, and a door opened. Whatever was climbing around my feet and crawling up my leg suddenly stopped.

"You goddamn bitch. That catatonic state was just a front. It fooled me but not for long. You know what gave you away? Forget it. Doesn't matter now. I should have killed you then. But I wanted to talk to you first. You seem frightened. But why? You should have known this was going to happen. I have only just begun. Cassandra, you are first on my agenda. I am just not sure how this will end. Let us just call this a work in progress. Not sure yet in what manner I will plan your demise. I can guarantee you one thing: there will be pain. Pain will reach a level where you will beg me to kill you. Yet maybe you won't. I know you're pregnant, so there is more to this than I originally thought."

Where have I heard that voice before? Somewhere. A frightening revelation occurred. *Oh God, how did he find me?*

18

Years Later: After the Event

It feels like so long ago when the memories become no more. The train ride is like white noise. It has a hypnotic quality that lures me into a melancholic state, and my thoughts retreat back in time. But it is as before, always the same. My memories carry me back to that certain time, when a wall rises up, shielding me from venturing further. Let me phrase it another way. There is not a specific point in time where the before memories, behind the wall, are completely lost, while the memories up to the wall are fully disclosed. It is a gradual process. More or less, the further back my memories take me, the more obscure they become, blurred by a gradually thickening fog. Initially, the memories are clear, as bright as the rays of sunshine on a cloudless summer day. When the memories recede further back, the fog bank becomes noticeable off in the distance, accompanied by a dark mass of thunderheads moving progressively toward me with a menacing discharge of lightning traversing between the fog bank and the massive hovering structures.

Eventually, the memories become cloudy, as if a mist is turning the sun-filled day to a darkened, overcast gray sky. The memories grow more vague, finally retreating into complete obscurity when I encounter the wall. It's a complete void, nothing except pitch-black darkness. Yet I sense something beyond the wall. I can feel the shielded, hidden memories with an awareness of something sinister, a place in time buried deep behind the wall. Amnesia is a mental block that prevents me from decades of memories. It sounds like a fatal disease, irrecoverable, but I have learned that the block is indefinite. It's not much to go on, but given time, I might have a full recovery. Or maybe not. At least that's what my counselors have told me. One thing is conclusive: a prior event in my life created this wall—a prior event of which I have no recollection. It's a total blank. When I inquire, I get no response, as if this is part of my recovery. At times, I almost convince myself that to eventually learn what happened, to peek behind that wall, would serve no purpose but to cause me pain. At first, I had trouble with reconciling myself just to the present and completely ignoring a past that is part of me but that I'm unable to remember. But eventually, I came to terms with it as my present situation became more pronounced, commanding most of my attention. Yet my curiosity, at times passively patient, waits in the background, never wavering. It persistently surges forward, always insistent, prompting me for an answer to the number-one question: What happened? The wall haunts me. I fear one day the wall will erode from time and disintegrate into just granules of sand, releasing a torrid flow of memories and revealing something so nightmarish that I too will break into fragments. The fragmented pieces will dissolve into windblown, minute particles diffused among the forgotten granules from the wall.

The wall is now part of my dreams, bringing with it a new element: fear. Pure, unabated fear has infused my dreams with a nightmarish tone. My mind becomes restless as I am pulled back to ponder further. A series of dreams come and go with no advanced warning and then suddenly end, followed by an indefinite lull before a new series begins. Each series seems to present a different theme, yet each dream within the series is distinct and unique, providing a sequence of images consistent with the theme. The images collectively resemble flashbacks from a foregone era. There is no discernible pattern to when the series of dreams are triggered. They begin purely at random and end with no advanced warning. I am unaware of the nature of the dreams until just before they start. Sometimes the series of dreams are fast and furious, each from a different era, leaving me breathless. At other times, they are methodical, filled with tension and terror. The ones filled with terror I fear the most. These ones are least predictable, revealing a tone of damnation and terror that lies behind the wall. There is something somewhere behind the wall—terror that defies what the mind can conceive—that soon will be released. I do not know when it will happen, but when it is revealed, I fear it will change me forever, and that change will be like facing hell itself.

My recent dreams are hanging on far too long, each weaving its web tightly, mostly with a reluctance to free me. Each seems endless as its silken fibers connect its surrealistic view to the fabric of my reality. Unaware of my dream's intent, the point where the dream flows into my reality is transparent to me. The resulting fused state of fantasy and reality persists until my mind detects the anomaly and attempts to correct itself. But even then, I am not fully aware of what part of the fused state is fantasy and what is real. This inability to discern reality from fantasy is becoming more frequent. My inability to determine when a dream has ended is more acute and persistent. Heavenly bliss and hellish torment combine in a constant struggle to dominate my senses. Can heaven and hell coexist? I may never know. Even when I am aware the dream has finally ended and am consciously awake, I still am unable to discern when the transitioned to reality occurred. It's an unknown that might be permanently undisclosed, resulting in a pseudoreality state.

Sometimes it feels as if the dreams hang on with the intent to reveal something but then realize it is too soon and wait for the right moment for me to know. Maybe that is when I become aware the dream has finally released me. There were instances when I thought a dream ended, and I found myself as a complete stranger to my environment, realizing my dream had not totally released me but was hanging on with adamant persistence. There were other instances when I awoke with minimum resistance, completely aware of my surroundings, yet sensed the remnants of the dream just ended. Despite all the variables in this malady of happenstance, the truth I must face is that even when I become aware of a dream ending, the dreams really never fully unleash me. I am always aware of them, regardless of whether my recollection of the dream is miles away or right beside me. They are always there, mostly submerged until the next episode begins unannounced to take me on a journey to a place I feel I have been before—to Cassandra.

When the series of dreams end, I miss her, but when they begin again, I become fearful. I'm fearful for her and for me but also, worse, fearful for her because of me. Recently, they have started again—dreams that carry me back in time. But this time, something is different; something has gone awry. I fear the dreams have ventured further behind the wall to the vortex of my hidden memories, a darkened maelstrom of nightmares, a hidden place the devil himself dreads, the underbelly of evil, where hell itself resides. Waiting, cloaked by dark shadows, it lingers for that one moment when I am most vulnerable. I am drawn back as a stranger to a time unbeknownst to me. The images are there yet have no significance to me. But the sudden diversion I feel is a precursor to a chilling revelation. Soon, I fear, it will happen. She is the link. That I am sure of. For now, they are just dreams, yet I feel that soon they will reveal more—oh, so much more when that moment of truth is revealed. Could it be that final retribution is nearer? Toward a full confrontation with the truth? May God help my soul.

I hear the conductor's muffled voice cry out that our final destination, Santa Monica, is near. It brings me out from my melancholic state. I shake away the cobwebs, refocusing on today. "Dreams," I whisper to myself. "Just dreams," I repeat haltingly as I break free from the containment shield that holds me close to these dream states. The terminal is in view, bringing my full attention back to focus on the upcoming workday. The scheduled tasks wrest control from my musing as my senses become keenly aware of today's commitments.

The train pulls in and slows to an eventual stop. We disembark to another daily adventure that awaits us with the usual unannounced surprises. My company, an architectural firm, is located in a new glass-enclosed, domed building just a few blocks away, across Route 1, facing the Pacific. My company, still relatively young, designs and remodels classic art deco homes off the California coastline, restoring the luster that showcased the classic architecture so prominently during the first half of the 1900s. The firm approaches the market with a unique strategy: to tap into a market that once defined the concept of individuality decades ago. We strive for creative uniqueness as it was perceived in generations past, when it was commonplace for individuality to be revered instead of viewed in a scornful way. Our market consists of homes along the coast, designed with an innovative flair.

But it was not enough to dedicate our plans to the custom homes that populated the coastline. The canyons that lined the Pacific Coast

Highway were a haven for these quality homes built decades ago. Some of these homes were classics. The cookie-cutter crews were tearing down these classics at an alarming pace and rebuilding with smaller condos to maximize the use of the limited land along the coast. Our company's total dedication was so entrenched in our mission to reverse the cost-cutting butchery that we expanded our reach to purchasing homes located in the surrounding canyons that symbolized the dominant, creative art deco era. We purchased several of the homes to preserve the quality that identified the architectural golden age that epitomized the California lifestyle. For those classics, we invested significant upgrades in order to be in compliance with building codes and to modernize without changing the original architecture.

It was not easy at first. We were lean, barely breaking even, before being noticed. We grew cautiously, adding an employee from the list of contractors for each contract we signed. We were selective, bringing on an employee who would add a skill that would resonate with our future plans. In our second year, the mainstream of society started to recognize us. We were fortunate, with some luck and much foresight, for it was the right time and place, and we have exceeded our expectations. Our dedication and research are extensive, and they began to pay big dividends as our efforts were rewarded with wide acceptance and recognition for our far-reaching concept while our creative approach took hold. Our homes were beginning to restore the California coastline to its former grandeur as a mecca of avant-garde art.

A large part of our success was due to Linda, our vice president—a prominent position well earned. In retrospect, she was more of an integral part of our success than I was. She joined the organization shortly after it was formed. She started as a consultant to enhance our current market and promote our company's reputation. It soon became obvious that her skills and talent were far reaching and could be instrumental in every aspect of our business.

I promoted her to a position where she could help us in several areas: design, promotion, and marketing. I took special notice of her research and commitment to the art deco architecture that embodied our inclination toward creative expression through art during that time period. I recognized that her talent partnered well with her imaginative insight, as her creative vision was especially notable with her experience in upgrading homes built decades ago that reflected the architectural design from the golden years of Hollywood during the early 1900s. After several meetings, we decided to expand our market to include the classic homes scattered throughout the canyons that overlooked the Pacific coastline. I promoted her to vice president and placed her in charge of the updated business model that promoted the preservation of the art deco architecture still prevalent throughout the canyons.

Linda's promotion to VP included equity partnership—a partnership well deserved for her insight; commitment; and invaluable, necessary contribution to the company's commitment to the success of our new initiative. I did not inform her of the partnership when I announced her promotion. I hoped that would be an unexpected surprise.

This morning, I am meeting with her to discuss the partnership and sign the necessary documents. I really do not know much about Linda, the person behind the work facade, and this meeting will also allow me the possibility to learn more about Linda and her past. I remember well our first encounter. My mind drifts back to that time when we first met.

We met at a convention and started conversing about architecture and how the designs have changed over the last few decades. Our views resonated on change and the direction of our professions. We both realized the focus now was on generating profit and increasing margins to the point of forgoing individuality. Custom design, creative taste, and artistic flair were the exceptions now, as compared to decades ago, when the focus was on individuality, artistic expression, and creative recognition, vital components of unique architectural designs that extended the buyer's personality and perception.

Design was once a statement of the buyer's value on individuality, a statement of uniqueness and creative perception. Nonconformity was valued and readily accepted. Now cost-cutting measures dominate the industry, readily reflected in the cookie-cutter approach, which dismisses the consumer's individuality, stripping the purchaser's creative approach to just a one-dimensional view. We both realized that the current direction is a stark reminder of the individual's loss of identity in a diminishing middle-class segment striving to save every penny to cope with an economy that is starving the average consumer from any hope of a quality life. It is stripping the middle class of any form of dignity and pride, turning our population into one large pool of overworked, hopeless individuals disillusioned by their dreams from when they were teenagers, when innocence shielded them from life's harsh truths.

Our company's approach is aimed at reversing this trend and bringing the individual's unique ideas back to the residential home market, where they can become most prominent at an affordable price. It's a goal well within reach once the recognition takes hold and results in a large enough quantity to level out the cost factor.

During our discussion, I learned about Linda's experience. She was in total agreement with me about the loss of individuality and creative expression within the housing market, a loss most exemplified by the cost-cutting approach that now dominated the industry. Her direction was to preserve the architectural style from the early 1900s, when creative flair was in its prime. She showed me her portfolio, which contained before-and-after photographs of historic homes purchased and restored as a reminder to future generations of the architectural designs prevalent in the last century and the way architectural design relates to our individual expression and perception as a society. In other words, it provided an insightful view into society's impression and attitude toward life at that point in time. It was a snapshot of society's social and emotional health. She felt her approach was instrumental in reversing the current trend and encouraging potential buyers to either purchase existing homes or, when building new homes, express their individuality in the designs of the homes. Her thinking was that if the mind-sets of the buyers could adapt to that viewpoint, then over time, the builders would follow suit. Her message was geared toward empowering the buyers with new, creative ideas for their homes from both exterior and interior views.

Our discussion could have lasted for hours as we listened to each other's ideas, both realizing we shared the same insight and passion. We both became aware of the day's scheduled meetings, surprised at how much time we'd spent conversing with ease. With haste, we got up and returned to the afternoon's first scheduled meeting. It turned out we were late for the first meeting, and we both took seats toward the rear, relieved that we'd missed only the introduction of the speakers. Fortunately, we'd made it on time to hear the first topic on the agenda.

After the convention, we continued our discussion for hours over several glasses of wine, and during our conversation, I recognized her genius and creative talent and was impressed that we shared the same ideas. I told her I'd formed a company that specialized in restoring art deco architecture. I impressed upon her that the company's goal was to reverse the current direction and told her we had been successful so far, as evidenced along the California coastline. I showed her some of the homes we'd designed as well as homes we'd remodeled, which obviously impressed her. I told her how inspired I was with her approach and said we both could be influential forces toward reversing the stagnant, conformist mind-set in the housing sector. I then asked her to join my company as an architect, which turned out to be instrumental toward the continued success of the company. We have been together since.

From the beginning, it was apparent her addition to our organization was the best decision for our company. It was sheer luck that we crossed paths, which led to our partnership. Yet there was something that kept nagging me, triggering my instincts to dig further. It seemed that upon meeting, everything was too perfect. There was not a hitch anywhere, which was uncanny. Despite her genius for creative insight, I have never encountered any write-ups on her work, except when she showed me her portfolio. Someone with a gift such as hers would have eventually been noticed by one of the industry journals—not once but, I would imagine, several times. Our goals and aspirations, which fueled our vision, were in complete harmony, bordering on perfection. There was more. I felt a bond with her as if in some way she were a part of me. I felt a certain protectiveness toward her, which added to the seemingly perfect partnership. That was what kept nagging at me. It was too perfect.

I then realized I had to put a halt to my overindulged suspicions. I was overthinking the scenario, and it was not fair to Linda. I should have felt blessed for the fortunate luck bestowed on our connection. My paranoia was getting out of hand—a problem that has repeatedly raised its ugly head as far back I can remember. It was due time to put my suspicions to the side and accept the good fortunes that had been handed to me.

From the start, we worked together from early morning to early evening and sometimes late evenings, preparing designs and preparing bids on the homes we decided to purchase. During that time, my dreams returned with an intensity that had not been there before. It felt as if my connection with Linda triggered an onset of recurring dreams. I experienced a series of dreams with a new twist that drifted in a different direction from the ones I had dreamed before, dreams that both enticed me yet terrified me. I had a haunting sense the dreams were connected to that missing chapter in my life. The truth lies hidden in these dreams, somewhere in a forbidden place behind the wall. I felt my personal survival and my relationship with Linda were somehow linked to finding the truth.

With a surprised suddenness, I break free from my reverie upon hearing the conductor call out to me. I am still seated in the passenger car. I'm not sure how long we have been here and notice that I am the only remaining passenger. I look out the side window and realize the platform leading from the rail yard to the station has only a few people walking to and from their destinations. "Sir, are you okay?" asks the conductor.

"How long have I been here?" I ask, my alarm reflected in the urgent tone of my question.

"Sir, we arrived at the terminal ten minutes ago." He eyes me with curiosity that grows into concern when I do not immediately reply. "Are you sure you are okay?"

Detecting the concern, I immediately reply that I must have fallen asleep and then get up and depart with a hurried step to my pace. "Thank you, and have a great day," I say right before stepping onto the platform. This is the day I scheduled a month ago with Linda to meet. It's a meeting to promote her to an equity partnership. I look at my watch and realize I have just fifteen minutes to get to the restaurant we chose to discuss her promotion and plans for the future. I picked the restaurant rather than the conference room at work to avoid interruptions. I want us to have an open exchange to relay whatever is on our minds during this discussion, and this restaurant has the right atmosphere, which is more appropriate than the imposed conformity of a work-controlled environment. I look at my watch again. Ten minutes are left. To be late for Linda's promotion would be construed as a sign of disrespect for her commitment to our success. I pick up my pace to a trot as I hurry to the restaurant.

I arrive just as the clock hits nine o'clock. There is Linda, dressed more casually than usual, which is comforting since I want this hour to be an open forum. We sit down, and over the course of the next hour, we exchange ideas on how to promote our market strategy to our current market and adopt a more aggressive approach in our campaign to renovate the classic art deco homes along the California coastline and throughout the canyons along the Pacific Coast Highway with our vision. My announcement of equity partnership follows. I am sure she expected this, but her surprised look is so genuine it would have convinced a jury. We spend another hour discussing and signing all the papers giving her a 15 percent share of the company. I then tell her to take the rest of the day off after we meet with the contractors at one of the classic homes we just purchased on Canyon Ridge Trails, high up on a cliff overlooking the Pacific. She gladly accepts and notes jokingly that she will go shopping in celebration of her promotion. I laugh as we get up from the table and walk toward the exit.

I call in to work and leave a message with the receptionist to let her know that Linda and I will be at the new site for the remainder of the day to inspect the property we just purchased and to discuss plans with the contractors. We take a taxi to the company garage and use the corporate car to drive to the site. The meeting at the site proves most beneficial as we tour the property with the contractors to ensure they are aware of every detail in our designs. We bring the contracts with us into the house and spend the remainder of the afternoon reviewing the terms and finally signing the documents.

It is still Friday, late afternoon, and the hectic traffic ordeal is just an hour away as I drive to Linda's home. Even though it is still early compared to our past weeks of working late, she wants to go shopping, and I have to get the company car back to the garage in order to beat the rush and still have time to catch the express home. By the time I pull into the company garage and lock the car door, it is past late afternoon, and Friday evening is approaching. I already missed the express train, and the next local train is an hour away. I walk to the train station and stop at the lounge for a vodka martini while I wait. Before I know it, it is already eight o'clock, and I am bone tired. This week has been an especially busy one; Linda and I have worked until midnight on preparing blueprints, project plans, and a contract for the property and home we purchased on Canyon Ridge. I pay for my drink and hurry to my ride as it makes its last announcement for departure. I am peculiarly antsy during the ride home. I'm tired, yet I keep sensing an internal alarm that detains any form of sleep. I have a feeling of urgency about being home tonight, and I jump out of my seat as the train arrives at my destination. Without a second to spare, as soon as I leave the train, I jog to my car and then start my drive home.

I feel unusually tired. But there is something more to tonight that causes me even more unease. I can't quite put my finger on the reason, but I feel something instinctively, an element of change, something linked to that missing chapter in my life. It's odd, but I have a sensation that my enduring quest for some answers could begin soon. A thread from the past will begin to unravel, a start to the discovery of the truth. The unnerving question is whether I can handle the truth. Curiosity, doubt, and fear all beset me with tension. But if the truth lies here in these dreams, then I must confront them to set myself free. I have to know. My biggest fear is wondering what will be revealed: demons from the past, an opening to a revelation beheld by the angels, or both. I pull into my driveway, too tired to park my car in the garage, and walk to the front door. I go through the foyer to the living room and toss my case onto the couch. I climb the stairs to the bedroom, turn on the light, and toss my clothes onto the nearby closet hanger.

I can hardly keep my eyes open. My dreams will again present themselves, as they have since I can remember. Impatiently, my dreams wait to carry me back to the wall. The blanket of drowsiness pulls me into the twilight zone that is the gateway to one's reservoir of dreams. I wearily draw the covers back, and as soon as my head hits the pillow, the reservoir releases the dreams that sweep me back to somewhere behind the wall—to Cassandra.

19

The Dream: Cassandra

The dream enclosed me in its grasp. I was swept into a vortex of unknowns filled with vague glimpses of apparitions reaching out toward me before retreating back into the dark void, leaving me held captive in my own web of apprehension. A mist was creeping closer. I felt it enclose me, drawing me into its own enigma. I was lost with the mist swirling around me, its tentacles closing in, entangling my feet, crawling up my spine, curling around my throat, and inching up toward my eyes, to imprison me in its grasp. I was frozen in place, unable to move, waiting for the inevitable. Then the tentacles started to back away with a suddenness, as if obeying a command to retreat, clearing the mist and revealing the wall, which reached upward as far as I could see. The wall had a surface that no longer seemed solid but looked like a liquidy substance with a watery ripple effect, filled with images that were partially obscured. I had no fear this time. I felt an unnerving calm, a restless peacefulness. The scene was too serene; the silence was deafening. I stood there waiting for something but was not sure what that something was.

I was no longer frozen in place and moved in closer, reaching out with my fingertips. But when I came within inches, the wall move farther away, avoiding my touch. I withdrew a few paces, surprised. *Strange*, I thought. The wall never had retreated before. *But why?* I tried again with a more forceful thrust, but it retreated again, this time farther away. I stood there waiting for something to happen. Then, suddenly, an opening appeared, a doorway that revealed a glimpse beyond the wall. I walked closer to the doorway, expecting the wall to back away again, but this time, it didn't move, as if it were expecting me to enter through the open passageway. I peered into the opening only to see nothing but a bright golden glow that radiated an energy force that seemed to be pulling me through. I closed my eyes and gave in to the force, letting it draw me in.

Once through the doorway, I opened my eyes, and at first, I saw nothing but empty space, but then the images appeared. I saw foggy, hazy images that triggered a vague recollection of memories—memories that both enticed me and made me feel afraid. They were too distant, and for some reason, I backed away in a desperate attempt to keep the memories from getting too close. Moments later, a silver halo of light moved toward me and enveloped me, leading me to another place, a place that harmonized with beauty and purity. A majestic image from within the halo appeared, moving me to a state of wonder. I stood in awe, realizing that the materializing view in front of me was of a heavenly messenger who defined the quintessence of miracles. I had no fear this time but a feeling of peaceful content, a sense of closure, as if a part of my soul I had been searching for finally had arrived to unite again. I closed my eyes to capture the essence of the soulful binding, healing the part of me that had been empty for so long. I sensed something moving near me, and I opened my eyes with the hope that it would be her again.

With a breathless gesture, I stood in awe, overwhelmed. There she was again, Cassandra, more exotic than before—a breath of fresh air backed by an aura of glimpsing light. Her image had an ethereal quality as she stood alone with unmatched perfection of angelic purity—a symbol of pure resplendence to be captured by the poet's eye, a beautiful perfection of such proportion that it symbolized immortality.

It was difficult to find the right words to describe her, for when I looked directly into her eyes, I became transfixed with a different view. There was more than just her physical appearance of elegance and refinement; her soul exuded a tranquil purity, giving a poetic fluidity to her appearance. When she was in front of me, I was presented with more than the blue-black hair falling effortlessly over her shoulders and more than her symmetrical face with high cheekbones, a sculpted nose, a smooth jawline, and full lips. Beauty would not justify her presence.

There was another quality to her that elevated her presence to a level of spiritual perfection. She was an angelic spirit that cleansed my soul of all my imperfections. An exuberance from within gave tranquility and harmony a new meaning. A innocence of soul, an aura, captivated me. She was a soul mate that defined immortality. It was a love that had persisted since the dawn of the heavens. Her perfection in spirit was entirely reflected in her eyes with that magnetic quality. Her eyes were sapphire and green but would change to an aqua blue with a hint of emerald, drawing me toward her to reengage, for now was the moment for us to reemerge for our next soulful journey.

I closed my eyes just for a second, hoping the view of want and desire was real. It was more than just a wish of heightened grandeur. I opened my eyes again. Slowly, I stepped forward, watching her eyes' movement as they locked onto mine. I waited for her hypnotic look to draw me in closer as the mystical moment in time unfolded into a harmony of untested proportions.

I moved toward her, each step bringing me closer to heightened anticipation, yet I was wary that the maiden before me would suddenly disappear, shattering my hopes once again for this vision to be more than just an illusion. The air was electrically charged with emotion as I took another step forward, hoping the magical juncture would evolve into a moment of truth that would materialize the scene into permanence. As I took my next step nearer, I realized I'd crossed the threshold of space off-limits in my prior dreams, which would dissipate before I entered that sacred sanctum. This time, the dream did not fade away but became even more distinct and vivid, with Cassandra hypnotically drawing me in toward her. Relief flooded my senses as I drew nearer with the anticipation of finally removing the veil of mystery and revealing the ultimate truth of the recurring theme.

But before I took my next step onto the consecrated place before Cassandra, I was suddenly confronted with a sequence of fleeting images unfolding around me. The images projected a surreal aura that one normally associated with a dreamlike state. The images provoked distant memories partially obscured in a hazy fog. Intermittently, the fog would lift, revealing the images with more clarity and triggering more memories, which were more dramatically distinct. Collectively, they formed scenes, each one extracted from a prior interlude that was inherently linked to this dream.

As I recalled each of my previous dreams, I realized that en masse, the scenes mapped out an obvious pattern that reinforced the fact that the dreams were somehow connected. Their connection formed a continual chronological sequence; each was from a different era, with a peculiar, haunting setting; the same characters; and distinct beginnings and culminations. As each sequence unfolded, the scenes became more vividly enhanced with a prism of colors that reflected a common theme of mystery and intrigue woven with a background of ambience, romance, and passion suffused with tunes of nostalgic interludes. Strangely, at unpredictable lulls, the level of imagery alternated in clarity, vacillating between opposite spectrums of complete vagueness and then infinite detail, as if a pulsating light would only reveal the explicit levels of detail at random intervals. During the cycles of brilliant clarity, the scenes were presented with electrifying intensity, vividly defined as they became solidly entrenched into my yearning for the vision to be real. Each detail etched firmly into my realm of hope, and my passionate craving progressed beyond the invisible boundary where wishful fantasy emerged into a reality. Yet when the scenes became subdued with partial obscurity, my passion for Cassandra to be more than just a dream retreated from hope and optimism to haunting doubts filled with questions as I struggled to continue my pursuit to unveil the cloak of mystery.

Cassandra, this woman of inherent eloquence who exemplified the very essence of saintliness, truth, and purity, a soul that had always defined the core of me, was always at the center of each dream. Her presence was central to a reoccurring pattern from distant times, wherein each interlude represented a karmic connection from past eras. It dawned on me that each dream, each encounter, was symbolic of a consummation of each of our past unions, wherein our souls would reconnect to become one brilliant celestial star taking its rightful place in a universe filled with unbounded magical dreams. Immersed in my fog of wonder, I pondered the haze of memories. A faint echo edged its way from a distant obscurity to an acknowledgment, like a faint reverberation of an even more distant past when Cassandra and I were first joined. A new vision appeared before me, enclosing me with a 360-degree panoramic view of our universe, where the wonders and quests for all our answers were portrayed as prominent symbols, each with its own colorful revelation as to the birth of our universe. When combined, the symbols revealed the truth of our origin and destiny. They revealed the birth of our souls, when the heavens were just forming at the dawn of eternity, when Cassandra and I were first aligned to become permanently sealed, bonded for a timeless journey.

My mesmerism at the revelations shown to me prompted a total immersion of my entire psyche into a different dimension, the genesis that encapsulated the birth of our souls. I suddenly felt weightless as my soul freed itself from my physical embodiment. I felt without limitations imposed by a physical being. *I can see the light of eternity. I can feel everything now. Everything in the universe is in motion. Death is not a cessation from existence but a transference to another state continually in motion. I feel the motion. I feel the energy. I absorb the energy. I can taste and smell everything. My senses are boundless. I feel weightless, with total freedom. My soul has been reborn to where the unthinkable is now possible. An endless stream of knowledge infuses me. Peace, harmony, and beauty encapsulate my soul. I feel, I hear, I sense, and I absorb the very essence of her spirit since the dawn of time, when our souls first became one. I can taste the thousand tastes of her. I can capture every sense of smell of her. I can feel her heartbeat. I feel her soul as it meshes with mine.* Our soulful union immersed me into a wealth of spiritual guidance to bind our souls once again as we sailed effortlessly to another realm of divine aspirations and hope encompassed by endless miracles bound by unconditional love and harmony. It was a coming home to my soul mate with whom everything was possible, to a place in time's boundless infrastructure where I finally had found what defined me: Cassandra.

After that brief, reflective, hallowed glimpse into the genesis of time, the portal then swiftly closed and faded into obscurity. In a bewildered state of wonder, I suddenly became overburdened with that newest revelation. Even though my dreams had revealed a pattern that was reminiscent of a soulful union, that was the first time I'd become visually aware of the birth of our karmic connection. I was overwhelmed and fearful of sensory overload, and I had to refocus to regain my composure. After the portal closed, the scenes from my prior dreams reappeared, allowing me to realign my focus toward the view before me with a resolve of heightened emphasis that stemmed from the new revelations. My doubts started to fade with increased speed, and I felt a renewed sense of urgency, realizing now that the dreams, somehow connected, might be more than just a fantasy.

I cannot recall exactly when the series of dreams began. It was long ago when the dreams started. They became fused into my soul, which was ageless, making it virtually impossible to discern when they first were conceived. The pattern was always the same: Cassandra and I were intricately linked. Even though each dream commenced within a different era, each episode began with a unique fervor of hope, signaling a new beginning, a chance to start once more with renewed, reinvigorated passion. Each was a reawakening from a past union from a foregone era. Each episode had its own culminating ending before giving way to the beginning of the next rendezvous. Those that ended prematurely were encapsulated with tears of sorrow and despair, as we were mercilessly torn apart repeatedly by the randomness of fate only to eventually reunite, reengage, and respond to our unsurpassable desire to connect, realign our bonded souls again, and reconnect through the powers of the heavens, as if the heavens and fate were in a constant struggle over our predestined connections. With each engagement, we were personified into another layer of perfection, as if we were being sculptured by the Greek gods from Troy. Each engagement was born in a twilight of haze that ultimately revealed a window of visionary clarity wherein we both manifested as embodiments of perfection, ready to embrace, anticipating another lifetime together. Our perpetually evolving bond would continue in that mode of spiritual engagement until the sands of time dissipated once again into a fate unknown.

Suddenly, the parade of images that encompassed me stopped as swiftly as they'd emerged, followed by a silence, as if the entire universe had halted, waiting with anticipation for my next move. The scenes collapsed into a tunnel that closed with alarming speed. Cassandra was again before me. She was not a mirage; the soulful depth revealed in her eyes validated her physical presence, vanquishing all doubts. Her appearance had an angelic glow that radiated a rapturous brilliance. As the eerie silence settled upon me, consciously aware of the vacuum of stillness, this time, I held my breath with hope when I reached out to caress her face to ensure that she indeed was not a mirage, not a hopeless fantasy. My touch upon her face felt real, and her eyes turned a deeper shade of violet upon my caress. My fingertips sensed the heat of her passion. As my desire heightened with intensity upon my touch, a deluge of images once again surfaced high above her, and a projected view of our saga momentarily traversed swiftly before me—glimpses of fleeting moments wherein truth hung in the balance as the scenes of Cassandra from all the dreams inundated my senses, converging in my consciousness with a penetrating level of lucidity. Each image was extracted from a different era before spinning off until no longer visibly present. When the last image faded away, my gaze lowered, held steadfast to Cassandra's hypnotic lure, as intense as ever. The hue of her sensuality and passion infused her aura with an intensely magnificent, rapturous tone of intimacy as she responded to my caress.

With the feel of her face and lips against my fingertips, the magical moment upon my consummate touch infused me with the essence of her passion. My lingering doubts retreated again as the veil of fantasy began to lift, further convincing me that this indeed was more than just an illusion. It was as real as anything I had encountered. Her touch heightened my awareness, and every minute detail reinforced my yearning, penetrating the most sacred part of my soul. Each detail of Cassandra was fully absorbed into the depths of my inner core. I felt her pulsating hunger when she responded with a breathless gesture. Upon my touch, she did not wince; her eyes became an even darker shade of sapphire, welcoming my caress, and we both felt each other's longing to connect on a primitive level of passion. She reached out toward me with poetic ease, her motion effortless, to caress my face. Her sensual response engaged my senses totally, and I realized this dream was symbolic of all my dreams. This dream bridged the unknown, reconfirming that Cassandra and I were indeed lovers from a distant past who had prevailed through the vortex of endless cycles of time. This dream was truly the culminating event in which our physical embodiments would be permanently sealed as one heart and soul, never to be separated by fate again.

I savored each moment of her caress, and each passing minute drew us closer together and toward that paradox in time where our souls would finally unite again and, with a crescendo of enormous proportions, would reveal the beginning of time, the moment of truth when the true essence of love would be released. Upon her kiss, an electrical charge passed between us and encapsulated us in a prism-like glow. This continued for only a moment, yet to us, it seemed like an eternity in which each fleeting second was a view of each instance in time, and our karmic connection was consummated with an unparalleled passion. I suddenly found myself surrounded by music from somewhere near the front of an enormous ballroom. I heard people dancing to the melodies of the big bands, but the light from the chandeliers above obscured my view of everything except for Cassandra, whose body was pressed firmly against me.

Our desire to connect was driven by our primal hunger with fervor, as if our last departure had left us empty. Our souls were desperate to reengage, to bond once again with an intensity and on a level that defied even fate, never to separate again. Our souls were connected on every level with existentialistic dependency on our passionate charge, which was a defining construct of our soulful union, one with a perfect sexual harmony. Our lips slowly parted. Her breath was scented with an aroused fervor as I entered her. My tongue brushed her lips as I savored the lingering taste of her pheromones. Our lips connected with a sexual lust, our tongues reaching farther to satisfy our unquenchable thirst for each other, to savor each other's taste. Our lips met once again, this time with an intensity of pure ecstasy. With each kiss, we delved deeper to savor each kiss, escalating our eroticism to an even higher level where each kiss was infused with a sweet, sexual taste. The scent of our sexual lust permeated the air as our hormones exuded a flood of pheromones from our aroused passion throughout our pores. As our bodies meshed in harmony, we held each other close. She drew me in toward her to feel the heat of her passion as we harmonized to the songs that conveyed our memories from yesteryear. My hands caressed her face. My fingertips barely touched her lips as they glided across, gently sensing her velvety smoothness. I moved my hands higher, gently lifting her silky hair, which then fell back over her shoulders with an intoxicating fragrance. I massaged her gently across the back of her neck, drawing her closer. The warmth of her breathless exhalation against my neck ignited a passionate shiver through my entire being. I drew nearer, my mouth barely touching her lips, tasting her, before I pressed harder, reaching farther into her mouth as she welcomed me, giving in to our exotic lure.

Our bodies connected on a spiritual plane, and the heat of our passion was exchanged when I entered her as she took me in with earnest. We engaged in total ecstasy filled with a rapturous, passionate charge that exploded into a cathartic, climatic release. Our souls were reborn as one, never to separate again. After what seemed like an eternity, we pulled ourselves away, and our lips separated reluctantly. Our eyes spoke volumes as we strolled toward the music to dance slowly to the melodies.

20

Rhapsody in Blue

We danced until the hush of night. The sound of midnight signaled the finale of a night that would be forever captured as an imprint forged into the deepest recesses of my being, a night that held me in a continual euphoric state of delight and bliss. Encapsulated by our intense desire and passion, we danced past the stroke of the chimes, reluctant to let go as we moved as one with each melody, our bodies fused into one. We both felt the beating of our hearts and were both aroused with sexual desire. Our heat soaked our skin with sweetly scented perspiration. Her scent permeated the air as I moved lower, my lips touching her neck as I tasted her. I followed her neck down closer to her breasts as they swelled with anticipation. My taste buds were aroused by the sexual scent of her desire as my tongue glided over her nipples. Her taste was sweet and salty, and the scent of her sex was like an exotic perfume infused with her own juices. My lips and tongue tasted her nipples, lavishly absorbing her sweet taste. Her nipples hardened from our eroticism as I glided my tongue sensually over her skin.

As the hands of time moved further past the witching hour, we strolled from the dance floor and glided our way through the shadowy passageway. The lights above cast shadows of couples in highly erotic settings, guiding our way into the dimly lit atrium. The atmosphere was charged with ambience as we headed toward the candlelit table hidden in the corner. There were only a few couples sitting at partially hidden tables tucked away into the shadowy corners, where the moon's glow from the skylight provided enough of a filtered light to provide an exotic setting. When the couples turned around from aroused curiosity, I saw that each patron wore a simple mask. The masks depicted various moods, from serene bliss to the tears of sorrow. The strange setting was unsettling yet strangely added a heightened awareness that infused me with an exotic and erotic sensation in the surreal atmosphere. The filtered lights from above broke into prisms, with each color in the spectrum reflected on our faces, glistening with a mist of perspiration from our encounter. Our eyes locked, mirroring the depth of our connection. As she conveyed her wish for a glass of French wine, I moved away from the table, away from the prism of light, and as I moved farther back into the shadowy distance, the light from the full moon radiated through the domed ceiling's skylight and rested upon her face, enveloping her body with a white halo that magnified her angelic qualities. I looked upon her in awe. I saw a goddess with a celestial radiance, with eyes that changed from a brilliant velvet to a blue-green sapphire with the intensity of an ocean-deep blue. I knew then our souls were one, and I could not exist without her. I felt as if my own will were infused with her energy, and the absence of it would devoid me of my own life force of energy and will to continue. I felt as if my total existence were an extension of her soul. We had experienced limitless encounters filled with love. I was filled with a rapturous high, yet something continued to hold me from total enrapture. Something held me in a void from a previous encounter that continued to escape me. A torrid fear lay just below the surface of losing her, resulting in a need for her so overwhelming it was consuming me.

I ventured forth to the lounge, taking each step as if I were in a hypnotic trance. Approaching the counter, I asked for a bottle of French Marsanne to celebrate our journey, an adventure that would reshape our lives and forever bond us as soul mates from past millennia. Upon returning, I saw an empty table devoid of her presence except for a crimson rose petal resting on her chair, scented with the fragrance of her perfume. I looked toward the hallway that led to the main entrance. I searched the ballroom and swept the room with an intense urgency. I found no evidence of her presence. My euphoria and hopefulness from just moments ago transformed into a facade of desperation and hopelessness. A moment of intense agony shot through my heart, and I felt a wave of despondency and anguish sweep down on me, intent on devouring me with a shroud of infinite darkness filled with an emptiness of hell. I ran back to the table, which stood all alone. Moments ago, it had been filled with rapture and elation; now it was depleted. The void was now suffused with melancholy, forlornness, and desolation devoid of passion.

Emptiness and an eerie silence seemed to permeate the air, as if a fog bank of unknown origin were approaching, charged with ominous foreboding. Without warning, the lights suddenly blurred, the music from the ballroom became more distant, and the banquet hall dissipated with a translucent glow, as if I were being transported from a distant past to another era. My surroundings turned into a surreal image as the impending misty fog devoured the evening into a distant memory. With the last details rapidly being expunged from that euphoric night, I reached out and grabbed the rose petal, catching the scent as I placed the petal in my coat pocket as a token to carry with me as a symbol of her presence. I suddenly noticed a letter partially hidden under the velvet cloth on the table where we'd sat. I picked it up and hastily glanced at the contents: "Never leave without a promise to return." With a sense of urgency, I placed the letter in my pocket alongside the rose.

The Omninous Wall

The swirling mist swept away the last visual details of the magical rendezvous filled with unforgettable bliss, forsaking me to a forlorn state of dark despair tormented with a flood of memories.

I find myself back outside the wall. The tendrils of fog that cleared the path for me to the wall have now concealed the path in a dense murkiness, making any journey impossible. The wall is no longer visible, and I remain fixed in a pensive, alert state, waiting for a clearing, a sound—anything that will signal that I am still among the living.

The silence is deafening, intensifying the vacuity of the open space where I reside. An odor permeates the air and repulses my senses, similar to the acrid, burned smell of an electrical short. The air has a strange color, a pale violet haze that periodically seems to display a disruptive rippling effect, as if it is transmitting an electrical current. I call out and hear but empty echoes, realizing I am in another place, one that seems to be an endless chamber of open space. I seem to be suspended, waiting for my sentence to be passed. While fate decides on my verdict, the uncertainty and fear of my present state leave me paralyzed with trepidation; my mind is a whirlwind of scrambled thoughts. I have to do something, or else I will lose whatever sanity I have left. How did I get here? The question screams relentlessly inside my head. I can only focus on my recent episode behind the wall with Cassandra.

But how is that possible? I am not even sure if my present state is reality or a continuation of the same dream. I have been reminded repeatedly that I have a perception disorder in which, during these dreams, I am frequently unaware of when the dreams end and am unable to delineate between what is real and what is fantasy. I'm uncertain when the dreams become no longer dreams, when fantasy flows into reality. It is all one seamless path to me. If this is one continual dream, then is it plausible to be able to have a dream from within a dream? How can I recollect a dream if I am still in the dream? I realize the absurdity of my reasoning, but I have no recourse and resort to pondering what I have just encountered, waiting for whatever lies ahead. I feel that the scenes I just experienced are near, and the void I am in, in which I'm held captive for reasons unbeknownst to me, will soon vacate, yielding to the very scenario I have just witnessed.

The images and scenes I encountered from behind the wall with Cassandra begin to haunt me with a soulful loneliness. The details of my engagement remain vivid as I recall my initial dreams, pondering relentlessly. The memories trigger an endless barrage of unanswered questions about Cassandra. Does Cassandra actually exist, or was her presence real at some point in the past? Or is this all the result of my perception disorder, paramnesia? Yet she seems so real, and when I am with her, our souls become one. She brings a feeling of home, where I am destined to be. The passion and harmony when we're together are overwhelmingly powerful, as if the heavens preordained our connection.

Caution and uncertainty plague me. The doubts and optimism viscously circle me, each taking turns in an unending exchange between the clouds of wariness casting shadows of despair and the eternal flame of optimism filling my soul with convincing hope and desire. It's a constant fight, an ongoing struggle between promise and suspicion, between optimism and despair, turning my mind into a battlefield where a continual war is fought with the protective shields of hope and the daggers of doubt. Confusion and suspicion have returned, plaguing me with the same repeated questions. I'm always faced with the same preponderance. Were the images fantasy, or were they real? Was the source of the images of revealing detail from a highly volatile imagination or a reflection of distant memories from past engagements? Why was the setting behind the images changing? My mind wrestles with the implications of the next question. Is my condition deteriorating, and my mind is now solely devoted to conjuring up fantasies? Or were all my suspicions on the probable causes just exaggerated, overcomplicated responses blinding me to the obvious question? Are they real images from recent events? To speculate further on the plausibility of another dimension, an altered state, is another remote possibility, but I dare not go there, for to do so would strike a fear that maybe I am going mad.

I stand here, still waiting for fate's verdict. My mind wanders, looking for a direction to focus on while I wait. I find myself being pulled back to reexamine. My mind redirects my focus to once again mull over my dreams, incessantly bringing forth another stream of countless questions. The dreams are changing. They're changing from a theme of nocturnal bliss to a theme of defiant, hellish chaos. Why the changes to the dreams? I keep looking for significant clues. The clues to unravel this tangled web of mystery have to be hidden somewhere in these dreams.

This recent dream of Cassandra was a tormented reminder of the tone of my initial dreams when they first started. It dramatized the progression of the changes from my initial dreams to the most recent dreams. Initially, I took the shifts as random diversions. But upon further scrutiny, I was faced with a sudden revelation that slammed into my consciousness. These shifts might be following a pattern. They are becoming more dramatic, focused, and intense with purpose, as if following a predefined script.

The possibility of where they are leading me heightens my dread of the potential consequences. The setting of my recent dreams is always farther behind the wall, in a dark, hidden place where a haunting tone emanates from the depth of its inner core. It's a place filled with an atmosphere of pure terror, a place that could be the domicile of empty souls hell bound to the abyss of horror. It is emerging from a deep slumber, causing me an intense fear of the implication of the recent transformation. I fear the implication points to a reconfirmation of one certain fact: the recent dreams are transforming because the time to reveal the buried memories hidden behind the wall is approaching, evolving toward an ending with consequences that I cannot contemplate.

The wall seems more ominous now, as if it is signaling the changes. But there is something else about the wall causing my unrest. The wall has always been present. It was prevalent in the initial dreams, yet it was far enough away to pose no imminent threat. It was sturdy and unwavering, and even from far away, it cast an ominous shadow. But the wall in these recent dreams seems different. The wall is nearer. Its presence is more portentous. The sturdiness of the wall is not as pronounced. It appears taller, with less substance; at times, it seems to waver. The second revelation hits me with a suddenness. The differences are not only in the dreams but also inherent in the wall. I remember the initial dreams and the sturdiness of the wall, but gradually, I notice slight fluctuations in the structure of the wall as it edges in closer. With further insight, it dawns on me these anomalies are always paired between the wall and the dreams, as if the changes to the dreams are forewarned by changes to the wall. It seems the reshaping of the wall and the dreams is synchronized, with the wall foretelling these transitions. If this is true, then the wall has prophesied these transformations all along.

The reasoning becomes certainty upon my realizing that my flashbacks were also triggered around the same time—vivid flashbacks of memories from a time that still remains hidden, a glimpse of haunting snapshots from past events too horrific to fully confront. The connection was always there. I should have immediately picked up the prophetic presage, but the change was too indistinct at the start due to its inconsistency. There were interim lulls, temporary respites when one or more dreams that harmonized with my initial dreams would surface. Despite the inconsistency, the changes came about gradually, undetected, until eventually, they became so prominent that the pattern became obvious.

The wall, the dreams, the flashbacks—all are synchronized, making the correlation undeniable. It is now obvious. The wall symbolizes my mental block. The mutations are accelerating, as evidenced by the increased frequency of the changes in the wall. They're increasing at a pace at which the synchronized correlation between the aberrations in the wall, the dreams, and the flashbacks has started to become indistinct to the point where the synchronization has become instantaneous. This implication is obvious, leading to one important, undeniable, conclusive pattern: there is now no escaping the obvious. The wall, the obstacle that represents my memory block, is breaking down, eroding from time's endless pursuit. I am panicked by what will be revealed. I feel an instinctive shadowy hint that it involves Cassandra—and whatever it is, it is not good. But what and why? I can't fathom what inescapable truth will be revealed. Could I have done something so horrible that more than half my life-filled memories are blocked indefinitely? Are the blocked memories that horrendous? Fearful of the consequences triggering my obsession to retreat further back to my initial dreams, my mind frantically seeks refuge, an escape, to revisit the place filled with moments of rapture and uncover any overlooked clue connected to this quagmire of unknowns.

My obsession incessantly pulls me back for an encore reunion to that one place in time that provides the setting I desperately need, a reunion with that moment when I lose myself in a whirl of rhapsody, a moment consumed by these initial dreams. Each episode makes its onstage debut in a setting of rapturous ambience. I reunite with that well-traveled road down memory lane as I pursue these memories with renewed fervor, recalling the vivid, intricate details and the euphoric high revolving around the one central element that defines my soul: Cassandra. My obsession now consumes the moment, taking total possession of my senses and providing the refuge I seek. It renders the setting I desperately need that holds my perilous sanity intact with an intent to provide some clue as to what lies behind the wall.

The recall is instantaneous, filled with overwhelming details to reexamine from the initial dreams. Images come rushing back, flooding my emotions with both soulful elation and distress. The initial dreams, wherein each episode follows an unchanging, consistent course, progress in a continual direction. Each episode is a separate journey, an engagement wherein Cassandra and I traverse from one era to the next. Precious moments present as an embracing view of reflections, marking a new beginning following our immortal adventure. Each period is characterized by that time's unique nuances, including the distinctive innovations, changing fashions, and general mannerisms of the dream's characters. The images are presented at various interludes during our voyage that reveal our harmony—precious moments frozen in time, reflective of our soulful connection. Each excursion has no distinct beginning or ending, just a sequence of images provoking unforgettable memories that gradually fade away with no hint of despair, flowing into our next excursion to be reborn with a new start as we emerge into another era. Cassandra and I are always at the center of each setting, where the theme is unwavering, unchanging: a surreal vision of passion, adventure, intrigue, and mystery within a venue of melodies from yesteryear. These precious recalled moments are priceless memories, treasured moments that will be held in a special place preordained for the select few who will remain beyond that threshold when time itself becomes but an expired dimension. Yet I find no evidence of anything sinister. I detect nothing that would trigger an explosive outburst. But upon further scrutiny, I notice the dreams start changing, diverting to a different direction.

The dreams take a different tone when the change starts, continuing unabated. Dreams that reflect the harmony and intimacy of the initial episodes are still present, as evidenced by the images and scenes from this recent dream, but these instances have become less frequent. They rarely make an encore as the mutation progresses. The altered dreams that have evolved from these transformations have become more dominant, changing the mood to a gradually darkening overtone. A different tone is emerging, a tone that highlights conflicts as opposed to harmony. It is a tone infused with a negative overcast of something sinister, with a focus on disruptive forces. I cannot definitively say these are a new set of dreams. The same theme is there, but the flow has lost its continuity. The flow is now disruptive, presenting an incongruous swirl of aberrant behavior. Are the dream's aberrations the cause or result of some hideous deed? Are the altered dreams indicative of the wall breaking down? When the wall finally wears down into wind-blown fragments, will the truth be finally revealed? A truth that will either imprison or free my soul?

My obsession totally consumes me. I'm frantic for some insight. *When did the initial change start?* I ask myself, as I have done repeatedly without resolve. I cannot pinpoint with certainty when it first started. But that is a moot point now. The obvious certainty of significance is the symbolism of the wall, which provides a pattern that applies some rationale to this enigma. When I first encountered the wall, I did not realize it was the epicenter of the change. I didn't realize the true significance. As the small diversions continued, the change became obvious, and it was then when I remembered that besides my inability at times to separate reality from a dream's fantasies, I had also been diagnosed with amnesia, a memory block. The block appears to be unraveling, as prophesied by the tiny fissures forming within the wall. Each dream now draws me closer to the forbidden place behind the wall. The blockade will soon erode, bringing with it an unparalleled terror to my soul. *Cassandra. Whatever happened to her?* The truth is buried somewhere in that forbidden place.

When the wall appears, there is always a winding path leading up to the wall that I feel destined to follow. I travel the walkway not by choice but from an unconscious pull toward what lies beyond. The memories that have been hidden lie somewhere beyond that steadfast barrier. Once I am near the wall, I sense the closeness to the wall. I'm so close that I feel the magnetic force as it resonates with a tension-filled vibration similar to what one would hear near a transformer. I hear the distant memories as whispered voices that travel through the wall. I have listened intently to the voices. Mostly, the voices are too many to have any intelligent interpretation. The multitude of voices resemble what one would hear when fine-tuning a radio late at night only to encounter multiple frequencies, making it impossible to clearly hear to broadcast. The voices traverse through the wall, resembling echoes from someone's past—a past that I know is mine. The voices at times contain distinct phrases and echoes of terror-filled screams that strike a chord of recollection, a faint, instant remembrance of what once was, but it's still too vague to assemble with clarity. Yet these moments, when these triggered memories bring forth a feeling of pending disaster that's still too cloudy and dark to distinguish, are just enough to trigger a subconscious fear that trickles outward, bringing a torrid dread to my soul bordering on pure panic.

The messages inherent in these dreams are never the same. Each dream presents a sequence of unique scenes that portray a unique message. I am never aware of the tone of the impending message, not until I become close enough to the wall to hear the voices. Only then will the tone be revealed by the voices, when they are reverberated as echoes from within the wall. The voices foretell the message and tone of the scenes that will soon follow. The scenes filled with joy and laughter that marked the tone of my initial dreams have become more infrequent. The recent dreams follow a tone of hellish torment that weighs me down with unbearable fear, presenting varying scenes from hell—scenes that are filled with demonic voices, tormented cries, panic, and horrific screams filled with repressed hatred. These dreams have become more pronounced, gradually taking dominance.

The increased rapidity of the voices further confirms the changes are accelerating. After further scrutiny, I realize a deeper pattern is developing from these recent changes. The tone of the messages from within the wall has reached unbearable levels of intensity. The voices, cries, and pleas have reached a new level of fanaticism, obviously a tone that is nearing a cathartic release with unimaginable consequences. It's a precursor to my mental block crumbling into just fragments, releasing what I believe will be unbearable memories in a total, immediate recall. The full disclosure of my past will result in my own destruction with scenes that will utterly shatter me. Soon the wall that symbolizes my mental block will dissolve entirely. I fear this most of all as the changes to the wall accelerate at a frenzied pace.

I fear the wall because I fear what lies behind the wall. I fear what it symbolizes. I fear the unknown.

Yet I gravitate to beyond the wall. I dread the wall, yet I'm lured to it because it is where Cassandra resides. I am drawn to her with a revelation that my salvation from my past depends on my discovery of our soulful connection. Yet when I pass through the doorway, I am tormented by the elusiveness of Cassandra. When I reach her with heightened awareness to connect, Cassandra unexpectedly disappears. Each time, her disappearance is with a suddenness, as if I am racing toward her with total exhilaration only to unexpectedly drop off a cliff at the last second before we embrace. It is as if each episode ends with its own enigma. Each episode is coupled with a sense of imminent danger and foreboding intruding into my awareness. I remember the look on Cassandra's face just before her disappearance—of despair and fear, a pleading gesture for my help, as if I have the key to unlock this disjointed divide before she fleetingly vanishes. The suddenness of our detachment exemplifies the disparity between my initial dreams and these recent episodes, which only reinforces my alarm that calamity with potential tragic consequences is lurking in the shadows that seem to suffuse the passionately charged atmosphere. I sense these lurking shadows as somehow linked to the recent dreams' aberrant behavior—a deterrent to our previous harmony, an obstacle responsible for the divergent endings, a wedge in the flow that caused these dreams to branch out toward variant paths. I feel that these recent anomalous patterns, if continued, will have tragic consequences to Cassandra and me. If this recursive theme continues unabated, it could jeopardize our engagement, and our encounters could disappear forever, the last episode in this soulful saga.

22

Behind the Wall: Neverland

I come to my senses, exiting the fugue that holds me with discernible trepidation. I sense the wait is finally coming to an end. The verdict has not been disclosed out of respect for the tenuous hold on my sanity. The air surrounding me seems to be lifting; its appearance is transitioning from an obscured view to a cloudy substance. The substance becomes thinner, revealing the wall once more. The path has been cleared, with the wall now directly in front of me. The wall appears to be growing again. When I look upward, the wall seems to have become taller, gaining a menacing appearance and casting its shadow out farther. But as the wall grows taller, it becomes thinner, as if the wall, while stretching upward, loses its volume. The wall is dissolving more rapidly now. It looms over me, bearing down with its weight of unwanted memories. This time, I stand deep within the wall's shadow. Its shadow is so densely overcast that there is no noticeable significant light except for the single light from the one open doorway waiting patiently for my entrance. I draw closer to the heightened structure. The voices carry an angry tone, which seems to be directed toward me. I feel the anger as it pierces my soul with heated vengeance. The voices become rapid as I approach the doorway. I halt before entering the door, taking notice of how thin the wall has become. The wall has lost most of its substance and has a watery effect, which at first does not seem to be contained. But even though the wall now is almost totally dissolved into a liquid substance, it apparently is being supported by something that is not visible.

I lean in closer until the echoes are almost unbearable. The rapidity of the voices causes an endless stream of chaos, but one word has become pronounced: *Tony*. It is not just the word that causes me fear but also the tone of its delivery. It appears to be a desperate cry, as the tone carries a sense of urgency, a plea for help. I turn my head to stare directly into the wall, and I suddenly notice images floating toward me from within the wall. The images are humanlike, but their faces are turned away from me as they float by. Before they float out of my line of vision, they suddenly turn their faces toward me and scream, "Tony!" The clear, watery substance that fills the wall turns to a crimson red. Tiny drops of crimson-tinted blood slowly trickle down the wall and form a pool of blood that circles around my feet. With an alarmed sense of urgency, I immediately step out of the circle and leap over the widening ring encompassing me with oppressive confinement. The burgundy tone soon changes the entire wall to a bright red, and hellish creatures swarm viciously with their demonic eyes glued to mine, letting out forceful cries of torment. I draw back from the wall, watching the scene unfold with hellish intent. I close my eyes when I cannot bear the scene any longer. I bend my head down, too grief-stricken, and my tears of sorrow fall with a heavy burden. I sink to my knees, weeping as I have never wept before. I realize now that my future, once the past memories are revealed, will enclose my soul with unrelenting torment. I fear that whatever remains of my future will be contained in a chamber reserved for the tortured souls of the damned, imprisoned for reasons I will be forced to confront—reasons that are beyond forgiveness and without absolution. I bend my head farther toward the ground in a sacrificial gesture as I ask for God's forgiveness and beg for his mercy to end it now.

While I wait for God to answer my prayers, a voice calls out to me—a voice I instantly recall, a voice that fills my heart with hope. Cassandra is calling me. Her message fills my heart and soul with renewed strength. "Tony, I am here behind the wall. This is where you will find your salvation. I am the key to unlock your horrors. You must confront your memories that lie here behind the wall. Then you will eventually find me. Our souls are preordained, destined, to unite again. Never leave without a promise to return."

I open my eyes and look up toward the wall with a surprised, whispered relief. I cannot see any evidence of the crimson color. The scene is back to the way it was when I first entered the wall's shadow. I stand up. My legs are wobbly, still weak from my emotional turmoil. I see the door and start walking toward it with an even warier caution. I become more alarmed as I approach the door. I am both fearful of and drawn to the wall. As I am pulled farther behind the wall on each journey, I have always felt this suffocating, threatening force that wants to destroy me. Now I feel a weight of almost unbearable grief. It fills me with paralyzing fear that once I pass through the doorway, it will disrupt my will to live, and I will give in to its wrath and commit the ultimate sin. I will end it all. Yet Cassandra intensifies my inner drive, which compels me to continue through the doorway in search of her for salvation. I know she awaits me, for I am the one who needs to be saved, and there is only one savior who can commit and forgive, with whom I will find absolution. That savior is my soul mate, Cassandra.

I tread closer to the doorway, as I have done before in my prior dreams, wherein, once beyond the wall, my journey becomes a treacherous one. I pass through the entrance. I wait for Cassandra to appear. But this time, my wait is in vain, and instead, I must search for her. I must find the village where she resides beyond the wall. It is called Neverland, a small village where Cassandra lies in wait, a place where the unthinkable buried past is hidden. The journey to Neverland can be a treacherous journey filled with unknown horrors. The is only one path that leads to this quaint village, a village of lost souls. Yet the path changes with each journey, as set by the dream's theme. When the theme is joyous and light, the path is filled with the brilliance of a perfect summer day comforted by the warmth of a sunny afternoon and filled at night with a brilliant full moon. It is as if whatever I am supposed to face is not to be until it is time for me to confront these memories. This theme was mostly prevalent during my initial dreams. Neverland was a joyous community before it happened, whatever it was.

But as this theme has become less frequent, the sunlit days have become a rare journey. The recent changes to these dreams have brought a different setting, one that has disrupted the path with detours that will lead to an uneventful fate. These episodes encompass days filled with a strange aura, a harbinger of evil intent. It is here where the treachery lies. It is here where the sun never shines, and the moonless night is filled with voices from the wall, voices that become echoes as the wind carries them through the desolate, tormented village of Neverland in a misty haze. The village is a ghost of what it once was. As I proceed on the devious path, sobs of sorrow, pleas for mercy, and desperate cries for help immerse the night in the depths of hell itself.

I am well past the wall, venturing into a world of unfamiliarity. The dark, moonless night is filled with wails of despair streaming from the wall. My fear is heightened, and my thoughts turn in haste as my trepidation rises to the surface. The realness of my encounters and with the unexpected consequences fuel my caution, for when I enter the world of unknowns, my fortitude is partnered with the baggage of fear, which burdens my mind with a fresh onslaught of unease and portend. A new set of questions and uncertainties sprouts with each journey. They frantically need answers. I need any clue to help avoid a pending catastrophic event. Is fate masquerading its intentions within these lurking shadows? Did fate finally overrule the heavens with the intent to punish Cassandra and me with total obscurity? Is fate toying with us mercilessly before final judgment? Did the heavens forsake us? These are the fears that torture me. I suspect these imminent dangers and the recent dreams' repetitive patterns are connected, but I do not have any notion of how this is going to play out and have no idea what I could do to prevent a pending calamitous end.

My mind returns to this frigid night behind the wall. My search for Neverland has taken me on an even more treacherous journey as the night takes on a sudden change from a humid night to a frigid one. The lack of warmth and the icy chill in the air keep my instinctual sense of foreboding on continuous alert. I am consumed with overwhelming trepidation, on the edge of absolute terror of new revelations and the potential consequences. To calm my fears, attempt to slow this avalanche of anguish, and be able to think and resolve, I refocus my attention back on Cassandra, looking for any clues as to my next action.

I remember her note and reach into my pocket to reveal her message, which further affirms the realness of her presence. I read the note, remembering I picked it up hastily as it lay next to the crimson rose and inserted it into my pocket before the recent images of Cassandra totally dissipated. As I read her note again, my longing for her companionship becomes unbearable. Tears of loneliness overcome me, and each teardrop falls as if in slow motion, reacting to her words written with a forlorn longing, as if she knew that when the scene retreated, she too would disappear into the haze-encumbered fog. I bring the note closer to me to catch the sweetness of her scent, and the words written send an echo through my heart. *We will never leave without a promise to return.* The note further ignites my quest, which evolves into a hunger that can only be satisfied through the ultimate final consummation of our union.

Wave after wave of uncontrolled obsession returns, overwhelming me, and my memories take control of all my senses as I search for meaning and truth. Once again, I enter this realm of foregone memories with an urgency to keep my resolve afloat with hopeful desire of her existence. Yet once engaged, it always starts the same: with a feeling of utter desolation. My soul feels incomplete; my emptiness is an infinite abyss of unknowns. I feel the pain of unbearable distress without her. My heart aches with a yearning for her companionship, a need for her by my side to distance my loneliness. In her absence, I am devoid of being total and complete. In my soul, love, laughter, and compassion that only the angels serving as messengers for God himself could have conceived were the integral forces that defined our boundless journey and held our soulful union in perfect harmony. Now the essence of my soul lies buried under unbearable layers of utter loneliness. I'm desperate for her guidance to mend my heart. I want to look once more into her eyes, enter the depths of her soul, and feel her closeness, her touch that binds us to our endless journey. We must reunite and capture once again that defining moment when our consummation will at last secure our rightful place reserved for the select celestial beings.

Once again, I find myself in a fugue state. I force my thoughts back to the path I pursue. The fog has returned. The night has regained its humidity, and the echoes of torment have disappeared, leaving the night filled with an eerie stillness. I find myself at a detour in the path, one I have never noticed before, which confirms that I must be farther behind the wall. The main path is now shielded by a fog bank that cloaks the path with swirls of tentacles from the fog. Something is there, shielded by the mist yet noticeable, as shadows seem to move about within the fog. The shadows sometimes stop, and I notice a tinge of yellow peering straight at me before moving on. I stand there at the fork in the path, undecided on which direction to follow. I feel an isolation, as if I am the only soul left in the universe. I cry out, and my cries become weighted with fear as they travel out toward the dense fog, where they are devoured into silence. The solitude is unbearable. I feel myself perched precariously on the edge of saneness. I know this is the culminating chapter in which all the truths between Cassandra and me will be revealed. As I remember the mirage of images from last night, I become more certain of the realness of this voyage. This realization ignites an intense quest to find her, to satisfy my thirst for validation.

I choose the detour, a diversion, but remain steadfast in search of Neverland. However, that is not the end-all. The pursuit can only end when I find the place in Neverland that holds the forbidden memories. Then my fate will be decided. The detour is eerily quiet; I hear not a sound as I continue on this alternate path. Suddenly, I see something. I'm not sure until I come nearer. Yes, it is Neverland. The detour I have chosen has led me to a cemetery. I stop at the old iron gates, which are locked. I draw in closer to the gates. A tombstone is off to my right. I lean in, peering through the gatepost. I have trouble reading the name of the deceased. Just for a minute, the fog thins out, revealing a bright light that rests on the tombstone. *Cassandra.* I glance again just as the light extinguishes, and the tendrils of fog swallow the tombstone into obscurity. It can't be. I did not get a clear look, but the possibility haunts me. I then clearly see the village beyond the gate, beyond the cemetery—a dead end. But for what purpose still remains to be found. I stand there watching as the scene in front of me disappears. I am surrounded again by a vast, open darkness. Cassandra appears before me, and as I frantically reach out for her, her image retreats, her eyes pleading for me. She retreats farther until she disappears into the night, entering a world of darkness. Everything seems to fade away as my mind retreats, and darkness consumes me. I become nothing.

I feel weightless, floating in hyperspace. The night of remembrance has ended yet retained me in a suspended void that encompasses my soul, blanketing me with the cover of darkness. I enter the abyss of unknowns as I descend into its depths of enigmatic proportions. I continue on this relentless journey, an unforgettable quest that will soon determine my eventual fate in this daunting yet forever magical adventure. I ponder my destiny.

23

A Dream Episode's End to Another Place

Slowly, I was aroused from what felt like a deep coma-induced sleep. My mind was suspended on the verge of panic as I tried to regain my senses. Vivid memories from last night surfaced and floated on a pool of unease. Immediately, I contemplated my surroundings to quell my anxiety, only to have my trepidation intensify, as I had no recollection of my present terrain and was unable to recall any clues. I found myself a stranger lying on a strange bed in a strange bedroom. Everything seemed out of place. My mind was a complete blank. Even the air had a strange scent. The taste in my mouth was metallic from an adrenaline rush, and I heard a high-pitched ringing in both ears; my eardrums were popping continuously. My heartbeat was rapid, leaving me breathless. My breathing was shallow, I had frequent spells of chills, and my hands were noticeably trembling. I realized my symptoms were related to shock. I dared not move, for I feared if I shifted my position even slightly, it could have unforeseen consequences on my present surroundings or my coherence. My mind became a sponge, absorbing an endless barrage of questions. I was on the verge of becoming unglued with the realization that I had no answers. *How did I get here? How long have I been here?* Haunting questions consumed me, repeatedly pursuing me as if a battering ram kept punching me for answers. These unknowns engulfed me with paralyzing emotions, leaving me precariously placed on a tightrope without a safety net, struggling to maintain a composed equilibrium. But my coping mechanisms barely sustained my stress upon my sensing a presence in the bedroom in which I was a foreigner, which heightened my level of angst.

A cry of alarm escaped me when I caught a noticeable whimper, a sob of sorrow, and felt a caress touch my shoulder. A scented breath brushed my ear, and a teardrop fell, resting on my cheek and then cascading into a steam of several. I brushed my cheek with my fingers to capture the teardrops. Each finger was a resting place as the drops pooled, turning to crimson. I realized the tears were tainted with blood. My reaction was immediate: I jumped off the bed and landed firmly on my feet with my eyes sweeping the four corners of the room. Last night's engagement was still vivid, and my concern for Cassandra prompted me to cry out, "Cassandra!" with no acknowledgment. My repeated calls became hallowed cries of despair, empty pleas of desperate attempts to be acknowledged. "Where are you, Cassandra? Are you in danger?" Each question hauntingly reverberated with an echo, as if my questions were instead meant for me. Music hit upon my ear—the same melody Cassandra and I had intimately danced to. I searched for the source of the music only to realize it was materializing from the open air around me. I caught the scent of her perfume as it swiftly passed by, and then a shadow on the wall revealed a village, with a young boy and girl peering upward, before disappearing as suddenly as it had appeared.

Within an instant, another shadow passed by haltingly, revealing the same village haunted by neglect as a hideous figure stood by with an ominous look, its form changing shape as if something from within were trying frantically to claw its way out. The figure had an aura, a metallic gray wreathed with a hint of blackness. At its center, the hue was black. Its density alternated from a translucent appearance to an intense, pulsating darkness. Each pulse radiated a sensation of menacing discernment. For a brief second, from within the center, an opening appeared, revealing a grotesque view: a horrific, distorted face, its eyes casting a yellowish glow. I immediately perceived the image as a monstrously deformed creature from the depths of hell. The eyes were not focused upon me but were sweeping from left to right as if intently in search of something or someone. I tried to rationalize these images as hallucinations, which caused me to wonder if I'd somehow suffered a concussion.

The images were too horrific to bear, so I forced my gaze away toward the bed—and viewed a pool of blood surging up through the mattress, saturating the blanket. I just stood there transfixed by the horror of what I was viewing. The shadowy figure floated toward the blood-soaked mattress and plunged its left arm into the crimson pool. It pushed farther into the bloodstained mattress, and the blood level nearly swallowed its arm. Its forearm disappeared into the pool of blood before stopping. It was obviously searching for something, but for what, I had no clue. Moments later, it removed its red-tinged arm from the blood. Suddenly, Cassandra appeared on the bed, lying in the blood as she cried out, "Tony!" I fought for composure, realizing the urgent tone of Cassandra's call for help. I moved swiftly toward the bed to heed to her call. Before I reached her, the shadowy image and Cassandra dissolved, and the blood disappeared entirely.

I stood there staring at an empty bed, my mind reeling with uncertainty. Suddenly, a new set of images took form on the bed. I soon realized the vision was of me lying in an unconscious state, with Cassandra overlooking me, her face hovering over mine. Her shoulders were slumped with worry, and tears cascaded down her cheeks, tainted with blood as the drops fell upon my cheeks and shoulders. I was the one injured, not Cassandra—or maybe both of us were. But there I was, standing uninjured, confused by what I was seeing. I was paralyzed with horror, trying to rationalize what I was viewing. A premonition of what was to come? A hallucination from last night's dream? Was I still caught in the web of the same dream, a deranged continuation of last night's dream, or was there another possible explanation I was not prepared to accept? Nothing made sense to me; my mind was too frozen to rationalize anything. Everything seemed too far-fetched to further contemplate, yet I was unable to move; my mind was held captive by the images before me.

Within seconds, the images of Cassandra and me disappeared also, retreating into the open air. The blood funneled into an endless vacuum in midair, leaving but a drop that vanished during its downward flight. The music faded in the distance, yielding to a pretense of normalcy, yet I was not fooled, for what I'd just perceived was anything but normal. A conveyance, a transference of images—any explanation fell outside the range of logic, but that was not important, for I sensed the reason the images were conveyed was to convince me that Cassandra was calling for my help.

I looked around my immediate surroundings in an attempt to ensure that all remnants of the dream had ended. With a relentless flood of tormented feelings of helplessness, I paced around the room, searching for any clue, my eyes glued to search every inch of space. The hairs on the back of my neck stood on end as chills ran up my spine. I had a feeling Cassandra was desperate, frantically searching for my help with life-or-death consequences, yet I felt a torrid sensation that I was also being watched or, worse, probed, and at any moment, unforeseen consequences would be unleashed toward me.

I was uncertain if the dream had relinquished its hold on me. I had an uncanny sense that Cassandra's presence was there in the room. The instinctive feeling sent chills through me. I jumped off the bed upon hearing Cassandra's repeated cry. Her plea, filled with desperation and despair, seemed to materialize from somewhere behind me. I turned around and saw nothing. Another call came from the closet off in the corner, which was partly hidden by obscured shadows and distanced from the fading sunlight as twilight began to make its entrance. Frantically, I intensely searched the room again for any clue as to the source of her pleas to no avail.

The room was taking on a deeper tone, with the fading sunlight giving way to a twilight haze. I sat back on the bed with my head bent low and my hands held to the sides to shield me from more worry. I tried to gain some semblance of what was happening to me. *Focus. How long have I been here? Where is Cassandra? Is she injured or, God forbid, dead?* Questions repeatedly invaded my senses with no answers—unknowns that constantly plagued me. I pondered relentlessly the stream of questions. *Where in the hell am I, and why am I here?*

With nothing to go on, I reverted to my dreams for any plausible explanation. There was no doubt that lately, the dreams had been cast with a nightmarish state, one of alarm, uncertainty, fear, and a desperate longing. It wasn't just the dream's unsettling nature that alarmed me but also the fact that it was starting again. My condition was becoming more intense, a vivid reminder of the genetic flaw wherein dreams flowed into the conscious waking state, leaving me unable to separate reality from a dream's fantasies. When my mind defused the fused state, I was aware the dream had ended. Only then could I vaguely determine what was real and what was fantasy. It was obvious the dreams were beginning to flow into my waking state with a fierceness that was gaining momentum. The point when the dream ended and I returned to an awake state was becoming more indistinct. It wasn't just the dreams' endings that startled me but also the aftermath following the dreams. The nightmarish endings followed me upon my awakening. The dreams attached themselves to me with projected images of both heightened grandeur and hauntingly repressed evil.

I felt helpless, trapped, and isolated. At that moment, I felt unbalanced, as if, if anything else unexpectedly occurred at that exact instant, I would go crazy, race to the nearest window, and jump out, falling headfirst toward whatever lay at the bottom, intent upon ending the nightmare. Yes, a nightmare—that was what it was. I was desperate to heed the calls of Cassandra's alarm. But where was she? I agonized as I looked around me; everything was alien. I felt an exigency to be somewhere else in a time of need, to proceed to another place, to the source of the tormented cries for help. But the more I fought that dilemma, the more I panicked. Out of desperation, I found and reread the note from Cassandra, a convincing fact that helped stop the avalanche of irrational thoughts. With the last of my reserves to quell my level of panic, I hastily retreated from my emotional turmoil in an attempt to gain a more rational view. With renewed hope, I urgently set forth, determined to find a clue—any clue—to my whereabouts. I needed an immediate plan, a goal, some form of action to stem my anxiety and regain some composure. I decided to initiate my plan with a thorough search of the house, looking for any thread to start unraveling the enigma.

Off to my right, I saw an open hallway that led to a loft. I hastily got up off the bed, hurried to the hallway, and noticed the staircase leading down to the first floor. I cautiously walked to the adjoining loft, which overlooked the open room below, and I called out to see if I would get any response. I heard nothing but silence. I turned around, facing the bedroom again, and saw a connecting bathroom. I entered the bathroom to find an enormous spa. There was a medicine cabinet over in the corner, but I found nothing that would even give me a name.

I returned to the bedroom and spotted a patio off to my left. My alarm somewhat eased, replaced with a cautious wariness while I hesitantly walked toward the patio and opened the patio doors, which gave way to a vast ocean view. The scene off the patio would have been mesmerizing to the average person, but from the tilted state I was in, obviously still in shock, I viewed the ocean as both a majestic view and a potential threatening force. I walked out onto the overhang and gazed at the landscape below and the surrounding homes. Surprisingly, I instinctually assumed I was on the West Coast. My judgment was supported by the majestic adjacent homes that scaled the cliffs formed by the canyons along the coast. The creative designs and sizes of the oceanfront homes led me to believe I was probably in California, which, if true, meant the ocean view must be of the Pacific. But beyond that, there was nothing familiar to me, which only added to my conundrum. I had no recollection of how I'd gotten there, yet there I was, in a spacious condo overlooking the Pacific. The memories from last night were still clear and vivid yet haphazardly scattered throughout my subdued consciousness, leaving me dizzy, dazed, and confused. I knew that last night, something profound had happened, something of paramount consequence and enormous significance, resulting in a euphoric high, yet I was pained with a sense of unease and loss, which resulted in a wave of desperation leaving me emotionally drained. I again scanned my surroundings and tried to recollect exactly where I was. At a loss for an explanation, I was left with one vivid fact: I had blacked out and, upon awakening, found myself surrounded by a new set of infinite unknowns. As that one fact became more pronounced, I swooned like a lost soul, as vanquished as a lone sailor immersed in a vast ocean of unknowns.

My head pounded with a vengeance as I tried to focus on my circumstances. Desperate for a clue, I focused more intently, painstakingly reexamining the house, hoping I would uncover anything to provide some insight. I descended to the first floor and took in the spaciousness of the house. The house was large, approximately six thousand square feet, and my search would be exhaustive. There were three floors, with a spiral staircase leading to the second and third floors. From the inside, it appeared the design of the structure was unique in that each floor had a different size. The third floor was the most spacious, consuming the most square footage. The second floor occupied less space, while the first floor, though expansive, had the least square footage. The curvature of the overall architecture resembled a cone. There were no corners or angles; the connections took on the form of gentle curves, presenting a seamless lineage, a continuous flow between the floors and between the rooms on each floor. The seamless flow gave the house and the rooms a sense of continuous harmony.

The first floor was designed as one large room, sectioned off with a den, living room, dining room, and wide-open balcony overlooking the Pacific. The room was eloquently designed, and the furnishings had an expensive look and feel. The kitchen was the only enclosed room. It had enough space to accommodate more than enough appliances, with room to spare. Numerous abstract art pieces hung on the walls, adding a final touch to the rooms' eloquently designed decor. The house was superbly decorated, most likely by an interior designer who had a prolific gift for artistic taste. My initial assessment was that whoever owned the house had a creative flair for the visual arts, most likely a person who was used to wealth and had an eye for perfection. The open great room was artfully crafted, and the gentle curves provided the impression that the walls blended as one, promoting a vision of symmetry and openness. I further examined the living room and den yet found nothing of significance that would be of help.

I climbed the spiral staircase back to the second floor and then continued up to the third floor. From the hallway, I noticed a third bedroom. I cautiously entered and saw another patio, which jettisoned out over the deck below and provided an even wider ocean view. This was obviously the master bedroom, with a master bath. The house, if put on the market, would have fetched several million dollars, a fact I felt worth noting to gain some sense as to the character of the owner. I surveyed the rest of the third floor, which, besides the bedroom, included a connecting bath, a patio, and another study room and loft that circumvented the spiral staircase, overlooking the first and second floors. My exhaustive search of the third floor turned up nothing to give me a clue to my ordeal, forcing me to even more disappointment and adding to my downtrodden state. It was as if no one lived there. The place was not gathering any dust, and everything was orderly, with no obvious disarray. The house was immaculate, artfully furnished, and spacious, with a creative architectural design. That confused me even more. Finding myself situated in an expansive house richly supplanted with interior decor suggested the owner or owners were more inclined to be cultured, refined, and intellectual within an atmosphere of successful accomplishments. The place was definitely not indicative of anything sinister, unlike the recent episodes that had just occurred within the walls of the house. Assuming that was true, then I was perplexed even more, at a loss as to the how and why of my displacement. I let out a solemn sigh from the impact of the additional weight of the uncertainty.

Refusing to relent to my frustrations, I continued with my search. I descended the staircase, returning to the first floor, and walked out onto the lower patio connected to the living room. As I looked out from the patio, my weary mind was drawn to the view of the waves rolling gently toward the shoreline and the distant seagulls swooping down toward the ocean. The vastness of the view both threatened and mesmerized me, triggering faint flashbacks from last night, adding to my disoriented, exhausted state. I wasn't sure of anything about my present surroundings. I remembered a similar view from last night, a night that had had a profound, euphoric effect upon me. As I stood there with that memory still freshly imprinted, I felt desperate loneliness and unbearable weariness, feeling totally helpless. My longing for Cassandra was too weighted with grief for me to carry much longer, filling my soul with a desperate want and desire. To be back by her side, to return to the charged atmosphere from last night, was my obsession, regardless of the cost. My loneliness felt like a burning torch to my soul, and my only salvation was Cassandra. My quest for her became a compulsive need to reunite our souls, or else I would surely drown in my tears of sorrow and my tortured heart.

I retreated back inside the house to the kitchen, taking a much-needed breather for a few minutes before continuing my search. I rested my elbows on the kitchen counter, lowering my head to relieve the tension in my neck, when I noticed the wall clock in the adjacent den. I was amazed that with all my scrutiny and extensive search so far, I had not even thought about the date. *Odd*, I thought. There I was, feeling lost, wondering where I was, and frantically searching for answers, but I had not even thought about the date and time during my search. I excused the lapse as pure exhaustion and walked over to the den to get a closer look. The mounted clock above the corner of the desk displayed the day and time: Monday, July 1, 2020, 10:00 a.m. That held no significance to me. I realized I'd never searched the desk drawers and immediately searched each drawer for anything that would provide a clue.

As I continued my search of the first floor, my peripheral vision again caught some type of movement. I hastily turned around but did not detect any further movement or immediate threat. I knew my nerves were taut, vibrating with tension, and resigned my alarm to an overworked imagination. Within seconds, the movement occurred again. This time, it was accompanied by a flicker of light, followed by a hollow, barely audible cry of sorrow. As I turned around a second time, convinced there was imminent danger, my vision blurred, and my head throbbed with pain, as if someone were driving a spike into my frontal lobe. Immediately, the pain subsided, followed by a series of vivid flashbacks from last night's dream. The flashbacks were instant flashes, a quick sequence of visuals, a random succession of images: an elegant ballroom, melodic music, a candlelit table, wine and dancing, and Cassandra. Another brief recall brought a dense fog, an eerie glow that seemed to spin in a circular motion with increased velocity, emitting a blinding white light of alternating intensity traversing toward Cassandra and me. More quick glimpses flashed before me of last night's events, including finding the letter and the rose that I hastily inserted into my pocket before the light overtook me. The symbolism was evident. As I had always known, Cassandra held the key to this phenomenon integrally connected to my soul. She was a central force behind these events yet to be revealed.

Then the remembrances, the flashes from the past, withdrew and diminished. A panicked sense of rejection encompassed me, and my insecurity forced me to desperately search my pocket once again. I found the note and rose from last night—evidence that something real had happened last night. My obsession too overbearing, I read the note again and feverishly hoped her words—"Never leave without a promise to return"—would materialize to bring us together and permanently seal our bond. We would never separate again. It did not matter if she was just a dream or if this was another form of reality; all that mattered was our connection. If this was only a dream, then I wanted to be part of the dream for eternity. If this was real, then my search would not end until I found her.

Never leave without a promise to return. I had vague, distant memories of those exact words, connected to Cassandra and me from a long time ago. That phrase was tied to our connection as if it existed solely to define our commitment to each other. It was a message that could only be shared by our hearts. If only my memories were more distinct.

Again, I detected movement in my peripheral vision, and when I turned around, this time, I found myself suddenly confronted with a thick fog that radiated an ethereal glow. A blinding light at its center moved toward me and moments later enclosed me in what seemed like a tunnel. At the end of the tunnel was an angelic golden halo that moved toward me and then stopped a few feet from me. Within the center of the halo was Cassandra, who seemed lost. She looked forlorn, as if she were searching for something or someone. I reached out for Cassandra, and with each effort, she became more elusive, as if a shield prevented me from connecting with her. A claustrophobic feeling overwhelmed me. Panic seized me as I tried to back away from the tunnel of light, but I was unable to move, as a seemingly magnetic force held me in check, pulling me back into the tunnel.

Suddenly, I was propelled forward through the tunnel, as if I were moving at an alarming speed through time. The forward movement increased its velocity to warp speed. After what seemed like an eternity, the movement forward halted with a suddenness. The stillness in the air, a quietness that seemed to permeate the tunnel, held me in suspense. I lay motionless, captive in a tomb of silence, frozen in a state of confusion and anguish. A dark cloud enveloped me, making me feel confined in a claustrophobic vise. I reached out, desperate to escape my confinement, and as I touched the cloud, the cloud separated, revealing Cassandra enclosed by angelic light. Brilliant in color, the light emitted a wave of warmth that seemed to sooth my senses. The image then changed from a tranquil setting into a nightmarish scene in which Cassandra lay in a pool of blood. The warmth was replaced by a chilling cold. There was no movement from Cassandra, as if every ounce of energy were depleted from her soul. She then lifted her head, and I saw a forlorn look on her face, with tears of despair. Each teardrop descended into a pool of blood, falling as if in slow motion and dropping with a soundless splash, causing a ripple effect as the pool of crimson widened with each drop. I watched in agony, feeling helpless, as the magnetic force held me in check. The images then appeared with a suddenness, with alternating periods of clarity with increased intensity and near obscurity, before totally vanishing, leaving me stunned. Cassandra's image returned unharmed; her angelic glow was radiant, and the coldness retreated as the warmth returned. Unconsciously, I pulled my hand back, and the warmth from the light filled my body as I remained motionless.

Wherever I was, it seemed transient in nature, for I felt that my journey through the void would at any time continue forward, as if I were in a capsule waiting for a specific entrance for me to enter. The movement started again, and I felt myself being propelled forward at an accelerated rate, racing against the universe's internal clock, as if, if the timing were not synchronized with exact precision, I would be left in that time void for the rest of eternity. Suddenly, the movement stopped again, and I was jettisoned upward toward an entrance, another dimension of reality. When I reached the opening, my tunnel of vision closed entirely. My vision became useless; the dark extinguished my conscious light, and I lost consciousness.

24

Changes to the Dreams

My body ached with a nail-biting vengeance, as if I had been on a drinking binge. I had no recollection of how I'd wound up on the hallway floor. The last thing I remembered was waking up in that house earlier before blacking out, and then I remembered last night with Cassandra, when we'd been enthralled with each other as we harmonized to the tunes of rapture. Beyond that, I recalled nothing. My mind was an empty void. "My God," I moaned. "What the hell happened?" Was there a connection between last night and the house? Attempting to trigger any recollection, I viewed my surroundings for the second time, trying to jar a memory or recall anything after blacking out. There was a sense of familiarity, yet everything still seemed vague, just beyond my reach, like a hazy cloud obscuring any recollection.

It became difficult to keep my state of trepidation at an acceptable level. Each moment became heavier and more intense, weighted down with weariness and an increasingly paranoid, overwhelming feeling of being trapped. I felt a total loss of control and direction, as if entangled in a spiderweb's desperate nightmare. When the growing sense of entrapment became almost unbearable, the web's silken fibers began to slowly dissolve, revealing an opening, expanding my consciousness, and triggering a recall of revealing details of my current setting.

With each passing second, I felt a reawakening from a deep sleep. The weight of weariness lifted as I started to regain some awareness. My recollection of my current state cut through my senses with an ever-widening scope. When I became more fully aware of my present surroundings, that awareness fueled my alarm at another frightening revelation. The revelation had always been present, just below the level of acceptance, but now it was an unavoidable fact that refused to be kept submerged; it demanded to be acknowledged. Once surfaced, it was apparent, too obvious to ignore any longer, leaving me in a continual restless state.

My recent dreams were revealing events that lay outside the boundary of recognition. A vague sense of a connection was present, but it ended there. Was it possible the recent dreams were exposing events that had occurred during the time masked by my amnesia? If so, then the unexplained, disparate gaps were becoming more explicit, as evidenced in the dreams. *My recent dreams were taking me behind the wall to a place where the hidden events started to be revealed. Eventually, enough of the event is disclosed to where some form of recognition begins. Yet before more memories are triggered, the event dissipates, leaving me more anxious than before, because just prior to the event dispersing, something with tragic consequences is about to occur. Whatever the tragedy is, it keeps eluding me just before my recognition takes hold, when the dream suddenly closes.*

I had the oddest feeling, though. *Something is terribly wrong, and it revolves around Cassandra and me. It is not just this one event. Several prior events have been disclosed, each by a separate dream. Each in a different setting and where each event is of a different nature. Unlike my initial dreams, these recent dreams present fragments of my life that seem to be totally unconnected. Life impeding interrupts with no congruous flow. Time slices with no connection seem to contradict each other, causing a pattern of inconsistency, leaving any form of interpretation up to an overworked imagination.* It was as if each dream was encapsulated, with its own set of variables. Any resurgence of memories was of such a short duration that they could not be connected and remained in a state of distorted, vague, and scattered memories.

It appears these recent dreams are for now toying with me, and the objective of the game is pure torment. But there were more oddities. *These events seem real, and they sometimes carry over to my waking state before fading into the background. But the truth is, they never really leave. They are always there, just under the surface. What I fear most is*

*that at some random point in time, these obscured memories will fully
evolve, the seemingly separate events will connect, and the gaps will close,
evolving into apertures allowing me to view what was previously hidden
with alarming clarity, scenes that will haunt me endlessly to the depths
of my soul.*

As my mind further elaborated on my recent dreamlike episodes,
the current dream's hold on me loosened, releasing me from its grasp
as the recollection of my present state fully emerged, starting with just
a steady stream of facts and widening into a flood of revealing detail
surging into my consciousness as if a dam that had held back all the
intricate details suddenly gave way, releasing a torrid flow of revelations.
I could feel the dream's constraints lift. My breathing became more
relaxed as the containment freed me. My mind desperately sought some
rationale for the recent dream's hold on me, searching for a pattern to
provide some basis for an explanation.

Lucid dreams. That was my initial assessment in an attempt to
provide some valid reasoning for the recent dreams that held on. Not
all of my recent dreams persisted into my waking state, but the number
of dreams that did had become enough to cause serious concern and
raise new questions. At first, it appeared the web of entanglement from
the dreams was so tightly woven that the effort to disengage extended
the dream into my conscious state. Lucid dreams, I thought, but it
turned out that was not the case since only the remnants from the
dreams intruded into my consciousness. The other explanation was
that the residuals from the dreams were hallucinations—a concept that
had validity. The dreams were so intense that it wasn't simple to just
immediately unleash them upon awakening. But upon further scrutiny,
as my mind regained some form of remembrance, I knew part of the
dream's intrusion was due to my condition: paramnesia, a perception
disorder, a genetic flaw wherein I could not separate the dream's fantasy
from reality—not until my mind detected and attempted to correct the
disorder.

However, despite my condition, the main revelation was my discovery
of the rose and letter upon awakening. That alone implied the dream
residuals were not just hallucinations but encompassed an element of
reality. The rose and the letter were the main impetus that led to that
major implication. The recent dreams might not have been entirely

fantasy dreams after all; instead, they embraced a degree of realness that led me back to my original supposition that despite my condition, they might be an out-of-body experience or lucid dreams. I had to be physically somewhere during the dreams to retrieve the rose and letter. But where? Was the where Neverland? That was at the core of the mystery, for which I had no answers. If the rose and letter were connected to Neverland, then Neverland was real, and that was where I would find Cassandra. Despite all the variables and questions, despite all the doubts that took their turn in trying to pierce my protective shield of hope, there was one fact that held true to my soul: *Cassandra does exist.*

Despite my steadfast, insistent conviction about Cassandra, the unrelenting questions hung on with endless pursuit. *Could all this be just one journey, and my present state is just a short recess before a continuation of the journey?* I admitted that the initial and recent dreams were just that: a journey to all the remembrances of what once was. But it didn't end there. Last night's journey was connected to the existence of the rose and letter. The realness of last night bordered on certainty, and that realness gained a finality with the confirmation of the rose and letter, which proved a degree of reality with their physical presence. They were proof that the unbelievable journey was more than just past memories but a journey that included stops at the here and now in my present state. Those stops included Neverland, where Cassandra resided. Neverland and Cassandra were real. Both were at the core of that mystery. If somehow I could find more evidence as to where I'd been last night and find the location of the village, I could start to unravel the mystery and, most importantly, find Cassandra, who was the key to all my questions.

Yet despite the rose and letter, the truth was, until I could find Neverland and locate Cassandra, the dreams were just dreams waiting for me to unlock the puzzle. I realized I was at the point where too many questions were surfacing without any answers. I drew my attention back to my current situation and to the recent dream and its aftermath. I knew by then the dream had relinquished its hold on me, leaving me until the next episode. There were times when the episodes felt too cumbersome to bear. Their burden left me with no recourse but to make them part of my baggage. The episodes could not be expunged as if they'd never happened. Even when the episodes finally ended, they did not just roll off and disappear forever; they were retained to become part of my history.

The fact that the dreams flowed into my conscious state was the one element that caused me the most consternation. The dream's fantasies and the waking conscious realities melded into a fused state. Yet despite the melded state, it felt as if the dream's dimensions of fantasy versus reality were in a constant struggle over which would take dominance. The disparity between the integrated yet separate dimensions was tipping me closer to the edge where everything would appear as one continual fantasy-filled dream. I couldn't hold on much longer. I realized that at any moment, one state would take dominance over the other. If the fantasy dimension became the dominant property and completely consumed the reality part, that would cause my mind to exist in a world of pure make-believe and would surely find me a permanent place in a psych ward.

The last episode was worrisome. It had hung on for far too long, allowing the deformed images to venture further into my realm of reality. If that kept up, I would surely lose my foothold on reality, as I was already beginning to feel as if nothing was real anymore. Fortunately, up until then, my savior had been that eventually, the horrific imprints faded into the background, giving me the freedom to live my life with some coherence. The pieces of the puzzle were still there but without the disruptive influence of demonic intrusion. Yet I was in danger of losing that freedom if the fantasy part of my dreams finally consumed the part that was real. But my perceptions could not be denied. It was too obvious. The dominance of the dream's fantasies was, in fact, beginning, which led to a more serious implication. The oppression by the fantasies in the fused state was pushing the realities into complete submission. In truth, the reality aspect of the fused state was being compressed to a point where the compacted details would eventually explode outward with a cathartic release. If that occurred at the time when the wall came down, the avalanche of infinite detail would be too much for me to handle. It was obvious everything seemed to be heading to an expulsion, rushing at a blurring pace to a finish line where the trophy was a final release of revelations meant for me from behind the wall.

25

Sudden Awareness of Tony's Current State

The awareness of my current setting finally took center stage, as if a secret doorway had opened to reveal a vast array of facts supporting the reality of my current state. Immediately, I had a stark realization that I was in my own house. My unease subsided immediately upon that realization. That gateway, once revealed, released a tide of revelations. The feeling thoroughly grounded me, leaving me with an insightful observation. I felt I'd just returned from an extended sabbatical that had left me emotionally drained to the point of exhaustion. I had mixed emotions about my awakened state. I was both despondent and relieved to be back in my house, having returned from an unexplained journey filled with challenges and obstacles. I could not come up with any logical explanation for last night's unexpected events that had turned the dream's usual harmonious flow into one filled with numerous interruptions. Yet I was not convinced that last night was an isolated event. I relished the euphoric high from Cassandra's engagement and felt unbearable loneliness without her by my side. Yet I felt relieved to have returned safely from the numerous detours that had served as threatening barricades erected by death's own messenger as I'd maneuvered my way on the journey toward Neverland.

My feeling of relief was but a respite, an interim camouflage, a buffer from the internal conflict between two contradictory emotions: the relief from the journey's perilous obstacles and an emotional exigency to fulfill a soulful need for Cassandra. Each opposite emotion of the spectrum would lead to only one course of action: to ultimately return to Neverland to uncover the truth. But how, and when? That was the undeniable question.

Annoyed that I had no answers, I redirected my attention back to my house. I observed the exquisite, tasteful art and furnishings accomplished by a team of designers I'd personally handpicked. I'd chosen designers who shared my vision of architectural taste through an open design concept of curves instead of corners and angles, which gave the impression of synchronized harmony and added dimension.

I took in the surrealist art I'd purchased at several art exhibits over the last year. Yet, each time I scanned the surrealist images, I was brought back to the surrealism that encompassed my journey. I could not dismiss my obvious obsession. Too many unanswered questions compelled me to return to my thoughts about last night. But it was more than just the questions. For some reason, I had a feeling, a restless calm, that the place I journeyed to was my true destination, my home, where I was destined to be. I felt the journey was different now. It had been for weeks or months—I was uncertain when the disparities had begun. The journey had become tainted with a demonic force creating a journey filled with nightmarish scenes with hellish intent. My dreams now encompassed a journey of heaven and hell. The initial journeys had transported me to a destination filled with a serene peacefulness, a soulful harmony. One composed with divine happiness and rapturous ecstasy had sent me back home to Cassandra. Yet something alien had intervened, bringing with it sorrow, danger, and a fear of impending doom at a destination of doubt. I felt that my ultimate home, my true destination, was threatened; the core upon which our soulful bond was based might end forever unless I interceded.

The dreams had taken me on alternate routes, each with detours that resulted in unexplained destinations. Maybe I was just too weary from last night's events to apply any consistent logic and was defaulting to sensory overload, wherein any delusional reasoning would suffice for now. However, there were obvious facts and feelings I could not ignore, and it finally dawned on me the answers might be hidden here in my current reality. Maybe that was why my journey kept transporting me between two dimensions, between Neverland and this present state: to find the answers to my plaguing questions.

The heavens must have heard me. The next revelation hit me like a ton of bricks crashing through a wall of dismissal and breaking down the barriers to release a new barrage of intricate details of my current situation. The backlog of data caused by my momentary delay in absorbing the initial revelation must have been excessive, for the second wave of revelations deluged me with a vicious impact, resulting in an overwhelmed, shocked awareness and triggering total recall. The recall was almost instantaneous.

Deluged with the sudden avalanche of memories, I felt my hold on any coherent thoughts slipping. Doubts increasingly weakened my perception of what was real. The boundaries were becoming indistinct, and the delineation of my awareness was hardly present anymore; reality and imagination were merging into one surreal view. The questions had always been present from the beginning, hidden under the surface of my consciousness, but the underlying question had persisted with no answer: Were all the episodes just altered states of one continuous journey? It was paramount that I find the answer to that pivotal fact before I completely lost my grasp on reality. I realized that if there were answers to find, then those answers lay in the volume of information bestowed upon me in this current setting. My direction was obvious now. I no longer faced an aimless search; I could finally conduct a more thorough search for the clues to the mystery. The information was here somewhere. I needed answers. The open-ended questions and their parade of variables, flashbacks, and dreams were consuming me, constantly searching for answers. But there was something else nagging me. A hunch there was another wave of information, of self-awareness, which would provide a wealth of knowledge that may provide the clues I desperately needed to gain more insight into my quandary.

Within minutes my hunch was fulfilled. The acknowledgement was instantaneous when it became crystal clear to me upon realizing my profession. That one fact was immediate, a starting place to begin anew with an even broader search for a discovery. I was an architect specializing in renovation of custom homes. My company was a small architectural firm that was still relatively young and composed of a few employees; the rest were contractors. We specialized in custom renovations of houses along the California coastline, including hidden gems scattered throughout the canyons. We had purchased several homes in the canyons that overlooked Santa Monica and the Pacific. The homes were architectural gems from the art deco era, the prevalent theme during the first half of the 1900s.

I immediately recalled there was a meeting at one of the homes we'd purchased scheduled for one o'clock that afternoon. I was to meet Linda at the office, and then we both would drive out to meet the contractors at the site. With a sudden jolt of adrenaline, I rushed toward the downstairs den and looked at the clock mounted on the wall, which confirmed that it was late Monday morning. It was already ten o'clock. Suddenly, my cell phone rang. Surprisingly, I remembered it was in my upper desk drawer in the den. I looked at the number and realized the call was from Linda. Hesitantly, I answered the call, and before I had a chance to speak, Linda reminded me with a slight edge that there was a critical meeting with the contractor to finalize the details. She seemed taken aback that I had not left yet, and she strongly emphasized it was urgent that I arrive within the next hour to review the final draft of the design before the meeting. I responded by apologizing for the delay and said I was on my way, at which point we both disconnected.

There had been a sense of urgency in her tone, which was understandable. I felt there wasn't enough of me to give the necessary devotion to both research these dreams and fulfill the responsibilities of my profession. Both initiatives required extraordinary time and effort, presenting an obvious conflict. Yet it was this very tug-of-war scenario which I was trying to avoid. I was torn between the memories of last night's episodes, still reflecting on them and trying to make sense of them, and the demands of my profession. How could I focus, when both required immediate attention? The dreams had a realness to them, and I felt compelled to reach out and resolve the obvious conflicts. That feeling of realness held me fast to the dreams, compelling me to continually search for any clue to rationalize the enigma. Yet my current situation had the same degree of urgency. My involvement with the duties assigned to me was needed to keep things orderly. But it missed the passionate desire thrust upon me by the dreams. I felt as if I were in a vise; both demanded my presence. Fortunately, the details from last night retreated just enough to allow me to push the dream further into the background. This respite was just an interlude, for the memories would come surging back unannounced. Yet I welcomed the temporary reprieve. Those interludes saved my sanity. Without them, I would surely have been committed as a delusional psychotic.

Realizing I did not have any time to spare, I hastily took a shower, dressed appropriately, and walked toward my Maxima. I drove to the train station, which, fortunately, took just thirty minutes due to the late start. I would catch the last express to downtown Santa Monica, which stopped exactly one block from my company. I did not take into account the delay in finding a parking spot, and when I finally found an open slot, I hurriedly parked, locked up, and grabbed my briefcase as the express signaled its readiness to depart. With just seconds to spare, ignoring the conductor's warning, I hastily boarded the first passenger car just as the outer door was closing, and the train started its departure. The conductor, upon realizing I was halfway in, grabbed my arm and pulled me inside with just seconds to spare. I narrowly avoided a serious mishap with possible deadly consequences. Once I was secure on the platform between the adjacent cars, he gave me a stern reprimand, followed by a firm lecture, informing me that he should write me up, but this time was just a warning. Acknowledging his warning with a flimsy excuse, I opened the door to the passenger compartment on my right and found the first available seat. The adjacent seat had no passenger, so I used it to rest my briefcase. Taking a short breather to unwind, I gazed out the side window, taking in the view as the train accelerated southward.

The slow, rhythmic motion of the train ride lulled me into a subdued mood, allowing me to mull over the eventful twists and turns and the successes and failures over the last several years of my life—at least as far back as I could remember. Enough time had passed that I could now acknowledge fact versus fantasy in some cases. As I centered on each significant facet of my life—unexpected turning points, eventful and uneventful pivotal milestones—even more facts were revealed, triggering more vivid memories of events and pivotal decisions that had transformed seemingly uneventful moments into life-altering episodes. My mind pondered the impact of such determining moments on the paths we inadvertently choose while unaware at the time of how a particular event could alter the expected journey into diverted routes. These turning points are just luck. They're lucky for a chosen few and mostly not so fortunate for the rest of us. Fate arranges small detours that we take for granted, unaware at the time of the potential impact, which can haphazardly lead us down a misdirected, illogical route. It dawned on me that because most of life's happenings were just the result of random spins of life's wheel of roulette, it basically was all a crapshoot, and it was a miracle in itself if we had even a remote chance of a successful outcome.

I exited my musings over life's uncertainties, and as the train ride swiftly raced south alongside Route 1 with a mesmerizing view of the Pacific and the morning haze started to lift, my thoughts resorted back to elaborate on my current situation. Yes, I was the primary owner of Architects Elite, a corporation still in its infancy stage. Our mission was to preserve the homes that showcased the art deco architecture that had dominated the market during the early 1900s. The company was located in downtown Santa Monica, occupying the top floor in a new all-glass structure towering over the city as a beacon of prosperity and entrepreneurship. It was a small firm yet was vibrant, creative, and energetic, still in an entrepreneurial mode.

My mind drifted back to the approaching Santa Monica skyline. The express, thankfully, encountered no delays as it announced its arrival into the Santa Monica terminal. I looked at my watch. There were still two hours left before the pivotal meeting, more than enough time to collaborate with Linda on the amended contract and finalize our planned agenda for that afternoon's meeting. The express repeated its arrival upon entering the enclosed terminal, using track eight, and slowed eventually to a stop. The passengers left their seats and moved toward the front exit, anticipating the conductor's acknowledgment to depart. Track eight was close to the walkway that led upstairs to Ocean Boulevard, near where the office building was located. After waiting in line, I finally exited onto the walkway toward the escalator that led to the upstairs thoroughfare. As soon as I stepped off the escalator, I turned right and walked the remaining two blocks to the office complex.

26

Brief History of Tony's Employees

As I approached the front door and walked into the lobby's security gateway, I reached for my badge hooked onto my belt. The clip was still fastened but minus the badge. I waved to the security guard, Charlie, to have him buzz me in. While I waited for Charlie to respond, I pondered how I'd lost the badge. I had an uncanny feeling I'd lost it sometime over the weekend, and even more unsettling was a feeling that the unforgettable journey was somehow involved. Despite my feeling, I admitted that linking the missing badge to the recent journey might have had some merit but was a stretch. I thought further about the connection between last night's events and the disappearance of the badge. I broke out of my reverie, realizing the absurdity of that presumption, and pushed the thought into the background as I walked with a gait of uncertainty through the security door with my customary smile.

Upon entering, I said my usual hello to Charles, a retired vet from Iraq. As with most everyone in life, he had his own story of life's perpetual pendulum swing of fate's cruel, ominous encounters. He'd been a volunteer in the marines, decorated during a reconnaissance in which he'd been seriously injured. A mortar round had come within an inch of his heart; he'd been fortunate enough to survive but with life-altering consequences. His sacrifice had yielded a mangled leg requiring numerous surgeries to attempt to return to some form of normalcy. The results had been far from perfect. As tragic as it was, it was of no consequence to our group due to the company's commitment to employing veterans. Such was the case with Charles.

Charles was a widower, as his wife had died when he was in Iraq. He'd been wounded and in critical condition in a navy hospital, unaware at the time that his wife had died due to a coma sustained during a routine medical procedure. He'd not been informed about his wife until weeks afterward, when he started regaining his strength. As it turned out, it had been a wise decision, for upon learning of his wife's death, he'd spiraled into a deep depression that resulted in intense therapy both emotionally and physically. With any tragic event in life, eventually, one needed to forge ahead and adapt, and Charles eventually had returned to a form of acceptance.

However, as time progressed onward, even though he'd come to terms with his loss, he never seemed to overcome his grief, for when one talked to him, through the smile and hellos, his eyes revealed his internal pain, loss, and broken heart. A piece of him was gone forever. Sometimes I actually believed he was waiting to just serve out the remainder of his term, secretly wishing for the grim reaper to whisk him away to rejoin his mate in heaven, where the gates would open to accept him to his rightful place, a place where his soul would eventually rest, no longer in anguish and torment. Contentment would replace the pain, and he'd be reunited with his soul mate, presiding under a rightful protective veil provided by their guardian angel.

That day, Charles was his usual self: outwardly smiling, surprisingly optimistic, and willing to discuss military strategy with me in those rare moments when I had time to engage in stimulating conversation over coffee in our break room. Charles was in a talkative mood, but my usual warm response was lacking, and I sensed that maybe deep within, Charles sensed I shared the same cross of loneliness he bore on his shoulders. I said hello, smiled dutifully, and continued toward the elevator that would carry me to the war room of creative minds.

After I exited the elevator on the top floor, I briskly walked across the hall and entered the office door. Our receptionist, Alecia, greeted me, and I proceeded into Linda's office. She wasn't there. She was probably at the Xerox, making several copies of the design, I thought. I walked over to my office, which was adjacent to Linda's. I saw no note or instant reminder to meet. I turned on my computer to see if there was an email from her. As my computer took its time engaging, my mind drifted back to our staff and was presented with the same questions, which had no immediate answers.

Linda, my closest ally, was well groomed, sassy, smart, spontaneous, creative, motivated, and aggressive without being overbearing. Her smile was contagious. That and her girl-next-door look gained her acceptance to even the most wary soul. She had long brunette hair styled in a chic updo to highlight her high cheekbones, giving her a cute, people-friendly look. Despite her physically attractive appearance, her dark green eyes revealed a different view: a haunted soul who seemed devoid of genuine happiness. That haunting sense kept many from getting too close. Despite the distant strangeness, it remained a mystery to me why she'd never married, for she had everything to attract any gentleman on her level.

Putting my curious questions aside, I had one certainty about Linda. If there was one dependable employee, it was Linda, for she always had an intuitive sense to provide creative input when we were faced with a controversial issue as to which design to select. We were in tune, synchronized in our views of creative expression and the means by which the company would accomplish its planned growth. As a business partner, I was always fascinated with her far-reaching ideas and avant-garde vision of architecture. I'd promoted her to an equity partner, a pivotal decision that had brought the company to its rightful place as a creative, aspiring architectural firm.

As I was contemplating promotions, my attention was directed to Alecia, our secretary, a young lassie with talent to perform all the required and requested assistant duties with apparent ease. She'd been with the company for a year and was a proven asset. She knew what and when things had to be done without even being told. She was instrumental in arranging travel plans; meetings; and accommodations for incoming guests, potential buyers, and magazine representatives and reporters. She had a knack for multitasking. I always believed that the first thing a visitor saw when entering our company through the glass doors was instrumental in forming his or her initial opinion. Alecia fit that concept perfectly, as she was cute, bubbly, well educated, and well versed, enabling her to communicate on many subjects intelligently. If there was a happy gene, then Alecia was a shining example of how that gene exhibited its trait, given her natural optimism. She always wore a smile, and her golden-brown hair was cut to highlight her youthfulness but also emphasized her blue eyes, which shone with an exuberance that added to an overall cute, attractive appearance. She had a gift to interact seamlessly with our customers and potential clients with a polite, refined, professional mannerism that added to her attractive qualities and accompanied her inner glow and magnetism. She was definitely a people person. My ultimate goal was to promote her toward the end of the year to a sales or marketing position, a promotion she had well earned.

Finally, I thought about the contractors who went out to the homes and transformed them back to the decade when they'd been showcases. The contractors were all well versed with the art deco theme that had dominated the architectural landscape during the first part of the century. The collaboration of knowledge on an architectural theme helped maintain our focus on the company's primary mission and was instrumental in our expedient rise to a recognized firm. Without the contractors, our vision would have been just a pipe dream.

I was proud of our staff; each was uniquely qualified, and all were vital components in the successful direction of our organization. But there was one thing that unnerved me, which I refused to disclose to anyone for fear of the implication. I stopped momentarily to ponder the one plaguing question for which I still had no answer. I did not remember interviewing or in fact hiring my employees or contractors. I dared not share that with anyone, for disclosing that cognitive flaw would have earned me a trip to the nearest psych ward without any hope of release. For some reason, I did remember bringing Linda on board, but everyone else was a complete blank. Fortunately, everyone was committed to our mission and an integral factor to the success of the corporation's goal. It was a pleasure to work with them, and each provided a positive contribution to the company. Each portrayed the ideal candidate to bring on board. But I was concerned that I did not remember anything about the screening process or the actual hiring. Everything was just accepted without question. It was as if an audience attended a play that skipped to act two and started within a normal setting that the audience took for granted. No one thought of act two and its history or asked questions about the play's past. They just took for granted that the scene existed and was real, with the expectation of moving forward. However, at some point in time, those investigative minds would question the past and resort back to act one, where the facts discovered might have an impact on their perception. Such was the case with me. I found myself musing over the questions that kept pulling at my nagging suspicions of each employee's past.

I searched the HR personnel records and found nothing out of the ordinary. Yet I did not remember reviewing that information prior to bringing the employees on board. That had me perplexed and caused doubts about my mental health. Everything I knew now of each employee had resulted from my reading the employee's records, which included background checks, and from everyday conversation with each employee. I had learned that everyone had a story, and sooner or later, willingly or with reluctance, each story would be revealed.

Too many questions were pulling at me, distracting me from the main task facing me. As before, I intended to ponder the matter further when time permitted. For the time being, I was in the next scene in act two, and like one in a full house watching the act play out, I needed to accept the current act on its merit. I put the nagging questions aside and returned to the computer to review Linda's write-up on that day's meeting.

27

Linda's Dream

I rushed to the conference room and saw that Linda was there, already collecting the designs. Linda was in charge of the project. Her connections had been instrumental in getting us to the point of meeting with the contractors who specialized in art deco architecture. We'd worked day and night to prepare the design, details, and plans for the renovation.

I thanked Linda for preparing all the artifacts necessary for the meeting, and she responded with a warm, grateful, relieved thank-you. We traveled to the site and discussed the designs with the contractors. Linda and I remained in the home's dining room after everyone else had left, both elated with the signed contract. After congratulating each other for extraordinary effort, we made plans to reward ourselves after work with a celebration of dinner and wine at our favorite restaurant off Route 1, five miles south of Santa Monica.

After a meeting that had gone on without a hitch, the day seemed a bit brighter. Using our laptops, we focused on returning to the tasks at hand. The rest of the workday went well as I discussed the next task with Linda. My mind continued to fuel my exalted state from the contract signing. Last night's journey was taking a respite, masquerading as a distant memory blanketed by a seductive high from a stunningly successful meeting, waiting for the right moment to derail the celebration.

The next item for the day was to discuss with Linda her new plans for the house we'd purchased overlooking the Pacific high up on Canyon Ridge Trails, and then we'd drive the ten miles north of Santa Monica for an inspection. The home was situated high on a cliff, towering over a gorge that separated the cliff from its magnificent full view of the Pacific. The overhang extended out beyond the cliff, supported by metal structures that reached out from the house's foundation and connected with support beams drilled deep into the gorge's walls. Once you ventured out onto the overhang, you were presented with a mile-long panoramic view of just the Pacific and the lights of the multitude of communities that lined the coastal area. The initial plan was to shore up the overhang with steel-reinforced supports along the underside. However, after further deliberation, we decided to completely overhaul the design to blend in with the mountaintop and greet the ocean's majestic view with its own panoramic style.

The classic home, when finished, would truly represent the classic architecture from when art deco design was at its peak. Linda spent hours and hours nearly compulsively researching that special decade and ensuring that every unique detail was included in the design. The house had her completely obsessed, and she accepted nothing less than perfection in the remodeling or replicating the design as it had been when newly built. She was drawn to the house as if she knew every inch of it. Her design was complete down to the minutest detail. We took the plan with us as we left to visit the site to reinspect the overhang.

Our initial objective, once we reached the house, was to view the site, gauge the lot, and reinspect the pillars under the overhang. As we drove toward our destination using the company car, I expected her excitement level to heighten as we neared our destination. But instead, I noticed she was in an unusually quiet mood. Her gaze was directed out the side window, her mind seemingly miles away. I sensed that something was bothering her, as she had slid into those subdued moods frequently over the past few days. I asked what was bothering her and prompted her to talk about whatever problem was on her mind. She turned her gaze toward me and just stared directly at me, as if debating whether she should disclose the dreams that had plagued her nights with restless sleep. After further deliberation, she mentioned that something strange had been occurring, and she reminisced about her dream from last night, remarking on its intensity and nature. She mentioned that her dream had centered on a village, Neverland, which she'd never heard of, yet she had an uncanny sense of familiarity with the village. In an unexplainable way, she felt a connection to the dream and to Neverland.

Did I hear that correctly? I did. I couldn't deny it. The word blindsided me like a sucker punch, crawling up my spine with numbing effect. Keeping my look of alarmed surprise masked by a forced, steady voice, I asked her what she meant by a connection.

"Tony, it was the village. Somehow, I feel I have been there before. There was a stranger in the dream. I distinctly remember. I never saw him—he was always hidden in a shadow—yet I felt that we knew each other. Whenever I approached him, he retreated farther away.

"There was a ballroom and an old mansion. Within the ballroom, there was a back room, an atrium, resembling a lounge, large enough to accommodate at least twenty booths, all set along the perimeter. There were only a few couples situated in the corners. But the strange thing was, the couples were not conversing. There was no dialogue or movement. They just sat facing each other, as if they were mannequins used as stage props. Then, unexpectedly, the couples turned toward me, all wearing masks portraying various expressions of joy and sorrow. I was at a table, and there was someone else, a man near the lounge. Someone I cannot recall. He suddenly disappeared, and then a shadow appeared in the place he'd vacated.

"A sudden cry of surprise and alarm erupted from somewhere in front of me, tinged with a sense of urgency. A male voice spoke, his tone resolute with one remark: 'Oh my God, Cassandra.' It was too dark to discern the source. That is all I can recall, and the last item I remember is a fog bank rolling in from the nearby coastline. Then nothing. The voice had a European accent, a mix between English and German. He sounded very similar to you, Tony. But why did he call me Cassandra? I did catch a glimpse of him as he walked near the lounge, but it was just for a fraction of a second, because the rest of the lounge was lit by candles, keeping the entire room in a twilight. But I saw his mouth and his nose, just a side profile, before everything dissipated. Tony, in a way, I had the uncanny sense that the male carried a resemblance to you or was connected to you. Sitting in this vehicle, I see that your profile has an uncanny likeness to what I remember from last night.

"Then I was suddenly on a street that ran through the center of the village, and while I was walking on it, I would frequently see this stranger following me from a distance. I wasn't afraid, which was odd. In fact, I felt somewhat protected. There was a quietness, a dead calm, as if nothing were alive except me and this stranger. And something else—a series of melodies from years ago filled the air, flowing from a distant ballroom enveloped in nostalgic waves that soothed my senses. But the one fact that unnerves me is that it felt so real yet distant. The dream had a look and feel of ages ago. The houses, the ballroom, the clothes, the music—all were reminiscent of an era from a distant past. I feel I actually had a connection to this village. I can't seem to shake the images from last night, and it has me curious but anxious. I have had these dreams for a few weeks now, and every one is a repeat but with some variations. In fact, they started with the latest purchase of the house we have been working on. I feel drained every morning. Maybe I am going crazy. I don't know why I'm sharing this with you. But I am desperate, and I know you will listen objectively without passing an inane judgment."

I turned to voice an opinion and saw a desperate look in her eyes, a plea for help. I was her last recourse for insight and discovery. Desperate for some response from me, her voice strained from fatigue and exasperation, she reached out to me again anxiously. "Am I losing it?"

I didn't expect her words to hit me like a heavy hammer, sending shock waves spiraling through my nervous system. Every cell felt an icy grip akin to paralyzing trauma as the reality of what I'd heard took hold of my senses. I felt as if I were in a dream within a dream. Still momentarily stunned at her revelation, I drove on in automatic pilot, unable to think or feel. I felt as if my head were floating. I felt rambling restlessness as undirected thoughts scattered throughout my brain, scrambling endlessly, unable to connect to form any logical reasoning regarding what Linda had described to me. I had read of couples sharing the same dream. I could not say with unconditional certainty if that applied to Linda's dream, at least from her explanation, but the eerie similarities were close enough to cause me serious unease. I could not, for the moment, respond to her inquiry. I needed time to sift through Linda's details. I dared not yet reveal my dreams and the uncanny parallels. It was not time yet to cause such a diversion with everything else Linda and I were overseeing. At a later time, I decided, I would earnestly respond to Linda. For the time being, I had to respond with something to ease the sudden tension. "I admit it is odd. But there has to be a rational explanation. We are both overtired to the point of exhaustion. You have worked endless hours on the design and extensive research, and maybe it is catching up with you. Maybe a weekend of rest would help. Monday we can have lunch and explore this further. Could this in some way be connected to something you experienced before? There has to be a logical explanation. I suggest you wait to see what happens between now and Monday. I also suggest seeing a doctor in case there is a physical problem."

I realized my response resembled reading off a script, lacking any display of empathy. She just looked at me, unable or reluctant to agree. She stared at me for the longest time and then turned away to focus on the view through the front windshield before she finally responded with a weary "Okay, Tony. It probably is best that we wait until we take care of the immediate tasks this week." I nodded as I listened to her, acknowledging her agreement, but I felt the reluctance and a hint of resentment in her tone. I carefully tried to hide any sign of nervousness.

We both fell into a pensive quiet with our own thoughts. Perplexed, I wondered if there was any symbolic connection between our dreams. There was something there that unnerved me, and it took all my concentration to ward off any hint of desperate concern. I dared not think about it much longer, for fear I would find myself wrestling with endless scenarios while gaining no ground. There had to be a sensible explanation, and I too needed the weekend to attempt to digest all I'd heard and come up with some form of rationale. The problem was, I did not know where or how to begin. I was at the point where my thoughts became an endless loop, always returning back to a dead end. I needed more time to think, not just for Linda's sake but also to calm my own angst. Reluctantly, I returned my attention to the immediate priorities that required Linda's and my attention.

28

Linda's and Tony's Shared Dream

Approaching our destination along Route 1, we took the exit ramp to the stop sign and then turned right onto Canyon Ridge Trails, climbed up the mountainside, and made the final turn onto the private road leading to the house. We stopped at the far end of the wraparound driveway, which overlooked the cliff, giving us a mesmerizing view of the Pacific. We walked down the incline, circling under the overhang of the house. As we inspected the overhang, we discovered it had additional problems. A stress fracture along one of the support beams had to be resolved before we could begin remodeling the home. I wondered why we had not spotted that upon our initial inspection before our decision to purchase. But obviously, that would not fix the problem now. We circled around the house several times, looking for anything else we might have overlooked, and fortunately, there were no more surprises. We scheduled a meeting with the inspector for Monday at the site to examine the overhang to determine the additional work needed to shore up the underside.

On our way back, Linda and I stopped at a restaurant near Santa Monica, alongside the Pacific. During our celebration dinner with a full view of the Pacific, we discussed our unique memories of

times gone by and the relevant impact they had on our lives and our connection. In the back of my mind, I couldn't help but think about Linda's dream. Linda noticed my distraction. She mentioned that I too had seemed distant lately, to which I responded that it was nothing.

Upon further consideration, I decided to share some of the details from my series of dreams. She listened with avid interest and was intrigued with my descriptions and remorsefulness. I refrained from mentioning Cassandra's name. I wasn't sure what the reaction from Linda would be if I disclosed her name. I didn't want to go there. Her reaction would be either disbelief or the assumption that I was some kind of nutcase. Either way, the result from her reaction would most likely dissolve into a 'humor me' type response.

I needed to have a serious discussion with Linda about both our dreams because I sincerely felt there was a connection, and I was desperate to find any clue. Trying to avoid the intricate details for the time being, I briefly described the woman in my dreams, a woman I felt I had known forever and whom I felt a soulful connection with. Each time I dreamed of her, I was drawn in with a hypnotic lure, with her eyes leading me in like a magnet. I described my connection as a compulsion to be with her, as if our union were preordained. The more I described my dream, the stronger I felt about revealing everything. But as compelled as I was, I knew it was not the time to disclose any more intimate details of the dreams from prior eras. That surely would overwhelm her and result in pushing Linda away in fear instead of drawing her closer from curiosity. But as I continued, I decided to bring forth more detail than I originally had intended. One fact led to another over the next hour: the village, the dance, and the nostalgic melodies. The clincher, the one fact that could change the dynamics between Linda and me, was Cassandra. I then disclosed Cassandra's name without further detail to gauge Linda's reaction without overwhelming her. I could have continued on, but I elected to bring the discussion to an end to give Linda time to absorb and adjust.

Linda's initial response was impossible to read. She was at a loss for words, stunned. She held her emotions in check as she tried to remain stoic, attempting to grasp the impact of my description. The similarities were obvious, and she contemplated the likeness between our dreams. She had read stories about shared dreams in medical journals, but those were experienced between couples who had been together for a while, with emotional, intimate implications. There was no rational explanation as of yet, but evidence indicated that intense bonding between a couple was a common factor in the noted episodes of that phenomenon. There was no intimate connection between us, Linda remarked. There must have been a sound explanation. Before jumping to any formal conclusion, she decided to suspend further questions until the time was more appropriate.

My reaction was also muted. I confirmed that we both seemed to have experienced the same dream. However, they were most likely different dreams with uncanny similarities. We both were at a loss for words and needed to explore later, when we both were in a more inclined mood to discuss with a more logical frame of mind before formulating far-fetched theories. The idea that our dreams were uncannily similar brought with it an unease. We both tried to push the subject aside. To avoid the awkward feeling we were experiencing, we resorted to a simple explanation, a posturing to temporarily bridge the possible suggestive implications, a delay until we had more information to discuss on a more rational basis. We agreed that maybe we were overworked, and our loneliness was creating the perplexing dreams.

By then, I was unable to hold back on what I felt was convincing evidence of the possible realness of Cassandra. I dared to push one step further, taking a chance that Linda would remain stoic without becoming too overanxious. I brought out the enclosed rose petal and the note I'd found at the table from the weekend and said they were proof she'd been there. Upon seeing the rose and reading the note, she looked at me with a tinge of fear and, with a different tone, asked me if I was sure the rose and note had come from the dream. There had to be a rational explanation, and she encouraged me to look at all the possibilities. I could see that the more I explored that new revelation with her, the more it appeared to her that my interpretation of my dream was highly exaggerated, bordering on a hallucination, due to the exhaustive overload of work. I decided to end the discussion and reengage the conversation at a later time. At that time, I would disclose more facts related to my dreams. Linda took notice of my sudden desire to end the conversation and agreed that we both should discuss it at a later time, after we'd both had a chance to reflect.

I still detected the scent of perfume on the petal. It was a rare perfume fragrance, and I remembered Linda wearing the fragrance one time a while back. Before suspending the discussion, I handed the rose to her and asked her about the scent. She bent her head toward the rose and immediately recognized the scent. She acknowledged her familiarity with the perfume by responding, "It is called Sensual Delight. It is only sold at a few high-end boutiques and is very pricy. It used to be worn more frequently years ago. It is extremely rare now because of its price, and there is one place near that sells it on Rodeo Drive." If the perfume was so rare, I wondered about the coincidence of Linda and Cassandra wearing the same perfume. That fact, together with my curious nature, triggered a set of questions I decided to keep to myself for the time being to avoid pushing the discussion any further with Linda. However, this wass one more legitimate clue that echoed a connection between the dream and my present situation. I made a mental note to explore further by visiting the boutique tomorrow.

Realizing we had been talking for what seemed like hours, we stood up and walked toward the exit. As we walked to the company car, we both sensed a bonding, a strong connection of the type one would normally form over a period of years. We'd met just more than a year ago at the convention, which made our bond even more intriguing and surely a topic destined to be explored further in a future conversation.

29

Tony's Residence: Haleyville

We felt the mellowing effects from the wine as we drove back to the office. Our mood was quiet; we both were pensive with possible theories to rationalize the latest revelation. Upon reaching the office thirty minutes later, we were silent about our thoughts, but our eyes conveyed many more questions to be relayed in more detail next week. We turned to our separate directions toward our journey home.

I lived in the northern suburbs of Santa Monica, and there should have been an express train that evening that would get me back home within thirty minutes. When we returned to Santa Monica from dinner, I parked the corporate car in its usual spot in the underground garage. I looked at my watch, wondering where the time had gone and realizing I'd missed the express. The local was just forty minutes from then, and I could not miss it. I decided to forego my usual lockup routine at the office, knowing that my receptionist, always dependable, would take care of the task since I had been out of the office all afternoon. The local train would double my time to reach home. That was normally a nuisance, but that evening, I could use the time to ponder all the events that had occurred over the last few days. I hastily walked to the train station to catch the local seven o'clock train back to Haleyville, my town of residence.

Haleyville was a town with a medium-sized population, small enough to know one another by first name but large enough to have a private life. The quiet community was upper middle class, with an old-fashioned downtown that had a circular park at the center and shops parading out for several miles before the residential homes began. I lived in a three-level, three-bedroom condo with twenty-foot ceilings and connecting lofts, one for each level. It was situated on the oceanfront, which allowed me a priceless view. I had three decks, one on each floor, attached to each of the three bedrooms. The third bedroom on the top floor was the master bedroom and had a floor-to-ceiling window that overlooked the ocean. That night, my house would be a welcome sight, as I looked forward to a quiet evening to try to relax without the stress that had plagued me since that morning. Maybe Linda was right about the stress level and its impact possibly causing us to hallucinate the events in our recurring dreams. Maybe it was time to see a doctor for a checkup or even a psychologist who could help reduce the stress and analyze the recurring dreams I'd experienced the last few months. But I could not pin on the stress levels my condition wherein I could not separate dreams from reality. I didn't know when the dream ended. The dream's fantasy just flowed into my waking state to the point where, for an indefinite duration, I was unaware if what I was experiencing was still a dream or in fact a conscious reality. Despite the uncertainty, one fact was a certainty: I needed a checkup to determine if my condition was worsening. The dreams had been with me for years but had just recently taken a turn, a twist in their pattern. *Yes*, I repeated with emphasis, *a doctor visit should be sooner rather than later.* My immediate priority, however, was to plan on visiting the boutique tomorrow evening to inquire about the rare perfume Linda was wearing. Afterward, I would make an appointment with the physician.

I boarded the seven o'clock train feeling more tired than usual. My exhaustion had caught up with me, draining every last ounce of energy. The drain was instantaneous; my eyes were barely open. I dragged myself to my customary seat in the third car. On each departure, I always found the same seat, even with a carload of weary passengers eager to reach their homes. Even stranger, the adjacent seat was always unoccupied, no matter which express or local departure I took to my hometown. There was nothing to indicate that the two seats were reserved, and I could not think of any reason why they would be. What if fate, in its own mystical way, had a purpose to fulfill a destiny that revolved around a journey to rediscover and reconnect Cassandra and me, and in its own way, it reserved the two seats by projecting an image of Cassandra and me as if we were in a distant past, sitting there to ward off unwanted passengers. *I must be more exhausted than I realized.* I was stunned by the absurdity of that thought. I dropped into the seat, struggling to support myself with my knees strained from pure exhaustion. As tired as I felt, the emotional impact from the last several days left me restless with a sense of apprehension, and I thought about what might happen next.

Just when I started to close my eyes, the memories began to surface. While the train departed, the memories marched forward, advancing into a vivid awareness and bringing images of Cassandra—not just images from last night but also images from the repeated dreams I'd encountered over the past few months. It was evident the dreams from earlier had changed, resulting in the recent dreams. I couldn't let go of that thought; my mind was continually searching for a plausible explanation, always with the same result: no answers. The initial dreams had followed a repeated pattern without unforeseen surprises, but the recent dreams altered the pattern, promoting different paths that seemed to conflict, each leading to a disjointed, harrowing ending. I was not sure which theme I would dream, but I hoped the theme from my initial dreams would be my visitor that evening.

I felt as if the recent dreams were relaying an ominous message to me. The initial dreams had presented a harmonious message clearly, but the recent dreams confused me, and the message harbored something sinister with evil intent. The message was scrambled and dark. In fact, it was not a message but a warning, a portent. The harbinger had me on constant alert, and so far, I was unable to comprehend it. That night, I needed to experience the harmony from the initial dreams. But there was a more urgent need to reengage with Cassandra. I needed to reaffirm the rose and letter, confirmations once again that her existence was real. I needed more than a series of dreams; I needed confirmation from Cassandra. If there was a concept of the perfect, consummate partner that translated to an ultimate sensation of serene harmony and spiritual perfection, then my connection with Cassandra was proof of it. I felt that Cassandra and I were more than just companions; we were lovers from ages past, and a reservoir of cosmic memories had streamed into my subconscious, resulting in the initial dreams. If that were the case, then the dreams touched upon reality from generations ago or, to stretch my imagination further, prior lifetimes. Maybe Cassandra and I had a karmic connection as soul mates. I felt a sense of partnership, as if reuniting with a lost companion—a balanced symmetry with no conflicts. I felt ultimate contentment, as if I were a part of her, and our souls were meant to be united. My final destination was to be coupled with her, connected through a spiritual bond. The feeling was so overwhelming that if I pondered it too much longer, I would become totally consumed. I began to slowly drift away, falling into a deep sleep. If my encounters with Cassandra were indeed a dream, a karmic connection, then I welcomed the dream during my interlude of sleep.

30

Encounter with the Ghost Train

As anticipated, the dream returned more vivid than ever. The same blanket of fog appeared, clearing a path that led to the wall. I tried to resist, and as before, my compulsion to view the changes to the wall nullified my efforts. My compulsion was no longer from curiosity but from my protective instincts to prepare myself for the inevitable encounter that would occur once the wall completely dissolved, eroded from the tiny fissures branching outward and causing the wall to disintegrate into tiny fragments. When the wall totally withered away, I feared I would be at my most vulnerable position, unable to shield myself from whatever evil lay ahead. My only salvation to prevent that vulnerability was to find Cassandra. This time, the journey took me on an alternate path, a temporary detour leading me to the door rather than to the wall, where the changes were most prominent. Instead of a white light, the doorway was enclosed within a fiery red glow. I was propelled forward, expecting to feel a fiery heat from the doorway, but unexpectedly, I was confronted with a frigid cold. I was propelled through the doorway, preparing myself for bitter temperatures. When I passed through the doorway, the freezing air turned to a warm breeze, ushering in a swirling mist. As the mist neared, I could see an angelic golden light emitted from within. At the center of the golden light stood Cassandra with her velvety blue-black hair. Her emerald-green eyes were venturing me to come forth. I moved toward her, but with every step, she moved a step farther away, disappearing into the mist. I stepped into the mysterious light, searching for a glimpse, and called her name many times without a response. I longed to see her, yet she appeared before me for only an instant, only to then fade away before emerging again, repeating the same pattern. It was as if she were beckoning me to join her, but the connection was only possible when the timing was right, and I would only be allowed to enter her sacred sanction when everything was synchronized perfectly.

Suddenly, I opened my eyes and realized I was still on the train, headed for Haleyville, not sure if I'd missed my stop. As I glanced at the empty seat next to me, I saw a red rose petal, and I instantly recognized the scent. I discovered a note next to the rose. I opened and read the note: "Till our next rendezvous." When an ancient-looking conductor passed by, I asked who had been sitting there, and he indicated that no one had occupied that seat since the train left. The train seemed empty as I looked into the adjacent cars. I looked around and realized I was the only passenger in the car. *When did everyone depart?* I wondered. When I'd boarded, the car had been crowded with passengers. I glanced around to see if anyone at all was still onboard. While I viewed my immediate surroundings, I noticed differences that could not have been possible. The car was different. It was older—in fact, decades older. "We are not headed for Haleyville, or we passed my destination," I remarked to myself. The interior color was different—not the cream-colored panels but more of a brown wood grain. I noticed the smaller, more detailed inconsistencies. The passenger seats did not have the same comfortable, cushioned feel; they were made of a stiff, rigid material. Even the headrest was different. It did not pivot but was stationary. The odor seemed different. Rather than the new, fresh scent one would associate with a new vehicle, the car had a sweaty stench like the kind that developed from years of carrying passengers between destinations. There was a heavy, repulsive, stagnant odor of tobacco. The engine sound was different, and the smell was that of a coal-fed locomotive versus a diesel engine. The train whistle was of a different pitch, more of a soulful moan, akin to a warning of an approaching portent versus the welcoming sound of an expected arrival. With a look of confusion and longing, I again glanced at my immediate surroundings. I noticed other ominous differences. The car didn't look like a train. It didn't have the right feel. There was an eerie glow from within the compartments.

There was another odor present, barely detectable but recognizable: the smell of death. "That's it!" I exclaimed. The strange lights, eerie silence, and occasional sighs I detected were similar to the dreaded, mournful despair of the dead. This transport's specific purpose seemed to be to ferry passengers to destinations known only by whoever was engineering the journey. I looked again at the rose petal next to me and reread her note. I lifted my gaze from the petal and saw a glimpse of her. Cassandra was walking in the adjacent car, moving toward the exit door for the next stop. I was momentarily suspended from action because of my delayed response, but as the transport slowed for the stop, I shot out of my seat and ran toward the exit. When I neared the exit, I saw her enter the next car, depart, and then walk toward the depot.

I jumped from the car's exit onto the platform just as the doors were closing and ran toward the depot. There was another train coming from the other direction, and I quickly judged if I should cross the tracks with another locomotive bearing down. As it came nearer within my visual range, I noticed that it had no smokestack. In fact, it had no wheels. It seemed to be traveling just above the rail, following every curve as if it were held by a magnetic force. It appeared to be decades old. It was pulling just eight passenger cars, but only two were lit from within. Each carried only one passenger. The other cars, dark and forbidden, were empty, carrying no passengers. The two on board had forlorn looks in their eyes, which were glued to mine as they were ferried past me. As the lit cars passed by, their heads turned, and their gazes locked onto mine as they shook their heads with desperate gestures akin to warnings and then let out mournful, soulful cries of pain and loneliness one would expect to hear from hell itself. My reaction was immediate. The two passengers were from my company, Alecia and Charlie. *What the hell? What in the hell is happening?* Was it possible the recent dreams, as evidenced by abhorrent changes, had polluted the theme originating from my initial dreams? I tried to understand the implication but came up empty. There was an obvious message there, and the message was meant for me, but I was unable to come up with any plausible explanation.

As the phantom train continued its lonely travel, heading away from the tiny village, its lights becoming more distant, on route toward places I would not dare to contemplate, painful cries from both passengers filled the air, as if they knew their destination. The train's shrill departing whistle eventually consumed their cries, carrying a tone of depravity, as the train transported Alecia and Charlie on their journey toward a destination that I instinctively felt was too horrifying to contemplate. I watched the train disappear into the surrounding fog, leaving a sense of finality in its wake. I then caught sight of a figure standing on the rear platform of the last car; his eyes had a piercing, hollow yellowish glow that penetrated the darkness. I swore he was looking directly at me, and as he swung the gas-lit lantern before him, he let out shrill, insane laughter that must have come from the bowels of hell itself. The shrillness of the laughter pierced my heart with trepidation, sending a blast of icy chill through my soul. "A ghost train," I said out loud with my eyes following the last image of the train as it evaporated into the night, its whistle fading away off in the distance, calling out a last farewell. Then I heard nothing. Silence filled the void. Hastily, I returned my thoughts to Cassandra. My mind was not ready to ingest the implication of what I'd just experienced.

I swept my vision back to the depot, checking one last time for another transport, before I crossed the tracks and entered the depot. I looked around the depot and saw no one. The atmosphere within had the odor of decades of emptiness, and I wondered when the depot had last been used.

I heard an ancient voice call out behind me, "May I help you, Tony?"

I turned around in astonished surprise. There at the ticket window stood an ancient, weathered old man. I asked, "How do you know my name?"

He responded with a raspy voice, "Everyone in this village knows you, Tony. Welcome home."

Welcome home? It wasn't just what he'd said but also the tone of his greeting that caught me off guard. It sounded like more of a warning than a genuine greeting. I stood before him, uncertain of a response. I was still stunned but realized I had no time to inquire further.

I asked the decrepit agent if he'd seen a young lady just enter the depot, and he said, "You are referring to Cassandra. No, there hasn't been anybody here in years. She lies in wait for you."

"What do you mean?" I responded, my alarm more apparent now.

"There is no time to waste. Leave before your journey here expires. She is in the village," he replied, his voice fading to a barely audible whisper.

I turned toward the rear of the depot and found the rear exit. Before heading toward the exit, I turned back to the agent to ask one last question but found no one. I called out with no response. I called out again, but my voice carried throughout the room with a strange, hollow tone. I realized no one was there. *No time to think. Just act.*

Before exiting the ancient depot, I searched from bench to bench to see if there was any clue of her presence. My search was rewarded upon my finding another petal with a note on the rear bench. The note read, "Never leave without a promise to return. All my love, my dear Tony. I am your heart and soul." I again looked around, hoping to catch a glimpse of her, and could not help but notice the charged atmosphere. My skin was tingling as if an electrical current were coursing through my veins. The air was saturated with a tingling vibration similar to the sensation one felt prior to an incoming thunderstorm, when an exchange of electrical charges between the storm's thunderheads were on the verge of releasing their explosive power.

I ventured outside the depot, wondering if that village was Neverland. I again viewed the town with a perplexing dismay, as if it were my first visit, noting it seemed empty, devoid of any soul. Then I caught a glimpse of a sign nearby that confirmed the village was Neverland. I was drawn to that name, as it was odd but interesting. The place had shown itself in my dreams, but that was where the familiarity ended. I wondered why I'd never passed through that town. As I explored the village more earnestly, it seemed like a village of yesteryear. Old flame lanterns lined the street, their lights flickering with varying degrees of dimness, casting shadows over the street. They allowed just enough light for me to navigate my way through the village. Homes lining the street were of Victorian design; each was seemingly empty, and the streets were void of any sign of civilization. The atmosphere began to turn pale gray with a misty feel as I continued my observation. I noticed a fog bank closing in like tentacles encircling the village. The village had a centuries-old feel, as if from distant, forlorn times, with its Victorian design. As I took in the view, it became apparent that something was not right there, as if a plague had taken away the village's life force. I went back toward the depot, hoping the ticket agent had returned, to ask him more about the village, but as before, he still wasn't there. "Where am I?" I asked several times, each time with more earnestness, as if I were expecting some unseen bystander to assist me. I ventured farther out into the street and looked around.

A saloon stood out noticeably, out of place on a street mostly dominated by earlier-era Victorian homes. I turned toward the saloon and wondered if it was just another vacant structure. It was eerily quiet, yet a hint of melodic tone with a hypnotic quality floated toward me and lured me in with its suggestive draw. I walked through the entrance, a pair of swinging doors that swung open with ease, as if anticipating my visit. The place was absent of light, but upon my entrance, the lights came on, allowing a dim view of the interior, which looked like an aged old-time saloon. Gas-fed lanterns lined the walls. Upon further scrutiny, I noticed the bartender, who had a handlebar mustache and pin-striped shirt, wiping the countertop, even though the place was empty. I sat on one of the stools toward the front door for a hasty retreat if needed and caught a glimpse outside of the evening sun slowly dropping out of sight. I asked for a shot of bourbon, which the bartender poured without any response. I looked around and viewed all the posters hanging on the walls, each one displaying scenes from a century ago. I saw one sign advertising a Jim Beam shot of bourbon for fifty cents.

Maybe fifty years ago, I thought as I drank the bourbon with shaky hands and then asked the bartender where I was. He responded, "Wherever you want to be, Tony."

I asked, "How do you know my name?"

His response indicated indifference yet was laden with indignation. "Everyone knows you in this village. Cassandra is here, but you must hurry."

His remarks carried the same warning tone, as if relayed more from resentment than concern for me. I wanted to ask more about Cassandra and where I was, but as I started to inquire further, he walked toward the other end of the bar, not bothering to turn around to acknowledge further questions. I wanted more information but realized my attempt would be fruitless since he left so abruptly. I took the time to glance around and walked toward the rear of the saloon, where I encountered an old-time phonograph playing a nostalgic song on a 33-rpm Benny

Goodman record from the '40s, which must have been a priceless antique by then, I thought.

I finished my drink, left a buck on the bar since I had no sight of the bartender, and roamed the streets. The fog was becoming denser as the night settled in, adding to my sense of foreboding. It was getting late, and I wondered if maybe everyone retired early in that town as I contemplated the village's emptiness. I felt an odd sensation that my arrival was expected but with a cautious wariness rather than a receptive welcome. Even though the village seemed deserted, I had an uncanny feeling I was being observed, watched with wariness by someone with a lurking suspicion as to my motives. I felt that whatever obstacle was causing my dreams to recycle—each with a different ending and each perceived as a threat to Cassandra—was linked to this village. Even though the village seemed desolate, I had an unsettling feeling that from somewhere within or outside the fog embankment, an element of unforeseen fear and uncertainty was suspiciously lurking with ominous intent, ready to launch a vicious assault upon Cassandra or me once it felt threatened. My angst was in not knowing what trigger would invoke that threat.

I listened intently for any movement, anything that would glide with a stealthy maneuver through the twirling wisps of fog. Behind that ominous feeling of malice intent, I felt a protectiveness toward Cassandra, my comrade in a coupled love that shielded one from harm's way. If the threat was directed at Cassandra, then it was also directed at me. I wasn't worried about myself; my dedication was at all costs to protect Cassandra. Out of the steamy silence, I took notice of a whimper rapidly turning into a shrill cry, an unfathomable shriek of pain that bled into a forlorn desperation. The cry slowly descended into sinister laughter that defied normalcy.

I heard a man's voice echo throughout the village, escalating to a thunderous roar, causing the smallest rodents to scurry about: "I am hell."

Then a final sequence from Cassandra as she called out my name, "Tony." Her call of that one word, Tony, encompassed every sensation conveyed between us, capturing an entire set of emotions.

I turned in every direction, but the fog obscured everything. The calls came out of the fog bank in front of me. I stepped forward only to be drawn into a denser, thicker embankment, whereupon I retreated to regroup to listen for the source. The evening was again silent, leaving me clueless. I pondered everything that seemed relevant, overwhelmed as to what was real and what was unreal. Suddenly, a dense swirl of fog lurched forward toward me. As I became aware of the lucidity of the approaching mist, it swelled to an even bigger swirl, which opened, revealing a house perched high on a cliff. The view maneuvered its way toward an underground passageway revealing a huge chamber—a chamber of horror. Another view appeared: a small village bright with the optimism of a summer breeze. A boy and girl walked down an old country road, holding hands, with gleeful laughter. My senses acutely picked up a faint recollection, but it evaporated before it took hold. I reached out to capture the exuberance, but in my doing so, the small village retreated, as if fearful of my touch, and turned to a decayed, dormant ghost town of zero population. The village's name hung in disrepair: Neverland. Darkness ensued; the edge of night fused with the encroaching fog. I cried out, "Cassandra!" My earnest cry was consumed by the dead of night.

"You don't belong here," said a voice in the darkness with the same tone as earlier. Another figure appeared within view. He was impossible to identify because of the shadowy darkness that enveloped him.

Whoever he was, I sensed his intense stare scrutinizing me as if deciding my fate. I yelled out to get some acknowledgment, but before he could respond, the light from the view dimmed, and the view closed to just a small opening. Cassandra appeared, looking out toward the Pacific from a large master bedroom. It suddenly dawned on me that it was the house Linda and I had just purchased, perched high on a mountainside overlooking a massive gorge.

She turned toward me. "Never leave without a promise to return. I am here, Tony." She held her hands to her face and then lifted her gaze to meet mine as the last visage of her face dissipated. Her image narrowed to just a pinprick of light at the end of a long tunnel before disappearing.

The view then finished closing rapidly, as if it were hiding something that contributed to the village's decay. I looked to where the saloon had been when I'd first entered the village but could find no trace. Many questions perplexed me. I felt on tilt, dizzy with the vast unknowns overwhelming me, and fearful of tripping over the edge into a dark abyss of madness. I felt I was in some form of a twilight state, suddenly unaware of what was real and what was not real. Yet she was there, as real as ever, in the view before it closed. What if this was not a dream but reality? One where nothing made sense? Giving credence to that was the fact that it seemed so real. If it was a dream, then what was happening could be easily rationalized as simply due to a vivid imagination. But what if it was not a dream but a connection to a past, a genetic memory to another void where I'd existed in a prior life? The more I pondered, the more questions surfaced. I backed away from all the conjecture, realizing that my reasoning had taken a sudden turn toward unproven theories that were going nowhere and that I needed some rational thoughts concerning the here and now. I pushed all the postulations to the background and directed my immediate attention to my whereabouts. I had to get back to familiar settings where I had more time to predicate and formulate a rational plan geared toward unraveling the mystery.

I wasn't sure where Cassandra was, for there was no logic in that place. But the vision I'd just experienced was from the home I'd just purchased on the Pacific. Cassandra could have been anywhere, and within that setting, it would have been impossible to locate her. No matter the urgency, I needed time to plan. The vision had given every indication that she was in the house we'd just purchased, calling out to me. How was I to travel back to Haleyville? Once I returned, then I could proceed onward to the house. My sole intent now was to return to my hometown.

I suddenly heard a mournful sound from off in the distance. It increased in frequency as it neared. After a few seconds, I recognized the sound that had enveloped me before I'd fallen asleep on the train ride home. Still unable to determine its source, I glanced toward the direction of the sound. It was a fruitless effort, as the mist was thick, yielding just a few feet of visibility. The noise neared, and soon I recognized it as a train whistle, as if a train were repeatedly announcing its arrival. The last thing I remembered before falling asleep was the local train ride home from work. I'd dozed off only to reawaken to find myself in that village. If I'd arrived there by a train, then by God, that fast-approaching sound was my ticket back, my return journey to my hometown of Haleyville. Then I'd go back to the house where Cassandra might be in wait. For the moment, I had nothing else to go on, just a vision of Cassandra calling out to me from the domicile on Canyon Ridge. The vision propelled me to focus on one direction: home. The thought took hold, and I was desperate to grasp and hold on to that hope.

It had to be. I could not allow myself any doubt. The whistling was close now; my adrenaline kicked me into overdrive. I looked ahead, searching for any sign of the depot. I started forward, moving into the mist, virtually sightless. I continued onward, and my pace quickened with every step as I used the sound of the transport as my beacon. My pace turned into a trot and then a sprint as I threw caution to the side, knowing I had no more time to waste and hoping beyond hope that the beacon was not distorted by the thickness of the dense fog. The whistle filled the air around me as I sprinted, desperate to catch any hint of the depot. My frantic run became a torrid charge fueled by a release of adrenaline. I ran blindly ahead, with my heart thumping fiercely to keep up, my legs moving without feeling, and my lungs struggling to fuel me.

It seemed the distance back to the depot was significantly farther than the distance from the depot to the village. I didn't remember that long stretch between the depot and the saloon. But I reminded myself that nothing made sense in that surreal world. I shouldn't have been surprised at the oddities, for it seemed that logic did not apply in that void I had entered. Anxious to get back, I repeatedly told myself, *Almost there. Almost there*, yet I felt that at any moment, I would crumple, totally exhausted, surrendering to defeat. I could not feel my legs anymore, my mind was foggy, and my balance was unsteady from vertigo. With my will and desperation fading fast, reaching my wall of containment, I glimpsed the top of a structure barely visible above the fog's ceiling. Could it be the depot? If not, then I would be hopeless. The whistling was less frequent, which meant the train was slowing or was at a stop at the depot. The mist started to clear just enough for me to spot the depot. The transport was coming to a stop. I was almost there, breathing heavily, and I felt I only had seconds to spare. With a final surge forth, I encountered the depot's rear door, threw it open, raced through an open front door, and crossed the tracks hastily without caution, eager to return. The transport was bearing down, belching black fumes through its stack, which were ingested by the surrounded fog. The engineer waited until the train was almost in front of the depot before screeching to a halt with the wheels spitting out streams of flaming sparks as the brakes were firmly applied. The screeching noise from the locked wheels reverberated throughout my entire being as the train stopped right in front of the depot entryway. The locomotive spit steam loudly into the air much like a dragon spitting out flames with the intent of heated vengeance and destruction.

Finally, the noise and steam subsided into a rhythmical pulse, allowing me to hurry on board the transport and enter the passenger car. Breathless, I doubled over with cramps in my belly. My leg muscles quivered from the strain. I felt dizzy and nauseated, on the verge of vomiting, and my sight blurred from excessive tearing. Every last ounce of energy was drained. I felt weak from overexertion in the aftermath of the maddening, torrid pace. I lunged toward the nearest seat to my right and collapsed. I closed my eyes and felt everything spinning. I dared not open my eyes for fear of vomiting. My pulse was still rapid, my breathing was still shallow, and my heart was still beating too fast, with each beat reverberating as a heavy thump, causing breathlessness. I needed just a few more minutes to catch my breath and use self-learned relaxation techniques to normalize my body responses. Five minutes and then ten minutes elapsed, and I was able to detect my physical signs starting to recover. It took another half hour before I felt everything return to normal, except the overwhelming weariness. Another fifteen minutes passed before I was able to concentrate and open my eyes. I sensed the transport moving. I wondered how long it had been traveling and how far I was from the depot. *Well, hopefully, this journey will return me back to my hometown.* I was not able to tackle the events from that night. My mind was not capable of discerning any form of rationalization. *Not now. Not until I reach home. It will have to wait until tomorrow for me to digest this journey.*

I glanced around and took in my immediate surroundings with a weary mind. I quickly observed that I was not on the same transport that had delivered me to the village. This car had the look and feel of an old-time nineteenth-century western. Gas lanterns lined each side of the car, perched high above, near the ceiling, with one lantern for each row of seats. Each lantern burned dimly; the core of the flame contained within a small halo inside the lantern yielded barely enough light to keep the area around the seats and the middle aisle visible. It was a dusky, twilight-like setting. In front of each pair of seats was a small table with black leather enclosing the edges. Leather also lined the seats. Upon further inspection, I saw that the leathery substance had the appearance of liquid. Upon looking into its black gleam from above, it appeared I was looking into a pair of eyes with an endless soul, a soul in torment with malicious intent to devour the essence of who I was. As I stood motionless, staring at the grotesque view in front of me, I saw what I perceived as a set of enlarged ink-black pupils blinking multiple times as if in slow motion, and each time, the cloudiness that covered the pupil, a layer of a milky substance, would dissolve, producing another thinner layer. With successive blinks, the cloudy substance completely dissolved, showing an intense darkness, a demonic black pupil that, when fully dilated, portrayed an abyss into a bottomless pit of hell. The lining of the seat started to move, at first sluggishly, as if waking up after a period of dormancy. Then the movement accelerated to a rhythmic pulse. Each pulse got stronger as the leathery substance started to wrap around my arms.

I was paralyzed by what appeared before me, and time seemed to freeze as I fought to tear myself away from my seemingly hypnotic fugue. With an alarmed urgency, I looked around to see if anyone else was on the transport. I saw no one, not even a conductor. I jumped out of my seat and ran through the adjoining cars toward the front, searching for a conductor. I finally found an elderly conductor in the front car. He had an uncanny similarity to the agent I'd encountered in the depot. With a panicked edge to my tone, I blurted out rapid-fire questions. "The village we just left—was that Neverland? When is the next stop for Haleyville?"

He promptly responded, "What village? There are no villages on this journey."

I asked again, "When is the stop for Haleyville?"

He replied with the same tone of neutrality, "What stop? There is only one scheduled stop on this trip. Neverland, next stop," he proclaimed with earnest as if there was a sense of immediacy for a large crowd of passenger waiting to debark.

I shook my head with dismay, my gaze downward as I whispered to myself with utter disbelief, *"Where is everyone? What type of transport am I on?"* Ignoring his response, I asked him for a pass to Haleyville, and he said no pass was required; the next stop would be Haleyville if that was what I desired. Confused by his response, I wondered when this nightmare will end for nothing made sense anymore.

My imagination ran wild with my senses on overload as I hurriedly sat down on the first bench by the first door, ready to leap out the exit once the transport arrived at the next stop. It no longer mattered if the next destination was my hometown, Haleyville, or if the next stop was a return to where I embarked, surrendering to the possibility that this ride was just an endless journey with just one stop, Neverland. If needed, I would jump off the transport once convinced there was an element of truth to the conductor's reply. I just wanted to get off before whatever possessed this transport consumed me. Unable to keep my eyes open with the cumulative effects of the night's events crashing down on me, I started to doze off from exhaustion. Memories of Cassandra surfaced, providing a blanket of tranquility, even though I knew it was just a temporary interlude.

The core, the essence of the journey evolving from each episode, was Cassandra. I believed our connection was paramount to our existence, for without our bond, we would cease to exist and would wither away to a state of nonexistence, as if we'd never existed. Every memory, every image, and every journey would cease, dismissed entirely, expunged from reality, as if Cassandra and I were never born. There was no greater tragedy than to entirely erase one's existence.

The night's journey consumed me with horrific images. Fear dominated my thoughts. I was in a fight-or-flight syndrome, and I would resort to the latter. It seemed obvious that these sinister efforts were just a diversion aimed to misdirect my efforts and ultimately break our connection. For what reason, I was uncertain. What was there to gain if the diversion was successful? The demonic force behind that sinister plot was of a horrific nature, which meant there must have been a significant reason to break our connection. If the reason was that significant to destroy us, then failure must have carried a serious consequence.

I couldn't think anymore. My mind had hit a wall. I was in desperate need of sleep. I felt dead to the world. I closed my eyes, and fortunately, I felt Cassandra's presence as she bent down to soothe a weary mind, covering me with her protective layering of warmth and love as I closed my eyes to sleep. She bent closer to my ear and whispered, "I love you, Tony. Rest. Our journey is your destiny." I fell into a deep, much-needed sleep as images of Cassandra floated before me.

A faraway voice, barely reaching me and registering, floated just above my consciousness, skimming the surface of recognition. I felt submerged underwater, floating endlessly. Again, the message came, garbled by the time it reached me. I was unable to discern any meaning. I was slowly approaching the surface. Something was pulling me up closer to the surface. The light broke through just as the announcement was repeated: "Haleyville, next stop."

This time, it reached me, more pronounced. "Haleyville? Haleyville!" I exclaimed with conviction, breaking the surface, rising out of my submerged dream state, and taking in its full meaning. "Haleyville!" I repeated, this time with more conviction as the last remnants of my submerged dream state gave way to an awake, full awareness, and the revelation sank in. "Haleyville." With anticipation, I rose upright in my seat, taking notice of where I was. It was the same train and same seat I occupied after work on the local. Only a few passengers in the adjacent car were left, waiting to reach their destinations. I felt as if I had been on a sabbatical to a strange yet familiar village called Neverland. I'd had an engaging moment with Cassandra and was now just getting back. I didn't remember much of the train ride from the station.

My mind was still hazy as the announcement started again with an increased frequency. Haleyville meant only one thing: we were getting closer. I glanced around me to find the source but realized it was coming from every direction, an echo that repeatedly boomeranged against the walls that enclosed the passenger car.

"Haleyville, next stop." The announcement became more frequent, intense, louder, turning into an endless continuous stream of the same announcement. Each announcement higher in pitch until it screamed in my ear.

Was my imagination conjuring up more tricks? Had I really heard the announcement of my hometown? *Got to be*, I thought, sure we must have been almost on top of the village. I glued my eyes to the window for any evidence of familiarity.

31

Mystery House on Canyon Ridge Trails

A sense of déjà vu swarmed over me. I was anxious to view any early signs of civilization, searching for recognition, a familiarity to convince me that this was real and that Haleyville was the next stop. There, off to my right, was a city sign, but it passed by too quickly for me to discern the city name. The city water tower emerged. The full city name was just out of sight, but I saw the letters *Hal*. The train took a slight turn as the tracks curved, approaching the town at full speed. *Haleyville*. The word was clearly in full view, and then more early signs of civilization appeared. My hopes rose as I searched for more confirmation. The outskirts of the town came into view, and I recognized the landmarks, convinced now that it was my hometown. I soon saw the depot around the bend as the train switched tracks. It became apparent, however, the train was not reducing its speed. Its welcoming whistle was silent, ignoring any signal of an approaching train. My stop was just a hundred yards away, when the brakes were forcefully applied, and the smell of burned metal saturated the car with a foul odor while the train began its screeching halt up to the main entrance of the depot.

A few moments went by. I was frozen to my seat with uncertainty. The broadcast was now vacant. I listened to the uncanny silence in the car where I sat, picking up the intermittent, forceful sound of the heavy wheezing of the engine, its labored breathing fluctuating with a rhythmic pulse. The sudden jolt when the train finally came to a halt jarred my senses, and I ran toward the front exit and reached for a handle to pull the exit doors open. My panicked urgency kicked up a notch, and I ignored the door handle and instead, without any concern, eager to exit with haste, frantically pulled the rip cord above me, which immediately swished the doors open. I hastily jumped off onto the platform and turned toward the engine, which was completely enveloped in the steam and billows of smoke pouring from the engine car's smokestack. I looked in both directions, searching for other disembarking passengers. I was the only passenger on the platform. *Strange*, I thought, as that was the depot for several surrounding villages, and there should have been several passengers calling it a day and walking to their autos for the drive home. My senses picked up a sudden hissing noise from the engine car, signaling its impatience. Within seconds, the train became totally contained within the steam, entirely disappearing behind a white cloud of vapor. Even though it was not visible, I could hear the gasp and groans. The train took no time to rest; the engine roared back to life, firing up its burners and fully engaging without a second to spare. It charged past the depot into the night, rushing with haste to its next destination to disembark its next crew of passengers, whoever and wherever they might be.

My attention diverted back to the visage from my dream: Cassandra. She was at the house we'd just purchased. I did not enter the depot but started off with an unsteady walk that turned into a dash toward my car. I did not wait for my car to warm up in the unusually cool weather that had enveloped Southern California's coastline for days. Overwhelming memories both inspired and haunted me. My memories with Cassandra were fused into my soul, but the haunting memories of the stranger masked by the persistent shadows and the grotesque images from the journey left me in a cage of fear, unable to comprehend any significance. I undoubtedly felt the demonic images were somehow tied to Cassandra and me, and if left unabated, they would pose a threat to us in which our soulful journey through endless eras would be forever lost and result in a vanquishment of our bonded souls. I was constantly torn between my compulsive need for Cassandra and my fear of the unknown threat toward us. I knew I had to take the ultimate risk in order to shield her from harm's way and provide a safe haven. With a surge of urgency, my mind rapidly scanned the surreal events that had invaded my senses over the past few months, seeking any clue to the harrowing journey.

In spite of my fear of being followed, I accelerated, mindless to the speed limit, and upon reaching the town limits, my tension started easing as I drove below the speed limit through the downtown area, receptive to the joyful sight of civilization, with people conversing and laughing while seated on the number of outside verandas that lined Main Street, even though it was well into the evening. I felt a loosening of the tightness around my chest. A form of stability was returning. My insides were buffered by a renewed calmness, with a feeling of normalcy spurred by the welcome, familiar sights of my hometown.

I drove through the town, past the intersection that led to my house, and jumped on the coastal highway toward the canyons north of Santa Monica. I drove northward with a sense of immediacy, accelerating in overdrive without concern for my safety, and the exit ramp suddenly appeared before me after I came out of a hairpin curve. Without slowing, I took the exit ramp at full speed, with my Maxima just barely hugging the ramp. Ignoring the stop sign, I turned a sharp right onto Canyon Ridge Trails and accelerated upward, blindly navigating the narrow road winding its way toward the top of the ridge where the home we'd just purchased was located. I slowed down as I approached the home with trepidation. The twilight that followed my drive toward my destination had turned to a soulful pitch-black night. The only discernible light was from one streetlight, which yielded just enough light to allow me to see a few yards ahead of me. There were no lights on in the house. There were four timer lights in the house, and at least one was supposed to be lit throughout the day. Unfortunately, we must have forgotten to set the timers.

I turned into the driveway, cautiously exited my car, and walked to the front door. There was barely enough light to guide me along the walkway. About halfway to the entrance, I detected a reflection in the front upper window overlooking the walkway. I stopped dead in my tracks and peered upward at the window. The light from the street caused a slight reflection, but I was convinced I'd detected more than just a reflection. I peered upward again and saw a silhouette of a young lady with a rose tucked in her hair, peering down toward me. She raised her hand and threw me a kiss. Then she vanished.

My emotional fatigue from that night's journey quickly took a siesta as a surge of adrenaline spurred me onward with renewed energy. When I reached the front door, I immediately tried to open the door, which was locked. I looked for a doorbell but did not find anything that would announce my presence. I resorted to knocking on the front door but got no response. *If Cassandra is here, she should have heard me by now.* After waiting for a few more minutes, I tried to open the door again without success. My keys to the house were at my home, and I had no spare on me. I didn't have time to return to my home to pick up the key and then return there to unlock the door. I hurried to my vehicle, grabbed the tire iron from the trunk, and rushed to the rear patio door. I tried to open the patio door, hoping it was unlocked, but as expected, the door was locked. I looked around for another possible entrance, but my search was in vain. Time was of the essence because of my sense of urgency to search for Cassandra and disengage the alarm immediately once inside. I wedged the tire iron under the lock. I then forcibly pushed down on the iron until the lock disengaged. Once inside, I stumbled to the light switch next to the patio door and turned on the lights. With no time to spare, I rushed to the security alarm. The security alarm was on, within seconds of notifying the police, as I reset the alarm.

It seemed as if an eternity had passed since I'd jimmied the lock. I felt I was out of time upon reaching the stairway to the upper floors. I picked up Cassandra's fragrance while climbing the stairs to the top floor. Once I reached the top level, I headed to the master bedroom, from which I was certain I'd seen Cassandra peering out the window. Once inside the room, I felt for the light switch on the wall and turned it on. I saw nothing. The room was vacant. I searched the room for any clue of her presence. I walked to the window, hoping to find any clue. On the windowsill, I found a rose and a letter. I brought the rose up to my face to catch the fragrance. The fragrance was Sensual Delight, which was a definite sign she was there. I opened the one-page letter. It was from Cassandra. Instead of feeling ecstatic upon finding the rose and letter, I felt unusually anxious because of the continual elusiveness of Cassandra. I felt exhaustion returning with a vengeance. As I gazed out the window, my mind a web of a flurry of emotions, Cassandra appeared on the front walkway. Her eyes connected with mine, and then she threw me a kiss before she vanished. At that point, I was so exhausted that I felt nothing was for certain. I could not trust my own perceptions, and I needed downtime, or else I would totally lose it. I spent the next thirty minutes searching the house for any clue to Cassandra's whereabouts but found nothing. I could not trust my reactions anymore that night. It was obvious Cassandra wasn't there, and I needed a fresh perspective in the morning. I looked at my watch: 2:00 a.m. I was beyond being surprised at the lateness. I was so exhausted that I was starting to believe the visions of Cassandra that night might have been hallucinations from exhaustion. I wasn't sure about anything anymore, and I hurried to my vehicle and started the trip back home.

I used the last of my reserves to drive home and felt an overwhelming relief upon reaching my house and driving into the connecting garage. I entered my house through the side door that led from the garage to the kitchen. I glanced around the kitchen and walked out through the den into the living room, relishing the fact that I was home safe—safe from my trip home. The trip had left me numb and drained. I could not even begin to rationalize what had occurred that night. But the events had happened, as real as 2real could be. I knew something profound was happening, but for the moment, I could not fathom what or why.

Without any warning, an alarming thought hit me dead center. Was there more to this? A worsening of my mental disorder? I was already aware I could not delineate between fantasy and reality when I dreamed. Simply put, I could not detect the ending of a dream, which would flow into my waking state, where fantasy and reality would at some point merge together, creating one fused state wherein everything appeared as one surreal view. Eventually, the waking state would become apparent as the fused web of entanglement loosened and eventually released me from its grasp. But the fused state was already imprinted in my mind, and I was unable to detect what part of the dream was real. When the diagnosis was made, I was informed it could lead to other physical or mental disorders. That stuck in my mind. I was painfully aware that if I was experiencing any additional disorders, the cumulative effect might be enough to flip me over the edge. Was this a further symptom of a decline in my condition, a cumulative breakdown, or a tumor? Either this was actually happening, or I had a physical or mental issue, perhaps a tumor or a worsening neurological disorder of significant magnitude. A sense of urgency raised my panic button. There was one thing I had decided for sure: I needed to make an appointment with a medical specialist and schedule a series of counseling visits to get to the bottom of the matter for my own peace of mind. Either way, it was a task that required immediacy.

I wondered if there was more to this mystery that I just could not grasp at that moment in time. For the time being, there was nothing I could do but gain a sense of composure, push everything that had happened that night into the background, free up my mind, and put myself in a position where I could objectively rationalize this. I had to compartmentalize to unwind and release the paralyzing effect on my senses. I was overtired, which was keeping any form of sleep at bay, and I decided to turn on my classic songs from the Sinatra days to soothe my soul.

Hunger pains knifed through my gut from lack of fuel. I felt famished, wondering when I'd last eaten. I realized it had been with Linda earlier that afternoon to celebrate. *Celebrate? How ironic.* We were celebrating a milestone, and the reward was my journey into a debacle of unknowns. I was too exhausted to even make a sandwich and wound up pouring myself another shot of bourbon. I was unable to detach myself from that day as I recalled the day's events. Everything had been going as planned until I'd left work for the train ride home. Then the mystery had reemerged, ushering in the saga of uncertainty and illusion mixed with apprehension, and my fear had fused with unparalleled rapture, turning into an unabated frenzy.

Cassandra. The name ruled my obsession—an insatiable fixation that had transcended to a compulsive need. The obsession was taking hold again. Its dominance commanded center stage. Cassandra had become integrated into my psyche. She was part of me with every second I breathed. Despite my dubious nature, the one fact that kept me on course was that every instinct within me led me to an undeniable certainty: the bond between Cassandra and me was unparalleled, a soulful connection that could not be denied, a bond of souls that had been inseparable since time evolved. When we engaged and connected, we knew that together we were one; separate we were incomplete. Separation was a threat to our survival; death was imminent, making it paramount that we unite for eternity and beat fate's intervention to tear us mercilessly apart. I was certain the demonic forces that had invaded our journey that night had been fate's attempt to divide because it felt threatened by the purity of our bonded souls, which could possibly threaten its own purpose. That realization further fueled my determination to endure the incessant sinister force, overcome its persistence, and negate its power. It felt threatened by our connection, and to withstand its power, our connection would ultimately overcome. I felt powerless at the moment, but the hypnotic draw of Cassandra infused me with a passion to endure and meet the challenge.

That night, our passion from our soulful bond proved to be hypnotic, a draw that even the most potent drugs could not have emulated. It magnified my obsession to reunite and reengage the dreamlike fantasy. My obsession pushed the fear of whatever demonic forces existed into the background, to a distant memory. I was consumed with our interlude of ecstasy, which was tantalizingly erotic, an invited diversion from an otherwise dull, repetitive life. That eroticism infused a climatic high, invoking a deep sexual thirst I had not experienced in the years as far back as I could recall. I sensed our next rendezvous would feel as if it were a long way off, as if we had an eternity to wait until our next engagement. I longed to be near her side. Her physical touch was endearing to my soul and made me feel whole and complete; chaos transformed to contentment, and harmony overruled conflict. I wanted to caress her smooth, silky skin and watch her eyes latch on to mine, anxiously waiting for the kiss of eternal bliss that would allow us to willingly reengage in our own sphere of mystery.

The bourbon and music proved to be the perfect tonic to release my tension, and an overwhelming fatigue overcame me. I felt drugged. I used my last ounce of reserves to drag myself to the master bedroom on the third floor. I barely made it to the bed before I passed out from pure exhaustion. My mind became a total blank as the veil of darkness covered my soul.

Searching for Neverland

Another morning arrived. I woke up at dawn, left with only memories of our last engagement. My sleep had been uninterrupted, as if the note I'd found last night had put a temporary hold on any form of engagement, placed there just to tantalize and tease with anticipation. I searched the pillow and the bed linens for a petal and found none. There was no letter, which caused me further unease. The loneliness rushed back, and my heart yearned to find a small note, something that would reveal she'd visited me and had not forgotten me, a promise of connecting again. But I found nothing. With a sense of disappointment, my doubts returned with a vicious impact, and I wondered if my imagination was the source of the possible delusions. Yet my yearning poked through the veil of uncertainty, and I remembered the rose petals and note she'd left from our last meeting as souvenirs. I reached into my pocket and felt the enclosed rose petal. I retrieved it and the note to reassure myself that Cassandra was real and to capture her still-pervasive scent. My desire was reinforced by the seductive lure of her perfume. When blended with her natural scent, the resulting fragrance would have enticed the most resistant soul and invited a promenade of customers, satisfying their thirst for the ultimate elusive aphrodisiac.

With a purposeful intent, I rushed into the kitchen to pour myself a cup of day-old coffee and grab a Danish. Then I opened my patio door to retrieve the morning paper. I combed through the paper intently, searching for any newsworthy event that stood out, possibly related to last night's journey. My search yielded no results. The letter and note did give conclusive evidence of some form of physical intervention. The link between the note and last night's journey gave credence to one fact: Neverland did exist. Yet despite the facts giving indisputable proof of the reality of Neverland, I still was surprised that my doubts hung on. It was a vicious cycle further obscuring the boundaries that separated reality from fantasy. I reread the note in a last-ditch effort to notice anything I might have missed, any clue to Neverland's location. Again, my effort was without result. I logged in to my computer and used the internet to search the immediate towns around Haleyville with a population under fifty thousand within thirty miles. I recognized all the towns and had been to each one of them at least once. None came close to resembling where I'd been last night. I expanded my search to include any town within a hundred miles of Haleyville and still did not find the village from last night. I extended my search to within five hundred miles, dismissing the population filter, and still got no results.

I wondered if I'd read the village sign above the depot correctly, and then I searched for all towns within seven hundred miles of Haleyville by the village or city name. I could not find anything close to Neverland. With no results from my searches, I felt helpless in trying to locate the village. With a surging impatience, I pulled up the train schedule and searched all the routes only to come up empty. I finally resorted to searching every route that originated from Los Angeles but again found nothing close to Neverland. In hindsight, I should have done that when I first started my search, but hindsight made us all geniuses. However, that too was a fruitless effort. With my mind reeling from overload after the weekend journeys and an exhaustive search, I reluctantly shelved my obsession for another time to attend to current matters, impatiently making the effort to channel my energy to that day's events.

In the background, I heard the grandfather clock send out its melodic hourly signal: seven notes. It dawned on me that it must be seven o'clock in the morning. With alarm, I realized I had a meeting at ten o'clock with Linda to finalize the purchase of several homes located in Bryan Canyon, overlooking the coastline. This was Linda's domain, which was like stamping the label "Mandatory" to my invite. After months of research and negotiations, Linda had prepared the plans for modernizing the homes while retaining their classic art moderne architecture. The homes, built during the '30s and '40s, showcased the classic design that had gained prominence during the art deco era.

With a sense of urgency, I headed for the shower. As I showered, I temporarily shelved my pondering of the weekend obsession to focus on the scheduled meetings with Linda. Yet my compelling obsession refused to be ignored, granting me one final visit before my day ahead. My thoughts cycled back to Linda and her dreams. Was there a connection? Something did not add up. My gut was telling me there was a link between Linda and the dreams and Cassandra. But I had just instinct, nothing tangible to work on at the moment. It was just another riddle, another piece to fit into the puzzle. I decided to investigate further at a later time and forced myself again with painful reluctance to concentrate on the business's upcoming events.

The forthcoming meeting was in two hours, a fact that hastened my ritual of making myself presentable for the workday. With a flurry of last-minute grooming, I finished my shower, dressed for work, and headed to my car for the drive to the train depot to catch the early express, not taking a chance of the heavy traffic in the morning rush. When I heard the train whistle greet me, a sudden jolt surged through my veins from the memory of the old transport from last night's journey. Quickly dismissing the sudden flashback, I waited until the express train entered the passenger boarding zone, and upon its stopping, I boarded the first car. Hesitantly, I opened the passenger door, and for a fleeting moment, the ghoulish image from last night of the vacant, lifeless pupils staring at me flashed before me. Shaking my head repeatedly to dismiss the invasive images, I moved forward until I reached the plush seats with leather cushions and quickly found a pair of empty seats. Even though the train was crowded, no one sat in the sole unoccupied adjacent seat, another oddity added to the collection of strange anomalies that defied the norm.

Still feeling the exhaustive efforts from last night, I took a short nap in an overdue attempt to get some much-needed rest to recoup my energy and alertness before the critical meeting commenced in two hours. Thirty minutes later, I awoke with renewed vitality and was thankful that nothing out of the ordinary had occurred during the train ride in. Upon arriving at the main station, I got off the train and briskly walked to the office complex, aware I only had an hour to discuss the agenda with Linda and get the documents ready for review and approval. The office complex was only a few blocks from the Santa Monica station; therefore, I had time to breathe in the energy of the city during my walk. The sun was at its low peak, and people of all sizes and ages were walking toward their destinations, some already transforming their demeanor to a conservative, somber, businesslike mood and others laughing openly, eagerly anticipating the day's events. I viewed the Pacific off to my left, watching the yachts and sailboats slowly glide across the horizon. It was a beautiful, warm, and sunny day full of promises for those who dared to hope and dream.

I approached our building, turned left onto the main walk toward the front door, walked through the glass-enclosed entrance to the lobby, said my customary hello to Charles, and hurried to the elevator to go to the top floor, which was entirely occupied by my company. I exited the elevator, walking past the various impressive art collections placed expertly on the adjacent walls leading to the main entrance to the company. I opened the doors and walked past the waiting room for visitors and potential customers toward the reception area, which was Alecia's personal space. Alecia was already busily conversing on the phone among a flurry of incoming calls, and we both winked and nodded. I gave her a thumbs-up before I finally reached my office. Upon entering, I immediately gathered the blueprints and contracts for the upcoming meeting. With thirty minutes to spare, I walked to the main conference room, which had a magnificent view of the Pacific, and found Linda already situated with everything set. I greeted her with a warm hello but received no response. Linda seemed somewhat subdued that morning. "Did you have any rest last night?" I asked, wondering if she was okay. I was concerned not only because of the criticalness of the meeting but because of my genuine concern for her as my closest friend. As I got closer to her, I saw that her eyes were puffy, with a slight hint of dark shadows under her lower eyelids, apparently from lack of sleep. I knew she was distraught about her recent dreams. Over the last few weeks, she'd had moments when she seemed distracted, and her usual keen focus was somewhat subdued.

Linda returned a perturbed stare and said flatly, "I am okay, and what business is it of yours anyway? Let's just get down to business and leave it at that." I was sure her matter-of-fact, direct tone was because our scheduled discussions regarding the uncanny similarities between our dreams had been postponed twice. It was not the best time, though, to get into a heated exchange.

I took a copy of our mission statement prepared by Linda to serve as the introduction to the scheduled meeting. I realized the effort and time it had taken Linda to prepare the document, and I used the next thirty minutes to read the document while Linda waited for my response.

Our company's mission is to preserve classic homes that showcase the art moderne design that symbolized the art deco architecture theme during the 1930s and '40s. We believe the designs from that era defined the cutting edge of creative expression, which, unfortunately, disappeared after World War II, at the start of the 1950s.

Today's designs of new homes are the result of the cost-cutting approach, wherein a series of homes— or, in fact, an entire subdivision of new homes—are exact duplicates. This has had an impact on society. Compliance, clan mentality, and conformity are widely accepted and rewarded, while nonconformity and creative reflection of one's individuality are feared and rejected. This trend is reflected in society's lack of emphasis on the creative arts, in which creative expression, an individual's uniqueness, and the buyer's unique perception are well rewarded and flourish. Instead, the emphasis is now strictly geared toward a one-dimensional, linear mentality that emphasizes conformity, cost reduction, revenue growth, and increased margins at the cost of losing the buyer's individuality and unique taste as expressed in the design of the home. This trend couldn't be more obvious in the housing sector.

We seek to reverse this cookie-cutter trend by presenting a display of the art moderne architecture from the 1930s and '40s. To accomplish this feat, we expanded our business model to include purchasing and modernizing classic homes whose architecture exemplified the art moderne design from that time period. Displaying these homes, which have been modernized through upgrades yet have retained the classic art deco design, will hopefully be instrumental in reversing the current trend in the housing sector. Our plan of modernizing existing homes was targeted toward large, grand homes built during that era along the coastline and scattered throughout the canyons that overlook the Pacific coastline that highlight the creative, expressive architecture that epitomized the art deco design.

To summarize, our mission is to promote the design from that pair of decades, when architecture was defined by an individual's creativity and reflected the buyer's unique perception. This approach defined the years prior to World War II, when creativity was in vogue. In contrast, the cost-cutting approach, which emphasizes conformity, started during the war and continued through the postwar years. The clan-based, conformist mentality resulted in drastic cost reduction in order to maximize margins at the price of the loss of the buyer's individuality and unique perception. Corporate Wall Street has taken precedence over the buyer. Renovating these classic homes while retaining their art moderne design will help promote the company's plan to reintroduce the art deco design to the California housing market.

I was impressed with the mission statement and congratulated Linda for the superb write-up. Our celebration, however, was short-lived, as Linda withdrew into the morning's solemn mood. I again asked her if she was feeling well.

She responded, "I did not sleep well last night. I had a migraine that finally receded at three o'clock in the morning." Linda then asked me if

I'd mind if she left early for the day and if we continued our celebration the following day for dinner.

"Fine. In fact, take the remainder of the day off, and we will pick up on things tomorrow during dinner," I responded. With total exhaustion, she whisked by me, and I caught a scent of her perfume. "Linda, remind me again. What is the name of that perfume you are wearing? It is the same fragrance of the perfume I encounter in my dreams."

"What perfume?" she replied. "I have no perfume on, and I don't know which fragrance you are referring to. I really need to leave now."

Her response was nervous, and she seemed to be defensive about the question. *I guess our tension will persist until we meet to discuss our dreams. In fact, that should be a priority. Linda looks like hell, and I suspect the dreams are to blame for what appears a lack of sleep.* Yet the defensive posture and nervous answer to my question about her perfume led me to suspect there was another issue. I knew the fragrance, but since Linda was in no mood to talk, I let it go. After she left me alone in the conference room, I proceeded toward my office, and once inside, I pondered her adamant denial of the fragrance—not necessarily her response but the nervous, defensive posture attached to her denial. I reminded myself to visit the boutique on Rodeo Drive that Linda had mentioned during my initial inquiry last week, which obviously she did not recall or chose to ignore.

33

A Visit to a Boutique for a Rare Perfume

A healthy reprieve from last evening's episodes allowed me to entirely focus on the day's workload. I left my office and told Alecia I would not be back until tomorrow. "If there are any calls, please tell them I am out on business for the rest of the day." I took the company car and drove south along Route 1 toward the Rodeo Mall in Beverly Hills, taking in the gorgeous Monday late afternoon with the top down since it was not too cool. In fact, it was perfect California weather, with temperatures in the midseventies.

The traffic was still light as I headed to the boutique in the shopping mall on Rodeo Drive. I turned left, which led me to the garage under the mall, and I left my car with the parking attendant. As the attendant opened the door, I asked him where the boutique Empress Voyage was located. He responded by directing me to the third floor next to Macy's, toward the center of the mall. I thanked him and gave him ten dollars for his directions. I turned toward the elevator bank and proceeded to the third floor. When the elevator opened, I found myself facing a huge atrium with greenery and waterfalls on both sides of the floor. I followed the walkway between the waterfalls toward the middle of the floor and found Macy's.

It took a few minutes to find the boutique. I finally located it behind one of the waterfalls. I followed a small brick pathway that led me between two smaller waterfalls, and there it was: a small, cozy shop that tailored to the fashionable woman, specializing in intimate wear.

I walked in and found a female employee to inquire about Sensual Delight. "That's strange," she said immediately. "You're the second customer to ask about that rare fragrance within the last month. I carry that brand but by order only, as I do not carry it in stock. I still sell the brand because one or two customers still purchase the fragrance."

"When was the last time you ordered it?" I responded, trying to keep my fact-finding questions disguised as casual responses in a nonintrusive, light, and simple dialogue to avoid arousing suspicion.

"Well," she said while remembering the last order, "I remember it vividly. The last time I ordered it was for one of our most steady customers. She stops by four times a year. She was here about two or three weeks ago."

I laughed, continuing the dialogue in a positive, casual direction. "When a customer commits to a brand, it becomes almost impossible to convert them to a different choice."

"Yes, definitely true," she responded with an enthused, engaging response. "I do not remember when she started as a customer. I have only been here for a year. I remember when she first ordered from me. I tried to sell her one of the brands we carry in stock—fragrances that, in my opinion, are more mainstream with the same quality at a lower price. About fifty percent lower. And besides, it takes over a month for me to receive the shipment for Sensual Delight.

"When I first met her, I informed her that we do not carry that brand in stock but will order it when requested. When I showed her other brands, she was adamant about Sensual Delight. What sticks in my mind was the tone of her response. It was defensive, nervous agitation, like she was obsessed, pursuing with repeated questions on ordering the fragrance. She was obviously distressed, and to help her, I promptly filled out the order form while she gave me cash in advance for a quantity of two. Now that I am recalling, the details are coming back. She asked to use the restroom, and then I inquired about the fragrance on the internet. It was extremely popular during the early 1900s and was accessible to those who were more affluent. Even then, it was extremely pricy. But the popularity waned after World War II, when the cost escalated along with a decline in the economic climate. When she returned from the restroom, I reiterated that Sensual Delight is two to three times pricier than other extremely popular fragrances we carry in stock. The price did not deter the customer's decision. Her agitated, nervous response became more compulsive without a hint of hesitancy.

"There was a sense of obsession about her that compelled her to this one fragrance regardless of the cost. It caused me some suspicion. I remember clearly because her obsession with this fragrance did not correlate to her youthfulness. She seemed too young for such an obsession with a product that was popular decades ago and is no longer mainstream. Plus, there was the oddity of her additional comments. She must have noticed my concerned look because she followed with additional comments. She told me that product has been used in her family line since the early 1900s, and the fragrance had a tranquil effect on her. She mentioned something else that didn't make sense. She referenced a name I'd never heard before when referring to the 1900s: Neverland. Another name she mentioned with a faraway look was Cassandra. That was it, with no follow-up about Neverland or Cassandra. But you know, there was something else odd. There was a strangeness about her, a faraway, dreamy tone to her voice and a remote, distant vagueness to her demeanor, as if she were in a twilight haze."

"Was her name Linda?" I asked.

It only took an instant before she replied, "Yes, that was her name. Linda. Nice name for a strange young lady."

"Did she pick up the order?" I suddenly asked as she started to eye me nervously.

"No," she responded with a hint of impatience. "It will arrive about a month from now." She stood there with an apprehensive stare. "I already have disclosed too much information. Why the questions?"

Her voice had escalated from a tone of casual dialogue to one tainted with an agitated suspicion.

"Well, she is a distant relative. I wanted to surprise her with this product for her birthday present. But I wanted to see if she'd already purchased the fragrance, and this is the only outlet for this fragrance in this area," I replied, trying to keep my tone as neutral and sincere as possible to avoid further suspicion. "Sorry for the questions. The product is so pricy that if she already ordered it recently, then I'll use the money I was going to use for this purchase for something else I have in mind for her. I apologize for all the questions."

"No problem. And your name?" she asked with the same sincere tone.

"Tony," I replied, and then I thanked her for the friendly dialogue. I then left before she had a chance to ask me any more questions I was not prepared to answer.

I walked back to the underground garage with a renewed sense of purpose and gave my parking stub to the attendant. While waiting for my car, I thought about our conversation. While I'd listened to her, I'd kept my responses to a minimum to avoid any suspicions as to the nature of my questions. I'd listened attentively, trying to digest everything she told me. I'd come there expecting some basic facts I could use to help me learn more about Linda, our dreams, and the connection to Cassandra. I had not expected an avalanche of information that, besides adding some clarity, added another layer of complexity and additional questions to the mired set of variables of the mystery. Overall, the information she'd shared was another integral component to the maze, another clue I had been searching for to gain much-needed insight into the web of mystery. I was now sitting at the entrance to the enigmatic portal of charades. The newfound information was the next legitimate clue to provide a window into the portal. But I needed more information to connect the dots. I needed to meet with Linda. I felt an urgency to meet with Linda to finally commit to Linda's request for a discussion about the dream we seemed to be sharing. The new information also raised another question about Linda. Where was she from before joining our organization? I knew nothing about her past. She'd just appeared one day at a convention, and we had been partners since. I was still surprised by such a scarcity of information about a key resource so pivotal to the company's success. But the stark reality was undeniable. That was the extent of my knowledge.

My car arrived after a short wait, and I exited the garage, making a left on Hollywood Boulevard to head to the expressway. As I drove along Route 1, the memories surged to the forefront like a huge tidal wave before cascading mercilessly toward shore, unleashing an avalanche of ocean upon landfall. After my initial adjustment to the sudden onrush of memories, the recollections subsided to a steady parade before me, allowing me to recall selectively the moments that revealed significant events I felt were at the core of the enigma that engaged Cassandra and me. I then fast-forwarded to Linda's moods lately and the comments she'd made when I discussed my dream about Cassandra. The perfume was another clue I considered significant. Maybe a pattern was beginning to appear, and the core memories were the dots that, once connected, would begin the unraveling of the conundrum. Intrigued, I pondered further.

There were two primary facts that together supported a valid argument that my journey was more than just a dream: the rose and the letter: Those facts could not be dismissed and yielded a more perplexing, far-reaching scenario, one that required more to be taken into account to harvest a rational explanation. The oddities enforced the fact that I wasn't sure of anything except that when I added everything up, it was obvious there was more to the journey. Part of the journey was real. But where did the realness to the journey begin? That was the perplexing question. I could summon possible scenarios to rationalize the primary facts: sleepwalking, an out-of-body experience, or a lucid dream state. But when I surveyed everything to find the invisible boundary that separated fantasy from reality, the facts did not easily correlate to any one of those scenarios. Not one scenario could connect all the dots. Not one scenario could provide me the answer I was seeking. The answer lay somewhere else, and without my locating Neverland and Cassandra, the answer would remain elusive. Until I located them, the perpetual cycle of doubts and incessant questions would continue. I realized in that present state, there was no way I could find a direct path to Neverland and Cassandra, as the path to both remained obscure. The path remained elusive outside the realm of my journey. That path would allow me to connect all the dots rather than present me with more variables that defied logic. The true answer lay somewhere in that maze of detours and hidden variables. The maze required an exhaustive search of all the variables that would eventually lead me to the yellow brick road. Despite the overwhelming impact of what lay ahead, I had reason for hope. I finally had uncovered another essential fact: the dream Linda and I shared might have been more than a dream, entering the hybrid realm of fantasy and reality. If that were true, then maybe Linda would be able to discern what part of the dream was fantasy and what was real, which would prove to be invaluable and instrumental in leading me through the maze of detours. It was apparent that meeting with Linda about our dreams was of paramount importance.

My drive along the coastline provided a breath-taking view of the intense blue hue of the Pacific. I watched the turtle-like pace of a passenger cruise ship off in the distance, silhouetted against the horizon, wondering what it felt like to be ferried away toward a dreamland destination. As I watched the ship travel on, my thoughts returned to Cassandra and a curious desire to be transported by a one-way cruise to a dreamland with Cassandra where we could transcend our shared dreams to a level of undeniable truth of eternal oneness. I pondered with a desperate yearning the enormous impact of such a soulful bonding. Was it possible to even capture the grandeur of such a potent union? To be whisked away with a one-way ticket to a destination of immense beauty to unite with one who shared my soul? Would I miss my present situation? I responded with an emphatic no.

If only it could have been that easy, to be able to join Cassandra purely upon my wish and desire. But such was not the case; my connection with Cassandra was at the discretion of fate—a journey provided through fate's intervention for one passenger with one destination until I could unlock the matrix. The journey swept me through an arcade of unknowns. It was not just the where that escaped me; the hows and whys were perhaps more relevant unknowns. The disparity between the now and the journey to that village was an odyssey that perplexed me intensely. I currently held no clue as to the why for the disparity between the two different worlds. I was caught in a swirl of questions of how I'd journeyed to the village. The journey's transport ride was one of the strangest concepts of the dream. Why a transport? The clue that surfaced immediately was my fascination with the nightly sounds of a faraway train. I was always mesmerized, hypnotized by the sound of a faraway train whistle, imagining its passengers being transported to their favorite land of enchantment. The transport's ride was the only medium presented to me as the entry point into the vortex. Whenever that time warp occurred during the ride home, it served as the capsule to escort me to the other reality, to another dimension, one I felt connected to. I felt a sense of belonging there, a feeling of coming home, as if that destination were my true reality, and my current existence, the now, was instead the dream.

The obscured variables presented me with such an overabundance of unknowns that at times, the situation overwhelmed me. My imagination daily conjured up all the scenarios, some plausible and some not so plausible. My mind perused all the possibilities and ramifications, leaving me feeling like a caged rat caught in a maze with endless paths. Only one path, yet to be found, would lead me to the elixir where the truths lay. One truth was a certainty: I desperately needed to be with Cassandra again. I knew that other setting did exist, and Cassandra's presence was the focal point to the abyss. If those frequent interludes were the only way to be by her side, then I welcomed and needed those journeys as confirmation that the village and Cassandra were somehow real and somewhere existed.

My quest toward unraveling the quagmire was now more intricately linked to Linda. It was a turning point on my road to discovery. But the trail did not end there. Even with that added insight, the trail toward resolution would have numerous twists and turns. Even with all the clues recently uncovered, I still needed a more effective plan, possibly an improvised plan. If I could travel on the journey at will, by advanced knowledge of the schedule, then I would have more time to accommodate a plan and possibly explore a new path to the road of discovery. "Just more ifs," I declared with an impatient, weary sigh. I had mixed feelings of exuberance and apprehension during that downtime to rescind into the past. I suspended my thoughts and emotions and held them in check until my next journey.

34

History of the Mystery House on Canyon Ridge Trails

Traffic was picking up, and congestion was starting as I continued north along the coast toward the Canyon Ridge Trails exit. I took the ramp and made an immediate right onto the winding road that led to the homes perched precariously on the cliffs overlooking the Pacific. We were halfway finished with remodeling the house we'd purchased on Canyon Ridge Trails, a house built during the early 1920s. We'd scaled back the remodeling effort in order to retain its prominent architecture. It was a massive house in a heavily wooded area that had undergone several facelifts during its history. When we looked at the house initially, both Linda and I had an uncanny sense of a strong connection to the house. We inquired as to why the house never had acquired a new owner over the last two decades. We found there were rumors the house was haunted. Stories abounded about a missing couple who were the previous owners. The superstitions that filled the gossip-hungry rumor mill were never proven or supported. Yet the rumors captured our intrigue. A house with an abundance of history fueled our fascination with houses rich with an endowed past. The mystery surrounding the house gained our attention and was a key factor in our decision to purchase.

The house had a definite appeal, with an upgraded architecture one did not see much of anymore. Upon further insight into the history of the house, we found that the original owner sold the house a few years after it was built to the couple who disappeared decades ago. There were unfounded rumors involving murder and mayhem surrounding the missing couple. The rumors included insanity, the occult, and a threesome love affair that led to torture and suicide. There never was any evidence to support the circulated hearsay. However, the damage was irrecoverable. The house was foreclosed and put up for auction. With its history, it was a certainty that a purchaser would tear down the house and build a new home that fit into the current mold of the conventional, standard one-dimensional structures. Fortunately, there was no interest due to the rumor mill. Upon Linda's discovering the architectural gem, she immediately brought me to the site, and it took no time for me to recognize the immense value the house would have in promoting our vision. Despite the dark overcast of the house's history, Linda and I made a hefty bid on the house and assumed the back property taxes. Within a few months, we became the ecstatic new owners; we felt we'd hit upon a potential gold mine investment. The next task was to decide on our final plans for the house, which was a task still in progress.

That year, Southern California was hit by a monsoon-like storm that savaged the coastline with torrential rain, devastating a number of the homes along the cliff line overlooking the Pacific. The house we purchased sustained damage. The overhang incurred most of the damage and was precariously extended over the edge of the cliff with barely enough support from whatever was left of the receding ground supporting the overhang. Even though that part of the house was the most vulnerable due to erosion of ground under the overhang's support beam, the stress was partially relieved because of the extended foundation. The art deco architecture used back during the 1920s through the '40s allowed the support framework to be easily extended to support new additions, such as an added overhang. That classic innovative design was copyrighted, and it was one of the key aspects of art deco architecture that made it so prominent during the pre–World War II years.

Because of the house's tenacity, fortitude, and refusal to break under the storm's savage beating, we could not bear to tear down the rear section. Instead, we decided to preserve its core structure, repairing the damage it had sustained. The major repair was to the overhang's support. Initially, we thought about shoring up the rear with landfill, but then we decided on a more long-term solution: to complete the repair by using steel-reinforced supports that would be drilled into the mountainside and welded to the main structure of the house. Even if the ground under the overhang totally receded, leaving no support at all, the overhang would remain intact. That said, the landfill would supplant the underside and around the overhang for aesthetic reasons, providing an artfully sculptured landscape and giving the overhang the appearance of blending into the mountainside. We were in the early stage of the construction, and when finished, the home would be a showcase of our company's ingenuity and far-reaching imaginative designs.

35

Discovery of the Letter and Photo

I arrived at the site, which was in between two other homes. The back end of the house was shored off for safety reasons. I ventured into the house to inspect the interior and check for any vandalism. The brilliant day was entering its twilight state, and fortunately, we'd left the utilities on, so timed lights allowed me to conduct a thorough inspection. After ensuring that everything was as we'd last left it, I went to the bar to check for any remaining vodka in the fridge from our kickoff celebration upon closing the sale a month ago. I found a fifth of vodka in the minifridge and poured myself a straight shot on the rocks.

I sat on one of the barstools adjacent to the floor-to-ceiling window on the side of the house that had a magnificent view of the Pacific coastline winding its way north toward the northern part of California. The view was so captivating that for a few moments, the view seemed to push everything to the side, allowing me to be drawn into a private retreat where the only thing that mattered was the view's captivating beauty and perfection. It seemed as if some time had passed, but when I came out of my reverie, I found that my captivating diversion had lasted only a few minutes. I finished my drink, placed the empty glass on the bar, and then continued my inspection, proceeding toward the spacious living room that overlooked the Pacific. Entering the room near the patio, I was suddenly caught off guard by detecting a familiar scent. It lasted just for a fraction of a second, so I excused it to my overworked imagination. However, I caught a whiff of the fragrance again, recognizing it immediately as the same one Cassandra and Linda wore. *It must be Linda, as we were supposed to meet here thirty minutes ago.* With a modest effort to make myself heard, I called out, "Linda, is that you? I'm by the patio on the first floor." I waited for a few minutes with no response. "Linda?" My tone was more cautious now, with a hint of uncertainty. *Cassandra,* I thought without further delay. "Cassandra?" I called out, my tone raised a notch to a level of concerned alarm. My discerning awareness escalated to a dreaded unease. I stood still for a minute, listening for anything, but it was still too quiet for comfort.

The scent was still distinct while I hastily picked up my pace toward the center of the house, where the scent became stronger near the spiral staircase leading to the master bedroom on the third floor. Suddenly, a noise from upstairs froze me in place. It was subtle but detectable. My senses acutely waited to place the source. Something was dragging across the upper-level floor slowly. The noise stopped. I stood still, avoiding making any sound that would pinpoint my location. I could hear my own breathing and slowed it to barely a whisper. I felt locked in a duel wherein the first one to make a noise would disclose his or her location, resulting in unforeseen consequences. The dragging noise started up again, making it possible to determine the exact location. It was coming from the master bedroom. Someone was in the house, and it wasn't Cassandra or Linda—unless the noise was from someone dragging Cassandra or Linda. The fragrance of the perfume became more pronounced, drawing me cautiously up the winding stairs to the third landing, which encompassed the master suite. My curiosity was tempered with trepidation.

Upon reaching the third level, I glanced toward the master suite, noticing the door was slightly ajar, and I realized the room was dark inside. Upon further reflection, I realized it was the only room with no light—a perfect haven for an intruder, which obviously had come to fruition. My instructions to the maintenance crew were to make sure every light worked throughout the house and to program the timers at varying intervals so that two of the rooms would be lit, depending on the time of day. The master suite would turn on at dusk, along with the room across the hall. But the entire third floor was lit except for one room. The master bedroom's light was supposed to be on. The timer was set to trigger only the den and master suite lights at dinnertime. The timer could have been programmed incorrectly. Or worse, the timer had been purposely changed to allow the intruder to enter without detection. My concerns were bordering on obsessed worry,and I felt as if I were cast out on a sea of paranoia. I tried to come up with a more rational explanation. Maybe it was not maintenance's fault. Surely, I thought, it was just a burned-out light in the master suite. But why were the other three lights on, when it was just supposed to be one besides the master room? "This is crazy," I hastily blurted out, trying to rationalize the human error. "There is an intruder here, and I am wondering if maintenance was negligent." My mind was paralyzed with indecision, using the maintenance as a continued distraction while pondering my next action. I was certain I'd left instructions for two of the four lights to be programmed to alternately turn on throughout the day. Furthermore, I'd been insistent that maintenance frequently check the lights to avoid burnout. I'd made sure maintenance was to follow a schedule to change the lightbulbs every two weeks. There had been reports of vandalism in the area, which heightened my concern to follow a rigid schedule. For the time being, that was a moot point. There was a stranger in the house for reasons yet to be found out. I looked toward the master suite as I mentally psyched myself into the moment, ready to commit to my next step. *Did I really detect a noise, or was it just my overactive imagination?* I wasn't sure anymore. But I was sure about one basic fact: Linda was supposed to be there, and she wasn't there.

With a guarded stance, I walked toward the master suite's door, when I noticed something else in the room: a movement I had not noticed before. It was not obvious, but upon further scrutiny, I saw a subtle change in the density of the darkness that filled the room. I swore I could see a denser black form dart across. It was difficult to detect, but when I viewed more intently, I could discern a subtle change of contrast in the darkened room. I was not sure if it was just my imagination, but it appeared the slight opening of the bedroom door seemed a little wider now—maybe only an inch, but it was noticeable. I moved closer toward the room, wary of what might lie ahead. As I closed my distance to just a few yards from the door, a bony hand crept out over the outer edge of the door, its fingers curling over the trim. The fingers were as white as snow, and the skin was stretched tightly over the knuckles. The swollen blue veins were so visibly pronounced that the skin was barely noticeable.

A finger lifted from the doorframe, pointing in my direction, followed by a hoarse whisper. "Tony?" It must have sensed I was near, for its whisper turned into a high-pitched, edgy, cackling voice. "Cassandra is in here, Tony. Come in. Come in to see for yourself if you dare, Tony." Her crackling voice turned into shrill laughter, sending goose bumps up my spine. "Tony, come here, lover boy, and make love to me. I will be like nothing you've ever fucked. Fuck me until your penis rots, lover boy." The bony hand then withdrew away from the door, and the shrill turned into a whisper, repeatedly calling out my name until her whispered voice was barely audible when I drew in closer.

With only a yard left between me and the door, the whisper halted, and silence ensued, as if she were silently waiting for me to enter the room. My senses were sharpened as adrenaline rushed through my veins. My mind, however, was reeling from what I'd just witnessed. I wasn't sure of what I saw or heard, but I felt a sense of urgency to enter the room, half expecting to find Cassandra in harm's way. My thoughts became scattered in every direction, with each thread embedded in a blanket of fear. If she was in the room, was she held captive? Was she in danger? Was she hurt? Or was she already dead? My fears drove me to burst into the room, and I found myself enclosed in a tomb-like pitch-black darkness void of any discernible light. Treading blindly while trying to navigate through the darkness, I felt for the drapes, which I assumed hung over a patio door. My hands groped around until I managed to find the drawstrings, and I quickly opened the drapes, allowing the brightness from the full moon to fill the room. The light was enough for me to be able to glance around in search of any intruder. No one was in the room.

I stood still for a few moments, my senses acutely tuned. I again caught the scent but was still unable to pinpoint its source. I was frozen in place, motionless, waiting in the shadowy light from the moon's glow, listening for any sound or subtle movement, but I sensed none. I found a wall switch and tried to turn it on. I was surprised when light appeared. As soon as the lights revealed the entire room, the fragrance left me immediately. The bed in front of me was empty, but it held the impression of something or someone who had lain on it. A strong sensation crawled up my spine, a feeling that I was being watched by a presence somewhere in the room or an adjoining room. I turned toward the doorway and passed the bed, and in doing so, I saw a red petal on the bed cover, almost hidden by the pillow. I rushed to the bedside, and surrounding the petal I saw another impression of someone who had sat on the bed. I felt the area around the impression and noticed it was still warm. I searched for a note, a message to confirm someone had been there recently. If it was Cassandra, was my journey to Neverland to resume once again beginning now, or has fate decided otherwise, to swiftly end this journey once and for all? Was this the moment when my journey would continue and I would travel to that dimension with no constraints, to Neverland and Cassandra, so our souls could bond once again filled with varied emotions of wonder and discovery despite being disposed to apertures of horror? Or had fate's unpredictability finally decide to deal its final card to end the game, claim victory, and vanquish us, breaking the bond, with each of us cast aside, hurled in an opposite direction, contained within a vacuum with no definite purpose?

Wishing fervently that Cassandra was near, I called out, "Hello!" I heard the faint echo reverberating from the master bath. I felt I had to find the source of the fragrance. I visually surveyed the suite and the master bath only to find nothing else out of the ordinary. As I entered the bedroom again, I inspected the room and noticed the numerous paintings on the wall. *Odd I did not notice this before.* There was another painting hidden in the corner wall adjacent to the patio door. As I moved closer, I realized it was a picture. The corners of the frame revealed aged, worn edges. My eyes scanned the picture, taking in a sense of its abundant history. The picture was an old framed shot of a woman from an earlier time, decades ago—based on her clothes, I guessed the 1930s or earlier. As I looked closer, I became aware of the woman's resemblance to Cassandra. The picture was withered and faded because of time. I carefully removed it from the frame for a closer look. The picture was discolored, making it difficult to be 100 percent certain, but the resemblance was close enough that the woman could have been a close relative. I scrutinized the picture with more earnestness. A date was scribbled at the bottom of the picture, dulled from time. From what I could decipher, the date was from the early 1930s, or it could have been the 1920s. Behind the young lady stood a handsome, distinguished gentleman holding the lady in his arms. Based on their serene expressions, I assumed they were either married or a couple romantically involved. Upon further inspection, I noticed a slight swelling in the woman's midsection. It was not due to excessive fat, for the rest of the woman's physique was trim and fit. Was it possible the woman was pregnant? If so, then based on the morals from that decade, I assumed the two were married, and the gentleman was the father of the baby.

I saw an old newspaper clipping on the floor beside my foot. I assumed it had come loose and fallen while I was removing the picture. I bent down to the floor and picked up the newspaper clipping, which was a news story of several paragraphs. Unfortunately, the clipping was badly tattered and worn and revealed no date. The condition of the article didn't matter. Nothing could have deterred me as I proceeded to carefully open the folded article. I read it, trying to absorb every legible word, hoping for some insight and realizing the paper might be the first real evidence that could lead me down a path of profound discovery. The article was in much worse shape than I'd initially perceived. Only portions of the article were readable; it was almost impossible to combine into any form of relevant meaning. From what I could read, it was apparent three parties were involved in the news story: a female and two males. There was some form of altercation, and the police were called, along with an ambulance. Therefore, my assumption was some form of violence involving injury. I continued reading the article, which proved even more difficult to interpret with consistency. I read on and encountered a paragraph that mentioned the impacted parties. The article was torn in several places, making it almost impossible to discern the names and location. I was able to read just a few letters of one of the involved parties' names: *Cas.*

Could it be Cassandra? There was a resemblance in the photo, but it was too vague to say with certainty. Despite the vagueness, I searched the following paragraphs in the article with the hope of something more revealing. An address appeared, but it was too worn from age to clearly interpret except for one part of a word that was fairly distinct and devoid of any damage: *Neve.* Another word came into view with some clarity: *Canyon.* I could barely control my hope with the clues in front of me. There was something there that had enormous implications. Was there a reference to Cassandra and Neverland? My hope fueled my certainty that something profound was there. If what I assumed was correct, then my journey, at least in part, was based on reality, supported by facts that gave it a degree of authenticity based on the article in front of me. More importantly, there now was substantial evidence that supported the realness of Cassandra and Neverland. It was a stretch, I admitted, but it was the first legitimate clue that had verifiable substance.

My jubilance was dampened, however, by the photo. If that was Cassandra in the photo, then she was pregnant and most likely married. If that were true, why the intimate dreams? Was it possible this was the house the article was referring to? My heart was racing with the possibilities. But more questions abounded. If she was pregnant, was the man in the photo the father of the unborn? I viewed the photos again. *The man—who is he? The jawline.* I went to the master bath and looked in the mirror. I saw a vague resemblance. "No way!" I exclaimed in disbelief. The concept of the male in the photo being me was too far-fetched to be even remotely plausible. I reviewed the article again. The paragraph about the injuries was too faded. There was no further legible information on the results of the injuries. I had no clue what had happened to the two in the photo.

I read the portions of the remainder of the article that were still legible. There was enough decipherable information to reveal profound rumors. The rumors were plentiful—a deranged love affair, talk of a dark paranormal connection surrounding the female and her lover. The female's closest confidante disclosed that the woman had psychic abilities and was part of an occult group that dated back centuries. Rumor had it that the woman and her lover were involved in some form of ritual to connect with spirits of those deceased decades ago. I was well aware of how rumors could become exaggerated from the truth and took the rumors as fantasies, claims that could never be justified. But what if there was a connection? A part of me had an uncanny feeling that the rumors held some basis of fact that could provide insight to the unfathomable mystery. The notion consumed me. There was a paragraph toward the end that hinted at the possibility of paranormal involvement, but it went on to conclude that the innuendos were unfounded and just hearsay. It appeared the couple and the supposed lover vanished. There was no evidence of medical treatment. There were no emergency reports or rumors about the couple being treated by medics or of any transport arriving at the scene. The couple just disappeared without a trace. The husband escaped, leaving an empty trail devoid of clues; his whereabouts were unknown. My elated mood at discovering the article was inhibited by the new unanswered questions amid the swirl of unknowns.

I looked back on the bed, and the petal was no longer there. In its place, a trickle of blood formed—a few drops initially, followed by an unending flow collectively creating a maroon pool that seeped outward toward the outer edges of the bed. I fell back, nearly toppling over the floor lamp next to the balcony, and held on to the patio door to regain my balance. The blood, as red as the rose, spread out, covering the bed with a crimson blanket and nearly overflowing onto the carpet, when suddenly, the flow slowed. I stood there against the patio door, unable to move, transfixed by what I was viewing. The blood's coppery scent was prevalent, and within the blood, at the center, an image appeared of Cassandra. Her eyes were closed, periodically opening just enough to glance at me. Her eyes were a shadow, but there was a flicker of light upon her recognizing me, and slowly, she spoke. She let out a cry for help, followed by my name, before the scene disappeared.

A memory was triggered, brought forth with a jolt to my senses. One memory became several from seemingly nowhere; each carried an image and surged forward: a mirror with my reflection; a crazed look; a gun in my hand, pointed at myself; a distant voice; a cry from nearby; a shot; Cassandra; blood; and total confusion. I heard a vast array of noises around me. All called my name and screamed one word at me: "Why?" A shadow appeared in the corner; only the eyes were visible, knifelike beacons. The figure just stood there, waiting and staring at me. One final scene of me emerged. My eyes were vacant, frozen in place with no movement, not even a blink. The pupils were fixed in place, open wide. The shock of what had happened poured into my soul. It was too much to handle. I was unable to process it. I took a one-way journey to another place, a retreat into a time filled with laughter and intimate moments between Cassandra and me. The images, one by one, provided a brief glance into a portal of a time past before fading into obscurity, each dropping from sight. The first scene disappeared, followed by the next scene. The scenes collectively revealed more, prompting me to reach out to try to hold on, trying to remember in more detail. Each image of Cassandra was tentatively suspended for a few seconds longer, as though it responded to my earnest request. Those extra few seconds were enough time to reveal more detail, delivering just enough to allow me to absorb the impact and revealing a frightening recollection, one tainted with desperation from injuries and blood seeping outward.

The figure from the shadow off in the corner, his eyes sharpened like a knife, intense, focused on me lying in a pool of blood. The stranger came forward just enough out of the shadow to partially reveal his face. I looked in his direction just as he stepped back into the shadows. It was too sudden. It couldn't be. For that split second, his identity changed from one face to another. I knew each face, for one of the faces was mine. I shook my head vigorously, closing my eyes for a split second before reopening them. To my relief, the two-faced identity had resorted back to that of the stranger. I could not fathom why my face was connected to the stranger. I waited for a few more minutes to confirm that my face would not appear again as part of the stranger's haunting soul. Yet my fear was that once I could vividly recall the memories and any immediate details of the stranger, once the recognition took hold, there was the possibility, even remotely, that I was part of the stranger's profile. The instinctive part of me knew of the potential consequences, the horrid nightmares that would infuse my soul, if found guilty of a connection with the stranger. But for now, that recollection and the resulting verdict were vehemently held back.

But I couldn't shake what I'd just viewed, even though it had been for a brief moment: his appearance; his face changing, alternating between two identities; and the two faces, mine and the stranger's. Each prompted me to recall terrifying images just for an instant before they could fully materialize with horrific memories. For that split second, right before the image would present itself with shocking visuals, my instinct for self-preservation would suddenly kick into overdrive and force the image to close and disappear. My denial was immediate; my mind vehemently attempted to submerge the image before full recognition. My recollection was already fading fast from a deeply rooted reluctance to accept what I was viewing. The wall was slamming shut, absolving me of any traces of the revelations. I felt drained as remnants of my recollection still hung on. I was unable to trust the horrid, fragmented residuals, unable to comprehend the unthinkable, which left me drained. Their errand was accomplished, as attested by the anguished look on my face, where melancholy was firmly implanted as a permanent fixture.

The brisk night breeze coming in from the patio helped bring my senses full circle. The scene from that evening was vivid, and I immediately got to my feet and looked toward the bed. The bed was undisturbed, with no evidence of what I'd experienced earlier. Everything seemed normal, as when I'd first entered the house that afternoon. I felt faint, so I went to the bathroom, turned on the facet, and put my head under the faucet to help my senses reawaken. I grabbed a towel and wiped down my neck and face. I looked in the mirror and saw a ghostly image starring back: a stranger, pale and shaken. My eyes showed the strain of weariness. Cassandra was in trouble. My anticipation was fused with apprehension as to what my next encounter would bring. I walked out of the bathroom back to the bed and saw the picture from the wall on the bed, next to the newspaper article. I wondered how the picture and clipping had wound up on the bed. I hadn't been near the bed since I entered the master room that evening. But I could not say with certainty.

The scenes I had just viewed were a constant reminder of the recent dream's abhorrent themes. The themes reflected the changes that had violated the continuous harmony of my initial dreams. The dreams had changed, with unpredictable, aberrant diversions, transforming from a pattern of harmonious bliss to a theme of multiple dimensions, each infused with nightmarish scenes of demonic forms, murder, and mayhem filled with hellish intent. The suddenness and repetitious intensity of the diversion had impacted the journey between the alternate dimensions, making the voyage a nightmare of the damned. The maelstrom from the surreal vortex of the journey had impacted me with uncertainty, blurring the line between reality and fantasy. My doubts of my own sanity had me constantly guessing, and I feared the delineation between fact and fiction had fused into a virtual world of surrealism. I walked over to the bed with forced reassurance and bent down to pick up the picture and article. I saw a note resting under the picture. A drop of blood was on the top of the note, still wet to the touch. At that point, I felt unable to generate any reaction as I numbly swept up the note and unfolded it: "Never leave without a promise to return. Our next journey is the key to our salvation before time escapes us." Then it hit me. I sat down, stunned, too tired to think, but I knew our next journey would be filled with eminent danger.

36

Unannounced Visit from Matt

Too exhausted to expend another ounce of thought, I succumbed to a numbness that swept through my senses. I descended the stairs toward the main floor, set the alarms, and left through the side door. Slowly, I walked along the winding driveway, reached my Maxima, and started the drive home to whatever awaited me. Exhaustion overwhelmed me, numbing my senses and physical being. I felt as though my mental state were perched precariously on the edge, wavering in either direction, and the next journey would decide my fate. I'd either continue pursuing the journey with Cassandra by my side or trip over the edge, and the journey would end with no salvation to save me from the pits of hell— from damnation and an existence without a soul and with nothing but agonizing pain and despair for an eternity. But truth be told, my exhaustion was so consuming that for the moment, I did not have the energy to even care about the outcome.

I was ready to succumb to the weariness from the last few days. Though I was totally drained, I could not sleep. Unsteady at the wheel from the debilitating effects of the earlier episodes, I finally took a breath as I pulled into my garage and sat there while the garage door descended. I sat with my head on the steering column as the images of that night paraded in front of me in an endless stream. I closed my eyes, wishing the images would disappear so I could unwind and finally sleep. I recalled the stranger in the corner—a stranger with a distant recollection, a remote recognition too far away to recall. No matter the faint reminiscence, the memory was far enough away to still remain a stranger. The look in the stranger's eyes had been that of a madman, a look of pure evil, of hell's appetite for pain. His pierce had been so direct that it conveyed a portent of lunacy. My mind, at that moment, quit, unable to process anymore.

37

Another Letter from Matt

I dragged myself through the side entryway into the kitchen. The lights were on in the adjoining living room. Too tired to even be concerned, I assumed I must have left the lights on during my hasty retreat that morning. But upon further thought, I realized I normally made it a point to turn the lights off before I left, especially if for a prolonged period of time. I revisited the kitchen to detect any signs of intrusion. Everything seemed as it had been when I left that morning. Yet I had an uncanny sense that I had a visitor there—a visitor with the wrong intentions.

I caught a footprint off to the side by the kitchen wall leading to the dining room. The dining room wasn't lit. As I took my first step into the dining area, I turned on the overhead lights. The dining room table was set for a dinner for two. My thoughts scrambled, trying to make sense of what was in front of me. My vision distorted just for a minute, unable to grasp the view-facing me. I felt a faint echo of moments past. A slice of memory hidden for so long tried desperately to surface, breaking through one of the fissures forming in the wall that held back the memories. The wall of hidden memories was soon to collapse, its structure weakened from the multitude of aging faults. A memory struggled to break free, bearing a barrage of baggage of dreaded moments from a time past which I barely survived. My memory then cleared when that one moment surfaced. I had a mixed reaction and was unable to untangle my emotions until the cobwebs fully cleared. Then it hit me: that moment past when everything became detached upon that isolated event. *The letter. It couldn't be. Been too long. Cassandra's ex. The letter from Matt.* My mind seized up, remembering the letter. *Dinner for two.* I remembered his promise to show up as a surprise when I least expected it. Well, that part of the promise was obviously true. I saw a note by the head of the dining room table, next to a covered plate. I stood there with the same hesitation that had plagued me when I read his first letter from what seemed like ages ago. So Matt was here, assuming that was who'd made this visit. But who was I conning? Of course it was him. It was a surprise dinner for two, with him as the unannounced guest.

I backed up a few paces as a mental preparation in anticipation of receiving dreaded news from the letter I was about to read—just like last time. In a repeat performance, I froze with reluctance to face news I did not want to invite into my life, especially that night, when every bone in my body ached for some sleep. Yet Matt's visit would revolve around Cassandra and me. That fact drew me in as a sacrificial lamb to incur the madman's crazed notions. With a mix of crazed fear and pure hatred, I brought the letter closer to detect any hint of Cassandra's scent. It was faint, but from what I could detect, it was the same fragrance Cassandra wore. With nervous fingers, I was able to open the letter, and I started reading.

Well, hello, Mr. Prince. What happened to our planned engagement? I told you we would be meeting for dinner at your place. I just didn't mention when. That shouldn't matter, Tony. It is your responsibility to be here when I show up. But, Tony, you weren't here. I personally prepared and brought in a six-course meal just for this special occasion. Maybe you didn't take me seriously. You should have, Mr. Prince. Now guess who will pay the price for your no-show. Do I have to mention her name? Shouldn't have to. This is a continual habit with you, Tony. You keep fucking up. Not taking full responsibility for your failed appearances. How many times does Cassandra have to pay the price for your failures? Look at yourself, Tony. You promised her a field of dreams. Dreams that would provide a magical carpet ride for her adventurous soul. But the truth is undeniable. You have led her to a field of broken promises. To a field of nightmares. How does that make you feel? To be a continual failure to your princess? Yet she keeps telling me she loves you. That is not logical. Your actions and failed responsibilities, your continual broken promises, and your departures at the most inopportune moments, leaving Cassandra to weep with her own sorrow of loneliness, do not warrant such devotion from her.

You should be wondering if your fiancée is still alive. If I was there now at this time, I would expect you to ask this question. If you decided to remain mute, that would confirm my suspicion of you I have held since I first witnessed your actions with Cassandra. In other words, Mr. Tony, that would confirm to me and Cassandra that you are a phony. A complete lying bullshitter. It does not fool me. Cassandra may fall for your BS, but I see right through it. It is too bad you weren't here, for as you can see, what I had planned was at least an hour's dialogue. An hour over a glass of wine before we got down to business. I left the carving knives there as a remembrance. Be sure they are there when I show up again. And I assure you, Tony, that you will not want to miss our next engagement. The consequences will be deadly if you miss our next dinner invite. And this time, be sure you have that French wine you ordered for Cassandra and yourself when you were seated in the atrium at the grand ballroom in Neverland. I was there, Tony. Surprised? I am everywhere, Tony. When you least expect it. Except for this dinner engagement. I'm still deciding on your punishment. By the time you read this, I will have made that decision. Now, open the dinner trays. I will then let you be. Probably best to let all this sink in. Next time, Tony, be present when I arrive. Or else someone dies.

As suggested, I moved to where the dinners sat. I put the letter down, almost making a decision to burn the letter. But I decided to keep it to reexamine once my alarmed senses settled. I opened the side entrée. Hidden beneath lettuce were two fingers, the forefinger from each hand. I picked them up to find they were fingers from an infant. Bile rose from my stomach when I realized they were from the baby. I immediately turned my vision toward the covered main entrée. I couldn't bring myself to lift the cover. I suspected something hideous from a madman. No matter my devotion, I didn't have the nerve to see for myself. I was too exhausted and nauseated to handle what I expected.

I returned to the kitchen for one reason: to grab as many trash bags as necessary to trash everything on the dining room table. Then I would drive to a Dumpster several miles out to unload the pathetic nightmare. Yet there was something I needed to do before I started to discard everything. I walked to the end of the table and placed my hand on the cover of the main entrée. My hand rested there; I was not sure if my nervous exhaustion was able to handle what I suspected. If I didn't go through with it, then maybe the madman had a point. Maybe I was a gutless soul always looking for an easy way out. I dug further, trying to reach my inner strength. I had to know about Cassandra and the baby. There was no way out. There was no escape. I had to know the truth, even if the impact would crush my soul and drive me to a psych ward. I lifted the lid slowly at first, which only made the ordeal more painful. I then lifted the cover swiftly and saw what was on the plate: a decapitated head. I dropped the lid to the side from shock. I looked again and saw that it was a fake head. It was made out of synthetic rubber. I then picked up the fingers again and realized they too were fake. I threw the dinner plate across the dining room, and it crashed against the window. A *sick joke*. My anger lashed out, and I swept everything off the table. I then saw another note next to the object of the sick joke. I opened it immediately.

Surprised, Tony? As I said, next time, you will need to be here, or else this will be real. It will be Cassandra's or the baby's head. Your call, Mr. Prince. Cassandra is still alive. At least she is breathing. The baby—well, I mean your baby. You will know next time we meet. But as far as you are concerned, they might as well be dead, for you will never see them again. Your only hope now, Mr. Tony, is to save them from the executioner's blade. Until next time. Bring the wine. I have a feeling you will need it.

I was numb. I couldn't think anymore. I needed to sweep the mess in the dining room into several garbage bags and drive out to a Dumpster several miles outside of town. It took me a full hour to pick up the mess, bag it, vacuum the room, and lug it to the car. I hopped in my car and drove out to the dump several miles away. I was running on pure adrenaline by then, and my primary focus was on tossing that sick joke into the Dumpster. It took me just fifteen minutes to ditch everything and then another thirty minutes to drive back home. I had left the lights on and the doors unlocked, but at that early hour, I did not give a damn. I would have killed any intruder who made an entrance at that late hour. I reentered my home and went back to the same routine, refusing to let the sick joke invade my space that night. Fortunately, my mind was so numb that I simply put the incident out of my mind and resorted to labeling it a freak accident.

38

A Temporary Respite for Reflection

I walked through the living room toward the spiral staircase to the master suite on the third level. After climbing up with strenuous effort, I finally reached the upper level and walked into the suite. I was bone tired, still filled with a neurotic tension that kept any form of sleep at bay. I walked toward the wet bar by the patio and poured myself two shots of brandy. "To hell with the shots!" I shouted with anger, and I grabbed the half-filled bottle and drank the brandy listlessly, feeling the sudden tranquil effort with every swallow. After finishing the brandy, I undressed and tossed my clothes over the hassock in the corner. I switched on the bedside light and turned off the ceiling lights. I sat there on the edge of the bed, listening to the distant waves washing ashore. The curtains to the balcony were open, and I glanced out toward the dark expanse of the ocean, catching the reflection of the moon's glow upon the ocean's surface. I saw an image of Cassandra standing on the beach with the tide rushing in, covering her feet and rising up toward her calves. Her eyes connecting with me as she turned away and followed the tide, retreating back into the ocean. I stood up to take a closer look but realized it was just a hopeless mirage. I folded down the blankets, ready to succumb to a somber sleep, and quickly looked for any note before finally giving in to night's embrace.

The morning greeted me with what should have been a beautiful sunrise over the horizon. The sun cast a shimmering silver glow over the ocean's surface. But the harrowing experience of last night clouded my reception that morning. The seagulls were communicating among themselves as they swooped down to pluck their breakfast before another attempt with aerial precision. My exhaustion was still prevalent, and my mind was still numb from last night's encounter. The feeling was compounded by the effects from the last several nights of unsettling events. My mind was fragmented from the fog-induced traumatic episodes from the last several days of spent energy. My reserves were totally depleted, and I anxiously worried about my much-needed stamina required for the upcoming events at work. Maybe I should call upon Linda, I thought, for she had the necessary determination, commitment, and focus to assume my responsibilities for the next few days. But lately, she too had appeared as drained as I felt at that moment. There was no one else who had the wherewithal to assume the daily duties Linda and I carried out.

As I lifted my weary body from the bed, just that minimal effort felt like a monumental task, causing a vertigo sensation. The room tilted oddly as I tried to focus. I walked toward the bathroom with an unsteady movement, intent on taking a cold shower to stimulate me—a shock to my system to wash away the weariness. I stepped into the shower, turned on the freezing-cold water, and dowsed my head, which sent a shock wave through me. The weariness drowned as my body responded, rebounding with a surge. I turned the hot faucet on to avoid prolonged exposure to the icy water and felt an immediate relief as the warmth soothed its way through my system. The combination of cold followed by hot had an extraordinary effect of restoration both physically and mentally.

Feeling refreshed, with my senses totally aware, I picked up the fragrance again. It was the same one from last night. I stood there naked in the shower, not moving a muscle, expecting the unexpected. A tiny image appeared before me like a halo of light that opened to full size before me. Cassandra was there before me, naked. But something was wrong. As she stood before me with tears descending down her cheeks before being absorbed by the running water, her body turned to a deep purplish blue. As more time passed, I realized her body was covered with deep bruises. There was not a spot that was not covered with a bruise. Her face looked swollen. Her eyes revealed her pain and anguish, a look of desperation and surrender. I reached out toward her.

Upon my touch, she screamed out with holy terror from the pain. I withdrew immediately and stood there reeling from shock. "My God, Cassandra, who did this to you?" She couldn't speak. I saw blood oozing from a wound by her ribs. She came closer to me, carefully avoiding any painful embrace. She leaned her head on my shoulder, with her cheek resting close to my face. I felt her warm breath on my neck, and the sensation was soothing to my soul. "Cassandra, did he do this to you?" I received no response again. Her tears, burdened with despair, dropped painfully onto my shoulder.

She lifted her mouth closer to my ear to whisper, "I love you, Tony. Soon we will join for an eternity." Then her breathing became raspy as she struggled to breathe. I desperately wanted to hold her and protect her, but I couldn't. The pain would have been intolerable.

"I love you, Cassandra." My own tears formed at the sight of her bruises. She leaned in close to me, still avoiding contact, and softly pressed her lips to mine. Our kiss traversed through every neuron, fusing our life forces into one, and we became aware of the truth that defined eternity, back to the birth of the heavens, when our souls bonded. Our love was unmeasurable, my commitment was unconditional, and my passion was endless. Our lips parted, and I saw the miracle. Her bruises were disappearing.

She came to me, embracing me, and whispered in my ear, "Your love healed me but only for a brief time. I will die without you." Then she vanished, leaving me in stunned silence.

I didn't know what to do. I had no awareness of where to look for Cassandra and Neverland. But I knew both were real. What I didn't know was if they were real now. The answer lay in the journey and the house on Canyon Ridge Trails. There was nothing I could do by standing there under the shower. Still stunned by the recent episode, I left the shower and used the largest towel I could find to wrap myself thoroughly as I dried myself to retain the warmth that was seeping from my body. Feeling overwhelmed was a constant now, undermining my effort to ease my precarious sense of balance perched high on a precipitous tightrope over an abyss of my deepest fears. My keen, intuitive awareness heightened my alarm, triggering a level of urgency at the newest revelation.

I hastily descended down to the first level toward the kitchen. I felt I had one foot on the accelerator with my other foot applied to the brake as my mind raced frantically to seek a way to find Cassandra. I was without a direction to proceed. I had several facts floating on a reservoir of still-unexplored information I was desperate for. I just needed time, but time for Cassandra was in short supply. Rushing in would be a waste of effort and result in a closed-minded endeavor done with immediacy, a vain effort. I might overlook clues vital for a solution. I had to retain an objective perception while trying to uncover clues to provide more insight, which obviously consumed more time. My problem was now compounded because I had limited time to find Cassandra, but I needed more time. An interim answer was the journey, but the unpredictability of the timeliness of being transported to Cassandra made that option a risk with no planned alternative. For the present, I had to make time for fact finding and hope fate would arrange my next journey that day.

My apprehension curbed my appetite since the unsettled feeling in the pit of my stomach was still hanging on. I decided on just a cup of regular coffee. With coffee in hand, I walked to the outside patio to view the vivid greenery of the surrounding oak trees and the tranquil blue ocean. Standing there, recalling my initial dreams and everything experienced with Cassandra was simpler. My nostalgia took hold, and I realized how the simplest things in life were taken for granted and were the ones we missed the most when life's complexities took center stage.

The turn of events from the past weeks had presented me with a multiplicity of new complexities that had enormous implications, ones that would decide my outcome. The decisions to be made would impact the direction I took from there on. That I was sure of. The direction I sailed would depend on the course set for me by the direction of the winds of fate. Yet that part was still uncertain. A definite change was in the offering, but the extent of the change was still unknown to me. Cassandra was the centerpiece and catalyst of the change. She was the epicenter from which my new direction would evolve. The nature of the change I felt was still undetermined, and the action I decided on to untangle the aberrant circumstances to unravel the mystery would decide the extent of the change and the bond that united Cassandra and me. I had hardly anything to go on to start the decryption process, just a few clues. Upon further scrutiny, it was obvious from the imposed time constraints that the journey was my best option. But that premise was based on the journey beginning that day. I had to rely on fate's ultimate vision for Cassandra and me. If our soulful bond was to be eternal, then I had to believe the journey would be there for me at the usual place and time. The journey was the vital link. It was important to adhere to the same pattern and schedule that had been the 3he portal where Cassandra and the village existed.

I stood watching the peaceful setting of the morning sunrise, my heart torn in every direction and bleeding. I let out a longing sigh. If only I could wish for all the complexities to vanish, removing all the obstacles, so Cassandra and I could unite to finally find our rightful place where the only thing that mattered was the love we cherished. *Why is it that the greatest loves shared between two souls are always so tragic? Do we always have to go through a series of hellish trials just to test our devotion? Are these the rules set forth by fate? Is the treacherous run really worth the treasure chest of gold if we survive the hellish journey?* Each tale that presented two lovers who survived the challenges devised by fate's cruel sense of humor always resulted in a newfound treasure of the true revelation of love and devotion. That I was most assured of. I was convinced the cherished love that bonded Cassandra and me would exceed everything fate expected. Once we passed through the wall of hellish torment, we would not only surpass the gift bestowed upon us but also exemplify a new meaning of the true essence of love. Our love would persist beyond the end of time. We had a bond that could not be broken. I missed Cassandra with an aching longing. There was nothing I could do at the moment but wait for the journey to take me back to Cassandra and to that place, Neverland, which I felt was my home.

My soulful longing kept me in a hypnotic fugue, and I needed to push that reverie to the background to resume later. I realized I could do nothing now except push forward with the day's events. Catching up on the tasks facing me that day was necessary to be able to engage the journey when fate handed me the tickets for the next eventful trip to our soulful reunion.

I finished my cup of coffee, finished dressing for work, and drove to the train depot to catch the local train that stopped at each stop rather than catching the express. That would double my time to the downtown station and allow me the extra time essential to examine each event from the last several weeks. The local train arrived ten minutes later, and I boarded the last car, which, at that time in the morning, had the fewest passengers. Only a few of the seats were taken, and I took the seat closest to the car door.

My mind ventured back to each dream episode that had contained an aberrant diversion over the past several weeks, searching for any relevance or pattern, anything that could shed some light on the complex yet intriguing mystery. Each episode, at first glance, seemed unrelated, but upon further inspection, the connection, though faint, started to appear. The connection dawned on me out of nowhere: the midnight ghost train was the connection between the recent aberrant dreams. Each episode over the last number of weeks had included a scene from the ghost train or an element construed as a change resulting from the ghost train. It was a gradual change; at times, it was difficult to detect the connection, but it soon became obvious. The phantom train had one purpose in the dreams: to escort its passengers on a one-way journey to one destination, where judgment was passed for those whose current existence had ended. The judgment would decide the next final destination: one filled with heaven's wonders or with hell's torment of the damned. It was the phantom train of the dead. Death was the connection. Yet why did the pattern of the dreams change? Cassandra and I were connected and had been for what seemed an eternity. Yet there were many conflicts between the initial and recent journeys that could not easily be explained by pure logic. I felt that another factor was causing the aberration, something beyond logical reasoning, on a level that exceeded our ability to comprehend.

My mind sensed the complexities underlying the anomaly of variables, freeing itself from the constraints of conventional rationale and stretching its limits to a new set of logic that expanded our concept of our universe to a new level where our universe was just one variable in the theorem of quantum physics. A new revelation came into focus after further deliberation, one with an obvious certainty: something had happened along the way on the journey—a mixup in the universe's signals. I sensed that somehow, someway, the journey had taken a detour that wasn't meant to be—a detour through hell's front door that had allowed whatever abounded in that realm to latch on and be carried to the intended destination. The explained the sudden appearances of the ghostly midnight transports I encountered once in Neverland, ferrying passengers to hell-bound destinations. The universal mixup seemed to have resulted in a fused state of what was real and what was not real, wherein the elements had been shifted to form a different reality that was not meant to be. It was a displacement of the components caused by a slight miscalculation resulting in a fusion of heaven and hell.

My dreamlike siesta jolted back to the present when I heard the train whistle signaling the train's arrival at the main station. Before the train slowed, I rose to begin my hasty walk through the adjacent cars toward the front car to get ahead of the unusually heavy passenger traffic because of the late arrival to the station. I was due to be at the company in one hour to meet with Linda to make sure that all the documents were in order and that we were prepared to address the issues delivered to us by a courier yesterday afternoon. The main issue was regarding the schedule for construction. Because of our backlog, we'd originally planned to start construction in the fall, starting in September. However, because of the timeliness of their supply chain with their vendors, they had asked us to start in the first part of summer, which was one month from now.

I met Linda upon arriving in the conference room. She had all the documents and plans arranged. I was both upset and relieved to see Linda. "Where have you been? You were supposed to meet me at the house on Canyon Ridge."

Linda responded with a slightly exasperated tone, "Did I commit to meeting you? I honestly do not remember. I apologize for the miscommunication. You should have called me."

My irritation was short-lived, as I was relieved to see Linda safe, especially after the gothic experience I'd witnessed there. "A miscommunication. At least you are safe, Linda. I was worried about you. But there is something that occurred at the house that we need to discuss. It involves our dreams. We were supposed to meet to talk about our shared dreams. Unfortunately, that was delayed because of our hectic schedule. But we need to meet this week. I need to disclose what happened at the house and its connection to our dreams." Linda just looked at me with an inquisitive yet puzzled look. Before she had a chance to respond, I said, "Linda, we don't have time now, and we need some time to discuss. I was hoping you would be free on Friday to meet." Linda sensed the sincerity of my request and accepted my request with a relieved yes.

Linda and I sat down to discuss making her senior partner to head up the division for showcasing art deco homes situated throughout the canyons overlooking the Pacific. I expected an enthusiastic response, but instead, Linda seemed continually preoccupied with other issues that seemed to be draining her of her vitality. I finally decided to talk to her about her distractions. However, upon my doing so, she again complained of a severe migraine and asked for the rest of the day off. I told her to take a week if needed to take care of whatever issues she had. Without even a nod of acceptance, she just waved goodbye to me and took the remainder of the day off.

Weariness crept up on me as my adrenaline leveled off. The fatigue was returning, bringing with it a piercing headache, as if someone were driving a spike through my frontal lobe. I felt nauseated with a sense of vertigo, and wisely, I too decided to take the rest of the day off.

39

A Dialogue with an Acquaintance from a Prior Dream

Shortly after I left work, the headache disappeared, along with the nausea and vertigo. I felt better, but the fatigue stayed with me. It was Friday again, and I decided to use the free time for something productive. I would drive home from work, change into something less formal, and take the train from my town toward the last scheduled destination. I suspected the journey started sometime after my stop when I fell asleep. Usually, when I took the scheduled route to my town during the summer, it was still daylight, with twilight just beginning. It was a thirty-minute ride via the express train, and my home depot would appear just as the sun was within minutes of sinking down over the horizon. I usually fell asleep just after twilight made its initial appearance. That meant I was about twenty minutes into a restful nap before we came to my stop. On those occasions when the train ride was to be transformed into a journey to Neverland, I woke up and found myself a passenger on the journey well past twilight. Therefore, the journey must have started after my stop, which justified my decision to catch the train from my village and see when the journey would begin. Maybe changing the venue a bit would reveal a clue I desperately needed.

I knew the train's departure time from my village was at least an hour away. Putting that thought aside, I decided to take the next right off Route 1 and make a brief stop at the oceanfront restaurant to have time to think and concentrate without the constant interruption of traffic congestion. I needed time to think and plan for the unexpected. I also needed the temporary delay to shore up my nerve to face again the unexpected. Maybe I was losing my nerve. Enough had happened to wear me down to the core, and even the least unexpected event would hit me with an acute, hypersensitive reaction, resulting in pain and fear. That time, due to the Friday after-work crowd, the lot was busier than usual. I drove to the outer lot, parked, and briskly walked toward the entrance. Once inside, I waited until my favorite hostess appeared, and I greeted her with a kiss slightly on the cheek. As I did, I caught the familiar fragrance of perfume.

Shaken from the earlier image of Cassandra in harm's way, my nerves were on edge, too strung out to allow me a moment of solitude by the seaside table. I forewent the table and decided to take a seat in the lounge by the oceanfront. I ordered a double shot of brandy and sat there staring off over the blue Pacific, watching the sun drift slowly into late afternoon. My thoughts scrambled to Cassandra's image. If what I'd seen was indeed Cassandra, then she was close to the end. From what I'd seen, her reserves were near depletion, and I had to do something to save her. But what, and how? I had no way yet to locate the village or Cassandra. She was being victimized by Matt. Who was Matt, and what was his connection to Cassandra? But more importantly, why?

I rubbed my forehead, which was still tender from the acute headache I'd had at work that had prompted my early siesta. The other symptoms from earlier in the day, fortunately, refrained from making a repeat visit. A sudden chill hit me, causing me to shiver as if it were fifteen degrees cooler. The overhead lights dimmed, and it was difficult to see anything clearly. The lights soon returned to the comfortable setting, causing me to wonder why and who was adjusting the light settings. My distraction was soon interrupted when my peripheral vision noticed a couple arriving at the lounge. They sat off to my right, two seats from me. At first glance, they looked familiar, but my distraction took precedence. I was aware that my initial impression was most likely misguided due to the recent episode that morning. I heard an old melody striking a memory. It was a tune familiar to the melodies I had listened to before, but I could not pinpoint when. I absorbed the seductiveness of the saxophone's tune further with a hint of nostalgia. In front of me, toward the lounge entrance, I noticed a stage, where musical instruments rested against chairs situated in a circular fashion around a center podium that held a microphone. The arrangement resembled that of an orchestra, and the podium would accommodate a singer or band leader. Then where were all the orchestra players? I threw my hand in the air and let out a moan of exasperation. So far that evening, nothing made sense. I thought I was losing my mind.

The couple shifted their position, sitting adjacent to me. The male left for the restroom, while the young lady ventured out to the open patio to catch the view of the ocean. I saw a newspaper lying next to his drink. I'd not had a chance to read the news from that morning, so I slid the paper my way and unfolded it to the first page. Immediately, I noticed the main headline: "Manhunt Underway in Southern California: Two Seriously Injured." I did not remember anything from that morning's radio broadcasts about an incident of that magnitude. I read further and then noticed the date on the paper: 1930. I turned to the following page and saw the same date. *No way.* Maybe the gentleman was a hobbyist and kept papers from decades ago that were linked to a significant event. I kept reading.

> The attack occurred at the Paragon Ballroom, ten miles north of Santa Monica. A couple was attacked on the dance floor by an unknown assailant who is still at large. By witnesses' accounts, a couple was engaged in a suggestive slow dance, when a figure from a distant corner hidden in shadows turned on the victims and fired two shots. The young lady fell back, and the gentleman grabbed the assailant, fighting for the gun. During the struggle, the gun went off, and the intended victim fell to the floor, hanging on to the assailant's ankle. During the melee, with mounting chaos, the assailant slipped from the man's grasp and disappeared into the crowd.
>
> During the ensuing panic toward the exit, a few of the witnesses heard an ambulance off in the distance, with

each blip of the siren becoming louder as it neared the ballroom. The witnesses closest to the incident swarmed outside when the ambulance arrived, escorting the medics to where the bodies lay. But when the medics reached the ballroom, there were no bodies to be found, as if they had disappeared.

During the evening, several photographs were taken of the crowd, and there was one photograph of the couple who'd been attacked. I glanced toward the lower right corner below the article, and the photos were of Cassandra and me. I grabbed the paper and went toward the patio door, under the ceiling light, for a closer look. The photo was of me and Cassandra.

It was another jolt to my system, and my mind froze, numb. With a trance-like walk, I headed back to my spot at the lounge to inhale my vodka martini. I then realized the orchestra was back, and through the fog that permeated my senses, an image appeared before me of Cassandra, who spoke to me. "Hurry tonight." The orchestra played on with the same melodies Cassandra and I had danced to.

The gentleman returned from the restroom, joining his companion as she returned from outside by the oceanfront. I overheard them say the attack had occurred last weekend. As I heard their voices and caught a close look at their faces, I remembered them from the dream at the lounge; they'd noticed me while I asked for the glasses of wine. They recognized me and greeted me by my first name.

The lady turned toward me with dreamy blue-gray eyes and spoke with a hint of a southern accent. "Welcome back, Tony. Where is she? Don't act so startled. Where is Cassandra?" Then the gentleman turned my way, dropping his glass upon realizing I was one of the victims in the shooting. They went to the nearest pay phone on the wall to dial the police.

The room suddenly changed shape, and the two faded into thin air. The room took on a different shade of lighting, and I found myself at the table overlooking the ocean. The waitress came by and asked me if I'd made up my mind as to having dinner. I looked at her, realizing the waitress who normally waited on me was nowhere to be found. I asked where Claudette was, only to find out she'd taken the day off. I noticed the clock on the wall. It couldn't have been that late. I felt as if I'd just arrived. One reminder immediately surfaced: the train. *Can't miss the scheduled stop.* I had to get to my village depot. Too much depended on this excursion. After responding with a quivering voice that I'd decided not to have dinner, I finished the last of my drink, paid the bill with tip in cash, and hurriedly exited, realizing it was already past seven thirty.

40

Return to Cassandra, Neverland and the Ghost Train

It was imperative I catch that train, for I had an unsurmountable feeling of pending revelations that would uncover a critical link to the underpinnings of my journey. It was essential that my journey commence, as I was aware the revelations might only be presented on the journey. I ran to my car and tore out of the lot, swerving onto the outer lane. Narrowly missing a semi, I merged to my left to take the shortcut to my home. I'd had too much to drink. No, the shock to my system overloaded with adrenaline was causing sensory overload, driving me furiously toward my house. I looked at my watch and realized I did not have enough time to reach my house, change, and drive to the depot. That would have taken me thirty minutes out of my way. I jerked the wheel sharply to the right as the exit to the downtown depot came into view. An accident was straight ahead, and a traffic jam was starting, so I maneuvered my car toward the side street to bypass the accident. I had forty-five minutes left. I was at least thirty minutes away because I had to travel through reduced-speed areas. I could not afford to be caught speeding. I weaved from one street to another and finally caught sight of the steeple that sat on top of the village hall next to the depot. I had fifteen minutes to spare. I raced the last few miles, and I heard my train off in the distance, announcing its approach. I turned left into the depot parking lot, which, for some strange reason, was still full. I turned my car around, drove into the adjacent lot, and finally found a space. I could hear the train clearly as it entered the village limits. I jostled the door handle, opened the door, left everything in the backseat, and locked everything up.

I ran toward the depot as I saw the train pulling in and then grinding to a halt. I had just a few minutes to spare. There was no time to purchase a ticket at the depot. I would take my chances with purchasing a ticket on the train, hoping I could catch a conductor before my anticipated journey began. I caught the last car as I heard the train depart for the next stop. I searched every compartment to see if by chance I could find Cassandra or detect any clue as a reminder to meet that night.

I eventually found the same seat, the one with a black smudge on the bottom corner. It seemed odd that I always was able to find the same compartment and the same seat, which mysteriously was always vacant. As the train left, I looked out at the twilight-endowed sky, with the lights from my village dwindling into tiny, twinkling sparks while the train picked up speed. The day's tension eased as the frenzy of the workplace mellowed into a hypnotic draw of complete calm. The calm was a welcome relief, but the rapidity of the calm sweeping over me was similar to a drug-induced sedation. Alarmed by the suddenness, I was not able to resist the pull of weariness as the fog of sleepiness overcame me and opened the gates to the familiar dreamland.

It must have been less than an hour before I reawakened, since the night still hung on to the remnants of twilight. I looked out my window to catch the twilight slide into the night's camouflage to reenergize for the next cycle of dawn. When night finally took dominance, the recurrent feeling of unfamiliarity crossed me once more, and I knew somehow that I was entering that mystical zone again. I was keenly aware that I might be losing my senses, but a heightened excitement entranced me and kept the repeated journey into the abyss of the unknown very much alive. I looked at the seat adjacent to me and found the petal. Swiftly, I embraced it, lifting it with both palms as if it were so fragile the slightest breeze would absorb its very essence. I brought the petal close and caught its scent as it enveloped me with Cassandra's exotic fragrance. At that moment, it did not matter how or when she'd left that token. The anticipation dominated my senses with one hopeful thought: that night, my time with Cassandra would reveal the mystery.

The train signaling its arrival at its next destination broke the silence. I looked through the window to see by chance the name of the village we were entering. I was unable to recognize anything through the stifling mist that filled the night with a feverish pitch of darkness, wherein random swirls of a shadowy blackness lurked with sudden movements, as if in wait for the transport's passengers to depart. Whatever demonic forces had penetrated that once sacred place seemed to be more pronounced. A heaviness of intense energy thickened the surrounding atmosphere with an overwhelming scent of fear. The moon was full, though sporadically, it became partially obscured by the surrounding dense fog. The fog's misty tendrils extended outward, sweeping upward. It seemed to besiege the moon, casting the moon's glow into a crimson hue, until the misty tentacles dispersed into knifelike slivers that bled like maroon blood droplets when they crossed the moon's path.

My eyes were glued to the ghostly images, yet my obsession to be with Cassandra overruled the mounting fear of what I was viewing. The village sign forced its way through the blackness. It was visible just for a few seconds before disappearing into the mist but was visible long enough to announce that we were heading into Neverland. I leaped out of my seat, glancing around at an empty car devoid of all passengers. I was the one invited—or uninvited—guest. The transport slowed, and the depot neared. One light was dimly lit above the depot's entrance, casting just enough of a glow through the misty air to announce the village's name on an old wooden sign that swung loosely even though the air held an eerie, ghostly stillness. I jumped off the exit as the transport was slowing down.

Before I took my first step across the tracks to the depot, I heard the faraway, melodic, desolate tone of another train approaching. It was the phantom ghost train from last time, but only one car was lit this time. *A long voyage just for its one passenger*, I thought. *The VIP treatment*, I mused. I saw the one red headlight as the train approached. Even though the phantom train had the appearance of riding the tracks, the train was elevated over the tracks. The open space where the wheels should have been was consumed by burning flames lashing out with a heated vengeance. This time, there were at least a dozen cars, but all but one were dark. The melodic tone filled the air, becoming louder as the train neared, and changed to a mournful sound of the damned upon approaching the depot. The ghost train slowed almost to a screeching halt before coming to life again as it accelerated past the depot. Momentarily, I froze in place when the train slowed, fearful that it was coming to a halt to pick up Cassandra or me as its next passenger. My lungs nearly exploded with relief when I took my next breath upon realizing Neverland would not be its next stop.

As the train swept past, I saw the lit car toward the end but no passenger. As the car passed before me, I caught the odor of decay. Just before the last car disappeared, a bloody hand pressed on the window, and the sole passenger appeared and looked straight at me, her mouth wide open, letting out a cry loud enough to be heard above the train whistle. It was Linda, staring at me with eyes filled with terror. I cried out for her in vain as she shook her head as a warning to me. The train picked up speed, mindful of the delay of almost stopping at Neverland. As the train made its way through the misty night, the coachman stood on the platform of the last car, waving its red lantern and looking at me with a piercing stare. The red light soon was like a distant mirage, a red cursor piercing the murky night's blackness, leading the passenger through the camouflage of darkness into the abyss of the damned.

I could still see the lantern casting its glow on the coachman, giving the illusion of a disembodied demo. His eyes darted my way with a yellow tinge, and he cried out in a shrill voice, his message hitting me with a chilled suddenness, "Soon, Tony!"

The ghostly procession disappeared into the dark midnight sky, leaving in its wake the tormented, mournful cry of the sole person on board, who knew her destination. I was reluctant to accept what I'd just viewed, yet Linda's image crying out with mournful torment cut right through my reluctance. Even though the last image of Linda burned its way into my mind, one thought kept forging through: *It couldn't have been Linda.*

I dared to cross the tracks, picking up my pace to a sprint as I dashed toward the walkway leading to the depot. The atmosphere felt electrically charged, clinging to me as I hastily reached for the depot door. There was something ominous in the air, and I caught a sleek, shadowy form that seemed to follow my hastened pace. I felt my every movement was intensely watched; every gesture was heavily scrutinized. A endless mewing sound like that of a tortured cat pierced the air at random intervals. In the background, I kept hearing a slithering noise reverberate around me. When I stopped moving, the noise would temporarily halt. Reaching for the door handle, I felt an odd sensation of something sliding across the back of my neck and then sliding down the center of my back before, with a whiplash movement, it retreated with a slapping noise. I suddenly surged through the depot entrance, and instantly, I heard and felt a trashing against the entrance door. I backed away from the door, and the noise and vibration suddenly stopped.

I was filled with intense fear, but my overwhelming impulse to see Cassandra consumed me. I turned toward the rear wall and saw the exit that would lead the way to the village. Without hesitation, I headed toward the door. I stopped right before venturing outside, to listen intently for any distracting noise or movement. After a few seconds, I ventured out and noticed an eerie quietness unlike what I'd experienced at the front of the depot. The scene was of a distant wall. I could also see the village of Neverland enclosed in a bank of gray mist. At unpredictable intervals, the mist would clear, and a few twinkles of light would appear, presumably from a few of the village residents. The serene quietness was unnerving. I expected whatever demons were present at the front of the depot to soon find their way around back. The strange fog that permeated the front had yet to advance to where I stood. Maybe it was the strange mist that transported the swarm of uninvited guests. It was as if a barrier stood as an invisible partition, keeping everything at bay, allowing me a chance to escape toward the village.

I looked upward and viewed the full moon as a sliver of a cloud whispered by. Unlike the scene from the transport, the view of the moon was crystal clear and devoid of anything sinister. Instead, the moon's glow acted as a beacon that showed me the path toward the village beyond the wall. The breeze was calm, gently flowing past my face, carrying Cassandra's scent, which filled my senses. Instinctively, I knew she was nearby, and my gaze swept along the path illuminated by the night's moonlight.

I heard the sound of horses pulling an old-fashioned buggy along the lit path toward me. As the horses and carriage trotted nearer, I saw the hooded driver dressed in black. I moved forward to gain a better view and finally saw Cassandra dressed in a black satin gown, beckoning me to join her in the carriage. With hurried anticipation, I rushed toward the carriage. My senses were on alert for any disturbance behind me. I half expected the demonic visitors from hell to swarm around the depot and transform that eventful night into a terror-filled scene of tormented visions. I hastened my pace, eventually running toward the carriage. Every breath I exhaled was a vent of desperation and fear. I felt something grasp my foot and inch its way up my ankle. I looked down, expecting to see some demonic leech clinging to my ankle with its tentacles wrapping around my ankle and cutting off any circulation. Instead, I realized it was just a patch of overgrowth brushing along my feet.

By then, every alarm button was triggered, and full panic was just moments away as I reached the carriage and slid next to Cassandra, who informed the driver to hastily take us into the village. She reached out and caressed my face, and the instant she touched me, I no longer cared about the events leading up to that moment. Her physical presence and her touch were electric; every sensation was ecstatic. Every fiber of my being felt soothed, and a sense of coming home held me spellbound. I did not care anymore about yesterday or tomorrow, for it was now that help me captive. If this was heaven, then it was a glory beyond my comprehension, and I would have gladly stayed there next to her side for an eternity.

As the driver started hastily down the path toward the village, my peripheral vision caught movement off to my right, in the direction of the depot. The damp mist was edging its way around the depot, creeping up the doorway, its wispy little curls climbing like vines around the depot. Each vine lashed out with tentacles that extended their reach toward us. Each tentacle possessed an eye that followed us with an unblinking glaze, its pupil as black as coal. Unexpectedly, tears of blood would ooze from its lower eyelid, and each drop was swept up by a protruding, forked black tongue. The nest of undefinable creatures swarmed toward us at an accelerated pace. But suddenly, their movement stopped, as if they'd run into an invisible embankment. Their advance halted, and at times, the demonic eyes showed a reluctance to move forward and an uncertainty as they turned toward Cassandra. I turned around and caught Cassandra with a different persona, one that seemed to be mired in an elusive stance. She looked at me as if I were a total stranger, and her eyes had changed color with the intensity of a pending rage. Her eyes seemed soulless, as if she were possessed by a force empowered to defend us from the hideous creatures' malefic intent. She brought her head down, standing with her arms outstretched toward the heavens. She gazed outward toward the approaching monstrosities. She voiced one command, which carried an echo that reverberated with a forceful presence: "No more."

The sweeping monstrosities capitulated into a fitful frenzy and slowly retreated. I then realized the demonic force was fearful of Cassandra, as if she possessed some form of spell that could neutralize the forces to keep them at bay and shield us to keep us out of harm's way. Once the monstrosities retreated, Cassandra's body slackened, as if devoid of energy, and she fell back into the carriage seat. She had her eyes closed, seemingly in a deep sleep. I saw her eyes slowly open as she turned toward me. Her demeanor one of confusion, as if she were trying to get her senses back. "Where are we?" she asked the driver, who responded immediately.

"On our way toward the house." There was no sign of nervousness in the driver's response, as if he were used to the scene that had just occurred with Cassandra. Questions resurfaced, existing ones and new ones that were difficult to ignore. Yet for the time being, I put it all on a time delay, not giving my anxiety a chance to override that soulful respite.

I lifted her veil from her face and was totally captivated by her spiritual beauty. She possessed an innocent, untainted, pure, soulful saintliness I had never seen in my lifetime, one that resonated with me on a level that defined me from a distant memory. That connection, once secured, would save my soul from hell's eternal damnation. At that moment, time froze. Our need for each other gathered sole dominance. Our physical and sensual presence commanded our sense of urgency to engage with rapture. Our bodies yearned to reconnect and were unable to hold back any longer, as if our connection were vital at that moment to recharge our bonded souls, recommit to one another, and prove to fate that we were inseparable. Our passion reached a cathartic need as she came close to me, facing me without a word. Everything that could have been said was evident in her eyes and her lips as they parted, waiting for me to enter her world of magic. Our unquenchable thirst for each other was endless as we engaged repeatedly. Each engagement commenced with a primal need until the moment when we fused into one being, reaching our climax with a torrid flow of passionate release. The heavens applauded in unison as they too became immersed in the interlude of passionate foreplay. Our eternal longing to let our souls become one undeniable force led to an overwhelming obsession. Our compulsive passion, with such intensity, caused an incessant need to never separate again. We were adamant not to yield to our thoughts of what lay in wait for us while treasuring that rare moment of bliss. She laid her head on my shoulder, and her warm breath caressed my neck with an angelic softness. A soft, mellow, enraptured sigh escaped her. She never said a word but was content with delight. The carriage driver, oblivious to our lovemaking, drew us closer to our destination.

I saw the wall at a distance between us and Neverland. Its presence approached as the carriage proceeded down the path toward Neverland. The driver and Cassandra did not seem to notice, as if the wall was nonexistent to them. Even the horses trotting down the path showed no signs of restless nervousness. The wall was approaching rapidly as the horses' pace accelerated to a gallop once Neverland came into full view. The carriage continued into the wall's shadow, which blocked most of the sunlight from the view between there and the village. There wasn't a moment of hesitation from the driver or Cassandra as we became enclosed in the wall's presence. I felt an overwhelming, paralyzing fear as the carriage proceeded closer to the wall. Once the wall felt our presence, a door emerged and suddenly opened to let us through. The sounds went silent within the wall. No creatures were swarming from within the wall. The wall maintained its height, appearing taller and thinner. Its substance was now entirely liquid yet still contained. No one else seemed to notice. It was as if Cassandra's presence had a neutralizing, forgiving effect on the wall's dramatic response. I realized Cassandra was my only salvation who could shield me from whatever hell awaited me once the wall dissolved entirely and released the deluge of memories that had been blocked for what seemed like an eternity. Without her, my fear of what lay ahead became oppressive, with overwhelming guilt consuming my innocence as I was swept into a void where the verdict of guilty was pronounced with assured conviction. I was doomed to die or, worse, to be held captive in a hell constructed specifically for me. With Cassandra, I could find forgiveness and secure my rightful place in heaven with Cassandra by my side. Without her, I feared my soul was doomed to a future of unimaginable horror. My quest to finalize my journey with the discovery of Neverland and permanently join Cassandra was a quest for survival.

We passed through the wall's shadow without any resistance. Once we were on the other side of the wall, the overcast disappeared, letting the warm sunlight through where Neverland stood waiting for our entrance. I wondered if the protective shield from Cassandra would extend to the forbidden place of unwanted memories hidden somewhere within the confines of Neverland. I already knew the answer, as Cassandra had repeatedly relayed that our salvation could only continue once I'd confronted my memories. The fear of what would eventually be known to me returned to remind me that my salvation depended on my reaction to whatever memories lay in wait. The time for disclosure was approaching fast. I held on to Cassandra's hand for reassurance as we approached Neverland.

Despite the imminent confrontation with what lay behind my amnesia, I felt a soulful inner peace with Cassandra. Cassandra and Neverland together were captivating, for I was at home there, a place that resonated with me to a time forgotten except for a few glimpses from a hidden past of someone who'd captured my love and defined the very essence of me. That someone was Cassandra. In those rare moments when the memories surfaced even for an instant, the image presented to me was of Cassandra when we were younger, in a time and place where I found an eternal oneness with a maiden I treasured. It was an endless reservoir of tranquility, where everything I perceived was in complete harmony, perfectly balanced, and in perfect alignment with my soul. Then the unthinkable would happen: my memories would become totally vacant, as if I'd dropped off a cliff into a chasm of eternal darkness. But there with Cassandra, the heavy burden was finally lifted. She looked into my eyes and knew my every thought and desire. She responded with the one word that defined my immortality: "Forever." My soul relinquished all ties to prepare for a lifetime with Cassandra and Neverland. I needed to know more about that village, its history, and its location. "In due time," she said. The words I heard resonated with my soul. The tone was like a classic melody with the charm of wind chimes. Its melodic tone harmonized clearly nearby yet with a hint of nostalgia from far away.

We rode into another part of town, a strange part of town absent of anyone moving about. There was nothing to indicate that part of town was inhabited, except for a few homes that appeared vacant. It seemed I had reverted back in time. There was a faint light that seemed a mile away, but it was becoming clearer as the driver hastily headed toward our destination. All of reality escaped me when the seemingly ghostly, grandiose home became clear, showcasing its pristine condition. It bore an unmistakable, uncanny spectral resemblance to the house remodeled on Canyon Ridge Trails. I recalled the photograph I'd found in the house on Canyon Ridge. Was the woman in the photograph Cassandra? The couple had vanished among the commotion when an assailant pursued and fired several shots at the couple. The couple and assailant were never found, and the injuries were never disclosed. If she was Cassandra, then was the male in the photograph the stranger who uncannily always seemed to be hidden within a shadow? If so, then everything pointed to the same presumption: this was the same house Linda and I had purchased to remodel.

I wanted to ask her but restrained my questions for a more appropriate time, not wanting to disrupt the mood for fear of the possible consequences. The town was so familiar yet so distant. It was an era gone by, yet there I was, reliving it, sensing that in some way, I belonged to that distant past and was unable to relinquish my tenuous hold. I sensed a base of reality there, a distant life from decades ago in that surrounding, yet with laughter and mayhem. The fervent energy now was gone; the town was filled with only memories of what once was. Cassandra sat next to me, holding on to my love as if knowing that our departure was soon to be.

The house loomed in front of us. We disembarked from the carriage and strolled forward to that house of yesteryear. Once inside, she turned on the lights, and I caught a glimpse of others in the house, yet they vanished as I turned toward them. An overwhelming sense of fatigue enveloped me, and Cassandra led me to the master bedroom. With weariness, I lay down on the bed, and then she lay down next to me, whispering soft melodies in my ear. I fell into a deep, coma-like sleep with a remembrance of her whispers that she loved me.

41

Another Encounter with the Shadowy Stanger

Later that evening, I awoke and found myself listening to another Benny Goodman song. I was in the ballroom hallway. The tune soothed my alarmed senses. I felt a peaceful stillness soothing to my soul, but where was Cassandra? I'd just been lying next to her as the blanket of drowsiness comforted me and the tides of sleep swept over me, cleansing my fears and tears of longing, feeling the warmth of her, believing I had finally returned to my destined fate. But as fate would have it with its game of chance, I now found myself there in the ballroom without her by my side. My only companions were the melodies that scented the air with opulent memories. Unable to bear the desperate longing, I turned to my left and walked toward the dimly lit, exotic back atrium, where the melodies echoed their soulful tunes. I looked to my left and then to my right at the candlelit tables alongside the cushioned wall. My search was in vain, with no sight of her presence. I found it strange that the tables occupied were the same tables occupied during my last visit. The couples looked the same, turning around and wearing the same masks of pretentious joy and somber sorrows. No one said a word in conversation. They just sat there like stage props. My curiosity aroused, I started walking in their direction to ask about Cassandra. Then I detected a wisp of a fragrance float by, and the sweet scent of Cassandra descended upon me. I then heard laughter, followed by a sensual moan, a cry of ecstasy filled with a haunting purr of passion.

I walked gingerly, not knowing what to expect and half expecting another unexpected surprise, toward the ballroom, searching the dance floor. The dance floor was filled with couples. Each couple was engaged in an erotic pose. I walked closer and saw Linda enclosed in a rapturous embrace. I found Alecia, our receptionist, off toward the corner, dressed in a voluptuous gown, in the throes of heat, intimately embraced by her partner as he held her from behind, keeping tune to the music. Their bodies closely knitted the movements, keeping time to the music's pulsating harmony. I found myself becoming more engaged with erotic zeal and forcibly walked to the other corner of the ballroom, searching for Cassandra. I saw Linda staring at me, and I stared back, recalling the image of her forlorn look of terror as the sole passenger on the phantom ghost train. Seeing Linda there on the dance floor eased my alarm. I realized that the phantom train's passenger must have had an uncanny resemblance to Linda. Fortunately, it could not have been Linda. Yet I felt sorrow for the unfortunate passenger whose demise was no longer in her control. I responded to Linda with a relieved nod. However, I was not the object of her gaze; she was looking at the gentleman behind me. I turned to see who it was, and it was the stranger who consistently managed to be hidden in the shadows.

This time, I tried to catch a clearer glimpse of the stranger, but just as the shadowy light from the dimmed chandelier cast its glow on the stranger's face, he suddenly turned toward his left, away from me, staring intently at the figure standing in the far corner of the ballroom. He stood frozen, intently watching, as she moved toward the ballroom entrance. It was Cassandra. The stranger unleashed himself from his frozen position, and with what seemed like malicious intent, he darted through the crowd while reaching into his coat pocket and pulling out a long, thin razor with a pearl handle that he gripped tightly. His obvious purpose was to hurt Cassandra, and I immediately hastily pursued him. I rushed through the crowd toward the gentleman. I accidentally bumped into Alecia without a response. I turned toward her and saw but a mannequin, its expression a mask of rapture. The gentleman behind her was stoic, his posture frozen in place, his hands suspended in time, raised just slightly above her breasts. His appearance was a mask of lustful intentions. I turned toward the other couples, who were but mannequins filling in as stage props. They were exact duplicates of my company employees and contractors. Each couple faced me, wearing masks of exaggerated expressions, mostly of joy and lust. The remaining few had masked expressions of tearful sadness. I knew each one of them separately and wondered if their masked expressions were accurate depictions of how they felt when at work. Just moments ago, the couples had been dancing to the musician's beat, as reflected by their playful poses. But suddenly, as if a switch had been thrown, the frolicking couples had turned into a set of stage props, each wearing a mask of his or her true intentions. I looked upon them with mixed awe and fear, waiting for a sound, a whisper, or any movement that would reveal this as another sick joke. But my wait was in vain. I was not able to detect if the scene was real or just fantasy. The deathly quiet mimicked a horror flick in which, at any moment, the frozen mannequins would come to life as death's harbinger of evil intent.

I heard a commotion near the ballroom's entrance as the stranger briskly turned over one of the tables near the entrance. His hasty intent was suddenly kicked up a notch. My attention rapidly turned toward the stranger as his pace hastened toward the ballroom's main entrance. My pace in turn quickened as I pursued the stranger. I passed the lounge and found an empty champagne bottle on the edge of the counter. I picked it up with my right hand, holding it by the neck. I saw Cassandra enter the ladies' room. Without hesitation, the stranger changed his direction and followed her. His pace slowed, and with a sudden jerk, he glanced to his right and then his left. He then spoke with an Italian accent. "I know you are there behind me." He slowly turned around. Expecting to see the stranger's appearance, I encountered but a mask of contempt. I stepped back in frustration, wondering why everyone's expression seemed to be highlighted by a mask. The stranger moved toward me, his intentions communicated through a tightened grip on the razor he held in his right hand. Backing away, I moved swiftly to my side, surprising the stranger as I struck a blow to the side of his head at the temple area. Stunned by my response, I immediately ran into the ladies' lounge and entered a stall. I listened for Cassandra and heard a weeping sound from the last stall. Before I could open the door to my stall, I heard the outer door opening and recognized the gait of the stranger. I saw his feet moving toward the rear as the sobbing continued. I slowly opened the door and quietly maneuvered toward him. I saw blood seeping from his ear from my blow to his temple. He didn't seem to notice me, probably because of the damage to his ear. The tearful sobs of Cassandra were pronounced, drawing both of us toward her. He held the razor intently in his hand. I still had the bottle with me; the neck was broken, leaving shards of sharp edges.

In an instant, I swung the base of the bottle against the man's other cheek, and the shards of glass cut deeply into his temple. He staggered, swooning from side to side and leaning against the wall adjacent to the stall where Cassandra was. I told Cassandra to stay put, not sure of the demise of the stranger. In the midst of all that, I had yet to see the face of the stranger. As I walked past to get a first look, the stranger shook as if on the verge of a seizure. Suddenly, a strange gray mist eased its way out, enveloping him, and then took the shape of a grotesque face that screeched its dismay. I recognized the scream as it brought forth echoes reminiscent of the ferocious screeching from the depot and the train ride from last week's journey. The image lasted for just a few seconds before succumbing to unconsciousness and evaporating into midair. I heard voices from outside and then heard the voices of two females nearing the restroom. I called out to Cassandra, asking her to hurry, but received no response. I opened the stall only to find it empty. I felt unhinged, wondering if this was another sign of my descending into the depths of lunacy. Was I going completely insane? Was this to be my future, wherein I could no longer determine what was real and what was not real? I pondered my own state of mind, wondering if all the seeming delusions were just another journey descending deeper into the realm of insanity.

To further complicate my concern, I felt that the disruption of the bond between Cassandra and me was caused by a demonic force—a force I still didn't know how to combat, let alone defeat. I'd seen how Cassandra repelled the forces from the depot. Though it was apparent she could keep the hideous forces at bay, was her power enough to dispose of the forces forever? Hastily, I left by another side entrance. I was shaken by all the events that had occurred over the past few weeks, and this last episode was overwhelming. Feeling dejected and crazed with my mounting doubts, I trudged my weary soul to the back atrium, lost in my thoughts of the woman to whom I was connected by the very fabric of my soul and for whom I would engage in a life-or-death struggle to keep her safe from harm's way. I felt our connection was becoming weaker, with our bond slowly unraveling. The times without her by my side threw me more into the depths of despair, and the loneliness reached the point of total annihilation.

Unless I found the key to unlock the mystery, my journey of bliss and salvation would detour to another journey leading to a path of total obliteration. It was crucial to unlock the mystery and find the single thread, the one pathway, that would wind its way to the core of whatever evil had entered that sacred journey. I felt I did not have much time left. There were several clues, each a potential key to unlock the door to the mystery. Another clue, another key, was the stranger and his connection to Cassandra. The answer to the riddle did not reside with just one clue but could only be found by connecting all the clues. One clue led to another; each was a stepping-stone, and together they would form the path toward resolution. But how they connected was the well-kept, hidden secret. Every clue needed for my quest was readily available. I just had to connect all the dots, and therein lay the complex challenge. The overabundance of data was overwhelming. My initial question was "Where do I begin my next step?"

If I were drowning in my own sea of madness, if being with Cassandra was the culmination of my descent into insanity, then I would not only accept it but also welcome it. Cassandra was me; her soul was my soul, her loneliness was my loneliness, her despair was my despair, and her love was my love. There was no substitute for my salvation. I had to find the right key, unlock the mystery, and see for myself if the journey was destined for eternal bliss or the entrance to the abyss of hell. I realized that to determine if I was truly descending into the pits of craziness, I had to engage all the variables surrounding this mystery and meet it the mystery head-on either to resolve it or succumb to its further descent into the one-way trip to hell's inferno.

With renewed strength and a reawakening of purpose, knowing that Cassandra was the central connection to my hope for salvation and survival, I entered the lounge, where her appearance was most prominent. She sat off in the corner as if nothing had happened. Our eyes locked again. She sat there glued to me, a beacon of light cast as a tranquil blue aura that shimmered with an angelic purity. I was drawn in by her hypnotic presence. I reached her table, sat down on the soft cushioned seat, and laid my hands over hers, feeling her welcoming gesture. She breathlessly greeted me with her soft lips pressed firmly to mine with feverish intent, and I responded with a fervent desire. She felt hot, with scented beads of perspiration glistening on her breasts, which exquisitely filled her black satin dress. Our desire to engage swiftly aroused our need to fully capture that moment, yet the recent unsettling incident restrained me with questions that plagued me with doubts.

I needed to ask her about the stranger. Who was he? It was strange that she didn't seem fazed by the recent episode. There was no sign of anything out of place. Gone were her tears and the panicked tone of fear so pronounced when the attacker stalked her with intent of malicious harm. In fact, her controlled demeanor was unnatural based on what had just happened to her. There should have been some nervous anxiety in the aftermath. That would have been almost impossible to camouflage by her body language. Her expression should have reflected a sign of relief. But there was no sign of distress or hint of nervousness. Everything seemed too calm. Despite my observation, I refrained from inquiring further to avoid confronting my own state of mind. If faced with facts suggesting that the previous encounter had never happened and been purely imaginary, I would have serious doubts about the reality of Cassandra and Neverland. To admit the possibility that the journey, Cassandra, and Neverland were all just a fantasy conjured up by my delicate mind would most likely send me over the edge. The time was not right for me to take that risk of finding the truth.

42

A Journey with Hell's Creatures

The night was silent and still except for the music that seemed to play on forever. Then, from far away, I thought I heard the faint echo of a train whistle. *No, it couldn't be,* I thought. There was nothing I could do to dismiss the sound, which grew in intensity as the train neared the village. The echo emerged as a deafening shrill piercing the stillness as a warning that the train was running off schedule without a minute to spare to transport me back to a place I began to doubt was my reality. Maybe it was, or maybe it was another fantasy detour along this journey.

I looked upon Cassandra with a forlorn expression. She returned my gaze and said, "This is the journey back for us. This is the last trip back to uncover the truth of us. Only then will you be free to return to treasure us forever. I cannot return with you. Not until you discover the truth. Only then will we both be able to accept the truth without fear or concern. This time, you must return. Tony, the house—the answer lies there. The truth to reveal the fear that haunts you, to discover the ugly truth. Then you will be free. All this is not what it appears. Only truth and faith in us will give you the courage to make this final journey of discovery and return to me. You must go now, and I will be your final destination when your journey finally ends."

I listened intently, as if I were listening to the gospel, my faith hanging on every word. I asked no questions, for just one question would be a denial of my faith in Cassandra. I placed the essence of our survival in her hands, knowing that our journey had traveled the infinite road of destiny and somehow she would be the final destination at that particular juncture. I placed my own survival of saneness in her hands. There was no longer an alternate route. I finally admitted I was the passenger, and she was both the pilot and the copilot on this journey. I could only pray I would survive the ugly truth. The journey of reckoning had arrived for my return to discovery .

Lost in my thoughts, I turned to confirm my agreement but found myself staring into an empty, vacant seat. I glanced at the table and found her calling card: a red rose. I picked it up to catch its fragrance, which blended with the pervasive scent of her perfume. I searched where she'd sat and found the letter: "Never leave without a promise to return. I will be your final destination." My trust in the outcome of the final journey fortified with unconditional acceptance, I set out with a hurried pace toward Neverland's depot. As I neared with the depot's steeple in full view, I looked away, listening to the transport slow as it entered our village and feeling its draw pulling me back with trepidation. A brief image of her appeared only to dissipate into the mist. Before her image disappeared, I detected a slight shift in her appearance. Her voice carried a message of concern, a call for help, as danger awaited her. She called to me through the heavy mist, telling me to hurry and return to her before it was too late. I felt my soul being drawn from me as the mist disintegrated into another realm yet still held me in a captive state of overwhelming alarm. I was fully aware that once again, my torment had not yet ended, and I was prepared for my return journey to the house on Canyon Ridge Trails. I had a relentless feeling that I would find the key on this next journey.

I heard the exhausted response from the transport as it hastily approached the front of the depot. The pulsating breathing of the engine car picked up intensely, as if someone from the train were yelling out last call. I funneled my way through the rear door of the depot and flew through the front door, catching the handrail to the passenger compartment just as the transport picked up speed at an astonishing rate. I fell onto the narrow platform that separated the first two compartments. I opened the door to the second car and felt a force push me forward. I crashed into a dark void where dimly lit candles flickered on and off, keeping in time with the movements of the transport hurrying along the tracks to another dimension.

The candles transformed into gas lanterns, and the flames would vary in intensity between a harsh glare and a barely visible, dim glow. I paced haltingly toward the door that separated me from the front car. During those moments when the lights cast but a faint glow, I sensed the presence of unwanted shadows that darted back and forth before me as to warn me off and attempt to block me from entering the front car. But with each attempt, my persistence to find out what lay ahead in that compartment intensified. With the little light I had for guidance, I took each step carefully, my back tingling with a sensation as if my every movement was being watched. Something glanced my shoulder and then latched on and crawled onto my back, creeping up toward my neck. I reached back with my hand, trying urgently to sweep it away. What felt like a furry tentacle crept up my neck, reaching out for my ear, and then I felt another slimy arm sliding its way toward my other ear. I felt both reach my earlobes. With a panicked gesture, I swatted at my ears to dislodge the creatures. The one by my right earlobe fell off, but the slimy tentacle held on with its suctioned bottom. I felt a sharp pain in my neck, right below the ear—a needle-like pain trying to pierce my skin. I tried again in vain to dislodge it and finally ran with abandon toward the front of the car and propelled my back against the side wall. I heard a loud popping noise and felt something oozing down my neck. I reached around and swiped at the slime dripping down my neck. The smell was like rotten decay, releasing an overpowering, sulfuric stench that caused me to retch.

I turned around and caught a glimpse of two spiderlike creatures flattened against the wall, with green slime oozing out from their underbellies. I glanced back the way I'd come, and the lights strung along the sides switched momentarily to a brighter glow, illuminating the inside of the compartment to unveil a horrific view. Enormous, deformed creatures were crawling along the sides of the compartment. Their faces were half formed; one side of each was covered with shafts of hair that swayed unevenly over the surface, resembling the ebbing of an ocean tide. The insect bodies acted as a flotilla loosely coupled with the hairy attachments. The other side of each was covered with a milky substance that oozed from its visible pores, which periodically opened up to expel the milky substance. As the substance touched the wall, it adhered to it like liquid cement, dissolving the surface with an acidic odor.

Every inch of the walls seemed to be covered. Some areas overlapped with layers of creatures, their tentacles reaching out toward the wall in a feeding frenzy. The air suddenly gained a stillness, and each creature stopped. The clicking, swarming noise went silent. I stood there uncertainly, frozen in place, as my senses struggled to grasp the images in front of me. The creatures along the walls slowly turned toward me with their bodies angled upward. Each revealed a deformed eye with a jet-black pupil. There was no eyelid, just a blackness that moved to track my movements. The view was horrific, and I struggled to retain my balance both physically and emotionally. As if acting upon command, the creatures started relinquishing their hold on the walls and fell to the floor. A swarm of creatures fell in layers. They spread out to form a single layer and moved toward me. Without hesitation, I turned toward the compartment door and anxiously gripped the handle to open it. I passed through with an alarming sense of urgency and finally closed it, making sure the door was securely engaged. I opened the next door to the first compartment, hoping the creatures would be contained.

The next compartment was entirely dark except for one light overhead toward the adjacent engine compartment, which cast a reddish hue. I turned toward the compartment I'd just exited, and the windows were covered with swarms of leeches. I opened the rear door to the compartment I'd just entered to ensure the hellish forms were still contained. The noise was deafening. The sounds emanating from within the compartment were agonizing shrills followed by sucking noises. Those that were flush against the rear window were angled upward to reveal their eyes, which seemed to track my movements with a gleam of malicious evil.

I closed the front compartment door, double-checking to ensure the latch was firmly in place. I was at the rear of the compartment, and both aisles of seats on either side had headrests that prevented any view of any occupants. I ventured toward the front, glancing to my left. I saw Linda sitting there with her head against the headrest. She seemed to be in a deep sleep or trance. I walked over and called out her name with no response. I shook her, trying to arouse her from her sleep, again with no response. I felt her pulse and registered a feeble beat. I dared not try to evoke a response, for fear of causing her harm. I looked to my right and saw my receptionist, Alecia, in the same state. I moved forward to the next row and caught the receptionist from the Ocean Blue, my favorite stopover diner. As I moved from one row to the next, I found all my employees and contractors sitting in the same state. I reached the front row and encountered Cassandra in a deep sleep. Hovering over her, the stranger traced his fingertips over her cheek. He looked up with a wicked smile, and for the first time, I caught a look at the stranger. He was wearing a mask, but his eyes gave him away, for they were filled with torment. I rushed toward him, and the next moment, I found myself seated in the front row, next to the right window. I looked off to my left and then behind me and saw no one.

I could tell the transport had dropped its speed as I saw lights off in the distance. There was a rain storm, and raindrops were pelting the window by my side. Among the drops, I could see a glimpse of lights drawing nearer. I could tell by the vibration from the traveled rail that the train was decelerating. No conductor was in sight, but I knew we were entering the village limits. I looked again out the window with anticipation. Yet my anticipation was short-lived upon my realizing the familiar scene was not what I'd expected. It was not my hometown. I saw familiar lights, with a strange tinge to the town's glow. The night sky became permeated with a strange mist, a dense fog that would dispel for a brief moment here and there. I knew then that my ride back to my village was not on that train's schedule; instead, I was on a return trip back to Neverland. There were no stops in between, just a journey back to the same village without any further destination—a treacherous, nightmarish ride through hell's front door. What I already knew was confirmed during one of the moments when the fog cleared for a quick view. I caught the village sign of Neverland.

43

A Dialogue about the Events at the Mystery House

I suddenly woke up in my own bed, soaked with perspiration. Every vivid detail followed me into my waking senses. I shuddered with a sense of urgency. The dreams were occurring with an ever-increasing frequency, trying to reach out to me, requesting my presence, as if everything depended on me to solve the riddle before time ran out. I felt I had little time left; the hourglass was more than half empty. Time was slipping away as whatever demonic forces were involved in that game of life and death impatiently upped the ante. The images from my last dream were haunting, and I knew Cassandra's life depended on my being there by her side. The intensity from last night persisted; each image was crystal clear, a memory distinct in detail. I knew that not only was Cassandra's life in the balance, but also, I would surely die without her.

But how could I get back there, and were these indeed just symptoms of dementia, or was I in some kind of vortex that had yet to be explained? The endless stream of variables were suspended by a lack of conviction, wandering aimlessly without any solid direction, fueling the vicious cycle between my doubts and optimism. My doubts were driving me with relentless anguish into a deep chasm of anxiety. My forehead felt as if it were in a vise, and I felt extreme vertigo. I became nauseated to the point where I almost vomited. Everything seemed far away, and I felt as if everything were diminishing into thin air. My thoughts became scrambled, and I was bombarded with memories crashing in on me haphazardly with no pattern. Everything became dim. I must have blacked out. It must have lasted for only a few minutes. When I became fully conscious, the intricate details from last night withdrew into a hazy camouflage, taking a temporary respite. Only the image of Cassandra and her final message remained in the forefront yet with no conviction. The answer lay in the house on Canyon Ridge Trails. That was what she'd emphasized, as if my return visit solely rested on finding the one missing clue that would connect everything and unlock the mystery, allowing the journey to make its final return. The heaviness of that final pending journey weighed on me. I knew my being there was crucial to her and us.

As the memories entered into a lull, my current situation became my focal point, and then I realized it was Monday, and I had only an hour left to get ready for work. Instead of taking the train, I decided to drive to work. My thoughts were on the day's work schedule and vague details about last night. As I was driving, I decided I should make an appointment with a psychiatrist. It was apparent the journey had consumed me to a point where I was not able to run my company with a commanding effort, as I had when the company was younger. The maddening voyage I had been on had an unknown destination and an unannounced schedule. Too much was at stake that required most, if not all, of my effort as the journey grew in intensity and complexity. This was now a battle between life and death, between good and evil, between insanity and saneness. The question had always been there but had become unavoidable: Was I going mad? To that end, I had to seek out a psychiatrist to help assess my state of mind. It was of paramount importance to resolve and overcome the death match before it grew to a point where it became unsolvable and marked a permanent end to both me and Cassandra, culminating in the tragic end of a soulful bond from when the heavens had first formed. I doubted I would return to head the company; instead, I would serve as a part-time executive consultant. If I survived that nightmare, I would then decide upon my future fate. It was now imperative to hand the reins over to Linda until the journey concludes. The downsizing of my responsibilities would be immediate, with my workload reduced by 50 percent. The company would grow under her guidance. That day marked the day to meet with Linda.

My focus turned to the house on Canyon Ridge, where I'd found the photograph of a couple shot by an unknown assailant. I knew there was a connection between last night's dream and the news story I'd uncovered at the house, and I decided to go revisit the house at the end of the meeting with Linda. As I drove into the parking lot of my corporation, I was overwhelmed by various degrees of conflicting emotions. I felt a sense of urgency, despondency, a wave of anxiety, and a feeling of being in a vortex that could change at any moment. All I knew for sure was that I had to get back to Cassandra and find the assailant. Knowing I had no control of those events, I forced the unsettling thoughts out of my mind, postponing any thoughts about last night until I revisited the house within a few hours, and concentrated on the meeting planned for that morning.

I walked into the lobby and made my usual welcome to Charlie, the guard. I stopped and chatted for a while before fully focusing on the day's agenda, working hard to keep everything else running through my mind on leave. My ability to compartmentalize was my best attribute, and I used it to the maximum that day. Yet as I continued my talk with Charles, I felt as if I were a stranger not fully engaged. It took another jolt to my senses for me to gain my full composure as Charles took a call for me and informed me that I was needed for an upcoming meeting. I welcomed the intervention, and I excused myself from Charles and hastily headed to the elevator. I walked through our office door, and our receptionist greeted me. My thoughts retreated to last night's journey when I caught Alecia in a voluptuous mood. I wondered if that was indeed part of the dream's fantasy. Whether it was or not did not deter me; with a sly smirk, I averted my eyes to her physical attributes. I detected a slight flirtatious smile, as if she acknowledged my thoughtful stare and affirmative nod. Both realizing the sudden shift in mood, we refocused, and she informed me I was expected in the meeting room, where Linda was waiting. I hastily dropped off my briefcase in my office and headed for the meeting room.

Linda was there and beckoned for me to close the door so we could talk. She told me an unsettling event had occurred last night at the house overlooking the Pacific. According to neighbors, several violent screams, followed by gun shots, had emanated from the house. The screams had had a tone of urgency, as if someone were being murdered. The neighbors had called the police, yet they'd found nothing to report, except for two rose petals lying on the bed. According to the police, they'd heard a sorrowful voice calling out the name Tony. I could not believe what I was hearing. I entered into a state of turmoil, but I remained calm and indicated that the disturbance must have been due to vandals, and the voices must have come from the echoes of the Pacific winds. I asked if there was any more evidence of damage, and Linda informed me that the police had found no evidence of damage but would have a car drive by every few hours as a precaution. I knew then that I had to visit the house again and examine the news article.

I asked Linda if she was finished with the initial draft of the project we were working on. Linda conveyed that she had the initial draft done and wanted me to review it. I put that on the agenda and brought up another priority to her. I asked her to start drawing up the blueprints and cost estimates for additional remodeling of the house overlooking the Pacific and to get various quotes on shoring up the back side of the house. She replied with an enthused, eager yes but needed to get clearance from the police first, since they were investigating the incident from last night. I wasn't sure if the police had cordoned off the house. My immediate concern was the newspaper article behind the picture on the wall. I needed that article for reasons best undisclosed and made it a priority to make an on-site visit ASAP. I told Linda to call the police for clearance and work on the initial draft as a high priority, and I would review it with her at the site.

The next discussion triggered another jolt to my senses as Linda asked me if I was experiencing any unsettling dreams. "Why?" I asked, hinging my sense of distress on her response. She told me she was having some unsettling nightmares about my being shot, yet the incident seemed to have happened in a time long past. She had been having recurring dreams, and I was involved in them. I listened to her intently despite the vagueness about my recurring dreams. I wanted to further explore the matter with Linda, yet now was not the right time. The right time would be after I revisited the house and reviewed the news clipping one more time.

As the day moved on, I had more meetings, and then, as morning turned into noon, I took the elevator to the first floor. Linda walked in behind me and waited for the doors to close before she started to discuss the events with me. "Tony, what is going on? There is something occurring with these events that are related to my dreams, and I am sure you are having the same dreams. Please tell me what you know. I have a feeling that something with potential dire consequences hangs in the balance. Each dream seems to be more revealing, and you are in every one of them. I feel that you are not telling me everything, yet we are both involved."

While I listened to her, I caught the scent of her perfume, which was the same as the one Cassandra had worn last night. I looked at Linda and saw the resemblance between her and Cassandra in my dream—the same high cheekbones and the same full lips, yet Linda's hair was blonde and was cut short. But if the hair had been longer and the color had been brunette, there would have been a remarkable, eerie resemblance to Cassandra. I told Linda we needed to discuss the matter in more detail toward the end of the week.

I was now convinced I should hand over the majority of the corporation's workload to Linda. My intent was to make another short visit with Linda that afternoon and then hasten over to the house. However, not surprisingly, my intended short visit turned into one lasting for the first part of the afternoon, which heightened my angst to return to the house. I told Linda we needed to discuss something critical. Without further explanation, I told Linda I needed her help and would be assigning her more responsibility, and I would explain in more detail at the end of the week. I told her I needed to investigate the incident at the house again before I dwelled more on our discussion. She gave me an inquisitive look yet decided to let it be until the week's end, knowing there would be a lot to discuss.

As I walked to my car, I thought about Linda, wondering about many aspects of our relationship. We both felt a connection, as if we were connected by subliminal memories from a past, as evidenced by the uncanny similarities between our dreams. I felt there was more to the situation, which we hoped would be revealed when explored in more detail on Friday.

Review of Key Facts of this Mystery

I got caught up in traffic on the Santa Monica Freeway and decided to wait it out by stopping off at my favorite sanctuary, Ocean Blue, off the Pacific. I parked my car and greeted the hostess, who sat me at a table with a full view of the ocean. As I viewed the surf, I pondered the unfolding events, which had started what seemed like ages ago. I knew there were events that occurred in the world that remained unexplained enigmas. Why, I wondered, was there such a rise in mysteries that remained unsolved and beyond rational explanation? In the overall scheme of things, there were a myriad of mysteries that were beyond science and logic—too many to cite—and I realized I was in the center of one of those vortexes. I required more time to research and arrive at a conclusion. I felt overwhelmed by the barrage of variables that challenged the hellish labyrinth. But the one fact that might give me a decisive advantage was that I was at the exact center of the vortex; in my opinion, that gave me the advantage of seeing firsthand the complexity of the inner workings of the web of variables. The key facts I recited in my mind were the constructs of the evolving dilemma.

First and foremost, I have had recurring dreams about a woman, Cassandra, whom I am connected to, and our relationship appears to span several lifetimes. Second, the village of Neverland is where Cassandra resides. Third, Cassandra and I are lovers. Fourth, Cassandra's husband was a suspect after an assailant attempted to murder Cassandra and me. Fifth, Cassandra is probably in a coma. Sixth, my unexpected journeys to Neverland. *Seventh, the assailant will try to find Cassandra and me again to put us away since his first attempt failed. Eighth, Linda is experiencing the same series of dreams, which, on the surface, seem to be connected. Ninth, the house we purchased overlooking the Pacific on Canyon Ridge Trails is included in this scenario. Tenth, the house may contain the answers to the mystery.*

The how and when still remained a mystery. In fact, everything I recalled was a mystery to me, and none of it seemed to connect. It was apparent, though, that those critical elements were somehow connected. I felt like a caged mouse in a cruel experiment, faced with a complex web of passageways, and just one sequence of connections would bring a successful outcome. The element of chance was so remote that the solution had a small to nil chance of an approachable solution. However, in order to solve the mystery and hold on to my sanity, I had to accept the facts and try to put them together, or else I feared I would perish and vanish forever.

Nothing made sense anymore. My world was composed of fact and fiction fused together, with no boundaries providing a landscape in my surreal reality. I was positive that if I discussed the issues with a psychiatrist, he would consider me deranged, even potentially dangerously delusional, and have me committed to an asylum. I was at the point where I had to resolve the puzzle, even if the outcome was a verdict of madness. Or perhaps the variables were valid facts, related yet unexplained, events that challenged explanation. I was at the point of just accepting what was and trying to fit the pieces together. However, a part of me was convinced the facts were real, and the task to resolve them was solely on my shoulders—but only if I was able to return to the elusive village of Neverland.

I pondered those facts while watching the waves thrash the shoreline, contemplating my next move. A sense of urgency weighed heavily on me. I was waiting for fate's arranged journey to return me to that village, a place where I had an uncanny connection, as if I'd once lived there. There in Santa Monica, I was helpless, able to plan yet unable to execute the plan. Maybe a clue would surface from further inspection of the house. As I sat there mesmerized by the hypnotic effect of the ocean waves, I suddenly felt my mind racing back in time to a place surrounded by frenzied energy from the chaos of events. I saw total darkness shredded by a brilliant flash of light, followed by a commotion somewhere in front. People were frantically fleeing the ballroom. A detective gave chase to an assailant, and doctors attended to Cassandra. I heard and saw the concern on their faces. I was faced with flickering images of the assailant coming in and out of focus, searching for us. I saw the gun in his hand, and I knew from his look that he was bent on killing both of us, not waiting for any updates on our condition. The images were all in slow motion, with intermittent moments of stillness, as one would experience with satellite reception that seemed to have problems picking up a steady signal.

I then saw Cassandra hovering above her physical body and beckoning me to come to her before it was too late. Her hand extended outward, pointing to the house overlooking the Pacific. Her voice reached me with one message: "What you seek lies in wait at the house. This time, look for what is buried, and the truth will soon be revealed." She said, "Hurry!" and then the images faded, with an inky blackness filling the void.

When the images withdrew, the blackness lifted, and I found myself at the ocean-side lounge with a glass of vodka broken in my hand. The hostess and bartender attended to me, both asking if I was okay. The hostess had an emergency kit available and returned with gauze and bandages to care for the cut on my hand. She carefully took care of my hand and asked me again if I was okay. It appeared I had almost fainted, yet I told her I was fine and had had a dizzy spell. Despite the concern on their faces, I walked out the entrance toward my car and then ventured back into traffic with one objective on my mind: to return to the house overlooking the Pacific.

45

Servants' Quarters: Discovery of Clue to Cassandra

I drove with careless abandon toward my destination, alternately weaving in and out of traffic, only half aware of my reckless driving. There was something at the house I must have overlooked. I could not pinpoint specifically what it was, but every instinct in me was screaming that I'd missed something. My mind was racing at an unbelievable speed, and I drove at a torrid pace, as if Cassandra's life depended on my solving the riddle. The one elusive clue to unlock everything had to be at the house. I finally reached my exit turnoff and climbed the canyon roads, winding upward toward the homes perched high on the cliffs. The house Linda and I had purchased was on a particularly high cliff. As I made my final turn, the house seemed to have a somewhat ethereal glow, and somewhere in the recesses of my mind, that whole stretch and the house seemed oddly connected to me, but any memories were just faint whispers of remote recollections mostly obscured by the passage of time. As I ventured forth into the house, that vague sense of familiarity became more vivid. That distant awareness, which I'd acknowledged upon the first visit, had been an influential factor in the purchase of the property. But now that uncanny sense had more relevance. There was something there of significance—a clue, a vital puzzle piece to unravel the cluster of winding entanglements leading to the core of the mystery.

I first caught the scent of Cassandra's perfume originating from the master bedroom upstairs. As before, I could not rest until I went upstairs to see if Cassandra or Linda was present. I called out for them with no response. Not surprised, I finished my climb upstairs to the master bedroom only to find it empty. Because that was not the first time I'd detected the fragrance without a hint of their presence, I was not immediately alarmed. After I searched room by room upstairs, I investigated the surrounding rooms on the lower level. I speculated on the history of the house and wondered why the house had been on the market so long. There were rumors that the house was haunted, but at the time, I'd just treated the rumors as hearsay. It was true that the distant neighbors who drove by at night heard disturbances and saw lights in the upstairs bedroom windows, where apparitions would fleetingly appear, transforming back to their former selves with horrific malformations, standing there with vacant stares and insanely shouting profanity before returning to their disembodied souls. I thought those sounds and visions were because of the Pacific wind winding its way through the canyons and the reflection of the moon on the windows. The apparitions, I reasoned, were just products of an overactive imagination.

But last night, the complaints from the surrounding neighbors lent more credence toward the credibility of the rumors. Added to that, my sense of familiarity with the house and the news clippings gave me enough information to support my belief that the house was part of the evolving mystery. There was a link, and there was something there that supported that premise. I just had to find it. I looked out through the glass-enclosed patio entrance, my gaze following the backyard's downward slope toward the edge of the cliff, which was gated with a sturdy oak fence to avoid a serious accident of tripping over the edge.

I stepped outside, studied the landscape, and walked down to the servants' quarters off to the left of the house, located close to the fence. The servants' quarters had been included in the purchase of the main house, and we planned to remodel them. The first level would be used for recreation and solitude, and the upper level would be dedicated to providing a creative arts center. What made the endeavor intriguing was that the design of the structure would follow the art deco theme from the 1920s and '30s. The architectural style would parallel the main house's design from the same pair of decades.

The police had thoroughly searched servants' quarters while investigating the complaints from last night, but they'd found no results that could help explain last night's disturbance. The place was a modest two-level structure with enough room to house a small family. I went inside and saw that it was entirely empty. The place seemed as if it had been vacant for centuries. A layer of dust covered the first floor, which provided no sign of disturbance except for tiny mouse prints. I wondered why the real estate agent in charge of the property hadn't hired a cleaning crew to keep the dwelling clean. I inspected the first floor, searching every room for any sign of disturbance, only to come up empty. I walked over to the stairway to the upper level and climbed the staircase carefully, testing the railing and each step for structural problems due to the age and obvious neglect of routine inspection. Again, everything seemed to be in order. Upstairs, I checked the bedrooms, which were uninhabited. The house had a hollow feel to it; it was totally empty, without a trace of ever having had habitants, except a few mice. *How long has this place been vacant?* I was curious about its history and decided to do some internet searching later on the house's and servants' quarters' past.

I exited through the front door and walked back to the main house. I saw a small reflection of light near the quarters' foundation, which changed in intensity depending on the angle from which I was viewing it. I reached down and sifted through the dirt with my fingers, wondering how much more dirt was required to shore up the overhang. My fingers felt something metallic, and as I cleared away the dirt, I found a metal necklace partially buried in the dirt. I pulled on the exposed part of the chain and discovered a green stone attached to the necklace. The stone and necklace, on further inspection, had the look and feel of quality. There was something else about the necklace. I felt an odd tingling sensation through my hands, traversing up my arms, when I came in close proximity. I felt a shivering awareness that provided a calm, harmonious bliss—a fleeting moment when all my anxiety dispersed, replaced by unquestionable faith, as if everything had a positive purpose. The concept of negativity didn't exist. There was something else undeniable. A sensation emerged just for a brief interlude, a vision of a time and place down memory lane: a boy and girl deeply in love were walking on an old blacktop road, displaying a mood of soulful peace and ultimate harmony.

I wondered how long the necklace had been buried without being noticed. It must have been buried deep, and the Santa Ana winds and torrential rainfall from a few weeks ago, along with the start of our shoring up the overhang, seemed to have unearthed the object. I found that the stone was a green emerald. A locket was attached to the bottom of the gem, partly covered by a layer of grime. I was able to mostly wipe the locket clear of debris, revealing an engraving on the locket's front cover: "With love." I opened the locket, and the date appeared as 1935. There was another engraving on the inside of the locket, together with a tiny photo. The engraving was also partly caked with mud. After wiping the locket clean, I read the print: "To Cassandra with love." I looked at the piece in stunned silence. I held the piece closer to view the tiny photo. It was difficult to view because a portion of the photo was damaged. A couple was standing in front of the house, but their faces were not clear enough to discern any resemblance to the photo I'd discovered upstairs. A portion of the photo was too grainy due to age, and I would need a magnifier to see more clearly and look for any resemblance. I then realized 1935 was the same year as the newspaper clipping upstairs in the bedroom. My feeling of urgency picked up pace, and I briskly walked toward the back door of the main house.

Midway between the quarters and the back door, I felt a hand on my shoulder and a whisper of breath in my ear. I caught the scent of Cassandra's perfume. I felt a sensual touch on the back of my neck. A whisper near my ear said, "Hurry back to me."

I rushed in through the main house's doorway, and again, I caught the scent and went upstairs but with a heightened awareness. My pace quickened with a hint of concern. When I reached the upper landing, the scent seemed as fresh as ever, coming from the dressing room. The master bedroom was a large, spacious room, and the back wall was all glass, which allowed a magnificent view of the Pacific. I went to the dressing room and found the night-light on, with the scent of her perfume fresh. By then, I was becoming accustomed to those signs of her physical presence. Before, the cryptic messages had triggered a relentless, frantic search for her, but each time, my search had proven fruitless. The emotional impact never changed. But now my response was more of a planned, measured search versus a frantic search with an uncontrolled wildness driven by raw emotion.

I followed her scent, which led me near the bathroom. I ventured into the bathroom, where the scent disappeared. I felt a sudden drop of hope and expectation, a rapid descent into despondency, leading me to the verge of a panicked cry for Cassandra. As I turned around to exit the bathroom, I glanced at my reflection in the mirror and saw the impact of the tension and anxiety on my appearance. My haggard image reflected my inner turmoil, as if I were precariously perched on a narrow ledge and viewing the depths of hellish madness below. I felt I had one foot on the ledge and the other perilously suspended in midair over the abyss of insanity. *Am I going mad? Or am I already there? Have I crossed the line with a slow, gradual descent into the hellish hole of madness?* I had asked myself those questions countless times with the same response. Once again, I realized I had no choice but to continue forging ahead, clearing a road of discovery to unravel the enigma—to discover the reality of lunacy or to discover the truth behind the swirl of mysticism.

I walked toward the bed and saw a new pair of crimson petals lying on the pillow. I picked them up and caught the scent of her perfume. I shouted into the vacant air, "If you are here, Cassandra, let me know! Give me a sign. Show me the way back." I then went to the picture on the wall and removed the picture from the back canvas. I pulled out the photo and newspaper clipping and started reading again with the intent of discovery.

I first saw the date: 1935. The story began with an assailant assaulting a couple with a firearm. Several shots were fired in the ballroom of a resort in Santa Cruz, California. The victims' names were withheld for security reasons. The condition of the victims was unknown at the time. They were taken back to the lady's house, where they summoned several medical personnel, including a well-known surgeon. The house was located in the canyons, in a new area known as Ocean View. The assailant was taken into custody, but a commotion occurred, and the assailant escaped. His whereabouts were still unknown. The condition of the victims was still undisclosed. That was the essence of the news clipping. The article was brief and ended with photos of the couple and the house they were taken to. I did not recognize the address and assumed it might have changed over the past decades from the 1930s until now. The community of Ocean View was a fact, I knew. After World War II, in the late '40s, during the housing boom, Ocean View was renamed Canyon View. If they'd renamed the community, it was almost certain the streets had been renamed, which led to my assumption of the victims' address.

The photos of the house were badly faded from age, and to make things worse, the sections of the newspaper clipping that contained more photos was torn, making it impossible to determine with certainty if the house was the same house Linda and I had purchased and if the woman in the photo was Cassandra. I was not surprised that any resemblance was only a probability. Everything related to that enigmatic world of mine was an uncertainty. Upon further scrutiny of the house photos, I found a lot of similarities. The architecture of the house was based on the art deco theme common during the decades prior to and during World War II. The servants' quarters also were designed with the same theme. Servants' quarters during that decade were in more affluent areas, which included Ocean View.

The photo of the couple was as faded as those of the house. It was difficult to identify the couple, but from what I could view with some clarity, I was able to identify several items that added some significance to my assumptions. The young lady in the part of the photo that was still relatively clear had a striking resemblance to Cassandra. She wore a necklace with an attached emerald. If the photo had been clearer, I could have used a magnifying lens to check for an engraving. But that was a big if and could not be erased because of the damage to the photos.

46

Inside the Servants' Quarters: Possible Demise of Cassandra

There were enough clues for me to be reasonably sure there was a connection. Whether the house was the same as in the photo was one variable that required more insight. With renewed determination, I went back out to the servants' quarters. I stopped near the place where I'd found the necklace and bent down to search for anything I might have missed. I shifted through the loose dirt with my fingers, digging deeper, searching for anything that might have been loosened by the work of the construction crew shoring up the overhang to the main house. There was nothing else I detected. There had to be something. I had a gut feeling there was more there; my instincts were acutely attuned, as if something or someone were directly connected to my senses, conveying to me an urgency to keep on searching, telling me there was a connection that, with vigilant pursuit, I would soon discover.

I stood up and took another look at the area surrounding the servants' quarters. I felt that I wasn't seeing something because it was too obvious. I walked in front of the servants' house to get a broader perspective. There was nothing unusual. I walked to the side of the house, continuing toward the rear. I bent down to sift through the dirt, searching for something revealing, but the ground was hard. I walked toward the back of the home to discover the same thing. I walked toward the other end, where the construction was, and saw where the ground had been broken into solid chunks. Once I got to the end of the rear of the house, I turned the corner and walked along the other side of the house. I continued along the side, examining the ground around the foundation. I saw that the ground was torn up in spots but not to the point where I could easily comb through the loose dirt. I continued to examine the area around the foundation until I reached the spot where I'd found the necklace. Sure enough, the ground was loose. I bent down near the ground and reached in with my hand. My hand easily pushed its way through the loosely filled earth until I was in up to my elbow. That loose soil was not the result of shoring up the overhang, I concluded. Instead, I assumed it was the result of some intervention by animal or human. I pushed farther and still did not encounter anything. The earth against the foundation at that spot was too loose, not a hard surface, as it was around the foundation. My suspicions emerged; I believed that someone was digging for a reason.

I started to pull my hand out, and it brushed against something solid. I moved my hand farther to the side to have a firmer grasp. Despite the loose dirt, getting a hold on the object was difficult. My hand was numb, and getting a firm grasp proved to be a challenge. With my other hand, I reached down, and I grasped the object with my fingers from both hands. I rapidly brought the object up to see what I had. A heavy coat of dirt and grime caked the object, and it took thirty minutes to clear all the caked debris away. It was a diamond ring. The stone was a yellow diamond. On the back side of the ring was an engraving: "To my princess with love. Until next summer." I looked again, as if I were drawn to the engraving. Those words held a significant implication for me. But I couldn't place when and where. I felt the engraving pulling on a hidden memory frantic for recognition. I felt it tug at my heart with heavenly bliss and a painful sorrow. The ring conveyed both emotions to me. But the lure wasn't strong enough; the years were hidden, frozen in time, and I needed more time, which I didn't have.

I picked up the ring and held it in the sunlight. An image came to the surface of the diamond: a young girl who had a sketch pad, looking toward the heavens. It lasted but an instant; it too was locked in time. I took the ring with me, knowing it held a precious memory that would reveal itself when the time was right. I carefully inserted it into my pocket. I needed to look at the picture at the main house to see if the woman was wearing a yellow diamond. However, that most likely would be a challenge because of the condition of the photos.

I headed back to the front door of the servants' quarters to look for anything else that could be related or provide a possible connection to the one area by the foundation. I walked up to the front and stood there, pausing before opening the door. A subtle shift in the elements around me caused me to take notice. I felt a sudden chill in the air, which was highly unusual for that time of year. A sudden frigid gust of wind swept past me, causing me to hunch over, before the air returned to a dead calm. Twilight was setting in fast. I watched the sun sinking rapidly over the horizon, and the quietness of the early evening immediately became apparent. It was too quiet. There was not a sound. There were no signs of any movement. Everything felt hollow and hauntingly silent, as if the sunset were absorbing the very essence of life energy from everything that immediately surrounded me. Night's creatures were eerily hushed, and there was not a whisper of a breeze. Everything had an unnatural silence, like the calm that encompassed the dead after a soul departed to other spiritual domains. A sudden chilling breeze carried the moans I'd heard from the ghostly transit I'd experienced in Neverland. Whispers from a breeze said one word: "Beware." Every hair on my neck stood on end. Then everything stopped; there was no movement and no sound except my own breathing—a moment frozen in time, with me enclosed in its vortex. "Something is wrong," said a whisper. The whisper was from Cassandra. Her shadow, carrying her scent, quickly passed before me.

I heard a commotion behind the front door. "Impossible," I said out loud. I'd just checked the inside earlier and found nothing—a complete void absent of life's energy, like the nothingness of a cemetery as the clock struck midnight. I heard two voices. Cassandra was one of the voices. The other voice was a male who seemed to be threatening Cassandra. I heard a struggle ensue, followed by a silence. Worried about Cassandra, I quickly opened the front door and rushed inside. The view in front of me defied normalcy. I didn't see anyone on the main floor, yet the house was completely furnished. The furnishings had the look and feel of the fashionable 1930s.

I heard the same voices but could not pinpoint the source. I heard another commotion and then felt the vibration when someone or something came crashing down on the upstairs floor. There was no guessing this time as I felt another vibration from above. I hurried upstairs and stood still, trying to determine the source of the commotion. Once again, the noise became nonexistent. Exasperated by the dreadful silence, I searched the upstairs room by room. Suddenly, I picked up a noise. *Where did that come from? Was that upstairs or downstairs?* If the source of the noise was downstairs, I surely would not have missed it. I heard someone climbing the stairway from the first floor. I retreated toward one of the rooms. I saw a glimpse of a male reaching the upper landing in the hallway and then entering an adjacent room.

I followed him and saw his back side. He had his shoulders hunched tightly, and his walk was hesitant; he was treading cautiously with his head titled slightly, assuming a prowler's prance. I yelled for him to turn around. I saw a slight twist of his head while he hesitated, and then he cautiously turned around. There was no doubt in my recognition: it was the stranger from the shadowy corner of the ballroom. He had on the same mask he'd worn when I last encountered him, the same type the couples had worn in the atrium lounge. The only difference was the expression. The expressions on the couples' masks had been those of clowns' smiles or tears of sorrow. The stranger's expression was more of a crazed look.

He must have seen my surprise. "Recognize me? Of course not. You don't want to see what is behind this mask. Not yet at least. It is not time. But soon. I promise. Very soon. I am always there when you are with her. In the shadows."

I was not surprised. I'd suspected it when I first noticed him mostly hidden in the shadows.

"And you are Tony? Looking for Cassandra?"

I just stood there with my eyes and ears glued to his every movement, hearing every word and processing everything—flight or fight. "Yes to both questions," I responded.

"Well, Tony, you will never see her again. I am Cassandra's husband. I have her at a location you will never find. As far as you are concerned, consider Cassandra dead."

A fiery hatred charged through my soul, and my posture took on an assault demeanor. His eyes beheld my pose; his own stance was one of wariness, jockeying for a strategic position to ward off any assault. He reached under his coat, pulled out a pistol, and raised it slowly, pointing it in my direction. I approached him, and he stepped back, his grip on the trigger tightening with each step.

We both halted in a moment of hesitancy as our defensive posturing got in our way temporarily. I surged toward him, and he fired off a shot, hitting my shoulder. The impact stunned me, knocking me to the floor. I surged for him again as he eluded my grasp. I saw him retreat toward the lower level. Desperately, I got up, stumbled out into the hallway, and descended the stairs. When I reached the lower level, he wasn't there. I overheard a distant scream from Cassandra. I advanced to the den, following the source of the scream. When I reached the den, I heard Cassandra scream again. This time, it was a high-pitched shrill. The scream was near, but I could not pinpoint the exact location. I heard another shot behind me and felt a sudden jolt of pain in my upper leg. My leg went numb, unable to support my weight, and I came crashing down onto the floor.

I became light-headed, and my vision blurred. I was just able to make out the assailant descending a flight of stairs. My vision dimmed, and the tunnel of light became a narrow beam. I must have dozed off for a while. The bright late afternoon had turned to a clear twilight. I remembered the assailant descending another flight of stairs before I dozed off. The stairway must have been near that section of the house. Using the wall for leverage, I managed to push myself up to a standing position. Some feeling returned to my left leg, allowing some movement.

I searched the lower level, unable to find any stairway leading to the lower level. I searched again, feeling the walls and avoiding making any noise that would attract the assailant's attention. Any area on the wall where I detected a distinct temperature change could have been due to an absence of insulation behind the wall, leading to a possibility of a stairway to a lower level. If that were the case, there had to be a way to reveal the stairway, whether through a panel or a hidden device that would trigger an opening to the staircase. Once I found an area unusually warm or cold, I tapped the surface a few times, keeping my movements as stealthy as possible to avoid alerting the assailant's attention. I found a spot near the small fireplace adjacent to the den. There was an area on the wall where there was a distinct change in temperature. The area had a frigid feel to it. "This has to be it!" I exclaimed in an excited tone infused with forced hopefulness. I searched next for a panel, a switch, or any form of a trigger to reveal an opening to the stairwell. My efforts yielded no results.

However, the assailant must have heard me. I heard some commotion downstairs. A male was shouting, and then a pitiful mourn came from Cassandra. She was there in harm's way, and I needed to find the entrance to the stairway. I hammered on the wall to distract the assailant, redirecting his attention from Cassandra to me. It worked, for within a few seconds, I heard footsteps climbing up to the main floor. I had to conceal myself in a place where I could detect the entrance to the lower level once he arrived, and besides, hiding would give me the element of surprise. Using the rest of my reserves, I was able to reach the doorway of the den and drag myself through. I found a place by the bookcase, where I waited once he started his search upon finding me missing. Some time passed without any sign of him.

My reserves were depleted, and I fought a losing battle to stay alert. My exhaustion and weariness overcame me, and I withdrew to the Land of Nod. Cassandra suddenly appeared, her image hovering over me. Her hand gracefully caressed my face. Every brush of her fingertips against my face soothed my soul, igniting a need to be by her side. Her touch exceeded a desperate want, igniting a long-awaited, desperate, necessary connection for our survival. "Tony, my love. Your turmoil and anguish are well founded. But there are things unknown to you that rationalize what you perceive as an endless conflict of realities. There exists a underlying pattern that you cannot perceive until we are together again. You are entering the precipice of a reservoir of knowledge that will reveal everything. This journey is nearing an end. It is our way of moving on. We shall exit this journey as a couple. At the same time, our departed souls will rejoin and rejoice. This marks our journey in which we wait to take our rightful position in the chamber of gatekeepers. The end is near. Soon you will realize this, and once the recognition takes hold, embrace it. It marks a new beginning for us."

I reached out with my fingers to respond and tap into her surge of energy. Her presence gradually withdrew, yielding to a shower of crimson rose petals. They floated around me, carrying the fragrance of her perfume. I reached out toward the petals and pushed them to the side, revealing a new image of Cassandra thrashing about where she lay, nearing the end. I knew the end was near, and my heart watched. Every moan was a searing pain that reached the depths of my soul. I reached out to sooth her pain, aware that our separate journeys would end only for us to begin a new journey together. The darkness enclosed me again, revealing a band of bright images that paraded before me. I saw images of our past eras, each carrying delegate cargo of precious memories of Cassandra and me. Now I knew that Cassandra was real. A unparalleled loss encapsulated me, with memories past yielding to a vast array of new, yet-to-be-experienced wonders. At that moment, I knew Cassandra finally had died. Watching her soul racing toward me, I cried out with anguish and despair. My torment was unbearable as glimpses of memories became just distant echos from a past, quick to disperse before any assimilation took hold. For an instant, I felt my heart breaking, as it had when we were younger and had to depart from those precious summer interludes in Neverland. At that moment, I wanted to die to forego any more heartbreak. I had nothing left. It was my time now to join Cassandra and walk that path one more time to our fishing pond, where our love protected us. I had to travel that old country road again.

I rose from a deep sleep to discover I was outside on the ground by the foundation of the servants' quarters. I looked around and heard the noises of a typical, normal day. The deathly quiet from gearlier was no longer present. In its place, a sense of normalcy filled the gap. It wasn't twilight anymore but late afternoon. I climbed back to the doorway and returned to the den. The house was empty, as I'd found it during my initial search. There wasn't anyone present. I didn't hear even the slightest moan. I walked over to where the stranger had exited the stairway from the lower level. I pounded on the wall, heedless of the noise. At that point, I invited a confrontation with the assailant. The wall seemed solid, with no differences in temperature. There was sufficient insulation.

I exited the servants' quarters in a quandary. Nothing made sense. It all seemed unreal, with no consistency. What appeared as real in one setting was thoroughly disputed or nullified in another setting. It was a world of contrasts. It wasn't just an occasional disparity between the presented views of reality but a disparity of entirely different worlds, each with its own separate view of my reality. Maybe this was the afterlife, a heaven born out of our disparate memories. Each distinct memory presented a separate domain of reality. Some encapsulated dreams of haunting demise, and others partnered with hope-filled dreams. That was my dilemma, a quagmire of enigmatic views, realities of heaven and hell.

47

Unexpected Discovery of the Cove and the Chamber

I walked down the gated fence for no particular reason except to look out over the Pacific. The peaceful setting was a soothing sight and provided much-needed insight. I was at my wits' end, feeling entirely defeated. I must have stood there by the gated fence for a good half hour as the last ten years of my life unfolded before me. Beyond that was a lost cause. I was unable to bring forth life chapters prior to my memory block. At that moment, it all seemed hopeless. I didn't know if Cassandra was dead or alive.

I stood by the railing, watching a cruise ship glide across the horizon, presenting a view of poetic harmony. Instead of providing a cushion of comfort to relieve my anxiety and provide more insight into the complex scenario, the view dramatized the contrast between the harmony I desperately sought and the reality of chaos that filled my world. It heightened my anxiety and feeling of desperation. I leaned over the railing, gauging the distance between where I stood and the landing below. A perilous fall would surely break one's neck if someone accidentally tripped over the edge. The word *if* stuck in my mind, serving as the linchpin for rational perspective, yet the crushing weight of pending disaster prophesied by the hellish visages that had demonized my journey had censured any rationality from my judgment.

I peered over the railing, more determined to yield to unrelenting dejection. My steadfast barrier that served as the break wall from the undercurrents of my propensity to thwart my instincts to persevere was crumbling. Frantic for a stoppage, I called out to Cassandra for a sign of hope. If there was a time when I needed her, it was now. I lifted my vision, peering out over the Pacific, waiting for any sign from Cassandra to no avail. I started to step down from the railing, when I detected an oddity along the side of the cliff, under the overhang. There was a cave-like opening in the mountainside about fifty yards below. That was not unusual; among the canyons that ran along the coastline, there were numerous coves, and several were connected to form a labyrinthine network of tunnels through the coastal mountain range. Most of the caves and inlets were camouflaged by nature's own abundant undergrowth. But that was where the discrepancy began. The inlet I saw had minimal underbrush, and what did exist seemed to be new. More convincing was the placement of the foliage. It was laid out too proportionately. The shrubbery did not follow nature's random pattern of sprouting new growth. It appeared an unsuccessful attempt to camouflage an inlet into the mountainside below. I needed a closer look. I searched the area around the fence that stretched from near the servants' quarters to the far end of the main house. There was no obvious way to descend to the inlet. I saw a partially hidden, narrow path several yards from where the railing ended. Some portions were covered by overgrown thickets, which implied it had been awhile since the path was used.

I struggled my way through the thicket. It was a difficult task due to lack of equipment. I finally cleared the path to end up at the edge of the cliff, where I perilously stepped closer to the ledge to view the Pacific pounding the shoreline below. I had a better view of the inlet from that angle but still could not determine an easy route to the cove. I scrambled back to the trail and scoured the perimeter around the trail. I saw several heavy limbs fallen from the vicious storms that had battered the coastline last year. I thrashed my way to the nearest limb. There by the fallen limb, farther back, was another trail that wound its way down into the dense foliage that covered the mountainside. My excitement level inched higher with increased anticipation, prompting me to scramble over the downed limbs to reach the hidden path. My hands were raw, and I had red welts on my arms from treading through the foliage. I stopped to take my shirt off and tear it into strips to wrap around my hands to avoid deeper cuts and possible serious infection. I used the remaining fabric to cover each arm as a temporary shield from the thickets, which were becoming denser while I continued following the winding path down the mountainside. After an hour of exhausting effort, I came to a small area where the undergrowth was sparse. "This is it!" I exclaimed with ecstatic relief. It was apparent that area had been leveled out and then filled in haphazardly with shrubbery. The cove entrance was several yards ahead, and with anxious anticipation, I headed toward the entrance.

Once inside, I discovered that the cove opened up to a large cavern the size of a huge chamber. The farther back I explored, the more difficult it became to navigate for lack of light. In hindsight, I wished I would have retrieved the proper equipment before I committed to exploring the mountainside. *But hindsight makes us all geniuses,* I thought in attempt to exonerate my oversight. I exited the cave and walked back to the trail to return to the house. When I reached the top, I paused to recoup my spent energy. I saw that twilight was settling in and decided to return to the cave in the morning with the necessary equipment. Before I headed back home, I wanted to go up to the main house to search for a light, gloves, and other equipment I'd need when I returned to the cavern to explore more thoroughly.

I trudged up the walkway that curved around the overhang to the steps leading up to the back door.

I didn't know if the house had anything I could use for the trip tomorrow morning. Probably not. I imagined if there was a flashlight, the batteries would be useless. But the maintenance crew might have the supplies on site somewhere. Once inside the house, I searched the downstairs for a storage area, but I only found rooms meant primarily for clothes and other personal items. I opened the back door to the outside by the overhang for one more look.

I hadn't realized the overhang extended out that far. Once under the overhang, I was surprised how far back it went before the open space reached the rear wall. The overhang had enough space underneath to accommodate two large storage rooms. There never had been a reason for me to search them until then. I was sure the maintenance crew had stored some basic supplies in one of the storage rooms, but I wasn't sure which one. Both storage areas were locked, and I didn't have the number for the maintenance crew. Impatiently, I retrieved the tire iron from the trunk of my car and used it as a wedge to open the first door. My search turned up landscaping equipment and gasoline containers, among miscellaneous items. I found a pair of work gloves that fit a little snugly but would be doable for tomorrow. Toward the rear, I found two large flashlights in good condition. I needed some sturdy equipment to handle climbing down the mountainside in the morning. Hoping for a hard hat, goggles, and possibly climbing gear, I tried the other storage unit, opening the door with the tire iron. Once inside, I encountered a vast open area large enough to hold an M60 tank. It was empty. I turned on one of the heavy-duty flashlights and saw that the back wall was set farther back, cast in shadows. I walked toward the back, and against the back wall was another door hidden in the corner. The floor around the door was littered with loose black dirt. I knelt down on one knee to get a feel of the dirt. It had the same color and fine consistency as the soil I'd found by the servants' quarters' foundation. I suspected there could be a connection. The door was made out of heavy, sturdy, solid oak and locked, which presented a formidable obstacle. All I had was a tire iron. I started to pry away chips of wood, hacking away for what seemed like an hour. Realizing the damage would be beyond repair, I was prepared to pay for a new door. More than an hour passed before I was able to dislodge the lock.

The door felt as if it were made out of lead. I hadn't been aware that oak was that heavy. Maybe *heavy* was the wrong word to use, but the oak was definitely dense, making the door a chore to open. I knew it must have been awhile since the door had been used, as the door hinges were covered with rust. Finally, I succeeded in opening the door wide enough to maneuver my way in. Despite the flashlights, the room was cloaked with shadows because the door was not open wide enough to let much light in. I left the room in order to pull the oak door wider. Finally, I was able to open the door wide enough that it would give me the space to enter and shed more light around the shadowed area. Once back inside, I viewed the size of the room. It was enormous, way too big for a storage shed. I walked farther inside, using my searchlight. There was a hallway on my left that extended out beyond the range of light provided. Using my flashlight, I followed the hallway until it ended, conceding to a smaller tunnel five feet in height. It was wide enough to accommodate two people side by side. I proceeded with curiosity tempered with caution, following the tunnel to a point where the tunnel took a turn, and the walkway made a sudden, steep decline. Off in the distance, I could hear the sounds of the ocean pounding the shoreline. I continued the downward trajectory until I reached the end. I found myself in the cavern I'd discovered earlier that day. I knew the canyons formed an elaborate connection of tunnels, but why was the other end reinforced with support beams lined with a cement wall? For what purpose? I couldn't tell when the tunnel last had been used. I couldn't find any fresh tracks except for those of a few rats scurrying about. I turned around and walked back to the chamber. I was weary from the day's exhausting effort, but my suspicions about a possible connection to the mystery had me committed. When I reached the chamber, I noticed an unusual contrast in the shadows that occupied the other corner of the chamber. My curiosity piqued and my suspicions fueled by the clandestine nature of what I had uncovered so far, I proceeded to the other corner of the chamber.

There was another doorway, and upon further inspection, I found the door was open by a fraction of an inch. With all of the secrecy, why was that door still open? The door handle was not attached, and as I tried to open the door wider, it moved with relative ease. I saw tracks from the doorway leading to the tunnel in the opposite corner. I walked into the room and detected an overpowering sulfuric smell. I switched on my light and saw a modern room with a platform in the middle, surrounded by several metal devices. I saw a wall switch and turned it on. There were no lights. The device at the foot of the table had multiple electrodes that emitted a violent electrical current. The air had an acrid, burned stench. I turned off the switch, walked over to the end of steel gurney, and noticed splattered blood on the floor by the foot of the bed and on the end of the gurney. I brushed the blood spots with my fingertips and found the blood dry. The blood had a flat tone, which meant it had been there for a while. I walked to the head of the gurney and saw numerous strands of hair. I bent down to see if there was blood. I caught the fragrance of the perfume Cassandra wore. I also detected the sweet scent that could only have belonged to one person:

Cassandra. I searched the room for any sign that Cassandra was there. I found a note that had one word: "Cassandra."

So Cassandra was there. Everything looked as if it had not been used for a while. Dust coated everything. I searched the room for clues and found a single set of tracks leading from the platform to the chamber door. *What is this place? What happened here?* It was obvious that whatever had happened there had not been recent. The trail of evidence to support my assumption that Cassandra had been there as a victim was also not recent. I was too exhausted to think anymore and decided to call it a night. I felt torn; my search for Cassandra was drawing me forward, yet the lack of sleep was too overpowering, consuming my attention and pulling me away to reenergize for another day. I knew from the evidence found in the room that something had happened to Cassandra, and it wasn't good. But the blanket of fatigue was too heavy to carry anymore, at least for tonight. I couldn't focus anymore, let alone keep my eyes open; staying there to look for more clues would have been fruitless because of the weariness. It was best if I started anew and fresh with an alert mind in the morning to examine the room with careful attention. Too drained to focus, I left the chamber, exiting out onto the elegant green lawn. I closed the doors leading to the open chamber as best as I could; my exhaustion was so intense that sleep became my only focus.

I wearily trudged my way back up to the main house to check the rest of the locks and security timed lights. Once I felt everything was secured, I walked to my Maxima, sat behind the wheel, and looked at my watch. It was well past eleven o'clock at night. *What the hell?* My words tainted with lassitude and my impatience filled with venom and vindictiveness as the weight of my fear and worry bore down unrelentingly, in a fit of rage, I tore out from the circular driveway onto Canyon Ridge Trails, mindless of any pending traffic. I needed sleep before I succumbed to a vein of vicious contempt.

I reached my house in record time. I pulled out the remote and parked in the attached garage. I was tense and overtired; nervous anxiety was triggering a rush of adrenaline. I was tired from an endless barrage of unknowns, yet restlessness kept sleep at bay. I laid my head on the steering column to mentally unwind. I needed a double straight shot of brandy. I opened the car door and got out on wobbly legs. I stood and stretched my legs before walking to the side door leading to the den. Once inside, I reached for the bourbon resting on the middle shelf of the hutch. The effects were immediate. My eyes weary, I pulled myself upstairs to the master bedroom on the third floor. I threw my clothes into the hamper, turned off the lights, and collapsed onto the bed, oblivious to the mystery as sleep pulled me into a comatose state.

48

Another Dream Episode:
Approaching Neverland

I heard the sounds of movement—rhythmic noise akin to white noise, always a pitch with slight variation. Something was moving on wheels, and periodically, a clicking sound interrupted the steady hum. The sounds were muffled at first, but they were becoming more pronounced.

The transport, the vehicle that seemed to be my transporter between the fused states of realism and fantasy, was slowing down, and I looked out my window to see the depot drawing near. I became aware of a vibration under my seat, which grew in intensity with each passing moment. With a jolt, the train accelerated upon its arrival. The vibration grew more intense, in sync with its increased speed. The village view became more distant, as if we'd reversed our direction, but as I looked out the window, I knew that was impossible, for our forward movement was marked by the swiftness of the clouds as they retreated. The logic of reason was no longer applicable. Sanity's last hold on me seemed to be on the run, and I was fearful of the consequences of its tenuous hold. The bands that had the flexibility to yield to enormously tumulus pulls on reality were stretched to their limit. I could hear the stretching sound as the tension approached its limit to hold on to its grasp of sanity. The tearing sounds from the tension became noticeable as the threads tore loose from the fabric of reality, the wire taunt leads breaking free from the infrastructure supporting reality's framework.

Again, a flash of light reappeared as the beacon reapproached the train with an even greater luminosity. I sensed the train halt; its breath came in wheezes as it groaned with reluctance, as if it were waiting for a reprieve to enter the village limits. *Only room for one form of hell at a time.* I laughed out loud. The flash of light pushed forward. This time, however, it did not retreat but continued until it was adjacent to my window. I avoided a direct look because of the intensity of the light, fearful it would damage my retinas. The light dimmed to half its brightness, seemingly aware of my caution, and it spread open like an angel spreading its six-foot wings.

49

A Dream: Panoramic View of Scenes from Neverland

The wings opened to their full extension, giving way to a huge panoramic view of a scene. Cassandra was lying on a metal table with not a movement. I couldn't tell if she was conscious. It seemed she was barely breathing. Her sleep was too shallow, as if it were drug-induced. The scene changed to a large home situated on a cliff overlooking the Pacific. I looked again with intense focus. I remembered the house. In my vague recollection, it was the house on Canyon Ridge Trails. I saw myself walking the hallway and stopping at the top of a stairway leading to a lower level. That was odd, I thought, remembering that when Linda and I had viewed the house before purchasing it, I hadn't noticed any stairway leading to a lower level, except the outside overhang, where a steep set of stairs descended to ground level before circling around underneath where two large storage areas resided behind a pair of oak doors. That fact would have caused me doubts about the house being the same as the one we'd purchased, but the similarities were too convincing and outweighed any doubts. The scene fast-forwarded to me walking into the bedroom on the third floor. The scene diverted to a corner of the room adjacent to the upper patio door, where I retrieved the newspaper clipping from the picture I viewed. I read of the unsolved disappearance of a couple who once had owned the house. The scene abruptly stopped, giving way to a new view of a small village—Neverland. But the view projected a village abundant with vibrant energy, unlike the village downtrodden with despair that inhabited my recent dreams. Cassandra's image reappeared briefly before her appearance took a noticeable change. The change in her appearance was regressive. Subtle changes happened to Cassandra as time regressed backward from her present state to an earlier time when she was just a young girl walking an old country road. I was the young boy walking with her hand in hand as we strolled carefree without any concerns—a luxury provided by youth's shield of naïveté.

The scenes abruptly froze, followed by another series of images, each from a recent dream with Cassandra. Each image presented as a visual frame from each episode. The rose petal and the letter floated in midair, approaching me as I grasped for both. But before I connected with them, the scene gave way to another view: Cassandra and me on the ballroom floor, dancing to a favorite tune. Another setting urgently grabbed my attention. Cassandra and I were resting on the bed on the third level. A drop of blood flowed down the center of the scene and then gradually spread into a widening pool of blood that seeped over the side of the bed. Cassandra and I were on top of the bed. We were both wounded. But it was Cassandra, with her head bowed over mine, that drew my attention. Tears of resignation fell in slow motion, each drop descending on my face. My eyes suddenly opened, and the vision came to a halt. A new scene appeared. It was difficult to view, for it only encompassed a shadow; its intense cloudiness alternated between complete obscurity and a fraction of clarity. For a moment, I thought I saw a human form, but before any chance of recognition, it vanished. The panoramic view grew dark and closed when its luminous light drew to a pinhole and then dissolved into the empty darkness.

The beacon returned to normal, whatever *normal* meant. Its light reduced to a shiny star of hope and then disappeared into a darkness of desolation before cycling back and reappearing, regaining its cyclical pattern. The train whimpered with a hissing groan that grew with a mounting force of reenergized energy. I sensed that its period of stillness had been to allow me to experience the series of images, and now that the true essence of what I'd viewed had melded with my soul, the belated first act in that heralded mystery would begin. This time, the engine groaned with an exertion of force as if it were pulling the full load of the world's past events as baggage hooked to the passenger car I inhabited. It was as if the train stopped, waiting for my entire history of karmic existence to be loaded as my personal baggage. I heard a conductor yell out, "Boarding complete!" and the transport commenced its journey without a second to spare.

I held my hands around my head with my head buried low as I strained to filter in everything I had viewed for the last hour. I looked at my watch and realized it was just short of thirty minutes since we'd stopped. I laughed out loud, on the edge of losing it—my entire karmic existence had taken only thirty minutes to load. It made me feel minuscule to realize that I represented only a fraction of time compared to the infinite time of the entire universe. I felt like a grain of sand in a combined sea of sand from all the beaches in the world.

But besides my feelings of diminutive stature, my instincts told me I'd just viewed the hooks that connected everything. It was not a clue but a series of clues presented to me that gave me renewed hope. It did not make sense logically, but that was because I needed more time to connect the dots. I'd been presented with what I was seeking: bits and pieces of a giant puzzle that, with the necessary insight, would finally reveal the right path to navigate through that maze. I would be able to apply reason and logic to ensure that every piece connected.

As I sat in the passenger seat, the transport accelerated its forward motion. I repeatedly felt that at any moment, the torrid flow of hideous, freakish events that had turned my world into a twisted reality would drain my will to persevere. Despite the dark undercurrents of hell dismantling my sense of being, my perseverance had held on to reach this one moment of renewed hope that marked my first step of a lone journey toward resolution. I felt that the scenes I had just witnessed were the beginning of another journey leading to a discovery to unblock the enigma. I still was not sure how much of what was presented to me was real versus imaginary. I had to establish some baseline of reality to even have a chance of unraveling the mystery. That meant decoupling of fantasy from reality was necessary to build a baseline. There was only one place where that was possible: Neverland. A final trip to Neverland was necessary. With reluctance, I committed, in part because I had no choice. I felt I was enclosed in a spiderweb of hell, at its center, vulnerable to the venom of a spiderlike creature that could appear at any moment to travel down its web of entanglement to devour me and send any hope I held on to tenaciously into an eternal emptiness of nothingness. With unparalleled fear, I mustered my last reserve of nerve and courage to take the final ride back to the village. If eternity did exist, I hoped my journey would end there.

I felt the thrust of the diesel engines mounting to full capacity as if in acknowledgment of my renewed fortitude and resolve to finally finish the mission bestowed on me. As my resolve regained its obsession, I the train back to the village climbed to maximum speed with an alarming velocity. The village must have been farther away than I'd originally suspected, for I felt as if we were gliding in midair along the rails. I looked out at the window again and caught the revolving beacon of light drawing nearer toward my final destination. The memories from each scene became clearly etched into the foreground of my consciousness, where the connections were already forming.

The train started its descent, and from somewhere, I heard a conductor call out, "Neverland, next stop!" That was my calling card, the echo from somewhere in my past, a messenger from a deed long ago that needed closure in order for me to salvage my resting place with Cassandra in whatever place fate had in store for us.

I took a few precious minutes to collect myself and prepare for my reentry. I looked out the window again before the final stop. I could see behind the depot as the transport made its swing into the village along the curved track. I saw a carriage and realized the beacon of light was the lantern that swung back and forth on top of the carriage as it slowed to a stop and waited for me to embark. There was a light from within the carriage, and I saw Cassandra within.

My transport slowed to a stop in a surprise departure from my previous rides, which had screeched to a halt with a forceful jolt. I walked toward the passenger exit, aware of the wheezing groan of the engine catching its breath from its frantic marathons. I stepped onto the platform, directly facing the depot entrance. Unlike last time, the scene had an eerie sensation of silence. The silence seemed like a weight, a false sensation of calm. It was too quiet. It felt like the eerie stillness before the approach of a tempest with malicious intent that would breed an avalanche of torrential calamity.

50

Cassandra Held Captive

Precariously perched on a cliff of wariness and caution, I approached the depot entrance. I opened the door with trepidation and walked toward the rear exit. Midway, I stopped when I heard and felt a slightbrush alongside my neck. A feeling of fingertips feathered its way up toward my scalp. A voice whispered into my right ear. It was too soft to hear—more of a vibration against my inner ear, causing slight vertigo. The room spun, on tilt momentarily, causing me to sit down on the young nearest bench.

The dizziness ended as abruptly as it had started, leaving me with my senses acutely attuned to the slightest distraction. I directed my gaze to my right and saw a red petal lying next to a letter. I picked up the rose petal and felt it go limp as it withered between my fingertips. I brought it to my nose to catch her scent but instead caught the scent of decay, as if the rose petal had atrophied from the artist's loss of artistic expression. I unfolded the note and glanced at what was written. The handwriting had a different look, as if written in haste. I read an alarming message: "Tony, I am near death's front door. Before it is too late, the carriage will be your transport through our memories, with the final stop here at my bedside."

With haste, I rushed to the rear exit, and there off to the side was the familiar carriage, with its lantern perched high, casting a strange yellow tint with intermittent flashes of a red glow before relinquishing its warning facade to a background of forebode. I looked for Cassandra but caught no glimpse of her within the carriage. The driver seemed to voice a sense of urgency, but his words would fade before reaching me, as if they were dispelled by a windstorm, even though the air was eerily still. He held his whip high, ready to bring it down on his steeds to hurry off toward a destination of certain alarm. I gripped the door to the carriage, and as I closed the door, ready to settle in for the journey ahead, he lashed the whip downward, striking the rear of the horses, which surged forward at an alarming pace. With the sudden acceleration, I fell backward on the passenger seat, listening to the repeated lashings against the horses, which signaled that time was of the essence.

"Where to?" I asked the driver.

He responded, "Memory lane." I looked out the carriage window, noticing a full moon that cast a similar shade of a yellow warning. Fragments of a haze that swept by masked the yellow with pigments of orange that graduated into a fiery red before the mist swept past the moon's crescent. The air had an unnatural appearance, with a total absence of stars. The night was a chasm filled with a dense blackness pierced by just the moon's presence.

Another lashing from the driver's whip reached my ears as the vision suddenly changed. I stood alone at the ballroom's entrance. Cassandra was nowhere in sight, and I swiftly turned to the lounge. I entered and saw Cassandra sitting at the corner table. A candle's flickering glow illuminated an ethereal sheen around her face. It radiated a velvety blue glow as her glance beckoned me toward her table. I approached her, bent down to catch her scent, and gently caressed her lips as I sat next to her. "Tony!" she exclaimed. "Our journey is in haste, and we must depart now to the next moment." She bent her head and whispered in my ear, "I love you, Tony. Our destiny is in your hands. Now we must depart toward our carriage." She stood up, holding my hand, and I joined her as we departed back to the carriage.

I was suddenly in the carriage as we sped along. I wasn't sure of the time lapse; it could have been seconds, minutes, or hours. The carriage ride could have traveled for an eternity; at that moment, I did not care. I felt that ride was the journey toward salvation. The carriage ride seemed to hasten, and I felt the swiftness of the pace. The stillness previously prevalent now was filled with the echoes of the wind currents sweeping by the carriage's sides.

I heard another slashing sound of the whip. The driver's voice was distorted by the wind's currents as a three-story house perched high on a cliff came into view. All the lights were on, which was a sign of imminent foreboding. Upon my seeing the house up close, my body alerted to a staunch position, prepared to leap from the carriage in a frantic pace to the front door. Unexpectedly, the carriage slowed before arriving at its expected destination in front of the house, as if it detected my intent to exit the carriage at a perilous speed. Impatient with the pace of the carriage's rate of decline, I jumped out the side exit, not waiting for the carriage to stop. I ran up the steep walkway, and upon reaching the door, I found it ajar. The lock was hanging along the frame, and the wood was splintered. With heightened alarm, I crept into the hallway off to the side, peering around the corner. I moved toward another doorway, which led to a parlor; the kitchen was off to my left. I found no one in sight.

I heard a rustle below me. I stopped to pinpoint the source of the noise but instead was greeted with complete silence. The stillness was interrupted again by a muffled voice. With stealthy movement, I crept toward where I heard the voice. I stopped near the back of the house, where the muffled sound was directly below me. I searched for a stairway leading to a lower level. I tapped on the back walls to detect any secret panel that would reveal a stairway leading to a level below. My effort yielded no results. I walked to the patio door that led to the outside overhang. The view was a tranquil setting that reminded me of Cassandra. I heard the muffled voice again, which became more of a moan. This time, the noise seemed to come from my right. In that direction was the patio door that stretched across the rear wall of the house, yielding to a magnificent view of the ocean. I walked over to my right, near the corner, with my senses acutely tuned to detect any noise. Moving toward the corner on my right, I walked over a section that had a hollow sound to it. I pulled back a decorative oriental rug, which revealed a trapdoor. "What the hell?" I said with concern. "Another entrance to the storage area below?" That made no sense. I reached down and pulled on the attached ring. Surprised the door opened with relative ease, I discovered a steep set of stairs that descended to the level below.

I caught the scent of the special fragrance worn by Cassandra. However, there was another scent that seemed to permeate the air: a coppery smell. I soon recognized the scent as I descended down the stairway. It was the scent of blood. There was no light, and I hastily returned to the first level to find a flashlight. Within a few minutes, I was back with a heavy-duty light, which revealed a stairway that wound its way to the lower level.

I descended the staircase with stealth, each step accompanied by a furtive glance. I half expected a menacing blow to impede my progression downward. Each step was a hesitant tread down the spiral staircase. Halfway down, I found a light switch, which shed some light in front of me, making my descent more manageable. I turned off the flashlight to save whatever charge was left as the light seemed to sporadically lose its brightness. Farther down the stairway, the light had minimal effect, and the dim lighting cast shadows against the wall. The shadows seemed to oscillate in a swaying motion, as if a tree limb were casting its movement to keep rhythm to a furious wind. The farther down I treaded, the more intense the darkness became, causing the shadows to take on a more menacing look. The shadows reached out toward the circular stairwell. I tried turning on the flashlight in places where the light was too dim to be of use. I moved my right hand against the wall to balance myself, with my left hanging on to the outer rail. I heard a moan, a cry, and a whisper, and then the moan seemed to stifle to a muffled whimper. I took each step with added weight, and my senses were acutely tuned to even the slightest movement. I stopped halfway to the bottom level. I heard a sound behind me—no, in front of me—and then the direction changed. The sound seemed to create an echo that surrounded me. It was too soft to interpret yet not soft enough to mask the haunting tone. The echoes continued to revolve around me, and I turned my body, anticipating a sudden movement that would throw me off balance and cause me to fall to the bottom landing. The outcome would surely be death. The echoes became entwined with a dark, shadowy mass that increased its rotation to a frenzied spin. My vision blurred as a sudden, intense wave of vertigo jeopardized my balance on the perilous winding staircase.

Realizing that if continued, I would eventually lose my balance and plunge to the landing below, I treaded carefully downward, fighting to regain some form of equilibrium. I bent down to grab the staircase as I tried to maintain my balance, using each step as support. Step by step, I descended; each step was a tenuous hold on my fortitude. I was perilously teetering on the edge of a fear-induced meltdown. I looked down toward the landing and saw a light off to the right. I neared the bottom floor; I had just ten more steps to descend. With each step, the echoes became more distant, and the shadow became less intense, its circular spin noticeably slowing, which allowed me to gain a broader view of the bottom floor. I struggled my way down two more rungs, which allowed me a full view of the ground floor.

I carefully swept my line of vision throughout the hallway that circled the stairwell. I perceived no imminent threat and, with trepidation, allowed myself to relax my guard. Off to the right was a partially open door. Light was casting a dim glow from within. I couldn't be sure if the muffled voice I'd registered earlier had come from that room. I no longer trusted my senses, especially my hearing, and relinquished any form of logical conclusion since nothing made sense anymore on my journeys. The only fact real to me was Cassandra, and I now knew she needed help. It was imperative I find her and shield her from harm's way at any price. I shed tears of relief upon reaching the bottom floor. Again, I searched the area around the stairwell, where all seemed to be without suspicion, and my immediate fear was somewhat quelled, at least for the moment. Though everything appeared to be secure, I had an uncanny feeling that at any moment, I would once again be in harm's way. Forcing my trepidation behind a mask of security, I turned my attention to the double doors set back in the corner to the right of the vast chamber. I heard the soft whispers once more and then the muffled moan from behind the entryway. My courage and fortitude to pursue constantly wavered between aggressive pursuit and submissive retreat. This was the moment I'd felt would be presented to me, but my mixed emotions mystified me, as if I had no control over how my emotions would react. Another whisper escaped from behind the doorway, giving me back control, and I proceeded toward the entrance.

I felt the door handle while pressing my ear to the wall, attempting to assess any familiarity. Cassandra's voice reverberated through my senses as her tears of pain prompted her cry, conveying her emotions of terror. A sudden surge of urgency triggered my reaction, hastily forcing my entrance through the doors. The view within the room seemed to cascade shock waves through my inner soul. The ghastly scene overwhelmed me, leaving me breathless and desperately gasping for air. Vertigo and nausea threatened to overpower me with a blanket of unconsciousness. I fought to keep myself from blacking out, keenly focused on keeping the tunneled passageway of consciousness from closing totally. I strengthened my resolve, forcing that tunnel wider and wider until I regained self-control. The vision before me was unparalleled, with an impact of tumultuous proportions.

Cassandra cried out, "Tony, he will be back!" Her mouth closed with a shudder as a wave of pain traversed through her body, causing her to convulse before passing out. I walked to the metal gurney and saw that she was lying spread-eagle with arms and legs extended and tied to the four corners of the gurney.

"What the hell?" I shouted. "Who did this to you?" I asked without realizing she was unable to respond. I saw blood from under her midsection. The blood looked fresh, and I attempted to lift her midsection to get a clearer view but could not since the tied ropes were taut with tension. I would not know how serious the bleeding was until I could turn her over to assess the wounds. I searched for anything to cut the ropes with to no avail.

Off to my right was a patio located under the overhang. I went out onto the patio, hoping to find anything that would be able to cut through the ropes. There was nothing to be found. I started back into the room, half expecting to see the assailant who victimized Cassandra. I halted right before the patio window, and it occurred to me that the glass could serve as the cutting tool. I went into the room and found a metal chair. I grabbed the chair and swung it at the patio window from within to force the shards of glass out over the patio. On my first attempt, the glass held, and one of the legs broke free of the chair. The second attempt cracked the window, and a web of fissures swarmed toward the outer edge.

I swung the chair a third time with a resulting mass explosion shattering the entire glass panel. Most of the broken pieces were too small to be of any use, but I found several pieces large enough to serve as cutting tools. The problem was how to grasp a glass fragment without severely tearing my own hand to shreds. I went back to the gurney, searching for a blanket or sheet to use to protect my hands. There wasn't anything in the room substantial enough to protect my hands. I tore off my shirt and cut a large enough piece to wrap around my hand several times.

I suddenly heard off in the distance, barely detectable but audible enough to make out, the echo of my patron calling for the pending journey back to whatever realm was waiting for me. Surely, if I left before setting Cassandra free, that would leave her vulnerable to more unimaginable acts of terror inflicted on her with the ultimate threat of death. I knew I could not forsake my return journey with Cassandra in harm's way. I had to at least free her from the restraints and escape with her to a safe haven of impenetrable protection. Yet I could not conceive of what would happen to me if I missed my return journey. I felt that if the voyage back embarked without me, my destiny would be of despair and total solitude without Cassandra. That potential outcome was inconceivable to me, and I surely would have welcomed death over a future of such despair.

I came by Cassandra's side, and upon my touch on her face, she stirred slightly. A soft whimper escaped her lips. Her whimper turned to a moan like the type one made upon awakening from a deep sleep. Her eyelids tried to open, and with continued effort, they opened slightly. Upon seeing me, she tried calling out to me, but her voice was barely audible. Her voice, once soft with a velvety smoothness, came with effort, each word delivered with strained hoarseness. I glanced around the room, looking for a bathroom. Off in the corner was a small room consisting of personal necessities. The door was partially open, revealing a master bathroom. I turned toward Cassandra, signaling that I would fetch a glass of water. She acknowledged with a nod as I retreated to the room in search for a glass or some form of container. There was a faucet, and in the overhead cabinet, I found several plastic cups. I turned on the faucet, filling the cup to almost overflowing.

I returned to Cassandra and held the cup while she took a sip and then emptied the cup. The water helped; her words became more distinct yet still without the mellow softness. I asked her how long she had been there.

"It must be a few hours because the last detail I remember is the ballroom during the evening," she said. I turned my attention to the patio facing the ocean and saw the full moon. Its light barely pierced the eerie darkness. I turned back to her and asked if she had any recollection of the events leading up to being restrained to the gurney.

"Not a thing I remember, just a complete void between the moment at the ballroom and here now talking to you."

I lowered my head to hers with my mouth near her ear. With a compassionate tone, I calmly said, "Cassandra, we must leave this room, for whoever tied you up is due to return." With concern, my inner voice reminded me that the critical question was when.

51

The House of Corpses

A shrill whistle echoed repeatedly to signal to me that my passageway back was approaching. I helped Cassandra get up to a standing position. She held on to me as she regained her balance. "We have to leave this place immediately, Tony, before he returns."

I held Cassandra close to my chest and tried to escort her to the entrance. She was still unstable but was able to stand on her own, and each step brought her that much closer to full awareness.

The shrill whistle seemed closer now, and I realized I had at tops thirty minutes to board the transport for the journey back. I asked Cassandra if she was strong enough to go outside. She responded with a definite yes. I said, "I am taking you back with me, Cassandra."

She stopped halfway to the door and turned to face me so I would not miss what she was going to say. "Tony, I can't come with you. I am stranded here. I do not know my past or how I ended up here, and I feel I am marooned on this tiny island of a village unbeknownst to civilization."

"Cassandra, you have been here too long. You must come with me on board for the journey home."

"Tony, I do not think that is possible. I was told upon arriving here that there is no way back and that this place will be my endless sanctuary."

"Cassandra, I do not understand what you are implying, but this is just a temporary place, a place that we both can leave. You must follow me back to the village depot, for this journey starts and ends there. You have to consider this as your way of escaping this village that has entombed your soul. We have fifteen minutes until departure. You will surely die here if you stay."

"Isn't that my ultimate destination, Tony—to remain here waiting for death's front door?"

"No, Cassandra, I need you to come back with me."

"Tony, if I follow you back, there may be unforeseen consequences if this is not allowed."

I stood there confused, listening to her.

Cassandra saw my confounded look and said, "You don't have a clue why I am here. It is not up to me to inform you. You must find out on your own."

I stood there with perplexed surprise. Her unexpected response left me without a reply. A response would without a doubt have turned into a lengthy discussion, which, at that perilous moment, we did not have time for. I shelved my response and turned to Cassandra with a pleading gesture. "Cassandra, we must leave now."

Cassandra and I walked through the door and toward the spiral stairwell. The stairwell that had escorted me down to that level now seemed unsteady for no obvious reason. I concluded that my descent to that floor must have loosened the entire structure. The anchors that secured the stairway railings to the side wall were partially torn away, which allowed the stairway to sway from side to side with the slightest push. It was not safe for even one person to ascend. How could two climb without causing it to collapse? Cassandra and I searched for another escape route but found none. We both knew we had to chance it. I told Cassandra, "We both cannot climb the stairs together. We'll go one at a time." To minimize her risk, I asked Cassandra to be the first to go up. I would follow once she reached the top. Cassandra led with her right foot to take the first step. I held the bottom anchor against the wall, keeping it steady, while Cassandra cautiously ascended one stair at a time. The bottom was secured because of the pressure I applied to hold it steady. However, halfway up was another set of anchors that were partially loose from the wall mount. Cassandra stopped halfway up as the stairwell swayed to the left away from the wall. I saw the tension on the anchor as it tore a bit more from its mounting. If the stairwell collapsed with Cassandra halfway up, she would be seriously injured or killed by the fall. We had no choice but to follow through and hope fate was on our side.

Each rung Cassandra crossed caused a high-pressure torque on the anchors, which were already strained to keep the well from collapsing. Cassandra would wait a few minutes for the railing to settle into a steady position before taking the next step. With each step, I feared Cassandra's assailant would reappear, leaving me in a helpless situation. Two-thirds up, the stairwell was more secure, and Cassandra's pace quickened. Upon her setting foot on the top floor, it was my turn to ascend. When I reached a third of the way up, the stairwell shook violently, swaying away from the wall, causing the top anchor to pull farther away from the wall. If I stayed in my current position, my weight alone would cause the anchor to totally dislodge from the wall, making any further climb nearly impossible. I hastily ascended the next five steps to lessen the pressure on the anchors at the middle of the stairway, hoping they were secure enough to hold my upward climb.

Halfway up, I heard a sound. The anchors at midpoint could no longer sustain my weight and had torn loose from the wall mount. The railing swung heavily to my right away from the wall. The top railing was no longer anchored, and it too tore away from the wall. I swayed significantly to my right; the entire stairwell felt ready to collapse, but it held for the time being. I was not sure how it still stood without collapsing. I quickly ascended the next dozen steps and stood still, hoping the structure would steady itself. I had another twenty stairs to reach the top landing. I yelled out to Cassandra, "Cassandra, move away from the stairwell! If it collapses, it may cause a portion of the top floor to collapse. Please move over by the rear wall."

Cassandra immediately took my advice and quickly proceeded to the rear. "Please, Tony, be careful. The bottom anchors are still solid, and that is so far keeping the structure in place." I heard Cassandra, and while ascending the last twelve stairs, I held my gaze toward the top while hoping the bottom anchors would hold. I heard a wretched tearing noise when the bottom anchors started tearing away from the wall. The pressure of the stairwell was too heavy to maintain. I felt I only had a minute at most before the bottom anchors separated from the wall completely, causing the entire assembly to collapse. If that happened now, it would be a long drop and surely catch me in the collapse. I took the last ten steps up without hesitation, and as I reached the top rung, the remaining lower anchors dislodged from the wall. The staircase stood steadily for a few seconds, as if it were deciding what to do next. I took those few seconds to race to the rear wall, where Cassandra was waiting, and finally heard the stairway collapse behind me. The crash of metal upon metal sounded like a train wreck, and upon turning around, I saw that the adjacent wall had given way during the collapse.

What lay behind the wall was a scene from hell itself. Dozens of corpses were entombed between the beams that served as the support structures. The corpses were in varying degrees of decay. Each wore an expression of horror. Worms and rodents climbed out of their eye sockets, searching for a new source of food. A rumbling sound from behind the support structure tunneled its way forward and spread outward, traversing through each corpse and shaking each from its enclosed space so that it forward and landed on top of the collapsed stairwell.

I turned toward Cassandra and asked her, "Where are we? In some form of hell? Are we in hell?"

She looked at me and acknowledged me with a downward glance. "Who is to say what and where hell is, Tony? I can only tell you what you have already seen, and if you believe this is hell, then I agree it is hell. I do not know how I was sent here. My memory is a blank." We both turned as we heard the echo of our pending journey. We both wondered when and where Cassandra's assailant was. It was now obvious that if I left Cassandra there, she would surely be killed.

"We must go now, Cassandra. You cannot stay here, for surely you are in danger."

"But, Tony, I can't do that. It is not time yet. I can't explain now, but soon I will be able to depart this place."

"I do not understand, and, Cassandra, we do not have a chance. Rather, you will surely die here. Your life is not here but with me, and you must trust that fate is giving us another chance. If you die here, we may separate with no end in sight."

"Tony, my love, I don't know, for the powers that imprison me here may have other plans."

"Cassandra, I will carry you on this journey to another dimension, a different state where you will be with me. As long as we stay confined in this carrier to guide us through this time portal, we will be okay and safe from harm's way."

Cassandra paused for a brief moment, considering what Tony had just relayed. "Let me think, Tony. This may be the portal that was meant for me as a safe haven. Maybe you're right." We turned toward each other as the transport shrilled out its last call for the journey back.

"It's a train, Cassandra. The way back is by any means we can conjure. For some reason, a train is how I perceive this journey. But we must hurry. We have no time left. We must leave now."

"Okay, Tony." We sprinted toward the entrance to begin our journey home.

"Hurry, Cassandra, before he returns."

Cassandra hesitated for a moment. "I can't, Tony."

I repeated that we had to leave. The echo came through loud and clear that time. We did not have any time. I briskly swept Cassandra up and carried her through the entryway out into an intense dark night. The full moon was our only source of light. Realizing the urgent haste, she was by my side as we darted toward the village depot.

"Tony, there is something you should know."

"Later," I said as I grabbed her hand to guide her through the mist that permeated the air. Frantically, we picked up our pace, but we still could not gauge our distance from the depot. Outside, the air seemed denser; the fog was swirling rapidly. Deep from within, fragments with a green hue spun outward, desperately lunging toward us, before retreating and disappearing behind the blanket of mist. We took each step with caution as we attempted to weave our way around the mist, but we realized there was no circumventing the haze that surrounded the depot.

I turned toward Cassandra, and our eyes conveyed the obvious: the only way to the depot to continue our journey was through the fog bank before us. We both sensed an element of foreboding. Fleeting shadows darted with furtive movements, followed by the tentacles of light reaching out to lure us into their domain. We moved forward a step closer to the point where one was emotionally committed to continue without any retreat. Minutes ticked by, but to us, it seemed like an eternity before we found ourselves at the outer fringe of the swirling mist. We stopped to regain our fortitude, courage, and determination to face whatever lay ahead, for we both knew that once we took that next step, there was no retreat and no turning back.

Another echo sounded, distorted from the fog bank but clear enough to convey "Last call!" from a conductor. We had just fifteen minutes left before departure. If we missed that fateful journey, the consequences would be unknown, but we both feared the worst: there would not be a chance to journey back. The window of opportunity, the portal, would permanently close, and the consequences would be unparalleled. A succession of events that governed fate's outcome would be broken, with the resulting pieces unraveling with no destination or purpose, and the only possible outcome would be an event of such colossal magnitude that it would bring a halt to our universal clock, which would be forever frozen. The dimension of time would cease to exist.

We sensed the urgency of the call yet were aware that behind that wall, whatever menacing force awaited us would have the intent of thwarting our destination. Our moment of truth had arrived. We took our first steps past the threshold, entering that irreverent place, when an ungodly shrill erupted from deep within. We heard a painful moan and a mournful groan filled with pain, as if we'd just reopened a severe wound. A flash of light erupted; its green hue turned to a fiery red. We saw an image of a woman's head cradled in her hands as she wept bloodred tears. We moved a step closer, whereupon the woman raised her head, screamed in pain, and then returned to her cradled pose. She turned to us. "Hurry," she whispered. "What you both seek awaits you on this journey." She cradled her head again before fading into the mist, her cry of terror escaping with her.

We stood still, undecided. Our momentum was temporarily halted in our attempt to fully absorb the event that had just happened. We both were deciding how to proceed. Our caution and indecision were soon answered when the last-call warning was announced again, this time with a clear tone of urgency. The sounds of preparation for the journey emanated from somewhere off to our right. A heavy wheezing sound came with the pressure increasing from the engine's reinvigorated effort to engage the journey.

As we struggled blindly through the haze, a dark, dense shadow darted before us and reached out with a clawlike movement toward

Cassandra, attempting to grab her. It narrowly missed, leaving but a scratch on her arm. I pulled Cassandra free before she stumbled to the ground. Who knew what abominations lay at our feet? We could feel and sense that whatever was there at our feet was plentiful, providing an uneven tread as we strove forward through the mist. I feared if one of us fell, we would never be able to get up and would be subject to whatever wrath the menacing force had in mind for us.

Our only course was to move forward hoping we'd start our fateful journey before the window of time that fate had arranged closed forever. We treaded our way forward, glancing over our shoulders, our paranoid senses highly alerted. From within the dense path of grayness, echoes became prevalent, calling out to Cassandra. The air was filled with aimless one-way conversations, warnings intended for her.

The message was distinct though sporadic: "Cassandra, you are prohibited from this journey. You can't. Not allowed. Vortex of time will be shattered." Then it retreated back into obscurity, where the echoes faded into a mourning sound. The echoes became more pronounced, filling the atmosphere with a horrific noise reverberating with an intensity that pierced our souls. We covered our ears, trying without any measure of success to ward off the haunting sounds. The melodies we'd danced to for what had seemed like an eternity played to our senses but with distorted harmony, masked by an overtone of sheer madness and culminating in a torrential downpour of demonic commands directed toward Cassandra to warn her of eternal damnation once we were on board with our journey.

Cassandra, her hand firmly in my grasp, suddenly stopped, causing me to lose my footing. I stumbled backward and almost fell before regaining my balance. She cried out, "Tony, there is something you have to know! It is not my time to take this journey yet."

Through the dense atmosphere, the messenger cried out for the last time, "We will leave in five minutes!"

"Cassandra, we do not have time. Please trust me, for this is our time. Please let us swiftly proceed to meet our destiny. Our time is not here but wherever this journey takes us."

Cassandra held my hand firmly, came close to my ear, and whispered, "You are my future, my salvation. You are the essence of my heart, for I would surely die without you. Let's hurry before it is too late."

I turned to our right, as we noticed that the noise came from our right. The air grew thicker as we progressed farther into the mist. The farther we went, the more frequent the green lights became. Their amber turned the air into a dark green hue. Yellow eyes would periodically pierce the gloom and rapidly approach us before darting away. It seemed that whatever forces were attempting to thwart us were warnings for Cassandra. They were reluctant and unable to mount a serious threat of harm to her. I did not fully understand and had no time to pursue with further questions. I picked up my pace into a fast walk and then a run with Cassandra following me. I could hear the preparations underway off in the distance as the journey's wait for us neared a close. We weren't going to make it, I feared. My run turned into a rapid surge of adrenaline. Cassandra's hand pulled away from mine, as she was unable to keep up with my last surge forward. I stopped immediately and turned behind me to reconnect with her. She was nowhere in my sight. *How could I lose her in just a few seconds?*

"Cassandra!" I shouted frantically. I was running out of time, yet the reason I was on that quest was because of Cassandra. Without her, I could not take the journey back alone. "Cassandra!" I called out, hoping for some acknowledgment.

Off to my left, she responded. "Tony, help me!"

I turned slightly and wound my way in the direction of her voice. I reached out with my vision limited because of the thickness of the air. I felt something—a hand that latched on to mind. I pulled the hand toward me, and there in front of me was Cassandra. She wrapped her arms around me and held me fast, afraid to let go. I took her face and titled it up toward me, and our eyes conveyed what words could not convey. We were one soul, one beating heart, one entity on a journey that would bond our souls for the rest of eternity. We were on a mission to seal our fate. I took her hand, and we turned to continue. My hand held on to hers with firm determination.

Our walk continued. The air became less dense, and the fog bank somewhat dissipated into clearness, revealing the top of the village depot. "Cassandra, we are almost there." I saw the depot as we made our final thrust through the clearing mist. Within seconds, the air became crystal clear, with not a trace of any disturbance. The silence was almost deafening. A disturbing thought pierced the veil of hope: I feared this was the calm before the storm, a storm of unknown proportions and deadly consequences. It was a potentially deadly calm. There was no breeze. Not a star was in sight; the only light came from a full moon. I recalled that every night there had a full moon. That night, the moon's glow was unusually bright, which helped lead the way toward our transport to carry us on our journey.

Cassandra increased her pace to catch up to me and walked by my side as we neared the depot's rear entrance. I reached out for the door but stopped when Cassandra's hand rested on mine. I turned toward her, and we drew close to each other. She placed her hands on my temples and brought her lips to mine in a passionate kiss. With her lips near my ear, she pronounced her love for me. Then, with her hand meshed with mine, we entered the depot.

The depot too was unusually quiet. It had always been quiet, I recalled. I did not remember seeing any others waiting for their departures or expected arrivals. But this time, the silence that persisted outside penetrated the small room where Cassandra and I stood. We heard not a sound from anywhere—no humming or vibrating noise from any ventilation or cooling system, no background or white noise. It must have been ten degrees cooler in there than outside, but there was no evidence of any ceiling fan to circulate the air. The longer we stood there with suspicious caution, the eerier it felt. We half expected that at any moment, a sound would approach with alarming frequency, turning the void of silence into complete chaos. Before giving whatever lay hidden a chance to turn the scene into a hellish nightmare, we turned and hastily walked toward the front entrance.

Leaving Neverland with Cassandra

As we opened the door, the transit for our journey started its forward movement, accelerating every second in motion. I grabbed Cassandra's hand, and we ran toward the last car pulling out. The last car accelerated, widening the distance between us and the outside grab bar. With a burst of adrenaline, I reached forward, and my hand closed tightly around the handle. With surprising effort, I was able to jump onto the platform separating the cars and pull Cassandra with me. She landed on top of me just as the outer door sealed shut.

Only a fraction of time elapsed between when we departed the depot and when we landed on the platform, but the energy expended equated to a mile-long run. Both exhausted from the effort and the constant fear of hidden threats during our retreat from the house of damnation, we struggled to our feet and held on to each other to regain our balance.

Lights flickered within the cars. Each car's lights followed a synchronized pattern, beginning with complete darkness and gradually intensifying to a harsh glare. As expected, it appeared our journey was a ghostly evacuation from the mysterious village back to my familiar destination, and we were the only passengers. Even so, I felt a serene comfort, a blissful high with Cassandra next to me. However, behind that facade of comfort, we both still had a suspended dread that the dead calm would soon be ending. Too exhausted to mount sizable concern, we were not able to muster the energy to use our aroused paranoia to formulate a protective plan to avoid potential threats. We were at the point of mental exhaustion, bordering on blinded denial, throwing caution to the wind, mindless of any potential intrusion. Just the idea of succumbing to any threat would have been too much to bear. We had to sleep, if just for an hour, to regain some form of alertness.

Not sure where to go next, we opened the door to the last car on our left and found the first seats, where we sat, drained. One of us should have kept watch; we could have taken turns to allow the other to catch a hour's rest. But at that point, our defense mechanisms were in a frozen state. Not able to care anymore, we both surrendered to the Land of Nod. Our eyes closed, and we rested our heads together.

It felt like a prolonged, deep sleep, yet it seemed only a brief moment. I tried to shed the cobwebs that had dulled my senses. I got to my feet to get the circulation moving, trying to revitalize my awareness. I viewed my immediate surroundings, which seemed foreign to me until I looked at Cassandra, who was still deep asleep. That sight brought back full realization of our trek from the house of unspeakable horror. I let her sleep while I took stock, exploring my options. There was only one option open: to wait out the journey and, during the excursion, collaborate with Cassandra on a plan—any plan.

My journeys had challenged my imagination and confronted my rationale, triggering an avalanche of plausible and implausible causes. I was at a point where my mental faculties would accept any conceivable theory. Contrary to my previous journeys, all seemed calm—too calm. It felt as if whatever menacing force awaited us had temporarily halted, stymied because of Cassandra. Maybe it was not able to mount any serious threat for fear of harm to her and the consequences of thwarting fate's predetermined outcome. Maybe Cassandra had been trying to warn me that her journey back with me was not to be and that whatever had to happen would happen; altering any link in the sequence of events would cause a tumultuous event that would disrupt fate's synchronization of timed events, causing time itself to cease to exist as a dimension. Whatever portal we encountered, it was one that allowed access to our universe's own constructs. To intrude could cause those constructs to realign, throwing everything created by those macrocosms' support pillars to break away from their intended properties. One could not begin to fathom the potential consequences.

Cassandra was still in a deep sleep, too deep for my comfort. I temporarily panicked, for if I lost her, my soul would surely die. She was my soul, my destiny. Without her, my journey would exceed my threshold to continue. I would surely perish, as my soul would be devoid of sustainable effort to proceed with my life. Responding to my panic, I reached out to her, feeling for a pulse. Yes, it was there, weak but steady. I gently moved her shoulder to see if she would respond. There was no response. I lifted her eyelid, hoping for some eye movement, but I found none. Her eyes seemed vacant. If there was a word to describe them, it was *soulless*. She either was in a deep sleep or had slipped into a coma. I recalled what she'd attempted to tell me earlier about the journey: "I can't go with you, Tony, for reasons I will tell you later." Was her current state the result of her taking that journey with me? I had not given her a chance to tell me why due to my sense of urgency. I'd asked her to trust me, and out of love for me, she'd agreed and embarked with me on the journey back, knowing the uncertainty. Was this my fault? Yes, without a doubt. Before I assumed the worst, I tried again to arouse her. I saw a slight movement of the eyelid and a tremor of the hands. Her legs started twitching and escalated to spasms.

She screamed, "Tony, they are coming! They are coming for us. This journey changed things. Fate was denied." Her next words came in a whisper. "I love you." Then she retreated back into a hibernating state; her spasming and twitching vanished as suddenly as they'd started.

At a loss for action, I sat next to her, wondering where our journey would end. I wrapped my hands around my head, trying to calm my mind from the mounting uncertainty and escalating panic. Emotion mixed with anguish was not the ideal formula for any rational thought. But at the moment, I did not care. If my emotions were overflowing, so be it. "I am not a robot that can tune out any emotion and replace it with logic like turning a simple valve to an on-off position. In fact, robots do not experience emotions anyway, " I said angrily. Realizing my emotions were getting the best of me, I tried to keep them in check and attempted to refocus.

I heard a faint whimper. Was that from Cassandra? I turned toward her and bent my ear close to her lips. I felt her soft, warm breath against my ear. I tuned all my senses to an acute state, listening for any murmur or whisper. The whimper sounded again, this time a little louder. Where was it coming from? I turned around to catch anything but saw nothing. I turned back to Cassandra. I heard the whimper again, but this time, I saw a slight movement as her lips slightly parted. Her eyelids twitched again, forcibly trying to open. She moved her hands, reaching out. I took her hands in mine, and she took hold, bringing my fingertips close to her lips. She gently kissed them. I lowered my lips to hers and gently kissed her. My tears of worry and joy fell drop by drop onto her cheek. After my kiss, her eyelids fluttered again, opening slowly. When they were half open, she used her hands to move my head toward her. Our eyes connected, and I could see her regaining her strength. I stayed calm and silent, giving her time to become fully alert. It took a while for her to finally reclaim her senses. She looked at me. "There is something you need to know."

"What is it, Cassandra? What just happened? Is that connected?"

"Yes, Tony. It is."

I sat next to her with my attention fully tuned, anticipating but dreading what I was about to hear.

"I can reveal only so much, Tony. The rest you must discover on your own. You will not immediately understand, but eventually, it will become apparent as the truth slowly evolves."

I listened to Cassandra intently, absorbing every word, knowing and seeing her earnest gesture to guide me down the path of disclosure. There was more revelations to follow, and my senses were finely tuned to what she would unveil next.

"Tony, this here and now is not real. I was in our past. At that time, it was real, but our engagements are all moments from our past. This journey is your escape to those moments in which we were at our happiest. Something went wrong in that distant state. But this journey is yours; it is not mine. I came here not of my own will; I was forced here by the laws of fate. I'm not sure why, but I know that my present locale was my imprisonment for something I cannot remember. This journey—my coming here with you—will have consequences. I do not know what is going to happen. I lapsed into a deep sleep and was swept to a place completely new to me. I fear that was just the start. The series of consequences will continue, each escalating in severity. I do not know the outcome. But my being here with you endangers you."

I listened to Cassandra's explanation, wondering if what Cassandra disclosed was true or if her rationale was still mired in the last remnants of the deep sleep she'd been in. "Cassandra, I believe you, for I realize this journey is about us, and it will have an impact on us. I know the journeys have taken us between different states. I do not totally understand, but I believe what you are telling me. But, Cassandra, we are on this journey together, and if I am in danger because we both are here traveling back to whatever destination, then I accept that danger to me, for without you, my life would tragically end. If I have to die, then it must be with you by my side rather than alone, where my death would be accompanied with absolute despair."

"I saw something when I was under that threatened to take me further under. I saw you, Tony, in a debasing event. The destruction is total devastation. The devastation is what is revealed to you. There is someone with you, and that person is symbolic of the devastating revelation. Neverland is my place for eternity. You will know your fate from the revelations. This here and now is where you find me when you are ready. A basic construct that governs fate and our universe has been violated, and the consequence is what is revealed. This is what is behind the wall."

I listened intently, and the more I heard from Cassandra, the more convinced I became that what she was relaying to me had merit and yielded some element of truth. But I was not convinced that her journey was final. This was not her imprisoned destiny. No matter what I heard, I couldn't fully digest that notion with total acceptance. There were too many holes that needed to be filled to give the story more credence. I suspected there was much more that Cassandra knew, information she was purposely or unintentionally avoiding to protect us both from being overwhelmed. I suspected that information would fill the holes.

We both fell silent, suspended in a web of a journey that could evolve into multiple journeys, each with its own possible outcome. Both of us had an uncanny feeling that our destiny had not yet been determined. If my journeys had traveled down memory lane from eons ago and the current journey had both of us as passengers, then I felt this trip must be part of the chain of predetermined events that would culminate soon. Or a link had been provided to us as part of a chain of random events. But regardless of what had brought us to that present state, we would face whatever was destined for us together. Cassandra fell asleep again, but it was more of a natural, restful slumber. She laid her head on my shoulder, and our hands entwined tightly. I soon joined her as my eyelids closed.

53

Fate's Denial to Leave Neverland

I awoke from a deep slumber. I'd had strange dreams, all of which seemed related. Cassandra stirred next to me. She was still asleep. There was no sign of the tremors experienced earlier. The journey we were on seemed to be taking longer than any prior journey. I looked out the window and recognized that the journey had come to a stop. How long we'd been idle was not apparent, but we were at a dead stop. I peered out through the window again and saw nothing but pure emptiness. It was still dark as hell—too dark. The moon that had been so prevalent earlier was now absent. I turned toward Cassandra, who was still asleep. I felt her pulse, confirming a steady beat, which alleviated any immediate concerns. I stood up and walked toward the door that led to the platform that led to the adjacent car. The door would not open. Unable to turn the handle, I turned and walked toward the rear door, and it too was locked. We were trapped in the car, confined to a fate unknown. I turned to Cassandra to find her still under. I felt heightened trepidation as our journey continued. My apprehension kept coming back to my immediate concern. It had been awhile since we'd boarded the train—too long. The journey had never taken that long before. I looked outside again and was somewhat relieved to notice movement again. My relief was short-lived, for I then detected what I feared the most: I noticed the sign announcing our arrival to in the village we'd departed from what seemed like ages ago. We were in an endless loop with only one stop, Neverland. This time, the journey would not delivery us to our destination of Haleyville. It was taking us back to Cassandra's place in time. Cassandra had not been mistaken: she was not allowed to leave this place. This was her origin and destination. Why was I allowed to journey back to Haleyville, but with Cassandra, it was not allowed? There was no way to know by just standing there.

I decided not to share what I'd ~~found~~ just experienced with Cassandra. At some point during this journey, there had to be a departure toward our destination of Haleyville eventually for both of us. If this was true, then was I playing a game with fate? I tried to contemplate that scenario, but the enormity of the possible consequences resulting in a script that may challenge the fundamentals principles of metaphysics. A script large enough to make it impossible to digest in its entirety.

But what if my assumption was wrong and with Cassandra, the destination of our journey together was to be always the point of departure with no stopovers? Even if our destination was reserved to be only our point of departure, the fact that my quest to reunite with Cassandra for the rest of eternity had finally been honored would result in a rejoice in such a way that it was beyond my ability to define. The degree of ecstasy would be beyond definition. But at what cost? To forever lose my compulsive need to know what had happened prior to my amnesia? The emotional impact kept me in a dual state of denial and acceptance. I looked back toward Cassandra and found her still asleep. Since we'd begun that journey, she had been asleep for more than fifty percent of the time, which, to me, was a troublesome sign.

I felt a vibration for a split second, as if the phantom train had just traveled over a juncture where several tracks crossed. I looked out the window and saw that the train had traveled through our destination without stopping. That must have been the vibration I'd just experienced. Now my concern returned with a chilling thought: *Will we ever get off the phantom ride, or are we stuck here forever?*

As I turned and walked toward the exit door to see if the handle would allow us to exit the car, the lights dimmed for a minute, which I perceived as another warning. Near the front seat was the shadow that had been prevalent in every one of my journeys. The shadowy figure was moving toward Cassandra. Alertly, I moved quickly to intercept, but before I was able to reach Cassandra, the shadowy figure vanished into thin air. The reality of what I'd just seen hit me like a sledge hammer.

Cassandra and I were not alone. The figure cloaked in shadow who always seemed to be near whenever Cassandra and I reunited had never left. I realized now that he was always there. His presence was known purely at his discretion, and according to the pattern up to that point, he made his presence visible when he felt threatened. But threatened by whom? Then it dawned on me who the threat was: me.

I turned back toward Cassandra and saw her hands start to twitch. Her leg spasms returned. "No, please. No, I cannot stay. Here is my resting place." I listened to Cassandra voice her anguish repeatedly. I shook her, trying to rouse her from her prolonged sleep. I tried to talk to Cassandra, looking for any form of recognition. She opened her eyes, connecting with me. She seemed to know what I was thinking at **that** very moment. "Yes, Tony. I too have seen the shadow. There are reasons, which you do not yet understand. Can you accept that?"

"No, I cannot. What life would I have to endure without you? A life without meaning. A life solely immersed in just memories. No, that is not what I want. Why do you feel you cannot return? Why do you feel that you have to stay here?"

"Tony, for me to return, then you will come to realize with a suddenness the truth. The immediacy of the truth may destroy you. I dare not say: There will be no delay to absorb and digest. The exposure to truth without any cushion will lead to devastation and shock."

"The truth cannot be so horrible to prevent you from returning to me. Whatever it is, we can handle it together, Cassandra."

"Tony, please. I cannot reveal all the reasons why. I love you too much to see this destroy you."

"Let me deal with that, Cassandra. Whatever you are talking about, if it must destroy me, then so be it, for without you, my soul will be empty anyway."

"Tony. Oh, Tony. Are you sure you can handle the truth?"

"Yes."

I looked at her as she nodded in agreement. We felt a slight vibration from within the car like before, as if the transport had to cross over a junction from one track to another. This time, I knew our course was set; our journeys would unite with the passage home.

We heard a whisper intended only for the two of us: "Yes, Haleyville."

54

A Possible Answer to Tony's Dreams

I woke up, surprisingly, with a renewed sense of hope. It was as if my last dream had revealed a resolution, something of paramount importance. That something involved Cassandra, and it freed her from feeling she was destined to live forever in isolation in Neverland. The revelation gave me a new calm, as if I'd crossed a threshold that barred the location of Neverland and Cassandra, a barrier once erected to avoid a past soon to be revealed. Was I ready? Waiting was no longer an option. It was now becoming an eventuality of truth, one that would allow Cassandra and me to move forward to where we would resolve our separation and reunite—or dissolve our union forever. The time was approaching for absolution or dissolution.

Yet I felt a calmness, one that centered on hope-filled promise. A reluctance, to void out any doubts. The feeling of calmness fueled my optimism upon my awakening to another morning. I felt refreshed. The sun was shining brilliantly. It was a well-deserved weekend of rest. Last night's dream was still prevalent in my mind, allowing me a fresh newly formed perspective. *It was as though I were living two worlds. I was not sure anymore which one was real. I could not delineate between reality and fantasy. But eventually, over time, there usually were small, subtle hints that would provide more insight into what was real and what was fantasy. Yet this time, there were no underlying hints, suggesting that both states might be real. However, the two states were so different that it seemed impossible both were real, I pondered with heightened* emphasis. "However, what may be perceived as impossible today may prove to be possible tomorrow. Maybe there's another fact I am missing," I said, wondering out loud. "If both are states of reality, then there must be something that links the two dimensions together. If I discover this missing link with further research, then it will raise the probability significantly that Neverland and Cassandra most assuredly are real." *If, however, the results from further research did not yield any evidence of a link between the two states, then I would accept the probability that one of them was a fantasy dr*eam. The question then would become the following: Which was the fantasy, and which was the reality? The bottom line was I needed more evidence, more research to provide evidence that could explain how the two dimensions were connected.

With heightened enthusiasm, I looked forward to an afternoon that hopefully would reveal more clues. *Was there a vital piece of information I had overlooked that was the sought-after link that connected the two realms together? The long-awaited answer might be provided that sunny afternoon.*

55

A Search for Answers to Tony's Quandary

I returned to the house on Canyon Ridge with a different agenda to start the day. I was always torn between priorities. In this case, the two tasks requiring action had equal priority: urgent. The search yesterday had been vital, but the evidence was old and was of no immediate help in finding Cassandra now. I felt I was spinning my wheels, gaining no traction. Despite my compelling need to search again, I had to delay the task for a while longer to proceed in a different direction that might reveal a hidden clue to Cassandra's whereabouts. I eventually would return to the unfinished task of searching the area under the house, where I'd found evidence of Cassandra in the rear chamber. I believed that at some point in time, she'd been there, as I'd found strands of hair and dried blood. The note she'd left with a hint of her fragrance served as conclusive proof she'd been there. But how long ago? The dried blood indicated it was not recent. I had nothing else that would give me the added advantage I was seeking. I decided to first explore the background of the house, along with the servants' quarters; Neverland; and anything else that came to my mind that would yield something of value. Among the number of facts I hoped to uncover, there was one primary fact I needed to know: In the history of the house or the servants' quarters, had another room ever existed on a level below the main floor, and were the two domiciles linked in some manner? If so, the knowledge would give me an added advantage that was imperative to my search.

My intended research would hopefully give me more insight that would prove invaluable to find the one thread to start unraveling the mystery.

My living arrangements now included my home in Haleyville and the home we'd purchased on Canyon Ridge Trails. I'd spent the last few days at the home we'd purchased. I went to my office to access my computer. The office was located at the back of the house, enclosed on the top-floor patio that protruded out over the cliff with a view of the ocean. It was a Saturday midafternoon, and the skies were clear. The sunlight reflected off the waves pounding the shoreline. A flock of seagulls off in the distance were practicing aerial acrobatics, swooping down toward the ocean and, just before hitting the surface, gracefully spiraling upward.

The peaceful view provided a much-needed tranquility to sooth my senses, which were still in an alarmed state caused by the emotional roller-coaster ride I'd endured during these recent dreams, which had consumed me. The recent dreams had a haunting repercussion which heightened their impact, with lasting permanence. I was now more convinced the town of Neverland did exist, though its location was still a mystery.

Half immersed in a pensive mood, I engaged the browser to begin my search. As my computer woke from its slumbering state, the browser came to life with an unexpected prompt blinking in the foreground. The prompt was blinking with such rapidity that it was initially difficult to interpret. What made it more difficult was its intense color: a watery pool of crimson. There was a link that seemed to float unevenly on a churning current that was intensifying and close to overflowing onto the screen.

Suddenly, the churning slowed to an even ripple, and the intensity of the red diminished just enough to allow me to comprehend the message's content: "What we seek is here. Cassandra." *Cassandra* was underlined. The link was like a beacon for those lost at sea. The blinking prompt slowed and eventually stopped. The prompt just rested there, intensifying as it drew me in. I lifted my hand and moved it closer to the screen. The screen felt hot to the touch, as if it were on fire. The blinking started again, but this time, the word *Cassandra* expanded into a scroll of text. As each line progressed on the screen, the blinking accelerated, which I interpreted as a warning that if I did not respond now, I would be left with just a fleeting memory and would lose a chance to delve deeper into the mystery. I temporarily froze, unable to respond. Then I reached out toward the screen, sensing the warmth turn to a heated sizzle as the words ignited with an image of a blaze that slowly melted the words as they flew by.

I touched the screen, searing my fingertips, whereupon the screen opened up to a vast network of images that swarmed before my eyes, assembling into a view of different scenes from different eras that appeared to be connected. Below the images was a new link containing the words *Quantum Dimensions.*

I clicked on the link, which directed me to a new site that presented me with a series of articles about research conducted on altered states and astral projection.

I felt I was faced with a barrage of information that would require hours to decipher. It was a disappointing letdown, for in my naiveté, I'd been expecting a quick resolution, an answer that would provide immediate insight. Instead, I was presented with an avalanche of information that would require deep concentration to find the clue or pattern of clues to help lead me to a possible resolution.

I retreated from the task at hand and walked outside onto the patio to get some fresh air and gain insight into what lay ahead. With a desperate sigh, I regrouped and prepared for the exhaustive effort I faced. I approached my study with a revised approach. With a sense of overtired humor, I recalled a series of articles I'd read a while ago about astral projections, which were basically out-of-body experiences. I recalled a particular article about a female who had an out-of-body experience in which she claimed she left her body, and her soul traveled to a location several miles away. She observed several shoes off in a corner adjacent to an abandoned warehouse and noticed their shapes and colors. When she rejoined her physical body, she told her observer about the location and the shoes scattered alongside the warehouse. Amazingly, when she and her companion found the location, the shoes were actually there, in the same colors and shapes. I wondered why that thought surfaced at a time when I faced a monumental task. "Wait a minute!" I exclaimed. "An out-of-body experience occurs when the soul travels." I immediately recognized the possible parallelism. Was it possible my dreamlike episodes were somehow related to that phenomenon? Perched on an enthusiastic high, I dove into the browser for more insight.

Within hours, I was exhausted with the volume of information, but I finally got to a point where I felt I was onto something that could start to unravel the mystery. It was a stretch, I admitted, but it was a start. There were some amazing parallels. I tried to pace myself to make sure I absorbed all the facts. Key points were presented to me. With renewed focus, I returned to my browser to dig further.

Astral projection was the scientific term, but it was more commonly referred to as an out-of-body experience. It typically involved a sensation of floating outside one's body and, in some cases, perceiving one's physical body from a place outside the body. That did not help me much, but upon further reading, I came across some cases that intrigued me. A *possible link*, I mused, desperate for any clue that would provide further insight into my plaguing questions. The further I read, the more intrigued I became.

> This state could be induced by brain traumas, sensory deprivation, near-death experiences, dissociative and psychedelic drugs, dehydration, sleep, and electrical stimulation of the brain, among other things. It can also be deliberately induced by some. One in ten people have an OBE at least once. More commonly, people have several in their lifetime.

I concluded that the phenomenon was more common than I'd originally perceived.

> Some subjects report having had an OBE at times of severe physical trauma, such as near drownings or major surgery. Near-death experiences may include subjective impressions of being outside the physical body, visions of deceased relatives and religious figures, and transcendence of ego and spatiotemporal boundaries. Typically, the experience includes such factors as a sense of being dead, a feeling of peace and painlessness, various nonphysical sounds, an

out-of-body experience, a tunnel experience (the
sense of moving up or through a narrow passageway),
beings of light, a godlike figure or similar entities, a
life review, and a reluctance to return to life.

The more I read, the more intent I became. The tunnel experience
was definitely a clue. Several times, I'd experienced a tunnel effect in
which I was being carried swiftly toward a light, and upon nearing
the light, I'd encountered a being of light, Cassandra. So far, in my
experiences, there were parallels—enough correlations to warrant
further exploration.

I continued reading.

Writers within the fields of parapsychology and
occultism have written that OBEs are not psychological
and that a soul, spirit, or subtle body can detach itself
out of the body and visit distant locations. Out-of-body
experiences were known during the Victorian period
in spiritualist literature as traveling clairvoyance.
The psychical researchers referred to the OBE as a
psychical excursion. An early study describing alleged
cases of OBEs was the two-volume *Phantasms of the
Living* published in 1886 by psychical researchers
Edmund Gurney, Frederick William Henry Myers,
and Frank Podmore. The book was largely criticized
by the scientific community, as the anecdotal reports
lacked evidential substantiation in nearly every case.

Theosophist Arthur Powell (1927) was an early author
to advocate the subtle body theory of OBEs. Sylvan
Muldoon (1936) embraced the concept of an etheric
body to explain the OBE experience. Psychical
researcher Ernesto Bozzano (1938) also supported
a similar view, describing the phenomenon of the
OBE experience in terms of bilocation, in which an
etheric body can release itself from the physical body
in rare circumstances. The subtle body theory was

also supported by occult writers, such as Ralph Shirley (1938), Benjamin Walker (1977), and Douglas Baker (1979). James Baker (1954) wrote that a mental body enters an intercosmic region during the OBE. Robert Crookall, in many publications, supported the subtle body theory of OBEs.

The paranormal interpretation of OBEs has not been supported by all researchers within the study of parapsychology. Gardner Murphy (1961) wrote that OBEs are not far from the known terrain of general psychology, which we are beginning to understand more and more without recourse to the paranormal.

In April 1977, a patient from Harborview Medical Center known as Maria claimed to have experienced an out-of-body experience. During her OBE, she claimed to have floated outside her body and outside of the hospital. Maria would later tell her social worker, Kimberly Clark, that during the OBE, she had observed a tennis shoe on a third-floor window ledge on the north side of the building. Clark would go to the north wing of the building, and looking out the window, she could see a tennis shoe on one of the ledges. Clark published the account in 1985. The story has since been used in many paranormal books as evidence a spirit can leave the body.

In 1996, Hayden Ebbern, Sean Mulligan, and Barry Beyerstein visited the medical center to investigate the story. They placed a tennis shoe on the same ledge and discovered that the shoe was visible from within the building and could have easily been observed by a patient lying in bed. They also discovered the shoe was easily observable from outside the building and suggested that Maria may have overheard a comment about it during her three days in the hospital and incorporated it into her OBE. They concluded Maria's story merely revealed the naïveté and the power of wishful thinking from OBE researchers seeking a paranormal explanation. Clark did not publish the description of the case until seven years after it happened, casting doubt on the story. Richard Wiseman has said that although the story is not evidence for anything paranormal, it has been endlessly repeated by writers who either couldn't be bothered to check the facts or were unwilling to present their readers with the more skeptical side of the story.

Two hours of research provided some insight yet introduced another round of questions. *To speculate further, if there is a connection between OBE and clairvoyance, then there may be an implied connection to the etheric, spiritual realm. This being the case, if the etheric realm releases itself from the physical realm, then the etheric realm, if unconstrained, can traverse to different physical locations. But what if the etheric realm can travel to different dimensions, as in the spiritual realm? What if my dreams were actually my etheric realm traveling to different realms of different dimensions, making my soul a traveling clairvoyance? What if I am able to project my etheric realm to different locations?* Then the key word was *location*, which could have different implications. What if Cassandra and Neverland actually did exist in a different realm or in a past dimension? What if my dreams were actually my traveling clairvoyance?

But insight to what? I wondered. *Okay, okay.* I gestured with my hands, which flew up in frustration. I continued my dialogue with no interruptions. I mused with mixed laughter and sarcasm, surprised at my sense of humor, which was obviously my attempt to salvage some form of lucidity. *Let's say I did experience some form of out-of-body experience, and I took it a step further. Instead of traveling a few miles outside my body, I instead traveled to a destination that could be a thousand miles away or, to raise this theory up a notch to a stratospheric level, in another dimension. But if any of that is happening, how does that solve anything?* I still faced an unknown location of Neverland, Cassandra, and the mysterious stranger.

56

Tony's Illusory Companions

At a standstill, I slowly turned toward the corner, where I noticed a flicker of light. My peripheral vision had been extremely sensitive lately, with my awareness elevated to an unsustainable level. Sooner or later, the level was going to drop like an anchor at sea. Off in the corner, Angie appeared. Well, it was about time. I'd not had a visit from my acquaintances in a long time. I'd known it would be only a matter of time before they made their visit—a counseling session, I decided to call it. I welcomed it. I needed the dialogue, and the guests gave me valuable insight. I remembered the first visit. Angie just showed up one day shortly after Linda and I purchased the house and started the plans for remodeling.

My high state of anxiety had persisted for months up until we purchased the house. The abrupt change of pattern in my dreams had started taking its toll. My mind seemed to have conjured up the imagined companions as a release valve. When they appeared, I would engaged them in serious debate. I never questioned the appearance of the imagined companions. I was at the point of just accepting what was. Maybe I never questioned ~~the~~ their appearances because at the core of everything I had experienced, my successful or unsuccessful attempt to rationalize these companions would not have much impact on the grand scheme of things. I knew the implications but could not and would not accept the ramifications. I would gain nothing by admitting that my genetic condition of paramnesia might be triggering the fantasies or that the imagined companions were signaling that the condition was becoming chronic and causing additional maladies. It was no longer an issue of fantasy versus reality. The unexpected had become the expected. In other words, even if the unexpected could not be easily explained, it was just another event that made no sense, and instead of questioning it and looking for a rational explanation, it was easier to simply accept the unexplained in ~~that~~ this pseudoreality where nothing made sense. I just accepted the fact that Angie would show up when she felt it necessary. Truth be told, I welcomed her visits. I suspected why Angie was there but did not confirm my suspicion. To do so would have consequences I wasn't ready to accept. To make things more interesting—or complex, depending on one's perspective—Angie wasn't alone. Several companions were present, each with a name as his or her personal greeting card.

As I said, I was at the point where I felt there was no benefit to having a rational explanation for the unexpected guests, in part because when I did come up with some rationale, there was nothing I could do about it. How did that make things better? It didn't. So I just acknowledged my uninvited guests as my invited companions. Each time I was under duress, a different character appeared.

I had an inkling of what triggered the companions. I'd visited a psychiatrist and told him my story, and there'd been utter silence in return, except for an occasional "What do you think?" There were at least a dozen instances during the hour-long session. I informed him at that time of my dreams, and—surprise, surprise—"What do you think?" was the response. I was not getting any return on my investment. I could have gotten more results from having my own internal dialogue.

Bingo. That's it. If I could adopt multiple personas, that would objectify my theories, giving plausible rationale. That was when Angie showed up. Then Angie grew into others, each with his or her own perspective.

To complete the scenario, I purchased an African gray talking bird, one of the smartest talking birds. It could form an intelligent vocabulary with the reasoning capability of a three-year-old. He had already developed a vocabulary based on my discussions with my companions. I even taught him to say, "What do you think?" Thus, I had all the comforts of a psychiatrist visit, a companion as my sounding board for insight, and my talking bird to follow up with "What do you think?" If that didn't prove I was ready to commit myself, then nothing would. My peripheral vision caught another movement off in the corner. "Hi, Tony. Time we had a chat." It was Julie. She was the second companion who'd materialized as my guest.

I thought, Well, it seems to me that all the variables to this mystery are too much for one of these imaginary companions, so they trade off, taking turns while the others reenergize. Funny. When is the last time I reenergized? Unless these conjured companions are my way of coping, a form of compartmentalizing.

"Thanks for the visit," I replied.

Seemingly from nowhere, I heard, "So what do you think?" I realized the question had come from my African gray, Perkins.

"Not now, Perkins," I declared, which resulted in a mimicked laugh from Perkins. I wondered where he'd picked that up, but I let that thought go for now. "I am onto something," I told Julie. "Maybe a clue." I explained the out-of-body experience to her.

Perkins chimed in. "So what do you think?"

"Shut up!" I shouted at Perkins.

Julie just stood there in the corner, amused by the dialogue between me and Perkins, thinking about what I'd said. "Okay, so what is the next clue? There has to be something more to this. Why just on the train?"

"I just fall asleep, and pronto—there I am, closing in toward Neverland. Village of unknown location," I responded with a twinge of impatience.

"Tony, is it possible your dreams are patterned around this theory?"

"Way off the deep end, Julie."

"Well, Tony," she replied, "it is just a possibility, and you will not know until you investigate further."

History of Neverland

At a standstill, I slowly turned toward the corner, where I noticed another flicker of light. Off in the corner was Linda. "Linda, where have you been? I didn't hear you at the front door. Have you been here long?"

"Just got here, Tony. It is time we had a chat. So you've been researching OBEs?"

I looked at her, wondering how she knew. "Yes," I responded. "How did you know?" She didn't respond. She just sat there. *Weird*, I thought. There was something odd about her presence. A vague aura encompassed her, with a background that appeared as a grainy, wavering film. Linda's image was at times translucent, resembling a ghostly apparition. I ascribed the irregular perception to my overstressed imagination.

"Interesting premise, and I give you credit for expanding upon the theory. You are on the right track. What you have theorized is correct."

I had never seen Linda like that before, discussing subjects well with a confident, informed, self-assured tone. "How do you know this?" I asked.

"Not enough time to discuss for now," Linda responded. "Later, when we have more time. It's time now to change our direction and see where it leads." I just looked at Linda, a bit puzzled yet impressed.

"Tony, have you wondered why you are on this journey? Why do you think this complex web of variables keeps on expanding, creating new threads? Have you wondered why you have not encountered me in a while? More importantly, why do you think I picked the house on Canyon Ridge Trails? Have you noticed it has been awhile since you encountered the wall? Have you wondered why? Finally, do you remember anything prior to the wall? Could it be you are already behind the wall? Have you really looked at Neverland? Research Neverland as a start, and you will be surprised where it leads you. Answer those questions, and you might find a trail to resolving this puzzle. Remember, what seems most complex seems that way for lack of normalizing to its simplest forms. To resolve requires decomposition.

"Remember the cemetery you encountered when in search for Neverland, where you were faced with what you perceived as Cassandra's tombstone? Did you observe the tombstone next to hers? You must use this for your search for answers. Then you will be ready."

I moved toward Linda, ready to respond, but her image faded away, disappearing into the air. I stood there staring into open space. I looked around the room, expecting to see Linda, but she was gone. *Because,* I finally admitted, *she was never here.* Whatever was going on in my life, I conceded that she had been there in spirit only to relay words of wisdom. "OBE," I whispered cautiously.

I had a lot of information to absorb—too much information. The solution seemed impossible. I felt a dejection of enormous magnitude. I had never seen Linda pose such questions. I had a lot to consume and a lot to ponder. Many of the questions she'd posed were confusing. I didn't know where to start. But one thing was certain: I was going to research Neverland's history. Now.

I turned toward the computer. Despite the pressing urgency to research Neverland, my mind was too desensitized to fully absorb the impact of what I beheld materializing on the screen. The link to Pacific View, California, emerged on the screen, each letter highlighted with a searing crimson glow. Each pulsated outwardly before subsiding to a listlessness. The letters changed form, with each letter mutating into a grotesque eye with a pupil as black as coal staring directly at me. A leathery, lizard-like eyelid would slowly drop, covering the pupil briefly before opening to reveal a milky substance coating the eye before dissolving. It was identical to the nightmarish scene on the transport. I looked away from the ghastly sight, feeling the malevolence crawling up my spine. I felt something prick my neck, prompting me to turn around.

I half expected to see a hideous form launching toward me. When I turned back to the screen, the grisly scene was replaced with normalcy. A link appeared exactly in the center with bold letters: "Pacific View." Hypnotically drawn in, I reached out with my fingertips, anticipating the unexpected. Just before my fingers touched the letter *P*, the link engaged as an anticipatory response. A series of visuals appeared— scenes of the house overlooking the Pacific. A couple appeared with their backs turned toward me. The couple walked toward the cliff overlooking the gorge below. I glued my eyes to the parade of scenes presented, hoping at least one would reveal their faces. But my hope was not rewarded, as the scenes returned to the house.

Based on the collection of scenes of both the interior and exterior views of the house, there was more than a hint of a resemblance between the house I was viewing and this house. As the last visual withdrew, another page appeared, containing information on Canyon Ridge. The article summarized the statistics about the small community. To my surprise, the community had more residents and covered a larger area than I'd originally thought. *The board must have approved annexing the adjacent canyons, doubling the area and population of the community besides increasing the tax revenue.* I wasn't aware of the annexing, which surprised me since Linda and I had looked into the history of the community prior to purchasing the home. I wondered how we could have overlooked something essential to our research. I looked at the date of the annex—just twenty-five years ago. That was relatively recent and was a fact we should have easily discovered.

I scrolled, and my attention was riveted to the first paragraph. During the housing boom, a number of houses were built throughout the surrounding canyons that did not face the Pacific. During that time, the community was renamed from Pacific View to Canyon Ridge. That also surprised me. It was another fact we'd overlooked. I could excuse overlooking the first fact as human error, but finding two pertinent facts that should have stood out as part of the home's history raised my concerns a notch. This was a contrast to the depth of research our company was accustomed to. There had to be an explanation.

The name changed from Pacific View to Canyon Ridge at the time the adjacent communities were annexed. A few of the newly built homes in one of the annexed communities did not face the Pacific.

The view of the surrounding canyons was breathtaking, justifying the name Canyon Ridge.

So far, the newfound information was not earth shattering. It added no further light to the evolving mystery. I read on as my attention waned, and my impatience became more pronounced, until I reached midpoint in the article. Before Pacific View, the community was an unincorporated area. It was a lot smaller back then and had been known by another name: *Neverland*. My mind was riveted with this discovery, reeling from that one word: *Neverland*. The article provided a link, *The History of Neverland*, that would forward the reader to a series of articles about the history of this newfound discovery.

"My God," I said with astonishment and fear—astonishment because of the unexpected connection and fear because of what I was about to discover. I reached out toward the link. My hands were clammy and unsteady, pausing every few seconds before continuing their course to invoke the link. The link was plain, with nothing occultist, as with the previous link. It was just there resting on the screen, patiently waiting for me to unleash a flurry of information. Almost there, my fingers were just an inch away. I took one final moment of deliberation before committing to a pivotal event that might lead to a paradigm shift in my perception of truth. I reached out farther with my fingers, and they seemed to lengthen, frantic to begin the journey of discovery. I tapped on the link with no response. The Neverland link did not engage. I tried again with no result; the link was stationary, as if sensing my nervous gestures and deliberating how to proceed before delivering me to the fateful gateway to altering revelations. Before I reached out again, the screen suddenly came to life. Every image that had paraded before me when I first engaged returned before receding into the background and then dissipating in midair.

The screen then turned to an ocean blue, and a couple stood at a distance, making it impossible to discern their identities. They gradually paced forward toward the forefront, whereupon I was able to behold their faces. I was able to perceive only two identical masks approaching me, looking directly at me. I was fully aware of their intense gazes as if they were present in the room. As they came nearer, I could see teardrops descending down the front of the masks. Upon further inspection, I realized the teardrops were instead melted fragments from the masks as the masks dissolved upon their reaching the house's front door. By that time, their backs were turned toward me. My curiosity became so overpowering that I unconsciously reached out with my fingertips to turn them about. I stopped midway, realizing the absurdity of my intent. Unexpectedly, the couple turned toward me. Time froze for a while. My mind tried to cope with the impact. The couple was Cassandra and me.

The scene withdrew, giving way to another screen composed of text that began with a bold storyline. I couldn't deny what I saw.

> The critically injured couple disappeared. The assailant escaped, and a manhunt ensued. The assailant is still at large. The couple were taken to the woman's home with critical wounds. Officials called emergency services, requesting a doctor and surgeon. Upon their arrival, the injured couple had disappeared. Another search party ensued, searching for the couple. The search turned up nothing.

My mind couldn't absorb any more. I was at a point where I was numb. Fatigue overcame me, crashing down with the unbearable weight of exhaustion. I felt dizzy, and my emotions seemed paralyzed, leaving me feeling like the walking dead. All I could think about was sleep, an escape from the recent discoveries. My brain was worn out, still wrapped around such implausible theories. Enormously exhausted, I walked upstairs to lie down and try to find some solitude.

I looked at Perkins, my talking African gray, and proclaimed that he was a big help. Of course, his reply was "So what do you think?" With a helpless gesture, I turned to say goodbye to Linda only to see empty space. Once upstairs, I sat for a moment and then lay down, staring into open space with my eyes drifting. My eyelids felt like weights sinking me into a comatose sleep.

58

Shadows of Revelations

I thought I heard something—a muffled noise that seemed to come from far away. I opened my eyes, anticipating the unexpected. I felt as if I'd had just a hour of downtime. I felt worse—drowsy, as if in a fog bank. I looked toward the corner and saw an old grandfather clock. Startled, I looked toward the door leading to the walk-in closet adjacent to the clock only to find a blank wall. Furthermore, the bed did not feel right.

I gasped suddenly, as though I were in a vacuum depleted of oxygen. My fingers felt numb, and my vision blurred from a fog of weariness. I could not feel my legs as I tried to move. I lifted my head with a sensation of panic. My lower extremities were intact but with no feeling. I concentrated on moving one toe on my right foot, and still, I sensed no movement. I blocked everything out, concentrating on one toe. "Move. Please twitch. Anything!" I cried, and suddenly, I noticed a twitch, a jolt, as my right toe moved. I experienced a small sensation as the numbness turned into an acute pain. *Was that a spasm?* It started at my toe and moved up along my calf, followed by an uncontrollable twitch. Soon both of my legs were alternating between bouts of spasms and twitching. I felt as if every nerve ending were overstimulated.

At least an hour must have passed, as I noticed the last remnants of sunlight dwindling at a rapid pace. The twilight had just started a short while ago, yet the fading sunlight rapidly dissolved into obscurity, replaced by a soulless night void of sight and sound. A hush fell upon me. The quietness was deafening; the only noise I heard was the beating of my own heart. Then the silence broke. I heard a deafening shrill pierce the still of the air. I looked around but saw emptiness. Off in the corner, I saw a shadow—the same menacing shadow that had been with Cassandra and me in every dream. I finally perceived that it was not one shadow but three shadows, each with a unique shade and density. The three shadows presented as a melded, swirling mass, a revolving series of forms. Each form bonded to its shadow, each with its own unique pattern of swirls and its own distinct contrast, but together they relayed a shroud of mystery. The swirling mass reverberated with a discord of voices, each a prelude of forewarning and a hint of profound revelations. The swirling mass moved closer to me, allowing me a glimpse of an evolving form inside each shadow. The forms repeatedly changed shape, as if struggling to break free from constraints that prevented the forms from emerging into their true personifications.

The swirling forms stopped as one of the shadows emerged from the swirling mass as a single entity. It opened up like a gateway to reveal a human form. As the gateway opened wider, I could see the human form inside. Its head was bent down, as if to shield its face until the moment arrived to disclose its identify. Moments later, when the gateway fully opened, it lifted its head to reveal a mask covering just the eyes and nose. The facial features that were revealed brought a vague form of recognition. The photo of the assailant from the newspaper clipping surfaced in my mind. I immediately made a connection to the human form in front of me.

It finally spoke. "Well, hello, you bastard. Do you realize you can't be here?"

I was taken aback and just sat there as my numb mind tried to compose any logical rationale for what I was seeing. After pausing for a moment to allow my senses to wake up, he stepped closer. "You fucking idiot!" he shouted. "Where the hell have you come from? You do not belong here. There are things I know that you have not even imagined yet. I know all about you and have been aware of your existence for a very long time. Do you realize where you are?"

"I have no idea what you are referring to," I responded with an offensive tone, feeling vulnerable to his vented wrath directed at me. I tried to get out of bed, but my weariness caused me to stumble, and I just missed hitting my left leg as I swung it out for leverage. The unnatural, specter-like person in front of me, still half enclosed in a shadow, called out to me to gain my full attention. Heedless to his request, which was his attempt to take control, I responded by changing the focus unexpectedly back to him. "What shall I call you?" I yelped out with a feeling of uncertainty.

"Just call me Tony," he replied.

"That is my name. Try a different one," I replied with defiant sarcasm.

"You don't know," he responded. "Tony, we must have a serious dialogue. I know things that you have not yet been made aware of. Recognize the vehement anger? You should. I am the personification of your insane rage."

"You have lost me. What in the world are you referring to? You're mad," I said.

"Well, Tony, if I am mad, then you are admitting to your madness."

I sat there half rooted in the bed, staring past him into open space. *I don't want to be here. Either I have gone completely insane, or these recurring dreams have just taken a turn into the nightmare of all nightmares. A hint of the past. The wall in my dreams. Is that what lies behind the wall? This personification of me? Ludicrous*, I thought. I withdrew back into the bed and shut my eyes to any memories from that time.

After an undetermined length of time, the sounds of silence eased my tension, and I dared to open my eyes, not sure what was in store for me to see. My eyelids opened wide, and my vision was unobstructed. The assailant's haunting image was no longer present, having retreated back to his resident shadow. A new shadow was in front of me. Its shade and density were different; it was not as dark and forbidding but appeared lighter, not as discernible. The shadow emerged to the forefront and opened, allowing me a glimpse of what was inside. All I could detect was a form curled up into a ball. The shadow emerged farther out and opened up more to reveal a female. Her arms were folded around her legs. Her head was bent down between her arms, as if to avoid being seen. I knew it was Cassandra. But why was she so noncommittal?

When the shadow fully opened into a gateway revealing her position, less tense, she unwrapped her arms and stood upright. Her head was still bent down, as if to shield her face until the moment arrived to lift her gaze. Moments later, she lifted her head to reveal a forlorn look. It was a complete contrast to the assailant's ferocious lashing toward me. There was something different. Cassandra was looking straight at me but with no sign of recognition. Her stance kept changing, as if she were searching for something or someone. I called her name and waited for her response. She obviously heard me, as she reached out with her hands, looking in the direction of my voice, but she encountered resistance almost immediately. Her hands were pressed against an invisible barrier. She appeared to be talking, but her voice was distanced by whatever barrier was separating us. I assumed she couldn't see me, because there was no sign of her awareness of my staring right at her. I managed to rise off the bed and walked toward the gateway that staged Cassandra. I felt useless. I stood there with my gaze fixed on her and my body tense, anxiously hoping nothing would threaten her while I was in that state. "Cassandra, it is Tony. How do I get around this barrier that separates us?"

"You can't, Tony. You haven't accepted your demise yet."

"What demise?" I asked.

"You don't know yet because you haven't acknowledged the incident."

"What incident?" I asked, confused.

"I can't show you because I am part of your past. But you need to know. It is time, Tony."

I felt vulnerable as I continued looking at Cassandra. After what seemed a lot longer than it actually was, Cassandra backed away from the invisible shield. *The shield*, I thought. It finally dawned on me: the shield was the wall. It made sense now. I was looking at what lay behind the wall. Cassandra was behind the wall. I feared that realization might have unforgivable consequences once my memories gave me full disclosure. I could communicate with Cassandra. I was able to see her, but the wall prevented her from viewing me. *What is the symbolism?* I wondered cautiously. Did that imply the wall was dissolving, and soon, when my senses became fully aware, I would remember the before? Was the wall symbolic of the event? Was behind the wall the full disclosure of hidden memories prior to the event? The possible connection unnerved me; the association felt too close for comfort.

"No," I blurted out with an urgent, uncontrolled, pleading gesture. "I am not ready yet."

Cassandra just stood there looking at me, not saying a word. It was as if she'd never heard me. She finally spoke with a flat tone, not her signature tone of deep reverence. "We will join soon."

Cassandra sat down, wrapped her arms around her legs, and curled back into a ball. The gateway started to close as it pulled back into the swirling shadows. Before the gateway closed entirely, another shadow evolved, merging with the shadow that enclosed Cassandra. The gateway reversed its retraction and reopened, revealing a new image of a woman who stood tall with the same posture, with her head down. When the gateway fully opened, she raised her head to reveal her identity. At first, I saw Cassandra and Linda side by side. "You don't know yet, Tony," Cassandra said. Cassandra's comment puzzled me. Her tone relayed truthfulness. It was not what she said but the tone of delivery that unsettled me. Before I could reply, Cassandra vanished. I stood there dismayed by the neutrality of her presence. Her spiritual qualities that defined her soulful purity, a highlight of our previous engagements, had not been evident in our recent exchange. "That was not Cassandra," I emphatically said to myself. The contrast was too incongruent. "I don't know who that was."

Linda stood alone. She reached out with her hand and gestured for me to take hold. "We are going to take a trip of discovery. It is time. Tony, have you wondered why your dreams have changed their pattern? If you want the clues you are so desperately seeking, you will listen to me. I cannot disclose everything, for it is you who must go through the experience, and from there, you will know what to do. I will lead you on a separate excursion that will reveal what you need to know. First, Tony, your denial of the truth keeps you in this endless journey between the two dimensions. You keep coming back to the same dreams with the same scenario because you can't bring yourself to face what happened with Cassandra. Your escape from knowing is your repeated journey. You are locked in a loop that journeys between these two dimensions as a means of avoidance, your resistance to the harsh reality of truth. The journey returns you to the other dimension once you feel threatened by facing the truth. It'll be one endless repetition until you commit."

"Commit to what?" I asked.

"Tony, you will return again, and when you hear that beckoning summons to journey you back, this time, wait. The transport will keep coming back to the other dimension until you are ready to continue past the wall and face the truth."

I turned my face toward the pillow next to me and saw a red petal lying there alongside a note. I grabbed and held on to the rose and note as if they were my last hope.

Desperate for Cassandra and desperate for answers, I took Linda's hand, and she drew me into her gateway. The air seemed suffocating, as if the oxygen were being siphoned off. My consciousness dwindled like a tunnel of light closing swiftly, casting everything into darkness. A thick fog enclosed me. At times, the fog thinned out, and I could see various entry points, portals, each with its set of messages to announce the theme of the trip down memory lane. The messages carried forth to my ears, but by the time the messages hit my senses, all I heard was a discord of voices revealing their messages into one streaming channel. I closed my eyes to lessen the impact of the disharmony, waiting for the eventful moment when I was taken down one of the memory lanes. I wasn't in charge anymore, so I relinquished my control, giving way to fate's decision of which memory lane I would travel.

Fate had an insurmountable number of memories to critique to decide which one I was to travel. How ignorant of me to be blind to the obvious: there was one main memory from which the rest would divert as separate paths to reveal more as separate sidebars before returning to the main channel or disappearing for good with their purposes fully achieved and no longer traveled. There was a main thoroughfare from which the memories were just side streets; some would rejoin the main route, and the remaining branches were one-way dead ends. It wasn't difficult for fate to determine which memory I would travel. It was obvious, I soon realized. The wall signaled the primary path to choose, the one main artery of memories free of defects that traversed though the wall's entrance as it continued to that one place that was forbidden to me.

Amnesia—it was a label assigned to my condition, firmly stamped as one would brand livestock. It was a tattoo to coexist with me regardless of an unexpected recovery. It would always be there as a reminder of what once was. *Strange name for a forgotten set of memories.* My mind shut down everything once the forbidden place was in sight, a barrier to circumventing the branches that would reveal everything. Years of memories were divorced or separated indefinitely. It was as if a part of me no longer existed, creating a separation angst.

When the wall first appeared, there was nothing—a complete vacuum. The memories beyond the wall were carefully camouflaged. In front of the wall was a barren landscape. There were no memories. It was like being born again but with all the insecurities and fears. The human mind could not function in a vacuum, where a void existed with nothing to work from. Even when a baby was contained in the mother's womb, the mind was forming memories. That vast, empty landscape triggered my perception disorder, paramnesia, to instantly create fictitious memories to fill the void with no acknowledgment of the consequences. The memory disorder became fully active, playing a dominant role by turning to an interim solution of creating a pseudoreality, a devised reality conjured up with a foundation of newly formed memories that were cleverly connected and disguised as real life. Fantasy characters and roles were molded to a reality theme I could handle. Each actor, cleverly constructed, had a specific role to follow to appear as normal as necessary, connected to the main channel of memories. That gave each actor a form of authenticity.

All was well for a while. I lived in a reservoir filled with fictitious memories based on what my imagination devised. However, despite the defective gene, the contrived memories could not exist indefinitely. Sooner or later, the mind would acknowledge the defect and devise a resolution in an attempt to correct the defect. Sometimes the attempt to correct would become a private hell. A path was formed between the fact-based memories camouflaged behind the wall and the devised fantasy memories. On that path, the fantasy memories would cross into the others' domain before returning with deformities that gave hell a new meaning. The deformed memories were the result of my condition, which fused reality with fantasy. The nature of my genetic flaw was to form a new memory in which fantasy and fact were molded into one state. The contrived memories were encapsulated with real and fantasized experiences purely at random, resulting in deformed memories that gave the word *horror* a new meaning. Even the well-known horror writers could not have conjured up the horror that genetic mutation could devise.

My own creative tools became my salvation to survive during that interim nightmare. Even though my mind conjured up a pseudoreality, it was clever enough to realize the only path to total resolution was to return to reality, dissolving the entity consisting of devised fantasies. I had to wipe the pseudoreality clean and restore the fact-based memories from behind the wall to their original form. The fact-based memories had to be re-aligned to their rightful state. A state defined by the actual fact based elements of time and place. In other words, re-aligned by the fact-based elements of when and where. For this to occur, mandated that the wall which suppressed the memories had to come down. The mandate was passed down to me with heightened emphasis: dissolve the wall. Maybe it was fate that had the final say-so when it was time to find the truth. Maybe fate gave the directive to reveal the elements of certainty. It was about to happen with Linda and me, our paths soon to culminate to yield to fate's unrelenting effort to strip everything anyway except what is relevant. To encapsulate reality into one medium to confront the facts. The false landscape constructed of a fantasized reality would soon come crashing down, burying the devised schemes and revealing the truth. The time was near. Once the barrier broke down, I would be ferried to the one hidden place that held the horrible truth: behind the wall, which already showed signs of wearing down. One fact came into my mind: *You can't hide the truth forever. The wall is crumbling.*

59

The Approaching Macabre Event: The Turning Point

I reached out for Linda as she led me down memory lane, the road to discovery. She was there for just a brief moment before she vanished. There was no trace of her; she was nowhere to be found. The last I remembered before she faded into a void was entering her gateway, where the journey she'd chosen for me started. My immediate surroundings took form as my new journey commenced with me driving down the coastline.

I suspected nothing. I was not aware of the sinister plot behind the storm. Linda and I were heading back from our latest inspection of a classic house built during the 1930s. It was still in immaculate condition. We should have been ecstatic but found ourselves in an unusually somber mood during the drive back to the office. An eerie silence persisted between us. Yet despite the silence, we shared a strong feeling that there was more to the impending storm. It was a cataclysm with irreversible revelations, one that would result in a paradigm shift in our perceptions. As we peered out the window, we noticed the strange overcast that accompanied the brewing tempest of enormous proportions. We had never experienced one like it before. The air had an unusual appearance. I could see shimmering pockets of dense, humid air moving in a horizontal direction. For a brief second, through the dense mugginess, I detected something moving within the pocket of humidity, but I was not able to see clearly. Several images appeared at random intervals. The images' duration was too quick to discern any recognition. Each time, though, I picked up on the sounds of whispers that seemed to be emanating from the dense pockets: "Soon, Tony. Soon everything will be revealed." Refusing to acknowledge what I was viewing, I rationalized the scene in front of me as being due to the storm's effect on the atmospheric conditions. I rolled down my window to get a clearer view only to be swallowed by the oppressive heaviness of the hot, steamy summer day. It was late afternoon, when the heat was more intense. Dark, forbidding cumulus clouds moved in over the Pacific, casting a sweeping shadow of ominous intent that raced toward land with an eerie glow from within its bowels. Lightning bolts crossed the sea of heavenly bodies, their intensity escalating with rage, marching onward with malicious intent. Seagulls, sensing imminent peril, circled in close to shore, screeching out cries of alarm, a harbinger of unleashed destruction.

A black mass emerged from the nebulous sky, moving toward Linda and me. As the mass moved in closer to our location, we realized the mass was a swarm of black crows. Their cawing grew in intensity as they converged in midair directly in front of us while we drove southward toward the approaching storm. Their squawking became cries of alarm. They were warning us of imminent danger. Their constant screeching turned into a repeated warning: "Soon, Tony. The event. The storm. Total vanquishment of this contrived reality." The mass then vanished in midair. The first incident I could rationalize as an atmospheric anomaly due to the pending storm, but the recent incident challenged my own rationale. The fact that my name was mentioned in each incident implied the two incidents were warnings directed at me. But why? The two incidents added to my wariness that the storm somehow was linked to me. It would be a pivotal point that would have repercussions on my past and future. However, I could not fathom why such a powerful storm was necessary if I was the only primary intended object of such a climatic event. Yet based on the recent enigmatic events thrown my way, I could not deny what my suspicions alluded to, no matter how far-fetched the ideas were. My suspicions took me a step further into the twilight zone. *Could this be related to the wall?* It was a far-reaching suspicion, but my paranoia was on high alert, and I perceived that anything was possible, no matter how far my deluded reasoning took me. I turned toward Linda to confirm what I'd just witnessed and found her in the throes of a deep sleep. She opened her eyes and greeted me with renewed vigor. Impulsively, I started to describe what I'd just viewed, but just before I blurted out the first word, I elected not to mention the two incidents and continued our drive southward.

We proceeded with caution, hoping we would reach our destination before the storm unleashed its power. Several times, we were about to turn around to distance ourselves from the storm's advance but elected to continue, as if the storm were intentionally pulling us forward into the heart of its escalating threat. Off in the distance, water spouts twirled higher to connect with the thunderheads, refueling the massive structures in midair. The storm was mounting an even greater intensity. Electrical charges traversed the water spouts upward toward this bastille, illuminating a labyrinth of neurons providing a connection that funneled the water spouts through the massive network of spiraling structures. The winds pummeled through the formations, converging as one and, reaching unheard-of velocity, sweeping down toward towering waves, transforming them into a powerful ocean surge of massive proportions. The surge reached a crescendo with ferocity, as if fueled by the wrath of the gods.

As nature's elements made their final preparation for the massive onslaught, the color of the sky suddenly turned to an eerie green hue, and the smell of ozone was present in the air. The atmosphere was highly charged with a current of stillness and silence, except for a high-pitched buzzing sound, of which every creature took notice. All eyes were glued to the ensuing monsoon, waiting with dreadful anticipation. The atmosphere was scented with terror. There was nowhere to hide and nowhere to run to escape the impending doom. The air became saturated with electrical spirals of charged particles sent in as scouts for the front-line assault. They canvassed the area as if they were communicating with the thundering formations before a full-blown invasion.

The hurricane-strength winds blew inland first as the first monster wave hit landfall. The classic homes we'd spent endless hours remodeling along the oceanfront were the first line of casualties. They were virtually devoured within seconds as the surge erased the coastline. The force of the initial onslaught detonated gas lines, causing violent explosions, and fiery flames surged skyward, fueled by ruptured mains. Treetops from the canyons across Route 1 violently exploded into fireballs as the monsoon winds carried the gas-fed flames farther inland. An ocean surge rushed forward. A massive wall of water mounted to a towering height of twenty feet and, driven in by the gale-force winds, extended over the highway, devouring everything in sight. With a rampant fury, the storm vehemently heightened its march toward total vanquishment with unrestrained force while Linda and I watched with frozen horror as the storm picked up its intensity and crashed violently, extending its reach northward toward us and pulverizing the cliffs across Route 1.

The belated warning sirens signaling to take cover were too little too late as the tempest of undaunted proportions raced onward. Lightning flashed from deep within the cumulus thunderheads, and each bolt briefly carried an image. I saw Cassandra, the house on Canyon Ridge, Linda, and Neverland, and then the scene shifted to the inscriptions on two gravestones. The image started to fade, but I had enough time to discern the inscription on the first marker before the storm's fiery display retreated to a thunderous roar, its intensity traversing toward the tree-topped canyons overlooking the Pacific. Two names were included in the inscription. My wall of denial served as a break wall to lessen the impact once the names fully registered. Everything around me retreated to the background as I grappled with the implication of the two names: Cassandra and Linda. *Why both names on one tombstone?* I thought with concern. A thunderous roar commanded my attention as the raging storm demanded center stage. My mind did a double take as I looked at Linda next to me. We had no time to think; we just reacted. Linda and I, paralyzed with fear as the storm advanced, miraculously evacuated our vehicle and frantically retreated farther northward toward the elevated cliffs across Route 1 in search of a safe haven seconds before the monsoon reached the northern peninsula. Series of lightning bolts jolted our senses when the towering red oak trees around us exploded. Hurricane-strength winds forced the torrential rain into sheets of hail as the deluge of unmeasurable force swept between the canyons, erasing everything in its path.

The classic homes we'd purchased, including ones we'd remodeled and those scheduled for remodeling, nestled throughout the cliffs overlooking the Pacific were annihilated, each swept down the mountainside. The storm's destruction was widespread, yet the devastation was absolute when it confronted the homes we owned. To our amazement, the storm seemed to target with a deadly purpose the homes we'd purchased. It didn't make sense, but I realized that unfortunately, nothing seemed rational anymore. I became entrenched in the storm's destruction as its wrath continued. While the storm continued venting its rage, I felt a barrier coming down, revealing the wall. I looked on, taking in its enormity. I was no longer able to hide from its presence. Manifested memories chained to more memories were expunged from my contrived reality. Slowly but surely, the fabricated structure of conjured-up views of a pseudoreality was losing its substance.

Linda and I forged on to escape from the storm's destructive force and find a safe haven. Shielded from the treacherous winds between two canyons, we rested, catching our breath, deluged from the rains that pelted us with cascading sheets of downpour. The dampness instilled a freezing chill deep in our bones despite the eighty-degree temperature. There were moments when the storm's intensity hit a lull for a few seconds. We encountered one of the interludes, and through a momentary window of clarity, we caught a glimpse of what seemed like an opening mostly hidden by dense foliage high above us along the cliffs toward my left. We darted across the chasm between the canyons to start our treacherous climb. The torrid rain resumed with renewed strength, coming at us with hail pellets that caused welts on our arms and faces. With nowhere to hide, we continued to fight our way, able to see only a few feet in front of us, pulling ourselves through the deluge. After what seemed like hours, we landed in a small crevice midway up the mountainside, shut in by the ferocity of the storm, which was still at full strength, its winds attacking with life-threatening vengeance. The storm hit another lull, and the rain and ravaging winds decreased in intensity, allowing us a brief interlude to scale farther upward. We rested once more against a cliff hanging on to tiny nooks etched into the northern wall. We wound our way around, clinging to the fissures to finish our climb. We clung to each other with every step, hanging on with desperation. The wind suddenly picked up, hitting us with ferocity and making any communication impossible. We relied upon our frantic expressions.

For a brief moment, I thought I heard Linda cry out that she couldn't hang on any longer, and I felt her hand start to lose its hold from mine. I grabbed what was left of the grip and pulled with all my might, using my last reserves. We dared not look down, for the view of devastation would surely cause us to lose hope. Miraculously, my foot found a firm foothold in a crevice. I reached upward with my right hand and, amazingly, found a tree limb. With renewed strength, I took hold of the weathered limb and pulled again, and I landed on solid ground, perched at the edge of the overlooking cliff. My hope must have fueled Linda's drive, as she grabbed my arm with her other hand, and I painfully pulled her up using both hands. She toppled over and landed inches from me on the sacred soil. We only had a few minutes to spare to find a new place to shield us. The downpour turned our welts into bloody sores as we fought our way farther in and settled into a small indentation nestled into the mountainside. Once tucked securely inside, we were protected from the ravaging winds and torrid rain.

We shifted our gaze out toward the ocean with forlorn looks of despair, overwhelmed by the enormity of the destruction. There was nothing left. Everything was gone. No trace remained of the historic homes we'd purchased and remodeled along the coastline and throughout the surrounding canyons. The roads, the beach, the homes, the hotels, and the office complexes were savagely beaten by the storm, and the area was littered with debris. Most noticeable was the obliteration of the homes remodeled by my company. My company's years of planning, sweat, and tears were gone within a few hours. It felt like a mirage that had suddenly dissolved as if it never had existed.

More conjured-up memories were extracted from the pseudoreality serving as my barrier of denial, weakening its formation. The fabricated structure started to disintegrate, with tiny fissures spreading out from its core and dissolving everything in its path. As the fissures spread outward, the barrier began to disintegrate at an even more alarming pace. The wall of hidden memories became overwhelmingly apparent.

In the midst of total devastation, we saw a cove next to Canyon Ridge Trails. Its entrance was high above the flood line. Farther up above the cove, surprisingly, we found the home we'd recently purchased. It had extensive damage but not to the extent of the other homes we owned. From what I could determine, the homes we'd remodeled were totally destroyed, yet it appeared the home above the cove on Canyon Ridge was still intact despite significant damage. I looked up toward the home again with the hope that when we reached the cove with the next lull, Linda and I could find our way to the house to further shield ourselves from the storm's destructive force. My hope turned into a task for survival when, with uncontrolled savagery, the storm intensified its determination to vent its rage with malicious intent while we fought our way through the torrential downpour and the massive onslaught of gale-force winds. The brutal fierceness of nature's venom became horridly apparent when we saw the total devastation as we raced upward toward the towering cliffs, searching for the well-hidden trail that led to the cove. We struggled higher against overwhelming odds, and suddenly, through the trees masked by a web of overgrowth, we saw the cove entrance and thrashed our way through the web of entanglement to find a safe haven.

60

The Onset of the Dissolution of Tony's Fabrication

We fought our way through the dense underbrush, when suddenly, a fierce, blinding surge of fire spiraled upward. We turned and watched with horror while the storm demolished our vehicle with a fiery explosion. The fireball jettisoned skyward, forcibly thrust into the cumulus shapes, as our SUV hurtled across the highway into one of the mountainsides. Frantically, we pushed onward, when suddenly, directly overhead, lightning flashes tore open the heavens, and within the storm's thunderheads towering above us, we saw a flicker of grotesque images. Their demonic eyes followed our retreat into the canyonside. Racing against the storm, with each step frantic and each breath taken in agony, as if the storm were depleting the air of oxygen, we ran for cover, struggling against the hurricane-strength winds, fighting for every breath. It was a race against time; we knew that any minute, the messengers from death's front door would carry us through the gates of darkness.

With alarmed urgency, we dove for cover, and miraculously, the cove opening came into view. We stumbled forward and fell at the entrance to the cove when a series of lightning bolts swarmed toward us and landed with a thunderous roar at the cove's entryway. A final lightning bolt struck, landing a few feet between me and Linda. The surge of heat and energy propelled us upward, as if we were being transported through a funnel directly into the thunderheads. Suddenly, the upward thrust ceased, followed by a downward draft, and we were propelled back toward land at an accelerated rate. We landed with a sudden force that jolted our senses, toppling to the ground like lifeless puppets dangling from a puppeteer's strings. The ground on which we landed was charred, and the smell of burning flesh was rampant. We crawled farther into the cove entrance, exhausted and ready to succumb to death's folly. Suddenly, a field of electrical charges enveloped us and traversed through our bodies. I saw Linda grasping her throat and chest as she fell to the ground, and I reached out to her to catch her fall. Upon touching her hand, I too was enclosed in a wave of unmeasurable force. I fell, stumbled forward, and crawled toward Linda, desperate to shield her from harm's way.

A brilliant, intense circle of light appeared and encompassed me, permeating me forcibly, reaching into my soul as though it were searching for a dark, hidden secret. The blinding light revealed a pulsating stream of floating images that seemed to magically swirl around me as if I were *Fantasia's* sorcerer's apprentice. I grabbed my head from the dizzying effects when I caught visions from a distant past enclosed in a white halo that cast an eerie phosphorescent light moving in quantum jumps toward Linda.

The streaming images picked up their frenzied pace, revolving rapidly around me while becoming more obscured, until they vanished. Another view appeared, enclosing me in a picturesque scene that projected a dimension of realness. I saw a small, quaint town nestled in a valley surrounded by majestic mile-high mountains. *Neverland*, in bold letters, stood out on the water tower, announcing its presence at the southern edge of the village. The village must have been formed at least a century ago, I thought, because of the abundance of massive oak and maple trees, which gave the village an impression of a poetic postcard setting. I got up and walked through the town to a home that looked like one that would have been built in the 1930s. It was similar to the house on Canyon Ridge. Upon further scrutiny, I realized it was the same house. But the house seemed bigger from the outside. The overhang was larger. Someone was standing on the patio with her back turned toward me. Another male was in the corner; he seemed to be talking to her. The look on his face turned into a mask of hatred as he approached her. It was difficult to discern the atmosphere due to the vagueness of the images. The male moved closer to the lady. The image was still vague but rapidly becoming more distinct. She suddenly turned around toward her assailant. *It can't be.* I was stunned, and my emotions froze for an instant. Yes, to my shock, it was Cassandra at the forefront in each succession of images. At that moment, for a fleeting second, I knew something tragic had happened, and seeing Cassandra was not possible. It could not be. Somehow, I knew how the tragedy had impacted our lives with life-altering consequences. "Cassandra!" I cried out. I closed my eyes, wondering, and opened them again, acknowledging her presence just for a moment before the feeling of tragedy retreated, leaving me confused and perplexed. The images then instantly dissolved.

I realized the rain was hitting me with fierce pellets. The storm was worse, and Linda and I needed to find shelter farther in the cove before the major typhoon extinguished our lives' energy. I suddenly turned toward Linda. She gripped her throat and grabbed at her chest as she fell out of my line of vision. With a surge of urgency, I crawled toward where she'd fallen, reaching out with my hand to grasp as I heard her shriek pierce the silence with cries of alarm. She cried out, "Tony!" I then heard her plea once more before it distanced itself to just a faint echo. Then an eerie silence ensued.

Suspended in what felt like a vacuum, I remained motionless to detect any indication of a storm. There was nothing—no sound, no movement, no wind, no lightning. There was an absence of any irregularities one would have associated with a fierce storm. *The storm must have ended.* I relaxed my breathing, realizing I'd been holding my breath all that time. After another few minutes, as I gradually became more relieved, the lack of any suggestion of a storm further confirmed that the storm's vengeance was no longer present. I wasn't sure where I was.

In the shadowy gloom, the white halo reappeared, and another parade of images surfaced of Cassandra as the light traveled through past eras. Each image was unique to each era, and each showed an altered portrait of Cassandra while retaining her likeness. Each was tailored with separate and distinct features. The series of images continued with increased intensity and frequency, and then the halo of light disappeared, followed by a vacuum of vacuity augmented by a silence of complete stillness, thrusting my world into the abyss of darkness. My last memory before I succumbed to unconsciousness was, once again, of Cassandra enclosed by a circle of images, each turning effortlessly like a ballerina, until she abruptly disintegrated into tiny fragments of bloodlike droplets that dispersed among the encompassing visuals, transforming my view into a surreal stage of a crimson blood portrait of forlorn desolation. As the blanket of unconsciousness consumed the last of my conscious light, I felt my pseudoreality gradually dissolve, revealing the wall as it too continued to fragment. The remnants of my life prior to the wall of hidden memories perched precariously on the edge of total discovery, waiting for the moment to launch a vicious attack without warning or concern on my precious sensitivities. Despite my effort to distance myself from the wall's inherent threat to my hold on sanity, there was no stopping the advancement of the blanket of darkness. However, in a strange way, I welcomed the encroachment of nothingness, as it camouflaged my anxieties with a restful respite.

61

The Event that Delineates
the Before and After

Darkness surrounded me—pitch-black emptiness that was dense and suffocating, screaming in my mind. The darkness was so intense that it left me breathless and vulnerable. I felt a claustrophobic fear bordering on panic. I was devoid of any sight, yet I sensed movement. My inner gyroscope detected motion—not voluntarily movement but the motion of a passenger being carried somewhere with haste. I sensed the pace accelerating, as if time were of the essence, racing with an approaching deadline. As the velocity increased, a sequence of vibrant colors appeared that spearheaded the journey. Each sequence was a series of brilliant-colored streaks that accompanied my transport, acting as a guide. Each streak was short-lived, disappearing into whatever lay before me, replaced by its successor following in its wake. Eventually, the acceleration reached a velocity at which the series of vibrantly colored streaks appeared to fuse into one continual chain of lights bursting out before me, leading the way to an unknown destination. The light was my only point of reference to gauge our speed. As the journey continued, the pressure increased, signaling an upward or downward trajectory. Either way, I was sure we were on a significant journey with a destination of utmost importance. It seemed forever before I felt our speed decrease, and then we came to a complete halt, at which point everything stopped as time consumed me.

I suddenly emerged into what seemed like another realm, a different dimension, a void where I was suspended as if I were weightless. I quickly glanced around and saw no resemblance of physical embodiment. My line of vision caught Linda off in the distance. Her arms hung limply by her sides, as if she were suspended in midair. I called out Linda's name repeatedly, not knowing if she was even alive. Suddenly, Linda's arms moved upward as electrical charges passed between both hands. Her eyes opened wide, and her line of vision connected with me. She moved haltingly as her mouth formed words I could not hear. I heard only an eerie silence, and then, anemically, with a breathless whimper, she whispered, "Soon, Tony. You will know." Then she faded into an aura of light.

What happened? Where am I? I asked myself those two basic questions seemingly countless times. Then I knew. A blanket of opacity was lifted. An intense vulnerability surfaced. A barricade of weighted denials was no longer present. Instinctively, I knew the storm had dissolved everything. The storm's fierceness had swallowed my pseudoreality, my barricade of denials. The storm of cataclysmic proportions had torn down the barrier fabricated with layers upon layers of contrived realities firmly implanted to hold back the truth hidden behind the wall of my amnesia.

Shadows—recollections of my contrived life—were etched before me with stunning disclosures. One basic fact which held overwhelming implications became immediately obvious. My current life has been an act featuring me as the sole performer. My life to the point where everything becomes obscured was staged as a solo performance featuring me in a lead role in one continuous act to reveal every intimate moment to the audience of unknowns. My house in Santa Monica, my company where I was CEO, my employees and contractors, the transportation system of passenger trains ferrying passengers between their domiciles and work, and the homes we'd purchased were all paraded as stage props to give each scene a sense of realness. It was a stage setting where the theme carried a message of impermanence; each scene was a construct that withered away into obscurity. The events were never real. I faced a finality, the dissolution of a marriage between constructed fantasies woven into the fabric of a pseudoreality. There was only a semblance of preserved realness centering on me, Cassandra, Linda, Matt, and the house perched high on Canyon Ridge Trails, located in a quaint village called Neverland. The rest of the acts in the performance, well past the closing curtain call, were kept in a temporary, private place reserved for permanent conclusion. Slowly, I nervously glanced around and viewed the same light heading toward me. I feverishly whispered, "The wall. It is time for reality to take its promenade along the avenue of truths." The light then grabbed control and swept me into a time vortex, and I fell into an unconscious state toward a fate unknown.

More visions floated by. The cloak of darkness was now a semblance of shadowed lights. I heard a rumble and the shrill echo of a familiar sound I was unable to recognize, yet the ghostly roll was of something turning. I heard the constant clicking sound of something moving. The tone and frequency never changed, and it never altered its course, carrying me on a journey that seemed to have lasted forever with destinations held secret by fate. *How long has it been? Can't remember. I have nothing. All memories are absent, but there is something. Something that wants to break through. Something that, once unleashed, will be my harbinger of unspeakable, unimaginable consequences. Consequences that may impair me and enclose me in a dark closet—a closet with no doors and no lights, just empty darkness, the kind that suffocates and entraps you with total isolation. Yet I am not entirely alone, for I have a companion to make sure I never get lonely and to remind me of an unspeakable act that no words can describe. There is just that dark, empty feeling, something like a memory that is rotting inside your soul.* Just for a moment, those thoughts floated by, leaving me paralyzed with fear and panic. Then I felt the rumble of movement—a transport—and as the rumble faded away, the unimaginable force left me, and I finally succumbed to the last visage of light. Then there was nothing. *But something is there waiting for me, waiting for that one final moment when it happens.*

Time has passed, but I was unaware of how much time had gone by. My instincts assumed the elapsed time was at the most just a few hours from when I blacked out. There was the wall, or what was left of it. It was standing in a few places but worn down around the entrance. I had no control of my movement as I was carried forward through the doorway on a path to a disclosure of the memories that had been blocked for what seemed an eternity. This time, the echoes of torment from the wall were absent. There was silence. At times, a flurry of whispers prevailed, as if to ease the impact when the truth was revealed. The path was now encumbered with obstacles. Barriers would open up, allowing passageway. It seemed, though, that as each barrier opened up for me to pass through, it was with the intent to reinforce the constraints to restrain me once confronted with the truth.

It seemed forever until I gained sight of the small town of Neverland, the epicenter of my anguish, which, once disclosed, would lift the weight of the unbearable cross or crush me with unsustainable weight I could no longer conceal with denial. As I neared the village of mystique, the sky turned to a dark wine color-The omen-like eerie darkened sky crossed my path, descending upon the village. The village now overcast with a dark purplish violet tone that symbolized a mood of mystery and transformation. I was within a few hundred yards of the village, and the stench of death was unbearable.

The whimpering murmurs of Cassandra filled the atmosphere. Tearful sobs tugged at my heart. I searched for her, trying to follow the source of the sorrow. The path led me to the village limits, where the familiar village depot stood out as a greeting or a warning, depending on the reason for one's visit. It was more than just a warning I felt as I moved closer to the depot. I discerned a finality to this visit, and the depot was drawing me in with an urgency to fulfill a deed long overdue. I crossed the tracks, watching in both directions for any type of danger. The evening was turning into night, with a full moon that highlighted the maroon-colored atmosphere. Strands of cirrus clouds floated through the sky, crossing the moon's path and filtering the moon's glow into an unnatural aura of a purplish fog. Off in the distance, I heard the familiar sound of an approaching transport. The sound conveyed a soulful loneliness filled with despair and sorrow. The sounds of pain and guilt were more pronounced as the transport announced its presence, approaching the village effortlessly. Unmistakably, the phantom ghost transport was making its nightly rounds. This time, only one of the eight passenger cars was lit. The transport didn't slow down as it passed through the village. As the front car passed, three figures sat up and looked out in my direction. I stood there with my emotions held in check. What I was viewing was not possible and could only exist in a surreal setting. Cassandra, Linda, and I were the three passengers, all staring directly at me with forlorn looks. I stood in disbelief. My doppelgänger was on that one-way journey, but I was standing there watching the deadly look on each face as they voiced their concern. The implication stared at me with a horrified appearance. Each gaunt-looking face projected a ghastly visage. Once the lit compartment passed the depot, each turned toward me, echoing one remark: "We are dead, Tony. Dead. All three of us. You need to join us on this journey to a place known as the gatekeeper. Only then can our souls be released to move on."

I turned toward the depot door, valiantly denying what I'd just heard. "All delusions," I remarked. I dashed through the depot, mindless of the deadly silence coming from the village. No carriage was waiting for me. As I proceeded toward the village, the path led me through a cemetery. My wariness heightened as the path wound around tall markers, each tilted inward as if attempting to slow my progress and whisper its long-overdue anticipation and acknowledgment of my visit—one that would have a permanence to it. I dared not look down at the markers, fearful that the one I looked at would have my name firmly stamped into the gravestone. The night grew to a darker tone as I carefully followed the winding path. The sounds of silence turned to a flurry of whispers, as if I were waking the dead. Among the whispers, I kept hearing, "It's Tony. It's Tony. We can rest now. Justice will prevail. The event."

"My imagination," I repeatedly said to drown out the whisper. I quickened my pace, fearful of being caught and detained by the dead spirits.

I soon exited the cemetery and continued on the path until I saw the house high up on the cliff. There was no obvious evidence of any activity in the house, but I ventured forth to investigate further. I strenuously climbed the walkway up to the front door and found it unlocked. Heedless to any warning, I entered to find the house unoccupied. I stood still, as I thought I heard a voice. Yes, there it was—a cry. "Shut up," a male voice said. The male voice turned into repeated, mindless ramblings that seemed irrational.

The atmosphere in the house had a stench to it, though the only occupants were ageless memories. The memories were so devastating they filled the vacancy with the stench of fear. They permeated the surrounding atmosphere with a sense of hellish doom intent on persevering for ageless lifetimes. Instinctively, I knew. It was here. *The event. The turning point when everything tilted on its axis, when the polarization reversed life's order. This is the source of the wall's purpose—hiding everything revolving around the event. The point where the obscured memories will surface.* The recollection's outcome and impact on me were yet to be determined.

I followed the source of the rambling, which led me to a stairway that descended from the back patio to a level below the overhang. I descended until I reached the bottom, where I found another doorway, which led me into a large chamber. I encountered a tunneled path leading to a passageway that continued outward toward the ocean.

I heard a cry again, which led me back to the large chamber. I followed the source of the sound, which led me to another smaller chamber located toward the rear of the main chamber. At the entrance was a huge oak door. I put my ear against the door to listen to the whispers. The oak door was too thick altering the whispers to just muffled noise. I pressed in on the door with surprising ease and found Cassandra chained to a gurney. A male wearing the mask of a crazed madman was with her, obviously holding her prisoner and, based on Cassandra's bruises, torturing her. I called out to Cassandra. She turned her head but was unable to lift her body off the table because of the restraints. She was pregnant—more than just a few months, based on her size, but I could not determine exactly how many months. The male had a series of instruments one normally associated with surgery. From what I was viewing, it appeared he was going to use the instruments to abort the baby. I rushed toward the assailant, catching him by surprise.

He turned and immediately held a surgical knife over Cassandra's stomach. "One more move, sir, and both she and the baby will die."

I backed away and asked, "Why?"

"I assume you're Tony," he replied angrily.

"Yes, I am Tony. But why this?"

"Then it's your baby, Tony. And she is my wife. I am Matt. Recognize my name? You should, Tony. Your trip to hell begins with me. Your question should be redirected at you. So my question to you, Mr. Prince, is why?"

I had no answer that would make the situation any better. I came out with the only response that would convey any meaning. "Love. Because I love her."

"Well, Tony, I love her too. Maybe it is my baby."

I blurted out before thinking, "But you're sterile." I realized my mistake before I even finished my remark.

"How do you know that?" His face contorted with a hellish rage as he faced Cassandra and then turned back to me. I couldn't say any more for fear of pushing him over the edge. "Well, Cassandra, you can't keep anything a secret. So I am sterile. You just had to tell lover boy here. Who else knows? Besides cheating on me, you also go spilling your guts about my condition, adding insult to injury. Since it is not mine, the baby belongs to no one. It must be aborted. By the way, Tony, she has already come up with a name and is convinced it is a girl. Linda. Too bad Linda will never see outside her mother's womb. But, Tony, I have a little twist here. I just love it when my mind conjures up these sudden creative impulses. I am not going to perform the task. You are."

"You're crazy if you think I am going to do this. And neither are you!" I exclaimed, moving forward, trying to catch him by surprise.

But he was quick as he brought out a Taser, knocking me to the floor. Convulsing, I felt a sharp jolt to my arm, and a numbing sensation immediately set in. I lay there motionless, unable to move or talk. I heard him endlessly repeat that it was not his baby. His tone was deadly serious, frequently infused with odd, shrill, insane laughter. Cassandra had not said a word. He must have heavily sedated her, I thought. He walked to the front of the table and then administered something to Cassandra. Then he moved to her abdomen and placed his hand on Cassandra's stomach. "She is already kicking," he said. "Must be a fighter. Unfortunate that she will never need her ability to fight." My numbness wore off enough to allow me to be more cognizant. I lay there and listened to what he was saying. "Tony, you seem to have regained a degree of consciousness. It's your baby, so you abort it."

"You're insane," I replied emphatically.

"Doesn't matter what you think, as this was caused by you. So the result of what I require you to do is on your shoulders. If you don't do what I need you to do, then this scalpel will slice open Cassandra's throat."

With a strained effort, I raised myself up to a standing position. "Where is the scalpel?" I asked.

"No scalpel is required. Here is the tool you will use to abort the fetus. I will instruct you as you proceed."

"I will need some cutting instruments to cut the umbilical cord." He looked at me. "Yes, you're correct. Here is a scalpel to cut the cord."

As he laid it on Cassandra's abdomen, I lashed out to catch his wrist. However, in my doing so, he sliced open a six-inch cut across Cassandra's abdomen. I looked at the wound, realizing it was not a deep cut but superficial. He raised the scalpel again. His eyes bore a crazed look filled with an insane intent to inflict a deeper cut. I charged at him, and we wrestled to the floor. When we landed, he sliced open a deep cut along my sternum. The wound seeped blood immediately, and I knew I had a matter of minutes before the blood loss would weaken me. Realizing I only had minutes to spare, I attacked him, knowing I would be cut again, this time deeper. I had one chance to use my scalpel in just the right place that would be terminal. I charged him again and brought my scalpel under his chin, but he was able to make another deeper cut on me. My hold on the scalpel loosened, and it fell by my side.

He looked down at me as if I were vanquished, my effort to thwart his deadly intent lost to the moment. "What did you say, Tony? I am sterile? By impregnating Cassandra, you assumed the role of lover and father. So your decision to extend my sterile condition to a symbol of impotence, a castrated unicorn, to denounce my role to an impotent lover and husband. Initially, I was going to do a C-section. I changed my mind. Mr. Prince, how do you feel? Instead of opening up Cassandra's life to a wealth of happiness, you have sentenced her to a violent death. You are going to perform a C-section. I will instruct you. If you refuse, I will end Cassandra's life with a quick slice to the throat. Then you will be without the baby, Linda, and Cassandra. So it is your choice: lose the baby, or lose both Cassandra and the baby."

"You're crazy!" I blurted out. I took the knife and held it over Cassandra's stomach. "God forgive me," I said. There was already a cut along Cassandra's stomach. "What do I do now?" I asked, trying to buy myself time.

"Don't play games with me. You're stalling. Just make a deeper cut, and slice the cut wider across the abdomen."

I hesitated, unable to fully absorb his demands. It was a no-win situation.

"Now," he said.

My mind went numb as I became overwhelmed with shock. I was unable to think or feel. I responded as if I were a robot operating in command mode. I rested my hand on the cut already made by Matt. With the scalpel, I started making a deeper incision. I stopped. I could not continue with such an unthinkable demand. I felt paralyzed, already weak from a loss of blood, and my mind was dizzy with emotions. A piercing scream erupted from Cassandra. Blood rushed out from the wound, covering my hands and midsection with blood. I felt weak, fading in and out of consciousness. My knees buckled, and I was unable to sustain my upright position and fell to the floor.

"You are one worthless coward. I am going to finish this myself."

My mind exploded with a desperate plea. "No, you can't do this. I am at fault here. Punish me. Take my life, for I am the guilty one. Just leave her alone, you worthless coward." I reached inside to find my last ounce of reserve and pulled myself to the gurney. I strained with an effort I didn't know I had to pull myself up. Halfway there, I crashed back to the floor, the last of my reserves spent. "No, no. Can't be happening." My words were just a whimper now. I was exhausted from the effort.

Another scream like one I never had heard before emerged from Cassandra. It was a terror-filled scream that only tortured souls could make. It was as if the bowels of hell had opened wide to reveal the tormented cries of the souls sentenced to lives of infinite torment and unimaginable pain. What he did to Cassandra and the baby consumed me as my life force dwindled to nothing. What had I gained? Was Cassandra's wound deep enough to lose both of them? My focus became a tunnel of light; the opening became smaller, and then I saw nothing.

I was caught in a dazed state. A muffled moan reached me, as if I were underwater. I opened my eyes, and my vision blurred; I was only able to see shadows. Cassandra was still on the table. Her body was twitching. She was convulsing. The baby was out, covered in blood. Not a sound came from the baby. Something dripped onto my forehead, seeped down my cheek, and pooled on the floor by the base of my neck. I raised my hand to my forehead to catch some of the residue and looked at my fingertips: blood. I pulled myself up to a sitting position and saw the blood pooling beside me—Cassandra and the baby's blood. Their life forces were being extracted, and her baby was lying next to her as a farewell.

The horror of what had happened there hit me like an avalanche. I crawled to Matt, trying to pull him down toward me. Cassandra screamed, now fully awake. Matt pulled himself up to the table and lifted Cassandra up from the table. In the process, the baby, covered in blood, fell from the table and landed in front of me. I saw a small-caliber pistol beside me. It must have fallen out when I grabbed Matt's ankle. I fired a shot, which missed its target. I searched around me and could not find Matt. I looked at my hands; both were covered in blood. I looked down at the floor where I was lying and found a knife and scalpel. I looked around again. Cassandra was covered with blood. The baby was lying in front of me, covered in blood. I felt something snap inside me. I was unable to process the images in front of me. Something gave way, and my mind retreated into a shell, unable to process anything. My mind became a total blank, devoid of my previous memories. *Where am I? How did I get here?* The same two questions repeatedly plagued me.

I heard a commotion at the door, followed by another scream from Cassandra as she fell back onto the table. Voices came from everywhere. One voice in particular shouted commands to others. I was lifted onto a stretcher as a voice said I might be the only survivor, but my vital signs were fading fast. Everything went dark. Emptiness was now a constant companion as the tide of unconsciousness carried me further out. The raft I was in rode the tide as Cassandra came into view, her head barely breaking the surface. I used my hands to move the raft closer to her. I finally reached her and pulled her in. There was something else in the water, barely floating. I reached out and lifted it into the raft—a baby who obviously was dead. Cassandra, barely conscious, pulled herself closer to the baby, calling her Linda. She pulled the baby into her arms and gently kissed the baby on the forehead, holding it close to her bosom. Total silence ensued as I found both Cassandra and the baby, Linda, dead. I sat there listlessly, floating with no destination in mind, just floating in circles as my mind disintegrated into fragments of what once was.

62

Dissolution of Tony's Contrived Reality: Collapse of the Wall

Scenes from the storm's carnage were everywhere. The devastation was beyond words. Every aspect of my existence had been obliterated. I was adrift in midair, looking down at the mass destruction. The setting below seemed strange upon further notice. I shook my head to no avail. My interpretation of the view below was subject to my condition, a genetic flaw called paramnesia, which made me unable to discern reality from a dream's fantasy. To make matters worse, the genetic flaw had mutated, and now I could consciously contrive a world of fantasy. I knowingly was aware of my creation, yet sometimes, suddenly, as if a switch had been thrown, I might perceive my pseudoworld in a different light, unaware that the portrait was just recently sculpted and viewing it as if it had long existed, whether it was real or fantasy. The switch could be turned on or off without forewarning. Yet there was no mistaking what I saw below. Was that wasteland a hybrid of make-believe? A fused state of contrived reality, fantasy, or horror-induced fiction based on factual constructs? Was this another fused state of fact and fiction created by my condition? But for what purpose? I didn't have to answer that question.

The answer came to me from nowhere, suddenly making its presence known, staring right at me: the wall, the event. The myriad of destruction was the dissolution of my pseudoexistence, a prelude to the wall's final collapse, which would reveal the truth. The scenes below had a translucent appearance, as if they would dissipate at a moment's notice. The monster storm had finally abated, leaving a stream of destruction in its wake. All I had worked for had been eradicated, tossed aside like props for a stage setting. The homes we'd remodeled, my company, my house of residence, and the other physical aspects of my life were gone, thrown by the wayside, swallowed by the ocean surge brought on by the storm's fierceness. As I viewed the scenes below, I felt like a stranger faced with a wasteland of objects that no longer had relevance to my existence. It was as if the carnage from the storm's violent confrontation marked the dissolution of any form of connection to my pseudoexistence. All the tangibles associated with my existence, all the physical constructs, now were just toys randomly hurled into a wasteland of irrelevance. It went beyond the destruction of the physical components of my conceived existence. All the intangibles became obsolete, their purpose of relaying properties to my identity, providing a framework for my reverie was negated. Every aspect of my existence in this pseudoworld of mine had been erased.

The only remnants salvaged from the storm's rampant vanquishment were the remaining viable links from that quasiexistence that formed the bridge between my actual and contrived realities: Cassandra, Linda, Neverland, Matt, and the house in Neverland on Canyon Ridge Trails. They were the mainstays, the footprints treading up to and past the wall to the truth, the pivotal point where the memories of the event resided. From the current setting back to the wall lay an abundance of pseudo memories in ruin, conjured-up instances of fiction to simulate a structure with a storyline. Yet the area immediately beyond the wall resembled a myriad of hidden memories. Once visibly populated but now where memories were concealed, carefully camouflaged behind a mask of denial, secluded until the truth could be reengaged. The landscape prior to the wall which the contrived realities once populated was now barren leaving the wall as the only visible sign of my presence. Soon that hollow view would be populated with an abundance of real memories that were once hidden, ones filled with dreamlike fantasy and ones filled with fact-based reality. A lifetime of memories carrying their own baggage would settle in for the long haul. Each memory with its own nuances, yet collectively, as a whole, they contributed to one fact known for the soon-to-be certainty: there would be no vacancy.

63

Injection of Untested New Serum

I heard voices from somewhere outside. A medic urgently called out for help. I was barely conscious. My head was spinning. My equilibrium was absent. I was too weak to respond to their beckoning and too weak to cry out for help. A coppery smell was in the air. As I looked around, I saw blood everywhere. I was on the floor, dazed and confused. I faded in and out of consciousness repeatedly. A gun was in front of me, with ejected, burned shells off to my right. I picked one of them up. It felt hot to the touch and still had an odor of gun residue. It was obvious the gun had been fired recently. A pool of blood formed around me. Where was it coming from? I searched my head area, looking for any head wound. There, just under the scalp line, I detected significant blood. I was losing blood fast now. I looked at Cassandra, who was lying on a metal gurney. Something didn't look right. Too much blood surrounded her, especially around the midsection. I climbed up to the table's height for a different perspective. *This isn't Cassandra*, I thought upon seeing her expression. The look of pain and stress distorted her features. As the impact of what I was viewing hit me, I was stunned by how prolonged stress and pain could cause such a contrast in appearance. The human psyche was so delicate, with every ripple of emotion easily etched into our portraits. Sadness, strain, joy, ecstasy, compulsion, love, hatred, and jealously—each was expressively depicted in our outward appearance. So it was with Cassandra; her suffering was engraved so firmly in her expression that I could feel her suffering. With Cassandra, the anguish went beyond her. It was on a level only a mother could identify, at which the suffering grew exponentially as a result of her daughter's suffering and demise. The lines of suffering went deeper than one normally associated with one who bore no child.

The baby never regained consciousness. The violence from the torturous act was fused into my soul as a tumultuous emotional storm. I lay there with my eyes engaged with wild rage and my vocal cords emitting strange, guttural sounds, obviously the signs of shock. My mind was retreating into a remote stage setting of acute paranoia in which I felt all the props coming to life and advancing toward me with deadly, violent intent. The violent means of aborting the fetus had been ruthless and barbaric. The barbarism of the savage act had led to my current frenzy. Yet the careless, inhumane disposal of the aborted fetus, done without the slightest remorse, as if the fetus were not human, served as the linchpin that fueled my internal rage into a focused revenge. Despite being the trigger to my acute episode of paranoia, the emotional impact of the abortion attempt on Cassandra rechanneled my paranoia into an intense revenge, fueling the revenge's persistence to ceaselessly remain in the forefront of my consciousness.

My senses dulled. My surroundings all seemed distant, as if I were still held in a state of shock. I couldn't determine if the voices were coming from the room I was in or from outside. I couldn't see clearly—another sign of shock. The alarmed cry came again. This time, it seemed to come from outside one of the few remaining homes that still clung to the mountainside.

The voice was closer now, next to me, barking out orders, saying there was no time to waste. "I have a survivor who is barely hanging on. Need a helicopter up here fast." As I lay there, barely conscious, fading fast, the voice I heard seemed far away, a distant cry for help, but I was unable to respond. A team of medics rushed over and attended to me, checking my vital signs. I was hanging on to life; they detected a feeble pulse and immediately rushed me to the medical helicopter. Another team of medics rapidly rushed to the remaining two victims. A young lady lying on a gurney was covered with deep bruises. A deep cut in her abdomen seeped blood. No one detected vital signs. The area had several large wounds. A medic suddenly realized the incisions were from a botched abortion. He called out to another medic, who was kneeling on the floor, attending to a small victim. It was a fetus that appeared to be in the final trimester. From the look of the aborted fetus, the bungled, savage attempt was a scene from hell.

The medic saw the blood from the back of my head. I felt him reach around the back of my neck to gain a better view. He noticed the spent shells lying beside me. "May have a suicide attempt here!" he shouted to his team. The medic caught sight of the gun lying close by. He turned toward me and asked one question, which triggered my paranoia button: "What happened here?" I looked toward what he was referring to. I had no words. I couldn't remember anything. The scene looked like a crime scene, and I appeared guilty as hell as the perpetrator. I started to respond in an attempt to coalesce with his perception of the display of carnage before us. Before I voiced my first word, I froze at the scene's implication. It was a bloodbath. I saw the gun, the blood all around me, and the obviously mutilated bodies of Cassandra and the baby. *I am the only survivor. I swear there was someone else here, but who?* Was I the only survivor? My questions became more pronounced. I couldn't have done this. Yet I would be held as the primary suspect. It was just a matter of time before the gates of condemnation would close, holding me prisoner. The immediate questions started to recycle themselves into a perpetual stream of tormented echoes. *What in the hell happened here?* Lost in my thoughts, I felt a panicked alarm start to settle in as the questions recycled into a steady surge of tormented doubt, tearing loose the mountings that held my reasoning in place and pulling against the underpinnings of my sanity. I heard the ripping sound of the fabric of the infrastructure starting to yield to tumultuous stress. More commands from the medic next to me snapped me out of my fugue. "Get these victims aboard the med helicopter ASAP!" he said with an alarmed tone.

With a sense of urgency, the helicopter lifted us away toward the nearest hospital. The helicopter was equipped with advanced technology to keep even the most critical on life support until the nearest medical center was reached. They hooked me to the support systems and conveyed my vital signs to evac headquarters. While the medic team monitored my condition, they radioed in and asked for the nearest facility, as my tenuous vital signs were fading fast. The dispatcher radioed back to the team and acknowledged that a new research hospital was a mile away from Saciento, twenty-five miles south of Santa Monica. The helicopter team set their new coordinates, made their turn, and raced toward the hospital.

When the hospital facilities came into view, the helicopter made its final turn before descending onto the rooftop, where a team of emergency medics were waiting. Once it landed, the medics were informed about the possible suicide attempt and the horrific crime scene and told to keep a watchful eye on my actions, as I was the main suspect. A group of medics then immediately hurried me into the surgery room. The other group of medics moved Cassandra and the baby into the critical care room to check for any vital signs. The medics hooked me up to monitors, and the surgical team at once took notice of my neurological activity. The alpha waves were virtually absent, with only intermittent activity from the normally predominant beta waves. The neuron activity showed alternating swings of intense frequency followed by voids of activity, resulting in a dense black patch of preterition. Suddenly, a low-voltage wave known as a theta wave increased to a frequency level that extended well beyond its normal capacity. To the shock of the neurosurgeons, the delta and theta waves were at a hyperintense state as the two sets of brain waves became the predominant neurotransmitters, serving as the sole communicators between the neurons from both hemispheres. What they were viewing was an impossibility. The CT scan showed a portion of a bullet lodged between the cerebral hemispheres that seemed to be impacting the brain functions of both hemispheres. All who looked at the CT scan knew the severity and implications of what they viewed. They all made eye contact in a knowingly way without needing to say a word until, at a later time, the diagnosis was confirmed. Major surgery was imminent. Yet the surgery was a major initiative and required a stable subject, which was not the case at the present time. The brain activity was too elevated and needed to be induced into a subdued state to give the patient even a remote chance of a successful outcome.

I was immediately transported to the critical care observation room and hooked up to a set of special monitors. Barely an hour passed before the monitors echoed an urgent situation. The delta waves resurfaced with increased frequency and then virtually disappeared, displaced by the theta waves, which consumed sole dominance of the brain's activity.

As the surgical team disseminated the information, it became apparent that I had entered into a comatose state; the brain's vital functions were unstable, and the theta activity was exceeding the monitor's threshold. Suddenly, I began emitting electrical charges arching from my head to my toes. I started convulsing, thrashing with violent physical eruptions. The monitors then sharply declined to a normal frequency when the theta waves gained a rhythmic pattern, and the convulsions subsided. The top surgeons immediately called their associates in Geneva and discussed the effects of the theta waves' dominance of both hemispheres.

As the neurosurgeons in Geneva became fully engrossed in the conversation with their counterparts in California, the biotech assistant was already making travel arrangements to fly in the neurospecialists from the Geneva headquarters.

64

DNA Reaction from the Serum

Eric rushed into the observation room. "Have you reviewed the charts of the patient in critical care? The brain waves have escalated well beyond the critical range." He received no response, which did not surprise Eric. Brahn was so absorbed in studying the metrics of the patient that it was obvious to Eric his comment went unnoticed. Insistently, Eric said, "Brahn, did you hear? I have never witnessed such abnormal readouts. At the present rate, a stroke will occur, brain activity will cease, and the brain stem will cease to function. In other words, Brahn, he'll be brain-dead. Regardless of whether the patient is revived, there will undoubtedly be permanent damage."

That finally got Brahn's attention, and he turned around to face Eric with renewed concern. "What are the numbers?"

Eric handed over the results to Brahn. "In my opinion, this frequency, if unabated, will result in a irrecoverable state. The condition is critical. The convulsions are erratic, with increased probability of cerebral aortic aneurysm. Simply put, Brahn, the brain cannot sustain the overload. We must induce a coma-like state to slow the neural activity and decrease the cognitive brain functions."

Upon listening to Eric's summation and reviewing the charts, Brahn finally concurred with Eric. "Yes, I am fully aware of the potential consequences. One drawback: the effects from the excessive brain frequencies may have already impacted the brain stem, and there is no indication that any significant decline has or will occur to slow the brain's activity. With our traditional methods, we most likely will be at a loss. I had to refer this case to our associates in Geneva. After we conferred with our research staff in Geneva, it was suggested we use the new cognitive serum from the laboratory studies, which has shown to be highly effective in reducing hemispheric function in cases where the brain's activity has escalated to stroke range. Furthermore, our partners in Geneva have emphasized that we must inject the serum immediately to avoid complete cerebral shutdown. For lack of any other alternative recourse, this may be the patient's only hope."

Eric's expression was stoic after Brahn's explanation. Yes, they were at a stalemate, and he conceded to Brahn's suggestion, though with reluctance. "The new serum has only been tested on chimpanzees. It has never been used on a human subject. I understand that the results from the phase-one test have so far exceeded our expectations. However, Brahn, we will be risking any future grants if something goes wrong. And we could face a prison sentence and lose our licenses. The FDA will be at our front door with subpoenas when they find out. Besides, those initial tests performed during the beta stage yielded near-catastrophic results. Two of the chimpanzees became highly erratic, with their moods acutely agitated, before succumbing to a fugue state. Physically, the signs were normal, but something was missing, as if their mental faculties were displaced or misplaced. They gave no reaction to any form of emotional stimuli. The brain functions showed significant stages of erratic, agitated behavior, followed by a nearly dormant state. Physically, the subjects were here, but it seemed the chimpanzees were not emotionally here, as all vital signs were almost lifeless, fixed in a hypnotic state or fugue. The subjects weren't in a controlled, induced coma. They were near death's front door. We are just keeping the subjects afloat, but for what reason? We've done all the tests and found nothing. For all practical purposes, they might as well be declared brain-dead. We just gave up on them, and we never did find the underlying cause. We don't want to take the chance of the patient being inflicted with the same demise. Do we dare take that risk?"

"I am aware of this. What do you suggest, Eric? We have no alternative. At this rate, the patient will incur brain damage, coma, and cerebral hemorrhage. I am fully aware of the consequences. But what is our primary duty? To try to save lives or to conform to these overwhelming, suffocating regulations? I'm not sure about your sense of duty, but mine is with the patient. We are going to inject the patient with this serum. We have no choice. Would you rather sit here and watch him deteriorate until his bodily functions cease?"

He paused, giving Eric time to respond. With no acknowledgment from Eric, Brahn began directing orders. "We will approach this with a gradual progression. We'll start with a minimum dosage initially, increasing to a full dose over a twenty-four-hour period. This will allow us to monitor the patient's condition and any adverse reactions. If the serum does work, we will have preserved the brain and will have bought ourselves time to evaluate and attempt to bring the patient safely back to a conscious state. Furthermore, Eric, I have thought about the consequences of failure. But that can only occur if the FDA finds out. No one knows the patient is here except the crew who delivered him, and I can keep that from leaking out. So, Eric, the answer to your question is this: we do not disclose any information about our patient. If we fail, only we will know. Are you okay with that?"

Eric had no response. They were at a juncture where there was no one winnable course. Despite the immoral, unethical, unlawful aspects of Brahn's suggested directive, he felt he had no choice but to agree with Brahn's decision. Brahn was a genius in the neurological field and the author of an award-winning, recognized thesis on advanced neurological research. One of his efforts was up for Nobel nomination. He, however, had a reputation for taking risks and was a loner reluctant to adhere to FDA regulations. He had a rebellious personality with arrogance and ego to match. He took chances, but he was lucky or just smarter than the others, for at first glance, his risks seemed unwarranted. The truth was, his risks were always well thought out and meticulously planned and researched. He identified every possible risk, probability, and subsequent course of action. Even though his methods were viewed with disdain in the academic circle, his accomplishments had been inarguably instrumental in advancements in the field.

Within seconds after an affirmative nod from Eric, the monitors screeched out an urgent alarm from the critical care unit. The chief assistant hurriedly announced that the patient was convulsing again; the thrashing was worse, and the patient had started to hemorrhage. Brahn turned to Eric. "Where are the vials of serum? The patient needs to go into a dormant state immediately for fear of an aortic rupture. We need to inject the serum directly into the brain stem and monitor the reactions for the next hour. Continue the injections every hour on the hour in twenty-cubic-centimeter increments over the next twenty-four hours."

Eric relayed the order immediately to the chief assistant in critical care. Within minutes, two vials of serum were rushed to critical care, where the patient was injected with twenty cubic centimeters. The waiting commenced, with everyone poised for a sleepless night.

One hour later, Eric confronted Brahn and relayed the preliminary results. "No significant improvement. There should have been an initial decline of neuron activity. There has been no discernable decline after one hour." Brahn, without a second to waste, ordered two more vials of the serum for the patient. Within a minute, the vials were delivered and injected again into the brain stem. Ten minutes elapsed, and to their surprise, the second dose triggered a mild response. The monitor's indicator changed from red status to yellow status. It was a start, and the medical staff circled around the patient's bedside with intense, watchful eyes. Another hour of waiting ensued. The monitor's indicator was now in the upper range of green status. Brain function was within range of low frequency; reduced functions had been obtained. Now the objective was to sustain those levels for the next twenty-four hours. Their nervous state keeping exhaustion at bay, the medical team members all took a breather and then returned to the observation room. The night was just beginning, and they prepared themselves for an all-nighter. All seemed normal; they were unable to detect the hidden variables. The silent symptoms, a series of DNA reactions beyond immediate detection, were just beginning to surface. The double helix was altered, causing changes to the DNA sequencing.

The DNA reaction soon turned into an endless chain reaction. For the time being, the visible reactions were subtle, beyond immediate detection. Eventually, the symptoms would become more visibly apparent, but during that temporary respite, the observers were smugly wrapped in a facade of congratulatory moods. They were overconfident as they sat idly in the observation room, sharing a bottle of century-aged French wine. Soon the short-lived celebration would abruptly end as the countdown continued.

65

Tony's Genetic Flaw: Paramnesia

Brahn and Eric met in the observation room for their weekly Friday meeting to discuss the progress of each patient, along with any issues: good or bad. Lately, their meetings had been about the experimental patient. Brahn asked Eric if there had been any progress, expecting the routine response. This time, Eric brought something significant to Brahn's attention. Eric's tone brought Brahn to take notice immediately. Normally, Eric had to be persistent to get any type of reaction from Brahn. This typical delay was used by Eric to his advantage by giving Eric more time to prepare for an initial overview before drilling into detail. This time, though, caught Eric off guard because of Brahn's immediate reaction. The lack of a delayed response from Brahn was totally unexpected by Eric, finding no time to mentally prepare his weekly summation. Therefore, when Brahn responded immediately to Eric's update, he just stood there nervously staring at Brahn, mentally preparing an overview of the issue he wanted to relay to Brahn.

Brahn impatiently stood in place, waiting for Eric to start the conversation. "Well, what is it, Eric?"

"It is the patient in room three," he said, and Brahn didn't have time to pry for more. "Brahn, the patient started talking. He wasn't conscious and was still in a deep sleep, but despite the fact that he is still under, he managed to talk while under. It was more like a dialogue. He kept calling for Cassandra. Warning her of the Paragon Ballroom. He warned her of a possible assailant looking for her and him. He mentioned to meet back at the house on Canyon Ridge Trails. His final words were to go back home to Neverland. The intensity grew as his dialogue started to fade. The rest of the dialogue was not clear, but he said, 'Hurry. Linda is there, waiting.'

"That is not all, Brahn. There is more." Eric paused for a brief moment, giving Brahn time to respond.

Brahn just stood there, not saying a word, thinking. That was not uncommon. Many times, dialogue could occur while the subject was sleeping. But what caught Brahn's attention was that the subject had been in a coma for months. He needed to research the matter further before further deliberation.

"One more thing, Brahn. His remarks were the first real evidence we've had, an obvious possible starting point to learn more about his history, so I did some research on what he revealed. I looked up Neverland. There was a village called Neverland, but it existed in the first part of this century. The town was more of a summer retreat for the wealthy—a picturesque postcard setting, a quaint village. Never had a history of violence or any problems that I was able to research. But that was where the research ended. There was no further information. It was as if the village literally disappeared. The last article I was able to retrieve included another photograph of Neverland. The village was run-down. Streets were deteriorated. Many of the homes seemed to be in disrepair. There was a fog bank that circumvented the village.

"I then searched for the Paragon Ballroom. That too existed during the time Neverland was in its prime. It does not exist anymore. In fact, it disappeared around the same time as Neverland. I dug further into the widening mystery by searching for any incident that occurred at the Paragon. I was surprised when I hit upon something. There was an incident that occurred. An assailant assaulted a couple on the dance floor. The article I uncovered was somewhat hazy on the details. The assailant had a gun. He shot at the couple several times. That was where the article ended. The rest of the article was too badly damaged to read anymore. As it turned out, there was no more mentioned of the couple and the assailant. They appear to have disappeared. But that is not all, Brahn. There was no disclosure of the assailant's or couple's names, but there was a photograph of the couple.

"I printed what I discovered, along with the photograph. Here is the

printout. Here is a copy of the photograph. The male in the picture—
does he look like anyone we know? It is the patient, Brahn. The female
in the photograph is a twin image of the female patient we brought
here along with the male patient. But how is this possible? The time
discrepancies do not correlate."

"Great job, Eric. Thank you for taking the initiative and researching
this. I agree that this mystery for now seems to defy logic. But there has
to be a logical explanation. That will need to come later. For the time
being, we need to keep this within the confines of the hospital. We
now know through blood work the male patient has a genetic disorder,
paramnesia. We are deep into researching the effects of the interaction
between the serum and the patient's genetic condition. That research
may well result in a treatment for the patient's disorder. When I am
finished, we can then disclose the results of your research. For now, we
need no interruptions."

Eric took it all in. There was no sense in debating with Brahn when
he locked into a decision, and for once, Eric agreed with Brahn. They
were at a pivotal point in the research of the serum and in the patient's
hopeful recovery.

Brahn appreciated Eric's research. However, even though the facts
pointed to an emerging mystery, to Brahn, it was just a coincidence. He
was not disposed to anything that pointed to a supernatural theme. The
matter had to have a logical, scientific explanation. Anything beyond
that was just hearsay. For now, he had to concentrate on his immediate
priorities and delay the material Eric had given him to evaluate later.
Brahn entered the patient's room as part of his daily routine. He picked
up his remote device with the same routine dialogue. "I am at the
patient's bedside, and I do not see any sign of improvement," he said.
He picked up the patient's charts and studied them judiciously, looking
for anything he might have missed.

His peripheral vision picked up a sudden twitch, catching him by
surprise. "Did I detect a sudden twitch around the eyes?" Brahn said,
excitedly hoping for the long-awaited breakthrough. "Can you hear me?
I am your chief neurologist," Brahn said, trying to trigger a response.
There was no reaction. Despite what Eric had relayed to him, he was
not surprised by the lack of response. He was at the point of expecting
the same condition they'd seen over the past several months since the

patient was first injected with the serum. The victim was still under. They'd placed him in a coma when they determined the patient was in danger of a seizure. They'd waited until a determination was made because the serum was not fully tested but had run out of time and had to inject the serum to save the brain stem from further injury. At the time, he hadn't been entirely sure of the side effects. The serum was not designed to induce a coma for the long term. It was designed for a short duration.

Could it be he'd miscalculated the effects? It was true the patient had been near a seizure state, with a stroke imminent, before the serum was injected. Could it be he'd waited too long? Even though his reasoning might have had some validity, his gut feeling told him something else was at play there. He had a suspicion of what that unexpected variable might be. *The prolonged wait before the injection may have something to do with the situation now, but that is only half the story.* He soon discovered there was another factor, another unknown, in the equation that later would have enormous implications.

He retreated a few paces to recap his effort. Rarely did frustration enter his thoughts during intensive research. A noticeable trace of impatience caused him some concern as far as his losing a degree of objectivity, which was crucial to his research. *I have spent what seems like a lifetime researching the effects of this serum,* Brahn said silently to himself with restlessness. *In fact, it really has been years since my first dissertation on the effects of this serum upon cerebral functions and the brain stem. I have also written numerous theses on another disorder I encountered accidentally that could be a candidate for this serum, a rare neurological memory disorder called paramnesia. But due to funding, I was not able to proceed to the testing phase. Unfortunately, based on my initial stage of discovery of both the serum and paramnesia, I began to see potential serious reactions if the two variables did intersect. Regrettably, due to government fiscal mismanagement, I was never able to continue to the integrated test phase to prove or disprove my suspicions. The end result was that the two variables never fully crossed paths during my years of research. Therein lies the dilemma.*

He didn't know at the time that the patient was inflicted with that genetic flaw. Through numerous tests performed on the patient, he soon discovered that the patient had that condition. A new set of unknowns then faced him regarding the potential effects of the serum when it crossed paths with the genetic disorder. What highly concerned him was any serious new or altered side effects from the serum because of the genetic flaw that might jeopardize the patient's hopeful recovery. Since both the serum and the defective gene impacted the DNA helix, the possible reactions would be at the DNA level, but he didn't know the possible specific nature and severity of the potential reaction. *Maybe Eric had a valid point in that we did not spend enough time thoroughly evaluating the results behind the past failed experiments. But in retrospect, we did not have the time, and if faced with the same situation again, I would proceed in the same manner.*

For the past few weeks, Brahn had begun to suspect there was a potential problem since the patient was still in the induced coma state without any increase of brain activity. He should have been recovering from the induced state since the serum was designed for short-term duration only. Brahn suspected the patient was still in the coma as a result of a reaction from the serum interacting with the patient's condition. His suspicions of a potential problem only intensified, and he spent countless weeks researching the patient's condition and the effects of the serum when used on a subject inflicted with his disorder. The results of the study revealed added side effects, warranting revisions to his patient memoirs. He listed a sizable number of the effects from the interaction as subtle warnings, while he flagged the remaining effects as potentially damaging to the mental and physical condition of the patient. He didn't know if there were other severe side effects that could result in serious consequences and warrant round-the-clock monitoring. From his research, he was aware of the potential demise and had sufficient enough knowledge to record what he believed the patient would experience.

It took several attempts to record the findings of his research. The write-ups were to be presented on two levels. First was a detailed write-up that recorded the results of his research at the DNA level. Since both the serum and the genetic flaw impacted the DNA, his research focused on the impact to the double helix and the subsequent reaction from the DNA when the serum was introduced at the early stage and then at the advanced stage of paramnesia. The detailed recordings were for a more technical audience, hopefully to encourage an in-depth discussion to reveal any areas that needed further exploration. The summation write-up was a high-level view of the problem, the attempted resolution, and the results of what he'd attempted and accomplished so far, followed by next steps. It took him more time than originally expected to detail his recordings from his research on the DNA reactions resulting from the interaction between the serum and the genetic flaw. He made another attempt to record the results, with the hope that would be his final attempt to capture sufficient detail from the study to yield an accurate assessment of the expected and actual reactions when both variants crossed paths. From there, he would revise his summation and patient memoirs.

66

Interaction Between the Serum and Tony's Paramnesia

Despite all of Brahn's repeated research, there were reactions occurring that would not be detectable unless the patient was awake to reveal his sensations. Until that occurred, those deep-rooted reactions could not be identified. The patient was in a deep-sleep state. The serum's expected result was fully realized: it had impacted the DNA helix to slow the cerebral hemispheric function to a quasidormant state to save the vital cerebral areas from further damage. However, the doctors didn't know about the additional reactions occurring at the DNA level as a result of the interaction between the patient's genetic condition and the serum. To fully understand the reaction between the two variants would require a disclosure of the intended reaction from each variable isolated on its own. Brahn decided to review the summation again with the intent of detecting anything that did not correlate.

> The patient, Tony, has a genetic defect that causes a condition called paramnesia. The genetic condition causes a malfunction of memory at the cerebral level. The condition causes a disorder of memory in which dreams or fantasy are confused with reality. A more direct definition of this genetic malfunction is a distortion of memory in which fact and fancy

are confused. Typically, memories can represent two forms: one that is purely fictional from a dream state and one that represents reality of fact. With paramnesia, it is frequently not possible to distinguish between the two forms of memory. Therefore, with paramnesia, we have three forms of memories: one that is purely fictional from a dream state, one that is reality-based, and a fused state of memories composed by integrating reality and fantasies. What makes the fused state even more distinct is that the patient will not be able to determine which part of the memory is real and which is fantasy. Initially, the defective gene lies in a quasidormant state. At this stage, the implication is that the defective gene's behavior becomes activated at brief, random intervals during which time the person will not be able to delineate memories that are fact versus those that are fantasy dreams. This occurs infrequently, and the activation is just for a brief period. As the individual ages, the genetically defective condition enters a fully active state. The condition becomes continually active, and the individual, for the most part, cannot determine reality from fantasy-related memories and will fuse fact and fantasy events together as one memory on a more frequent basis. The fully active stage of the defective condition makes it almost impossible for the victim to be able to determine the origin of his or her memories. The memories contain both fact and fiction, unbeknownst to the individual, and even if it were possible to recognize this type of memory, the individual would not be able to delineate the part of the memory that was fact from the part that was fantasy. Besides being a serious defect that can cause havoc, this defective gene may trigger additional cerebral maladies.

The other variable in this intricately woven formula is the introduction of the serum. A newly formulated antidote still in the testing stage has been designed specifically for reducing cerebral functions by intervention at the DNA level. It was designed to protect the cerebral properties of an overstimulated hemispheric function. The serum is designed to immediately reduce the brain waves of a patient whose cerebral functions are near a seizure stage, which, if uncontested, will cause irreparable damage to the brain and brain stem.

If each variable had been introduced separately uncontested, there would not have been unexpected results. Each variable, the defective gene and the serum, would have provided the expected reaction. The serum would have accomplished its purpose successfully. The defective gene, unfortunately, would have functioned as expected. In other words, from a purely objective, scientific perspective, the intended results would have been delivered as predicted.

Brahn stopped his summation. He reviewed his summation several times, and each time, he felt something was amiss. He knew there were additional reactions that escaped him. The summation ended at that point because unbeknownst to Brahn, there were hidden symptoms from unexpected reactions due to the interaction between the serum and the genetic flaw. The well-disguised symptoms would emerge only through the patient's conscious recollection during the injection of the serum, which was an impossible scenario because of the patient's condition. Thus, the serum was a risk that had to be taken. Unfortunately, such scenarios occurred frequently in the medical field to save lives with new measures yet to be fully evaluated.

The first undetected reaction was the serum's impact on the DNA. The serum's intended purpose was to immediately slow the cerebral functions, which had occurred as expected. However, the defective gene and the introduction of the serum had caused a complicated twist. The serum would have an unexpected reaction on the DNA. It would cause the DNA to release stored memories. The serum's second unexpected reaction affected the defective gene. It would cause the defective gene to become fully active. The twist was that once the defective gene became fully active, it in turn would alter the effect of the serum by increasing the range of the serum's impact on the DNA. The modified serum then had the capability to impact the DNA's molecular structure and modify its sequence so that the DNA would have an additional impact on the person's memory. The DNA would have the potential to release all memories from the time the soul was first formed.

The serum's unexpected reaction was a two-stage approach: a short-term reaction and a long-term reaction. The short-term reaction would impact the DNA with the intent to hide all of the individual's memories. The DNA would hide all the memories by transferring them from the conscious mode to the subconscious area of the brain. It would be akin to suddenly moving everything to a holding area for later disclosure, similar to a victim with amnesia, for whom the process of removal was almost instantaneous. In essence, it would create a wall to shield a conscious awareness of all memories.

The serum also impacted the genetic disorder by triggering it to become fully active. The next twist was that because the defective gene was fully active, it would immediately detect the absence of memories in the conscious foreground and create a new set of memories, resulting in a contrived reality. Because it was in a fully active state, it would choose a set of hidden memories purely at random and fuse them together into a pseudoreality memory. The reaction of the serum on the genetic disorder caused the fused memory to be deformed. The integration was impacted to where the resulting memory was sometimes deformed to the point of resembling a haunted nightmare. It didn't matter if the memories being integrated were both fantasy and fact; the resulting fused state was a contrived memory.

The short-term reaction would persist until the long-term reaction was initiated. The long-term reaction would be triggered when the disorder, in its active state, impacted the serum, increasing its potency. The impacted serum would interact with the DNA again, and the DNA would begin a complicated process of unleashing all its memories. It would start after an unspecified time when the serum caused a reverse reaction in the DNA, to be triggered without advanced warning. As if a switch had been suddenly turned on, all the memories in the conscious state would be erased, and the memories stored in the subconscious would be released like an avalanche, flooding the victim's conscious senses and creating a potential overload of sensory awareness.

67

The Unleashing of Tony's Hidden Memories

The reactions between the serum and my genetic condition had almost run their course. I had undergone a transference in which all memories in my conscious state were moved to my unconscious state. In the interim, the genetic disorder had created a contrived set of memories to fill the void, resulting in a false reality. The final phase started when all contrived memories were erased. I was visibly aware of the removal process as my paramnesia disguised the process as a violent storm. Everything was wiped away except the core elements of my reality still etched in my conscious state: Cassandra, Linda, Neverland, Matt, and the house on Canyon Ridge Trails. The DNA memories had been prepped for emergence. Chemical reactions affecting the DNA helix unleashed all the memories, including the dormant memories held in the DNA cells. The interaction between the genetic flaw and the serum caused a complete download of all my memories, starting with the memories first formed when my soul first emerged when I was born. Memories that were just unconscious instincts were triggered through a universal reawakening, a full transfer of all experiences, resulting in an avalanche of sensory awareness. The result was a streamlining of past life events—a total recall of prior memories from the inception of the soul to the current state. The DNA reaction soon turned into a full chain reaction.

The enormity of the conceived reality was intimidating and fearful. The mind's attempt to sustain itself in the face of such an elaborate scheme was a daunting task. The fabricated memories at the forefront prior to the barrier, the wall, were gone, all devoured by the storm. The recent memories covered the staged years since my amnesia, sustained by an increasingly complicated infrastructure. It was such an elaborate framework that it took the perfect storm to obliterate everything associated with the barrier. The houses and company went first, with minimal reluctance from me, but I fiercely protected Cassandra and Linda. I held on to Linda with fierce determination. However, fate held fast and vanquished her image. I knew then that the barrier was no more. Before Linda vanished, she made one remark that would remain with me forever: "I never existed, Tony. I was just an invented memory. Tony, listen to me. Remember, Cassandra was pregnant. She knew it was a girl and had a name, Linda. I am your daughter. At least I am your image of the daughter you would have had if we had survived. If the event had never happened. Everything is gone. The barrier wall is gone, along with all the devised memories. Now you are faced with what is left of the wall. You know the event now. It was not your fault. Your guilt created your contrived memories. But they are not real. Your genetic flaw, paramnesia, created the fake memories. You are innocent. You must accept that."

The DNA got its signal to begin. It started as a trickle and then rapidly increased to a voluminous flow from the subconscious to the conscious state. The flow was overwhelming. The wall had collapsed.

68

Behind the Wall: Aftermath of the Event

The hour-long session ends. I first thought there was a breakthrough, but now that I have had time to evaluate the dialogue during the hour, my opinion has changed. There was hardly any dialogue between me and my counselor. As usual, the dialogue came from me. So where does that put me? The same place I was when I first started these repetitive sessions. I've made hardly any progress.

I remember his dialogue to his associate: "Very unfortunate is all I can reflect on now. I have never seen such a tortured soul. He blamed himself for her demise. But there really was no way for him to know. When the medics found him, his attempted suicide failed. But what he saw took him over the edge. At times, he referred to a place called Neverland and a violent storm that destroyed California. Found no evidence of this. But he has come a long way. Will most likely be here for quite some time."

That was the extent of the dialogue—a typical response. I've been here for what seems like ages. I'm part of the family now, at least those who are committed. That means I'm just part of the furnishings. Anything new just wait your turn. That feeling of urgency, here to help, and you will be okay. All is part of the script for new patients, but once you've been here for a while, well, let's put it this way: there is no script; you basically have to be a fly on the wall to hear any feedback. I was that fly overhearing the two doctors conversing about me. It's not much to go on, but I can infer what I need to know from just those brief comments.

The end result of what I overheard is, maybe I am innocent. I now needed confirmation. I just have to wait until my next appointment. As I already mentioned, I'm just part of the family.

The wall no longer exists. A flood of memories was unleashed, overwhelming my senses—too much to immediately absorb, creating an overload. So even if I recover from what brought me here in the first place, it no longer makes a difference as far as my tenure here. My stay now is continual because of the deluge of memories. It's a prolonged visit with an undetermined release date. My recollections seem endless. Most reveal the truth of Cassandra, as she warned would happened. I remember the pallid color that was cast over Cassandra's face. I have seen it before; it occurs when the patient is close to death or actually deceased. It's part of the decomposition process. Cassandra was dead or close to the end. I did not know she had been close to death for quite a while. I found out from the hospital psychiatrist who was treating me. She knew she would die. That was how it was always intended to end. Spiritually, she was alive, yet she was prepared to leave her physical form. I remember her words: "Tony, we will never fully recover. Not until we become passengers as a couple on this journey to our beloved small mountain town of Neverland. All three of us, Tony. You have given me my soon-to-be-born daughter, Linda."

My psychiatrist has helped me retrieve and make sense of the lasting memories. Through our discussions, I've learned that my dreams were played out repeatedly from guilt. The monsters that accompanied me on my journeys were my guilt and self-punishment. I was my own visualization of my own hell, which has been with me since that fateful day.

The transport that took me on the journeys to distant times to join Cassandra in moments of bliss was a passenger train. I chose that as a symbol of my retreat down memory lane because of the soulful, lonely sound made at night when a train whistled far off in the distance, a nostalgic, haunting call during a voyage to a destination unknown.

Guilt played a heavy toll on me. I agree with that. But there are many other things that the doctor does not know or that cannot be explained. Cassandra is a survivor. She is not here.-She is in the tiny village I so often have visited. She should be there now. The last journey we both took stopped one more time at her village, and that time, I let her depart, knowing the rest of the journey was mine to take. Now I know the truth, and my decision has come to full fruition. It is time for me to return to the village, not as a visitor but as a full-time resident. I am just waiting to hear that soulful whistle from that special trip beckon to me for the last journey back.

I will return to Neverland at the specific point in time when Cassandra and I felt the most protected, the exact moment when we consummated our connection. We made love with an intensity that fused our souls into one spirit. This time, our return to that magical moment will bring with us another companion: a soon-to-be-born baby. It couldn't be a better tribute to our consummated love to return to that time when our intimate confirmation gave life to a newly formed embryo. It will be poetic justice—a gift to bring into our lives that defines our soulful union. Cassandra knew the gender. It was a baby girl. I knew her name: Linda. Cassandra has always had an uncanny sense of predictions. It's a unique quality she's often exhibited since the first day we met. I have often wondered if she instinctively knew we would experience these journeys to hell and back.

This journey back will bring with it freedom. There is no baggage this time. This time, the only item I will bring with me is my heart. My heart belongs to her. I'll give it to her as a token, a promise of a lifelong connection never to be broken. My mind feels the overwhelming burden lift. For the first time since that last summer retreat, I feel a sense of freedom. My mind is no longer consumed with intense worry. It refuses now to be immersed in any weighted burden. My mind feels like a bird that once was contained in a cage but now is experiencing the weightless freedom of the cage's removal and can take off on short excursions at will. I have the freedom to roam from one thought process to another at will without constraint. Too spend enough time to recall but resisting any temptation to overindulge.

69

Tony Committed for Observation

My mind is lost in the moment—so absorbed with expectations of my return to Neverland that I almost forget my current setting. I look around with impatience. I've been waiting forever, it seems. Why am I still here? There's nothing left; I'm a ghost of my former self. Waiting to just fade away was never my intent. If my life became just a delayed approach to my final resting place, I had made an oath, sort of a promise to barricade that private roadway toward my fateful destination with a detour. Road no longer passable due to irreparable conditions, please use noted detour. That detour, the terminal stretch of this tormented journey, a shortened end which I should have known how it was to end a long time ago.

My condition is a catatonic stupor. I am comatose, languid, impassive, and listless. Those are the adjectives the medical team uses to describe my state. Oh, there are many more descriptive attempts to explain my remorse, inability to respond, and lack of reaction to subjected stimuli to no avail. Oh, I hear all right, and there are moments when I break free from my self-induced constraints and speak freely before retreating to my muted stare into a world of total remorse.

Yes, my interim breaks in silence have been enough to provide them with some explanation and allow them to give my condition a label they can now use freely when writing their journals. I saw their proud, joyful, self-congratulatory smirks, as if to say, "Look, Ma—no hands!" when their colleagues visited. Oh yes, my journeys. What did I hear? Oh, I heard everything, unbeknownst to them. I arrived in a near seizure state. They decided with optimistic naïveté to resort to a new wonder drug to supposedly bring me back over the long haul. It was supposed to induce me into a coma to save the brain and brain stem from further damage during the short term. But the drug pushed me deeper toward my own self-induced fantasy and triggered my paramnesia condition to its fullest active state.

Why do I persist in this survival mode, you ask? Why to what? No reply is necessary. Okay, I get it. It does need a little explanation. But I will keep it brief, for in the long run, it is not really going to change a thing. I can freely talk now, in case you are wondering. Yes, they were finally successful in bringing me back to a conscious, normal state where I can be a participant in my tailored dialogue between myself and my doctors. Normal state—now, that is an irony. Normal by whose standards? My return to normalcy came through the dissolution and breaking down of the protective barriers I built out of unbearable guilt. Now my burden of emotional pain knifes its way into the very heart of my soul, so I can relive the journeys that bonded my spiritual self to Cassandra. Is that normal? Can you even know where to start to try to identify or comprehend the pain I endure? Normal, they say. All my barriers are gone, swept away by weeks—or has it been months?—of endless diagnosis. "Knowing the truth will set you free" is their reply, an old saying gone by the wayside. I never put much faith in that saying. It is all subjective anyway. For me, knowing the truth imprisons me. The truth is my cell mate. It goes by the name of Pain.

Oh, I forgot I was beginning to shed some more light on how I found myself in an unending state of torment. Yes, I do believe—in fact, I know—that my dreams I endured for who knows how long were real. They were real to me at least. That is the doctors' conclusion: the dreams, the journeys, were just concepts I created to cope with what I knew really had occurred. It was I who killed Cassandra. Were we in love? Without a doubt, we were spiritually bound. But my love became my own imprisonment, for it eventually held me captive, and my soulful connection turned into an obsession. My purpose for living became too one-dimensional. My sense of purpose was living for her and only her. Can one love too much? Can people give so much of themselves to their partners that they become obsessed to the point where losing those partners would mean total destruction? Well, those are my crosses to bear, and you can make your own judgment. But back to my story. I blurted out that her husband was sterile. That drove him into a murderous rage. He took it out on Cassandra and the baby and murdered them both. So it was I who really killed Cassandra and the baby.

My journeys were all created by me as a way to cope with my guilt. My alter ego imagined the journeys as a coping mechanism, a salvation, to allow me to be a hero, her savior and rescuer. That's ironic, isn't it? I was her hero to rescue her. But at the time, it was my only recourse to free myself from absolute terror and guilt. The strategy worked much of the time. The monsters I encountered on the journeys, the hellish creatures trying to devour me, represented my own guilt bearing down on me to break me and devour my inner core. That guilt, at the time, was just too much to bear and endure. I almost became overwhelmed, but my resistance, my inability to admit to my negligence, was too fortified to overcome.

The journeys all occurred via a phantom train. I always had a fondness for the echoing whistle of a train far off in the distance at night. It would lull me to a peaceful state when I was just a child. I would lie awake many nights, unable to sleep until I heard that soulful whistle from an unknown distance, which provided comfort to me. I identified that whistle as an escape to free oneself from life's agonizing tasks. It was my escape to free my soul and carry away my spirit as the journey's only passenger to destinations that can only occur in dreamland. So as you can obviously deduce, my journeys were conducted by that phantom train.

On the last journey Cassandra and I took together, she told me our journey together could not be because of "unforeseen consequences"—those were her exact words. She spoke the truth, for I bear witness to those consequences; all have a hold upon me. I strove for that train whistle to give me hope and set me free, as when I was just a child, but in truth, that longing tone became a tormented whistle that would eventually imprison me for the remainder of my agonizing life as an adult. Beware of what you hope for. That is all I can really tell you when everything is finally said and done.

That final journey was the journey to my total recall. I had to face my own demons and pay retribution for my own deeds. That is when I blacked out, and upon awakening, I found myself here in a padded room. A straitjacket is no longer necessary. The walls are padded, and there are no sharp edges anywhere. I'm caged in this enclosed white room, waiting for my usual twice-daily consultation. The drugs have stopped, which, though they deny it, is why I have exited the comatose state.

My appointment is just a few minutes from now. They seem to be jubilant upon my return to verbal exchanges. They listen to me but keep telling me that for some reason, I still am convinced I was responsible for Cassandra's demise. I ask, "Why try to absolve me from this horrific crime?"

"Because she is not dead, Tony," they say.

I just look at them when they attempt once again to trick me. When I inquire, "Where is she?" they say nothing beyond "You are not ready yet, Tony."

I have often spent too much time pondering this question with little resolve: If what they say is true and if I were to face Cassandra again, how would I fare? Would it break my tenuous hold on my sanity? Would I be able to handle the impact, the sensory input, to an already overloaded system? Would that cause my house of cards to come crashing down? Am I beyond my ability to comprehend the truth—that I am insane with no foreseeable recovery? Would the impact of her survival be such a turn of events that I could let go of my guilt and self-imposed punishment, as if pulling the plug to an overwhelmed dam? Would the overflow result in a torrid flood destroying everything in its path? I have no answers. I'll just wait and see. This one potential fact keeps me resolute and holds my resolve to wait for that eventful day when I will bear witness to their claim. Maybe after all, that will be my salvation.

70

Cassandra's Presence In the Ward

Cassandra is enclosed in her own private room. Yes, she is still alive. Her memories have faded, but whispered recollections reappear in tiny fragments, snippets of time that just confuse her more. She dreams of a long-ago past, of journeys through generations of time. She recalls a small village and the voyage home. Distant recollections periodically surface. It is a miracle she survived, the doctors tell her. But that is the extent of her recall. From somewhere behind these walls, she hears a faint cry, a mournful moan. It is a shrill similar to the faraway, soulful whistle of a distant train on a journey toward a destination known only to its captive passengers. Somewhere within her, she somehow suspects—no, knows—the cry centers on Tony. She gets out of bed for the first time in ages with her legs wobbly and her knees buckling, steadying herself against the railings to press her ear against the wall and listen to the mournful cry. She recalls the trembles in the voice and the resonance. *Is this Tony?* Too weak to tap a signal on the wall, she presses her mouth to the wall and tries to speak. The words are hoarse but hopefully loud enough to carry. "Tony, is that you, my love? It is me—Cassandra." Her energy spent, she struggles back to her bed and lies back down, succumbing to another episode of sleep to recover from the aftermath of her miraculously surviving a tormented trip to hell. It is a miracle she survived it. Her last thought before returning to dreams of her journeys with Tony is *Tomorrow, Tony, we will try again to meet. Good night, my love.*

71

Tony's Discovery of Cassandra's Presence In the Ward

I hear a whisper from behind the enclosed wall—a barely audible female voice. "Tony, my love. It is Cassandra."

I'm too weak to move. Woeful cries escape me, along with a flood of tears, as I try to respond. I say in confirmation, "Yes, it is Tony." The extra effort drains my still-precious reserves. Before I fall asleep again, a new journey forms in my fertile mind. We both are waiting on a platform to embark on this new journey. Each of us will enter a different compartment, but upon the journey's commencement, we will find each other to reconsummate our union once again in a private compartment reserved in anticipation.

"Cassandra," I murmur, hoping she will sense me here in the next room. "We have to escape. There is a way out. We will get out of this place tomorrow night. We'll escape on a special journey back to a place called Neverland." I hear a soft whisper in return, an acknowledgment of my plan.

"Tony, I am here. Yes, Tony. We need to leave. I have the key. I know the place, Tony. It is our beginning, and we will be safe. Neverland can only be reached by this journey. And, Tony, I love you."

That thought gives me the impetus to finally rest my head once more on my pillow, but this time, I smile in anticipation. I've found my destination. "Good night, Cassandra. I love you."

72

Gatekeeper: Paradise Found

I feel free, weightless, with no constraints or physical limitations. I feel no remorse or guilt. In fact, I feel spiritually pure, as if my soul has been cleansed of all negative deeds that imposed any intrusion into my spiritual well-being. I feel as if I've been born again and am starting anew with a fresh slate. I have never experienced such an overwhelming sensation of peace. Yet a part of me sorely longs for my spiritual partner. True spiritual freedom can only come by my sharing this heartfelt journey with Cassandra, my soul mate.

Despite my feeling of longing, I feel no reluctance as I move effortlessly down a passageway toward my destination. It is more than just a passageway that will lead me to my fateful destination; it is a passageway filled with knowledge. There is nothing to read, and there are no exams, courses, or videos from which to learn. The knowledge that becomes available once one is admitted to this righteous place is knowledge we all have within our spiritual realm. We just do not have access to the knowledge until we are admitted to this passageway. Once we're there, a wealth of knowledge is infused into our souls—insight and awareness not given to us as individuals. It is not knowledge as we perceive it in our daily lives but knowledge that gives us a far-reaching awareness of all our souls and how we are all connected in the spiritual realm. From this awareness, we have a keen consciousness that becomes available, wherein our intuition lies.

The path I am on will lead me to the point where fate decides my next journey. The decision will be made once I arrive at my destination, which is where my guardian angel resides: the gatekeeper. Everyone has one. Those of us who are fortunate enough to have a soul mate have the same guardian angel, the same gatekeeper. The gatekeeper is a spiritual guide who is dedicated to aligning our adventure with our spiritual plane as we travel the roadway called life. We travel toward a gateway that has two exits: one reserved for eternal damnation and the other for eternal bliss. Fate will decide our next journey.

Despite the guidance, our adventure will encounter a number of detours. Some slightly alter our course with minimal or no impact, while others can lead us to pivotal moments, or turning points, that affect the outcome of our adventure. Our guardian angel helps us make the right decision by acting as our guide along the way. Our guardian will provide us the necessary guidance in choosing the right path. Sometimes our own faulty instincts override that guidance. That is when we get into trouble, when we enter that yellow zone where caution is required to avoid the unexpected pitfalls that line the detour we inadvertently chose. If we are not careful, the yellow warning area can lead us to a forbidden zone that changes everything. If we choose enough of these forbidden red zones on our adventure, then we risk the gatekeeper deciding to send our contaminated souls to a place called eternal damnation.

I see the destination ahead. It is a vast room filled with every color on the spectrum. I notice that the colors change every so often. I become aware that the change occurs when my mood changes. If my mood is one of caution, the spectrum will change. If my mood is one filled with hope, that too causes a change in the spectrum. I may exhibit a hundred different moods on the pathway to my destination, and each mood has its own color on the spectrum. As I proceed down the pathway toward my destination, I am well aware that my color spectrum is changing every second.

I reach my destination. I look up, and there in front of me is a throne filled with one seat facing me. There is no place for me to sit, and I kneel down to sit on the floor while I wait for judgment. Suddenly, she appears, the Gatekeeper. She walks toward me and touches my face. She raises my head so I can look into her eyes. I am in awe as I feel surrounded by a force that is beyond words. I am finally at peace.

My journey rests in her hands. She bends down to the floor and sits in front of me. "Tony, your life has been a challenging one. One filled with many detours. But I sense no regret, and you have earned the right to choose your next destination. But once you do, that will be your resting place for eternity. Now is the time to tell me your response."

I think about this for a second or two. The answer is obvious. Given the choice of a final resting place, I have to be with my soul mate in a place where we both feel protected and secure, a place where the ultimate gifts are eternal happiness and love. I choose the place called Neverland, during the last summer when we made love and were in love. I don't have to say a word, for my guardian angel, my gatekeeper, knows my every thought. "Is this what you want, Tony?"

"Yes, I do. But it has to be with Cassandra. When will she choose her destination?"

"She already has, Tony. She is in wait for you."

"What about Matt? He will kill us if he finds us."

"Tony, he had all day to ponder his destination by his own actions. He did not have a choice. My decision was for eternal damnation. His soul has traveled there, and he will stay there until redemption is made. For now, he has fulfilled his dinner request. But this dinner was with the devil himself. He will not be bothering you again.

"One more thing, Tony. There is someone else waiting for you besides Cassandra."

I look into my guardian angel's eyes, searching for the meaning of what I've just heard. I'm puzzled and confused but afraid to ask.

She must know my confusion and surprise, for she says, "Tony, Cassandra is bearing a child. She is pregnant with your child. A female. Linda." I stand there and weep silently. She rests her hand upon my head and says, "You can leave now. Cassandra and Linda are waiting for you." She removes her hand, and when I look up, my angel is no longer there. I stand up, turn around, and walk back the way I came. As I continue on the path back to where I began, I see a circular light directly on the path a few yards ahead. I walk up to the light and feel a force pulling me in. I close my eyes and let the force pull me in.

My last words as I'm swept up by the light are "Home at last."

A Final Journey Towards Lasting Harmony

I hear the sounds of movement—a rhythmic noise akin to white noise. It is mostly the same pitch, with slight variations. Something is moving on wheels, and periodically, a clicking sound interrupts the steady noise. The sounds are muffled at first, but they are becoming more pronounced.

I open my eyes and look toward the adjacent seat. I see no rose or letter. Instead, Cassandra is there with her eyes closed. I look out the window and see the familiar sight of the village depot. The water tower appears as we round the corner to Neverland. The transport pulls in closer, approaching the village with a sense of immediacy.

Cassandra opens her eyes and looks up at me. "I love you, Tony. I'm glad we're back to this quaint village, a place perfect to raise our newborn."

I place my hand over her stomach and feel the kicking. We both know it will be a girl—Linda. We both agree it's a perfect name for a perfect place. It has such a familiar sound to it. It resonates with our souls.

We both are enraptured with anticipation of this new world of a time past, one dear to our hearts. This moment connects us, bonding our souls in this chapter of our life experiences. It is a token granted to us by our gatekeeper. We both are filled with heightened awareness.

We near the depot and hear laughter from the village crowd attending a parade. The day is beautiful, with the sun filling the air with rays of optimism. It's a perfect day, followed by a perfect night for the festival carnival, which we both look forward to. This is our final journey to Neverland, a place filled with promise and happiness.

"I love you, Cassandra," I say.

Hand in hand, we stand, make our way to the exit, and eagerly disembark. We enter the depot with a hint of caution, feeling a sense of déjà vu. We leave through the rear exit and stand in awe of the magnificent view. There it is: Neverland, just as we remember it. A few cumulus clouds lazily float by in the picturesque, sunny blue sky, providing a tranquil, serene setting. We follow the one road leading toward Neverland as our gaze absorbs the view, believing the unbelievable and acknowledging with divine reverence that our wish was miraculously granted.

We continue on the road through Neverland, hearing the village residents cheerfully converse while they perform their daily errands. Soon our home comes into view, and we hasten our pace to a fast walk upon hearing a faint semblance of laughter coming from our home. When we arrive at the walkway leading to the wraparound porch, we stop at the surrounding old oak and maple trees. We both stand in front of one old oak tree and look at the engravings we made at a time when we felt most at peace. We turn toward each other, our eyes mirroring our deep love for each other, and kiss gently. Then we hold hands as we stroll toward the front steps. We climb the few steps to the porch, and before opening the front door, we both turn and look back at the exquisite setting of Neverland.

The front door is unlocked, allowing us to walk in unannounced. We stop at the hallway entrance, which runs the length of the house, ending at the kitchen. We then hear laughter from the kitchen area. The friendly sound brings forth pleasant memories. We decide that later, we will join the conversation and laughter. First, we want to head to the pond where we first made love. We turn around, walk back to the front door, quietly exit the house, and proceed toward the corner of our lot, where the old black tar road is. We take off our shoes and place them under the precious oak tree. We walk back to the country road and gingerly saunter toward the old pond. A special feeling of total contentment envelops us as we hold each other's hand while walking down memory lane. Soon the pond comes into view. We come closer to the water and sit at the water's edge. We lie back on the green grass, breathing in the summer warmth, our eyes connecting with the clear blue summer sky. We feel not a worry; we both are sure there will be no separation on this trip. Finally, a peaceful calm settles over us, and we hold hands tightly, never to let go again.

We see a huge cumulus cloud moving lazily across the sky. We see an image of ourselves nestled comfortably in the billowy structure. I am holding a sketch pad, as if writing a message. Cassandra is nestled next to me with two red roses in her hair, one on each side. Soon a message appears on the surface of the cumulus mass directly overhead: "Welcome home, Tony and Cassandra." There is no doubt as we peer at the cloud, following its course as it moves onward.

We look at each other, our souls in total unison, both admitting, "Yes, there is magic here in this special world."

My peripheral vision detects something. I turn my head slightly to the right and detect an unnatural movement across the pond. There by the overgrowth under the oak trees, partially hidden by foliage, I see another sudden movement, like something darting swiftly from the oak tree to the adjacent willows. I can't make it out, for whatever I notice keeps going in and out of focus. Whatever it is, it has a dark tone—almost black—projecting a sinister appearance. It is a menacing view. I sense the same instinctive feeling I had when I first detected movement as a teenager at this very spot with Cassandra.

It dawns on me. *Could this be related? The shadowy form. The stranger always unannounced. Did he follow us here? Not possible. The gatekeeper sentenced him to hell.* Yet this stranger has an uncanny way of persisting, as if he is obsessed with pure revenge, and Cassandra and I are the objects of his revenge.

My imagination and paranoia are getting the better of me. But what if it is? If the shadow is the hidden stranger, there will be no avoidance this time. If so, he will meet both of us soon, and when that encounter arrives, it will undoubtedly be the test of faith that bonds Cassandra and me. In the meantime, I just wait and observe. There is a wall, but this time, it's a wall of faith with one purpose: to protect Cassandra and me from evil's heinous attempts. Cassandra is unaware, and I will not tell her my suspicion, for there is nothing to gain.

I need to get off this paranoid track and trust what was revealed to me. The stranger is gone for good.

The undisclosed figure hidden across the pond, camouflaged by a set of weeping willows, is glued to our every movement. His eyes display a feverish glaze, projecting a burning rage, and his whisper is filled with venomous hate. "Still do not know who I am, Tony? Soon though, Tony. Soon. Yes, welcome home, Tony and Cassandra. Welcome back. Looking forward to our next reunion. Maybe this time the dinner engagement will be for a party of four."

To Be Continued
A Haunting Obsession, Part 2
Stranger in the Shadows

Printed in the United States
By Bookmasters